SHIP OF ROME

About the Author

John Stack was born and lives in County Cork. He has always wanted to write but has done a variety of jobs ending up in IT. He is presently writing the second book in the *Masters of the Sea* series. He is married with two children.

JOHN STACK

Ship of Rome

HARPER

Harper
HarperCollins*Publishers*
77–85 Fulham Palace Road,
Hammersmith, London W6 8JB

www.harpercollins.co.uk

First published in Great Britain
by HarperCollins*Publishers* 2009
3

A catalogue record for this book
is available from the British Library

ISBN: 978 000 728524 2

Set in Sabon by Palimpsest Book Production,
Grangemouth, Stirlingshire
Printed and bound in Great Britain by
Clays Ltd, St Ives plc

To my beloved Adrienne

CHAPTER ONE

For an instant the low sun shone through the surrounding fog to illuminate the lone figure on the foredeck of the *Aquila*. Atticus had been motionless but the momentary shot of sunlight caused him to quickly lower his head and close his eyes tightly against the light. He raised his hand instinctively and rubbed his eyes with his thumb and forefinger, trying to wipe away the tiredness he could feel in every part of his body. Slowly raising his head, he spied the winter sun, estimating it to be no more than an hour above the horizon, its weakened rays only now beginning to burn off the sea mist which had rolled in so ponderously the evening before, and so the Roman galley continued to be enveloped in the all-consuming embrace of the fog.

The *Aquila*, the Eagle, was a trireme, a galley with three rows of oars manned by two hundred chain-bound slaves. She was of the new cataphract style, with an enclosed upper deck that protected the rowers beneath and improved the ship's performance in heavy weather. As a galley she was a breed apart, the pinnacle of Roman naval technology and a fearsome weapon.

As the onshore wind freshened, blowing a cooling mist into his face, Atticus opened his mouth slightly to heighten his sense of smell. The oncoming wind and his position at the front of the trireme allowed him to filter out his surroundings, the salt-laden air, the smouldering charcoal braziers and the stench emanating from the slave decks below. The breeze would help conceal the *Aquila*, robbing any approaching ship of the opportunity of picking up the all-too-familiar smells of a Roman galley.

With his vision impaired by fog and, before that, darkness, Atticus had planned on detecting his prey by sound, specifically by the rhythmic beat of the drum marking the oar-strokes of the enemy bireme's two rows of galley slaves. He knew from reports that the galley they were hunting would be travelling close to the shore, passing the inlet that hid the *Aquila* from the main channel. The fog afforded the Roman galley extended cover now that the sun had risen, but it was fickle and Atticus knew he could not rely on it as he had on the darkness of the pre-dawn.

Hobnails reverberating on the timber decking indicated a legionary's approach, and Atticus turned to watch the soldier emerge from the fog behind him. He was a *hastatus*, a junior soldier, recently recruited and untested in battle. He stood tall with broad shoulders, his upper arms disproportionately developed from long hours training with a *gladius*, the short sword of the Roman infantry. He wore full battledress and, although his face was expressionless beneath the iron helmet, Atticus sensed the man's confidence.

The legionary stopped four feet short of Atticus and stood to attention, raising his right fist and slamming it into his chest, a salute to the captain of the ship standing before him. The sound of the soldier's fist against chain mail sounded unnaturally loud in the quiet of the morning. The silence was shattered, a silence needed to ensure the *Aquila* remained undetected. As the legionary drew himself to his full height in anticipation of addressing a senior officer, Atticus reacted.

'Beg to report, Captain,' the legionary declared in a strident voice. As per regulation, he was looking straight ahead, but his eyes dropped quickly as the captain suddenly lunged at him, his expression murderous. The soldier tried to react but the movement was too quick and he felt the captain's hand close over his mouth.

'Keep your voice down, you whoreson,' Atticus hissed. 'Are you looking to have us all killed?'

The legionary's eyes widened in surprise and alarm as both his hands wrapped themselves around the captain's wrist in an attempt to ease the pressure over his mouth. Panic flared as he realized that the grip was vicelike, the muscles in the captain's arm like iron, the pressure unrelenting. Atticus relaxed his hold a little and the legionary gulped air into his lungs, dread still in his eyes which moments ago had showed only confidence. Atticus removed his hand, his face expressing the warning for silence that needed no vocal manifestation.

'I, I . . .' the legionary spluttered.

'Easy soldier,' said Atticus, 'breathe easy.'

As if for the first time, Atticus noticed how young the legionary was, barely eighteen at most. Septimus, the marine centurion, had twenty such *hastati* under his command. Fresh from the barracks, and before that a Roman family, these boys had eagerly signed on at sixteen to fulfil their duty as Roman citizens.

'The centurion . . . ' the soldier began haltingly, 'the centurion wishes to speak with you.'

'Tell him I cannot leave the foredeck.'

The soldier nodded, as if the effort to speak was too much. He straightened up slowly.

'Yes, Captain.'

Once again he stood to attention, though not as sharply as before. He began to salute but stopped short of hitting his chest, his eyes locked on those of Atticus.

'I'm sorry, Captain . . . about before . . .'

'No shame, soldier, now report to the centurion.'

The legionary did an about-face and marched off, although this time with a softer step. Atticus watched him leave and smiled to himself. Ever since Septimus had come aboard the *Aquila* ten months ago, he had tried to impose his will on Atticus. As captain, Atticus was responsible for the ship and its crew of sailors, while Septimus was responsible for the reduced century of sixty marine infantry stationed on board. The ranks were, to all intents and purposes, equal, and it was the responsibility of both men to maintain the status quo between the commands. Atticus turned and took up his position at the bow of the trireme. He instinctively checked the line of his ship, satisfying himself that the four rowers, two fore and two aft, were keeping the trireme midstream. He became motionless again, rock steady, refocusing all his senses on the task at hand. As suddenly as it had blown up, the onshore breeze disappeared, robbing the *Aquila* of that additional advantage, shifting the odds again, this time in favour of the prey.

Septimus stood tall at the front of his assembled century in the aft section of the main deck. At six foot four inches and two hundred and twenty pounds he was a formidable sight. The centurion stood with his feet slightly apart, balancing himself against the gentle rolling of the deck, his right hand resting lightly on the hilt of his *gladius*, his left arm encircling his helmet. His dark Italian features were accentuated by a tangle of black curly hair, giving him a permanently dishevelled look.

The centurion had been standing ready since before dawn, over two hours in full battledress. The waiting never bothered Septimus. Over his twelve-year career as a Roman infantryman, he had developed the endless patience of the professional soldier. He began his career not long after the Battle of Beneventum, when the Roman legions finally routed the army of Pyrrhus of Epirus, the Greek aggressor who had sought to subdue Rome and expand his kingdom across the Adriatic. Where before the legions would have been disbanded after a campaign, the ferocity and swiftness of Pyrrhus's attack persuaded Rome that she needed to maintain a standing army, trained, disciplined, and ever ready. Septimus was one of this new breed, a career soldier, honed through discipline and battle, the backbone of the ever-expanding Republic.

The year before he had fought at the Battle of Agrigentum, the first pitched battle against the Carthaginians, the Punici, on the island of Sicily. As a member of the *principes*, the best fighting men of the legion, he had been positioned in one of the centre maniples of the second line of the three-line, *triplex acies,* formation. He was an *optio*, second-in-command to his centurion, and, after the first line of *hastati* had been over-whelmed by the Carthaginians, he had helped steady the line before the Romans turned the tide of battle and broke the Carthaginian front. His actions that day had come to the atten-tion of the commander, Lucius Postumius Megellus, and he had been rewarded with promotion to the rank of centurion.

'Alone, of course,' he thought to himself with a smile, as he watched the legionary return from the foredeck of the trireme through the dissipating fog. He had known that Atticus would not come to him. Before being assigned to the *Aquila*, Septimus had had no respect for sailors. His first experience at sea had been only four years earlier, when the Roman task force of four legions, some forty thousand men, were ferried in barges across the Strait of Messina to Sicily to counter the Carthaginian threat to that island. It was the first time the Roman legions had deployed off the mainland, but the sea trip had only been one link in a chain that saw the legions travel from their respective camps around Rome to the battlefields of Sicily. In his eyes, the sailors had been no different from the myriad of support people who serviced the fighting men of the legions, and their ships were unwieldy, uncomfortable hulks.

The *Aquila*, however, was a different breed of ship. Powered by both sail and the strength of two hundred slaves, she was capable of incredible speed and manoeuvrability, a stallion in comparison to the pack mules that were the transport barges he had first encountered. Atticus was the perfect foil for the *Aquila*. Completely at home on the deck of his ship, he had an innate ability to get the best out of both his crew and his ship. Septimus's respect for sailors was born out of his respect for Atticus. On the two previous occasions the *Aquila* had gone into action since Septimus had been assigned to her, the captain had proved himself to be the equal of any centurion.

Septimus noticed that the legionary was treading softly on the timber deck, and when he saluted it was not with the usual vigour.

'Well, soldier, where is he?' Septimus asked with underlying menace.

The legionary hesitated. 'The captain said he can't leave the foredeck.'

In the silence that followed, the soldier waited for the rebuke that was sure to follow, bracing himself. Septimus noticed his expression and smiled inwardly.

'Very well,' the centurion said tersely, 'get back to your position.'

The legionary saluted again and with relief retook his position in the ranks.

'Quintus,' Septimus called over his shoulder, 'take command. I'm going to see the captain.'

'Yes, Centurion,' the *optio* replied as he moved front and centre.

Septimus took off towards the foredeck, passing several of the ship's crew as he went. They had been busy since dawn, preparing the ship for action, a routine drilled so well that all work was carried out without comment or command. He approached the captain slowly.

Atticus stood at the very front of the foredeck, leaning slightly over the rail as if to extend his reach through the impenetrable fog. He cocked his head slightly as he picked up Septimus's approach, but did not turn. Atticus was three inches shorter, thirty pounds lighter, and a year older than the centurion. Of Greek ancestry, he was born the son of a fisherman near the city of Locri, a once-Greek city-state of Magna Graecia, 'Greater Greece', on the toe of Italy, which Rome had conquered a generation before. Atticus had joined the Roman navy at the age of fourteen, not out of loyalty to the Roman Republic, for he had never seen Rome and knew little of its democracy, but out of what he believed to be necessity. Like all those who lived on the shores of the Ionian Sea, his family feared the constant attacks of pirates along the Calabrian coast. Atticus had refused to live with this fear, and so he had dedicated his fifteen-year-long career to hunting pirates, a hunt that he hoped would bear fruit once again that very day.

'You wanted to speak to me?' Atticus said without turning.

'Yes, thanks for coming so quickly,' Septimus said sarcastically. 'Well, where are these pirates of yours? I thought they were expected over an hour ago.'

'I don't know where they are,' Atticus replied frustratedly. 'Our sources said their bireme passes this section of the coast every second day before dawn.'

'Could your "sources" be wrong?'

'No, the lives of those fishermen depend on knowing the movements of any pirates in these waters. They're not wrong . . . but something is. That ship should have passed by now.'

'Could you have missed them in the fog?'

'Doubtful . . . a pirate bireme? If she passed within a half-league of here I'd have heard the drum master's beat. No . . . she hasn't passed.'

'What if she were under sail?'

'She can't be under sail, not this close to the shore, especially with an intermittent onshore wind.'

Septimus sighed. 'So what now?'

'The fog is dissipating. We wait until it's gone and we move out of this inlet. Without a man on that headland,' he indicated the opening of the inlet, 'we don't have enough advance warning of any approach and we might be spotted in here. We can't risk being bottled in.'

As if by Atticus's command, a large gap in the fog opened around them. Septimus was turning to leave the foredeck when the sight off the bow arrested him. At this point on the Calabrian coast the Strait of Messina was over three miles across, and under the blue sky he could see the distant shore of eastern Sicily. However, it was not the magnificent vista opening before him that stopped him short.

'Now we know why the pirate ship didn't appear,' muttered Atticus.

In mid-channel, a league away and directly across from them, three trireme galleys were slowly beating north towards the mouth of the strait. They were a vanguard, scouting ships, moving ponderously under oars in arrowhead formation, unable to utilize their sails in the calm weather of the strait.

'By the gods,' whispered Septimus, 'who are they?'

'Carthaginians! Tyrian design, heavier than the *Aquila*, rigged for sea crossing. Looks like the fog hid us for just long enough.'

Atticus's gaze was not on these three ships as he spoke, however. He was looking further south along the strait. At a distance of over two leagues behind the vanguard, Atticus could see the darkened hulls of additional approaching ships, a whole fleet of them led by a quinquereme, a massive galley with three rows of oars like the *Aquila* but with the upper oars manned by two men each.

Septimus noticed Atticus's gaze and followed its line, instantly spotting the other ships.

'In Jupiter's name,' Septimus said in awe, 'how many do you think there are?'

'At least fifty,' Atticus replied, his expression hard, calculating.

'So what now?' Septimus asked, deferring to the man who now controlled their next move.

There was a moment's silence. Septimus tore his gaze from the approaching fleet and looked at Atticus.

'Well?'

Atticus turned to look directly at the centurion.

'Now we run.'

Hannibal Gisco, admiral of the Punic fleet and military commander of the Carthaginian forces in Sicily, was a prudent man. Ever since taking command of the Carthaginian invasion of Sicily over five years earlier, he had insisted that any significant fleet of galleys was to be preceded by a vanguard. This ensured that any dangers were detected long before the fleet proper stumbled upon them. The evening before he had transshipped from his flagship quinquereme, the *Melqart*, to the trireme assigned point duty for the coming day's operations, the *Elissar*. They were on their way to Panormus on the northern Sicilian coast, where Gisco planned to deploy his forces back along the coast in an attempt to blockade the Sicilian ports now in Roman hands, thereby hampering their supply lines from the mainland. The captain of the galley had naturally given up his cabin for the admiral; although the cabin was comfortable, Gisco had slept fitfully, the anticipation of the coming day running through his mind. They were to pass through the mouth of the strait, where Sicily and the mainland were separated by only a league, a mere two thousand five hundred yards, and a natural route for Roman supplies. As the commander of the vanguard he planned on being one of the first to draw Roman blood that day.

Gisco had arisen at dawn and taken his place on the foredeck of the *Elissar*. It felt good to be in command of a single ship again, a trireme, the type of ship on which he had first cut his teeth as a captain and one which he knew intimately. He had ordered the captain to open the gap between the vanguard and the fleet from the normal distance of one league to two. He remembered sensing the captain stifling a question to the order, but thinking better of it before moving to signal to the other two ships to match his pace. The captain knew the admiral's reputation well.

Only a year before, when Gisco was besieged in the city of Agrigentum on the southwest coast of Sicily, he had continued to resist against all odds, even though the populace, as well as his soldiers, were starving, and all attempts to alert the Carthaginian fleet about the Roman siege had failed. Gisco's tenacity had proved to be well founded, as relief did finally arrive, and although the Carthaginians had lost the ensuing battle and the city, tales of Gisco's fearsome reputation and determined aggression had spread throughout the Carthaginian forces.

Gisco had opened the gap to add a degree of danger to his position. Now if they encountered the enemy it would take the fleet just that little bit longer to arrive in support. He wanted the first encounter of the day to be a reasonably fair fight and not a slaughter. Not from any sense of honour, for Gisco believed that honour was a hollow virtue, but from a need to satisfy his appetite for the excitement of battle. More and more his senior rank of overall commander placed him at the rear of battles rather than the front line, and it had been a long time since he had felt the heady blood lust of combat, a feeling he relished and hoped to experience that day.

'Run . . . ? Where to?' Septimus asked. 'Those three ships obviously haven't seen us; maybe we should just sit tight. There's still plenty of fog banks, maybe one will settle over us again.'

'No, we can't afford to take the chance. The fog is too fickle. We've been lucky once, the lead ships didn't spot us, but their fleet is bound to. There's no way fifty ships will cross our bows without someone spotting us. Our only chance is to outrun them.'

Turning away from Septimus, he called back along the ship, 'Lucius!' Within an instant they were joined by the second-in-command of the *Aquila*. 'Orders to the drum master, Lucius, ahead standard. Once we have cleared the inlet, order battle speed. Get all the reserve rowers up from the lower deck.' Lucius saluted and left.

Atticus turned to the centurion. 'Septimus, I need ten of your men below decks to help maintain order. Our rowers may be chained to their oars but I need them obedient and the reserves guarded. I'll also need marines on the aft-deck – those Punic bastards are going to give chase and I'll need my helmsman protected from Carthaginian archers.' Septimus left the foredeck to arrange his command.

'Runner!' Atticus commanded.

Instantly a sailor was on hand.

'Orders to the helmsman, due north once we clear the inlet. Hug the coast.'

The runner sprinted back along the deck. Atticus felt the galley lurch beneath his feet as two hundred oars bit into the still waters of the inlet simultaneously and the *Aquila* came alive underneath him. Within a minute she had cleared the inlet and the galley hove right as she came around the headland to run parallel to the coastline. As Atticus hoped, there

11

were still some fog banks clinging to the coast, where the change in temperature between land and sea gave the fog a foothold. His helmsman, Gaius, knew this coastline intimately, and would only need intermittent reference points along the shoreline in order to navigate. After fifty yards the *Aquila* was once again hidden within a protective fog, but for how long Atticus could only estimate. Although he had told Septimus that he planned to outrun the Carthaginian vanguard, he knew that it would not be possible. One ship could not outrun three. He needed an alternative. There was only one.

'Runner! Orders to the helmsman, once we clear this bank, turn three points to port.'

The runner disappeared. Atticus tried to estimate their position relative to the vanguard. The *Aquila* was moving at battle speed, the vanguard at standard speed. He judged the *Aquila* to be parallel to them . . . now . . . now ahead. The longer the fog held, the greater their chances.

It lasted another two thousand yards.

The *Aquila* burst out into open sunshine like a stallion surging from the confines of a stable. At battle speed she was tearing through the water at seven knots, and Atticus noted with satisfaction that within her time enclosed in the fog she had stolen five hundred yards on the Carthaginian vanguard. He was about to turn to the stern of the galley to signal the course change when the *Aquila* responded to Gaius's hand on the rudder. 'Sharp as ever,' Atticus smiled as the galley straightened on her new course, running diagonally across the strait. Now the *Aquila*'s course would take her across the bows of the vanguard, Atticus estimated, at no more than three hundred yards. He gripped the rail of the *Aquila*, feeling the pulse of the ship as the rhythmical pull of the oars propelled it through the water.

*

'Ship to starboard . . . Roman trireme . . . bearing north.'

With an agility that belied his fifty-two years, Gisco ran to the rigging of the mainmast and began to climb to the masthead. Halfway to the top he glanced up to see the lookout point to the mainland. Following this line, he looked out towards the distant coast. Sure enough, some five hundred yards ahead, a Roman trireme was moving at speed along the coast.

'Estimate she is moving at battle speed,' the lookout shouted down after overcoming the shock of seeing the admiral below him. 'She must have been hiding somewhere along the coastline, invisible behind the fog . . .'

Gisco stared at the Roman trireme and double-checked his estimate of their course. It puzzled him. 'That doesn't make sense,' he thought, 'why not run parallel to the coast, why halve their lead on us?'

Gisco clambered down the rigging to the deck twenty feet below. The instant his feet hit the deck he took stock of his surroundings. The crew were frantically clearing the deck for battle. They were good, he noticed, well drilled and efficient.

He could see the captain on the foredeck, no doubt looking for him.

'Captain!' he shouted.

The man turned and strode towards him. 'Yes, Admiral?'

'What do you make of her, Captain?'

'Roman for sure, probably coastal patrol, maybe thirty crew and a reduced century of marines. She's fast, doing battle speed now, and she cuts the water well. She's lighter than one of our own, maybe a couple of knots faster at her top speed.'

Gisco wondered if the captain had noticed their course. 'Anything else?' he asked.

'Yes, she's commanded by a fool. If he holds his current course he's giving us an even chance of catching him.'

Gisco turned away from the captain and spied the Roman

galley again. She was ahead, about forty degrees off their starboard bow, but instead of running parallel to the *Elissar*'s course and maintaining her lead, she was running on a converging course that would take her across the bow of the *Elissar* at a distance of approximately three hundred yards.

'Captain, alter your course, two points starboard.'

The captain issued the order to a runner who set off at speed to the helmsman at the stern of the ship. The ship altered course slightly and Gisco nodded with satisfaction when he noted the other two triremes instantly responding to the new heading. He turned again to look ahead. The captain was right on one count – the Roman was a fool; but he was wrong on the other: their odds of catching them were a lot better than evens.

'Shall I increase to attack speed, Admiral?'

At first Gisco did not hear the question. All his senses focused on the Roman galley, now four hundred yards ahead on his right. 'He must know he is eating up his advantage with every oar-stroke by now,' he thought. 'Where is he running to?'

'Shall I increase speed?' the captain asked again.

'What?' Gisco answered irritably, his mind replaying the captain's words that he had heard but not listened to, allowing them to form in his mind.

'No, maintain course and speed. If we increase, the Roman may alter course and run before us, matching us stroke for stroke. We'll let him shorten his lead in his own good time. Then we'll take him.'

Septimus moved towards the foredeck. He had noticed the course correction when they emerged from the fog and had been instantly alarmed. What the hell was Atticus doing? He trusted the captain but their course seemed like madness. Atticus was joined on the foredeck by Lucius, and the two men were deep in conversation. The second-in-command was ten

14

years older than Atticus. He was a small bull of a man, solid and unyielding. A sailor all his life, he too was a native of the Calabrian coast. He was known as a tough disciplinarian, but he was fair, and all the crew, especially Atticus, respected his judgement. As he spoke with the captain, he occasionally pointed ahead to the distant shoreline across the strait.

'There,' Septimus could hear him as he approached, 'about two points off the starboard bow, you can see the breakers now.'

'Yes, that's where I thought. Lucius, take command on the steering deck. Have Gaius follow my signals once the Carthaginians fall in behind us. Make sure he doesn't take his eyes off me. The course corrections need to be immediate.'

'Yes, Captain,' Lucius said, and hurried past the approaching centurion.

'Your men in place, Septimus? Remember, once the Carthaginians get behind us you can expect some incoming fire from their archers. It's imperative that my helmsman has all his attention on his job, I don't need him worrying about taking an arrow between his shoulder-blades.'

'Yes, they are. But why the course change, Atticus? We're halving our lead.'

Atticus did not immediately answer. He looked back at the approaching galleys, two points off his port stern, a little over three hundred yards behind. Within seconds they would be running dead astern.

'Septimus, we can't simply run, they'll catch us before we breach the mouth of the strait. One ship can't outrun three.'

'Why the hell not? They're all triremes, surely you could match them stroke for stroke. I've seen how you run your slave deck. Those men are all fit. With your reserve of forty rowers they could maintain battle speed for at least another hour. The Carthaginians would never have closed a gap of five hundred yards before we reached the mouth of the strait.'

Atticus shook his head. 'Think it through. If you were one of three men pursuing another and all were evenly matched in stamina, how would you run your prey down?'

Septimus thought for a moment. He turned to face the three galleys astern. One was in the lead with the other two off its port and starboard stern quarters. They were matching the lead ship stroke for stroke, as if they moved as one. But they're not one, Septimus thought. They're three. The commander of the vanguard did not need to run his ships at the same pace. Even with two galleys they sufficiently outnumbered the *Aquila* to ensure victory. One ship could be sacrificed.

'We can't outrun them,' Septimus said aloud. 'They'll sacrifice one ship to run us down.'

Atticus nodded, his eyes never leaving the Carthaginian hunters. They were now dead astern. Three hundred yards.

'Septimus, clear the fore. I need line of sight to the aft-deck.'

Septimus hesitated, one question remaining. 'So if we can't outrun them, what's our plan?'

'We need to level the odds,' Atticus replied as he turned his full attention to the course ahead, 'so I'm steering the *Aquila* between Scylla and Charybdis, between the rock and the whirlpool.'

'Match course and speed, Captain,' Gisco ordered over his shoulder. He heard the captain repeat the order to a runner, and a moment later the *Elissar* heeled over slightly as she slotted into the wake of the Roman trireme. Gisco could not see the crew of his quarry. The Romans had erected a shield wall along the back of the aft-deck using their *scuta*, the four-foot-high shields of the legions, in a double-height formation, ostensibly to protect the sailors on the deck, Gisco surmised. 'That won't protect you for long,' he thought. He turned to the captain, his face a mask of determination.

'It's time to hunt them down, Captain . . . Signal to the *Sidon* to come alongside.'

Again a runner was dispatched to the aft-deck and the captain watched the *Sidon* break formation and increase speed, moving abreast of the *Elissar*.

The captain turned to Gisco. 'The *Sidon* is in position,' he said, but the admiral was already brushing past him to the side rail.

'Captain of the *Sidon*!' he bellowed across the forty yards separating the two galleys as they sped along, their oars once again matching each other stroke for stroke.

Karalis, the captain, identified himself on the foredeck.

'Captain, increase to attack speed. Maintain for ten minutes and then increase to ramming speed,' Gisco shouted with resolve. 'Push the Romans hard, Captain, whip your own slaves until they drop from exhaustion, spare no man. I want the Roman galley slaves spent. When your rowers collapse we will overtake you and run them down.'

'Yes, Admiral.' Karalis saluted and immediately turned to issue orders to the slave deck below.

Gisco watched the *Sidon* leap forward, unleashed, as if she had thrown off a dead weight, her speed increasing to ten knots.

He turned again to watch the Roman galley, the blood in his veins mixing with adrenaline as he sensed the approach of battle. It was now just a matter of time.

Atticus focused all his attention on the waters ahead, trying to read every nuance in the waves. His concentration was interrupted by the approach of a runner.

'The second-in-command begs to report, Captain, one of the Carthaginians has broken formation and has moved alongside the lead ship.'

Atticus kept his eyes on the waters ahead. The water was calm, the rock still two thousand yards distant. He had time.

His orders to Lucius could not be trusted to a runner, he needed to speak to him in person. He double-checked the waters off the bow again and then turned and ran down the length of the ship to the aft-deck. Lucius was staring through a chink in the shield wall to the galleys behind.

'Report, Lucius,' Atticus said.

The second-in-command turned and straightened. 'Just as we expected, Captain, one of the Carthaginians has broken off and has just increased to attack speed. She's already closing the gap. The other two have taken up flanking positions on her starboard and port aft-quarters, but they are maintaining battle speed.'

Atticus brushed past Lucius to look through the shield wall to see for himself. The three Carthaginian galleys were in arrow formation as before, but now the lead ship was outpacing the other two.

'Lucius, let him come to within one hundred yards and then let fly. Attack speed. Match him stroke for stroke. He's nothing to lose so he'll push us hard. He'll keep pace for a few minutes then he'll push to ramming speed. Hopefully we'll reach Charybdis before that. When we do I'll signal for ramming speed, then for the oars. We want him off guard, so keep them close. We can't allow them time to react.'

Lucius nodded. 'Understood, Captain, I'll watch for your signal.'

Atticus reached out and clasped his second-in-command on the shoulder, feeling the calm strength there, trusting him. 'See you beyond Charybdis,' he said.

'Or in Elysium,' Lucius replied with a smile.

Septimus had watched Atticus outline his orders to Lucius without comment. He did not understand the strategy that Atticus was dictating, although the captain had been right about the Carthaginians. They were sacrificing one ship to wear down the *Aquila,* to leave her helpless, unable to even limp away at standard speed. The captain turned and ran once again to take up position on the foredeck. Lucius returned to looking through the shield wall at the approaching galley, the marines holding their *scuta* in place grimly as arrow after arrow struck their protective wall. Septimus stood beside the second-in-command.

'Lucius, what are Scylla and Charybdis, the rock and the whirlpool?'

'Scylla is the rock and Charybdis is the whirlpool,' Lucius replied, never taking his eyes off their pursuer. 'The ancients believed that both were once beautiful sea nymphs who displeased the gods and were punished. Scylla was transformed into a rock that reaches out into the sea to claw at passing ships, and Charybdis into a whirlpool that would swallow ships whole as they tried to avoid Scylla.'

Lucius paused, judging the distance before bellowing down to the slave deck, 'Drum master! Attack speed!'

Septimus could hear the drum master repeat the order to the two hundred sweating slaves as their pace increased perceptibly, the *Aquila* instantly responding. Lucius looked through the shield wall again and grunted his approval before continuing as if he had only paused for breath.

'Any ship that doesn't know the strait – and we're counting on the fact that the Carthaginians don't – may find herself running along the Sicilian coastline. On this side of the strait you have to run between Scylla and Charybdis, between the rock and the whirlpool.'

Karalis thought for a moment that the Roman ship would not react, perhaps resigned to her fate, or perhaps wanting to fight and die with honour rather than run. Maybe he would get the chance to bloody his sword after all. Karalis was Sardinian by birth, as were most of his crew, and although he respected the strength of his country's Phoenician masters, he despised their condescension. He fully understood the admiral's strategy, but this did not assuage his anger, as he knew it was because he *was* Sardinian that his ship had been chosen to be sacrificed. Just as a smile began to creep onto his face, as he relished the idea of robbing the Carthaginians of first blood, the Roman craft responded, increasing to attack speed. The captain cursed. The *Sidon* was still one hundred yards short of the Roman ship. He would never catch her now. Even from his initial vantage point at the rear of the vanguard, he could see that the Roman trireme was a faster, sleeker ship than his own. He estimated that she was at least two knots faster, which meant his rowers had to worker harder to keep pace. None of that mattered though, he thought. Even the best galley slaves could not maintain attack speed for longer than fifteen minutes. At ramming speed they would collapse after five. The captain would follow orders. He would keep the pace unrelenting. He would push his slaves past exhaustion, past endurance. They would tear the heart out of the Roman galley slaves, and then both ships, Sardinian and Roman, would stop – the Sardinians to rest, the Romans to die.

Atticus wiped the spray from his face as he refocused his eyes on the sea ahead. The *Aquila* was now making eleven knots, her attack speed. He stuck out his right arm, a signal to Gaius to make another minor adjustment to the ship's course, keeping her just right of Scylla, the rock. Atticus estimated that they had increased speed some ten minutes ago. He knew the measure of his slave crew, knew their worth, and knew that by now they were reaching their limits. Once again he swept the sea before him with his eyes.

'There!' he shouted to himself. 'There she is . . . dead ahead, eighty yards!'

He quickly turned and looked back the sixty yards to the aft-deck. Lucius was staring directly at him. 'Now, Lucius!' he shouted, and pumped his fist in the air, the prearranged signal.

Lucius's order carried clearly along the length of the ship: 'Ramming speed!'

Karalis glanced at the two Carthaginian galleys one hundred yards behind him. They were drawing further behind with every stroke the *Sidon* took, although the captain knew that once the Roman vessel was stationary, the Carthaginians would be upon her within a minute. He walked quickly back along the deck to the steps leading down into the slave decks below. The drum master was seated at the foot of the steps, keeping the rhythm a notch above attack speed in order to match the Roman trireme. It had been ten minutes; time to increase to ramming speed. Even though he knew his ship would miss the action of the final kill, he could sense the blood rushing through his veins in anticipation of this final part of the chase. He had never continued on ramming speed past two minutes. Normally that was all that was required to bring his galley to its top speed of twelve knots, enough speed to drive the bronze ram of the *Sidon* through the heaviest timbers.

'Drum master, ram—' His words were cut short by the sight of the Roman trireme increasing her pace to her top speed. He hesitated for a second, perplexed, then gathered his wits: 'Ramming speed, drum master, ramming speed!'

Karalis ran to the foredeck to confirm what he saw. At only one hundred yards' distance the Roman galley filled his field of vision. She was drawing ahead slightly, her faster lines giving her the advantage at top speed. Karalis was dumbstruck. Why by the gods would the Romans increase speed unprovoked? Surely once she went to top speed her rowers would only last mere minutes? The captain of the *Sidon* was still trying to understand the Romans' lunacy when suddenly, within one stroke, all two hundred oars of the Roman trireme were raised clean out of the water.

At ramming speed the bow of the *Aquila* tore through the water at thirteen knots, the drum master pounding eighty beats a minute, forty strokes for each of the trireme's two hundred oars. Atticus leaned forward over the bow rail, measuring the distance between the *Aquila* and the rim of the whirlpool ahead. He stuck out his right hand again for a minor course adjustment, the ship responding instantly to Gaius's expert touch on the tiller sixty yards behind. He dropped his arm and the ship steadied on its final course, one that would take the galley to the very edge of oblivion, the gaping maw of Charybdis. Atticus afforded himself a brief look over his shoulder to the pursuing enemy galley. The shield wall was obscuring his vision; however, he could tell by the line of her oars that she was matching their course adjustments, point for point, wary that her prey might suddenly make a drastic course change in a bid to escape. He turned to the bow again, refocusing all his attention on the point where the *Aquila* would skim the edge of the whirlpool, now forty yards away. . . now thirty . . . twenty . . .

He had to be exact. Too soon and the ship would not have enough momentum for steerage; too late and the starboard rowers would fall victim to the currents of Charybdis.

It was now, the moment was now, the bow of the Aquila was ten yards short, Charybdis was upon them. He spun around, looking for Lucius, finding him riveted to his post on the aft-deck. Their eyes locked.

'Now, Lucius!' he roared.

Lucius responded, 'Drum master, raise oars!'

The order was instantly repeated below in the slave decks.

The drum beat stopped. The slaves threw themselves forward, pivoting their oars, lifting the blades clear out of the water.

The *Aquila* sped on, at first her speed checking imperceptibly. Atticus sprinted the length of the galley to the aft-deck, barely registering the terrified faces of many of the marines who had never witnessed the fury of Charybdis. To his left the churning waters of the whirlpool were speeding past the *Aquila*, only six feet from the hull, running counter to the direction of the trireme but not hindering her progress.

Gaius stood immovable at the rudder, his gaze steely as he sought to keep the tiller straight along the axis of the ship, the true course of the *Aquila* vital if she was to avoid becoming the victim of her own trap. The captain took up station beside him, his hand resting lightly on the tiller, searching for a telltale tremor that would betray any pressure on the rudder's blade.

Atticus saw Gaius's reaction a heartbeat before the minute tremor under his hand confirmed the helmsman's incredible reflexes and he gripped the tiller tightly. Beneath the *Aquila* an unseen tentacle of current, too weak to attack the seventy-ton hull, was building against the rudder, threatening to force the blade off true. Within seconds the pressure had multiplied tenfold and the muscles in both men's arms were tensed and flexed as they struggled to keep the tiller aligned.

Time slowed as Atticus's mind counted the seconds it would take to sail past the whirlpool. Beside him Gaius's face was mottled from exertion while beneath him speed bled from his galley as the enemy closed in. The sound of Lucius's voice filled the air, sounding the ever-decreasing gap between the two galleys. 'Seventy yards . . . ! Sixty yards!' and all around him the faces of the crew were frantic as they witnessed the struggle of their captain and helmsman. Underneath it all, Atticus felt the rudder shift slightly under his hand and for an instant a panic flared in his heart that he had cut his course too close to the vortex.

Hold your course, Aquila, his mind roared, trying to connect his will to the ship.

Almost within an instant the pressure on the rudder was released, and Atticus knew the *Aquila* was through, the waters around her hull becoming calm once more as the whirlpool fell off her starboard stern quarter. He spun around to his second-in-command.

'Lucius, prepare to get under way. Get below decks, have all the reserves assigned plus any additional crew available. Do whatever's required, but I need attack speed immediately.'

'Yes, Captain,' he replied, and was instantly away.

Atticus moved to the stern rail to watch his pursuers. Now, he grinned with satisfaction, the Carthaginians would feel the wrath of Charybdis.

The *Sidon* cut through the water at twelve knots, closing the gap on the Roman trireme by ten yards every five seconds. Karalis had wavered for an instant, unable to comprehend the Roman captain's actions, before his years of command experience took over. He realized they would be upon the Roman ship within a minute. Karalis shrugged his questions aside and began issuing orders to his assembled crew.

'Prepare for impact! Assemble the boarding party!'

They would ram the Roman galley through her stern, a killing blow, taking her rudder and holing her below the waterline. While the Romans were recovering, his boarding party would spill over the stern rail, killing the senior officers who would be stationed there. He would lead his men personally, they would spare no one, and when his ship finally disengaged, tearing her bronze ram from the hull, the Roman trireme would drag her chained slaves beneath the waves.

The gap was down to fifty yards when the Roman vessel re-engaged her oars. You're too late, fool, the captain thought. The

Sidon was at the point where the Roman crew had inexplicably raised oars. He would be upon them within fifteen seconds.

On the slave deck of the *Sidon*, the galley slaves were oblivious to the action above decks. Chained to his oar, each of the two hundred men was enclosed within his own private hell. For many of them, years at the oar had brutalized them and they worked in silence, their whole world focused on the constant rhythm of their oar-stroke, the backbreaking pull, the quick release to bring the oar forward, a second's respite, the muscles straining again through the next pull. Sweat poured to mingle with fresh blood raised by the taskmaster's lash across their backs, as man after man collapsed in exhaustion, to be savagely beaten where he fell as a reserve took his place, the unrelenting pace never abating.

The thirty rowers of the starboard fore section of the *Sidon* were the first to strike Charybdis. Not six feet from where they stood, on the other side of the hull, the current of the whirlpool sped past them at twenty knots. Keeping to the beat of the drum master, the rowers brought their oars forward and stuck their blades into the water in unison. Instantly the oars were ripped from their fingers as the current took hold of the blades and pushed the oars parallel to the hull. The slaves on the lower two rows screamed in agony as the oars of the upper row, fifteen foot long and fifty pounds in weight, spun on their mountings and slammed into them, killing many instantly. Within the instant marked by the drum master's beat, the second section of thirty rowers endured the same fate, fuelling the destruction of the slave deck. The starboard side was in chaos, a mayhem of broken men. The port side never missed a beat, the rowers continuing at full tilt, completing the trap.

The air around Karalis was split by the sound of shattering timbers and cries of pain from the slave decks below him, and the *Sidon* heeled violently as momentum was lost on the starboard side. He ran to the starboard rail in time to see the second section of oars collapse against the hull, the air again ripped by the sound of his ship and her rowers being destroyed beneath him.

'By the gods,' he whispered as he saw the cause, fear coursing through him.

The ship heeled further to the right as the left-side oars continued their stroke, pushing the bronze ram into the current of the whirlpool. The *Sidon* was gripped as if by the hands of a god and whipped around to starboard, throwing Karalis and those around him to the deck. The archers stationed on the foredeck were thrown into the maelstrom of the whirlpool, their cries cut off as they were sucked beneath the tortured waters.

Karalis looked frantically towards the aft-deck, praying for respite but finding none. The helmsman was dead, his chest staved in where the tiller had struck him a killing blow. The *Sidon* was out of control.

'You men, to my aid!' Karalis shouted to three sailors who were lying on the deck around him, realizing that, if he did not check the *Sidon*'s momentum once she cleared the current, the galley would spin her stern into the whirlpool and the ship would be lost.

The sailors were dumbstruck, petrified, unable to comprehend the forces attacking their ship.

'Now!' Karalis bellowed. 'Before I cast you overboard to the monster beneath us!'

They were instantly on their feet, their fear of the captain and his threats overcoming their terror and confusion. The men followed the captain to the aft-deck, the violently spinning ship causing one to lose his balance and fall over the side rail.

The force of the turning ship was pressing the rudder hard against the bulkhead, as if it were nailed to the very timbers of the ship. The three men took hold of the six-foot-long tiller and, with all their strength, attempted to heave the rudder back to true. The resistance was incredible, the twenty-knot current gripping the bow of the *Sidon*, causing water to rush past the stern, engulfing the blade of the rudder, transferring its energy up the shaft to fight the strength of the three men. The resistance lessened as the bow cleared the whirlpool and, although Karalis and his men fought hard to bring the rudder to true, he knew the fight was hopeless, the momentum of the eighty-ton galley too great. With his fears echoed in the cries of his men, Karalis felt the whirlpool grip the stern of his ship, sucking the vessel deeper into the maelstrom, dooming all on board.

At only sixty yards' distance, Atticus could hear the screams of the slaves and the snapping of their oars as Charybdis took hold of his enemy. Within seconds the galley had swung her bow into the vortex, which spun the enemy ship until her stern was facing the *Aquila*. Atticus watched in dread fascination as a group of men fought the tiller of the enemy vessel, their forlorn efforts overcome by the power of the whirlpool, the Carthaginian galley inexorably drawn into Charybdis as the current took a firm grip of her stern, dragging the ship ever closer to the centre of the vortex. The cries of terror were beyond any that Atticus had ever heard.

'Septimus!' Atticus called.

The centurion approached. He was shaking his head in amazement. 'By the gods, Atticus, I have never seen such a sight. What might does this sea have, that it can take a ship and devour her?'

'Charybdis has taken one for us,' Atticus began, 'the Carthaginian on the lead ship's starboard flank is heading directly for the whirlpool. They'll realize the danger so they'll either break off their pursuit or try to navigate around. Either way they're no longer a threat. We're still too far from the mouth of the strait to escape the last ship. She'll run us down, knowing that the rest of the fleet are not far behind. Our only chance is to attack and disable her and then disengage before reinforcements arrive. Once we clear the mouth of the strait we'll raise sail, using the trade winds sweeping south along the Tyrrhenian Sea. The *Aquila* can outsail any Carthaginian trireme.'

Septimus nodded, agreeing with the captain's logic. He looked back over the stern rail again at the two remaining Carthaginian galleys, picking out the one they would need to attack. Atticus had levelled the odds. Now it was the turn of Septimus and his men to take the fight to the enemy.

On the foredeck of the *Elissar*, Gisco watched the scene before him with mounting disbelief. He couldn't accurately judge the distance between the *Sidon* and the Roman galley from his position on the portside aft-quarter of the chase, but he knew it had to be close. The oars of the Roman galley had been suddenly raised from the water and before Gisco could question the action they had re-engaged and were once again moving as if nothing had occurred. Then, without warning, the *Sidon* seemed to buckle and swing wildly to starboard. Even now she continued to spin at incredible speed, her hull breaking up under the intolerable stress. Gisco was staggered by what he saw.

'What sorcery is this?' the captain beside Gisco muttered aloud. 'It is the work of Pluto. We must abandon the chase.'

'No!' Gisco bellowed, the captain's words allowing him to give vent to his frustration and fear at what he had just witnessed. 'There will be no withdrawal. Give me attack speed now and signal to the *Hermes* to continue the pursuit.'

'Yes, Admiral,' the captain blurted, caught between his fear of the man before him and the unknown forces attacking the *Sidon*.

Gisco now fully understood the actions of the Roman trireme, from her erratic and seemingly suicidal course to her inexplicably raising oars, and the thought of how they had played him for a fool fuelled the anger within him. Armed with the knowledge that the Roman ship had passed through these waters at attack speed, he gambled that the way ahead was clear, driven now by a desire for revenge.

Captain Maghreb had watched the fate of the *Sidon* with equal horror from the aft-deck of the *Hermes*. The doomed galley was one hundred yards ahead, the sound of snapping timbers as the hull disintegrated mixed with the last cries of her crew as they were consumed.

'All stop!' Maghreb roared, his own fear consuming him. The oars of the *Hermes* were raised, the galley instantly losing momentum. Maghreb looked across to the *Elissar*, expecting to see her oars similarly raised. He could only stare in disbelief as the order to continue the pursuit was signalled from the admiral.

'Steerage speed, lookouts to the foredeck!' Maghreb roared as he immediately tore his eyes from the *Elissar* to scan the waters ahead, expecting any moment to see the vortex that would engulf his ship. The galley slowed to two knots, steerage speed, feeling her way through the water as she edged forward, searching for the rim of the maelstrom. Maghreb could only hope that the *Hermes* could navigate around the whirlpool in time to join the *Elissar* in full pursuit.

'Come about,' Atticus ordered, his gaze steady on the approaching Carthaginian galley, her partner now trying to manoeuvre around Charybdis.

'Be ready, Gaius,' Atticus added, 'she'll try to manoeuvre to ram. That's where her strength lies and our weakness.'

Gaius nodded, his entire being focused on the enemy galley. The Carthaginian vessel turned three points to starboard in an effort to run diagonally across the *Aquila*'s bow. Gaius knew that the enemy would try to turn tightly to come at them from the beam, to ram them amidships. He turned the *Aquila* three points to port to counter the enemy's move, keeping the bows of both galleys on an intercept course.

Septimus had assembled his marines on the main deck, preparing the boarding parties that would sweep over the rails of the *Aquila* onto the Carthaginian galley. They had separated into two groups. The first group of twenty *hastati* and twenty *principes*, new recruits coupled with seasoned soldiers, were moving to station themselves on the foredeck. The second group, the older *triarii*, were ranged across the main deck, ready to counter any boarding party from the enemy ship. All had discarded their four-foot-long *scutum* shields for a *hoplon*. The lighter rounded shield was a Greek design, perfectly adapted to the speed and agility needed for boarding, and the marines had trained hard to overcome their past allegiance to the legions' standard shield.

'Steady men,' Septimus said, sensing the aggression coupled with nervous tension in the soldiers assembled at his back. The enemy galley was only one hundred yards away and closing fast.

The *Elissar* tore through the waves at eleven knots, every turn of her bow matched and countered by the approaching Roman galley. Gisco had not anticipated the Romans would turn into the fight so soon, expecting his prey to continue their headlong rush for the mouth of the strait in a vain hope of making their escape. The reversal brought instant, instinctive commands as the galley was prepared for immediate battle. The helmsman worked hard to manoeuvre the *Elissar* into a ramming position, but his skills were evenly matched by those of the Roman helmsman. The Roman galley was now fifty yards away, her bow pointed directly at the *Elissar*'s. There would be no opportunity to ram. As the bows connected they would be made fast by both crews, each looking to board the other.

Gisco turned from the approaching galley to look out over the stern rail. The *Hermes* was skirting the northern rim of the whirlpool, her tentative steps enraging the admiral. He had ordered the galley to join him in the pursuit, their combined strength initially needed to ensure the Romans would not escape. Now the *Elissar* would face the Romans alone and Gisco could not suppress the blood lust rising within him, the chance to gain some revenge for the loss of one of his galleys. Further behind, the Carthaginian fleet was advancing at battle speed. Once the two galleys engaged, Gisco estimated the fleet would be upon them within fifteen minutes.

Gisco left the aft-deck and strode determinately to the fore-deck, leaving the helm in the charge of the captain. The admiral would command the boarding party himself, standing firmly in the front line. Gisco tightened his grip on the hilt of his sword, feeling the unyielding iron in his hand. He drew his weapon in one sudden release, the blade singing against the scabbard.

'Prepare for impact. Make ready to board!'

His men roared with naked aggression. Gisco let them roar, let them fill their hearts and nerve with anger, a rage that he would throw against the Romans.

'Prepare to release!' Septimus ordered, and his twenty *hastati* hoisted their *pila*, their heavy javelins, up to shoulder height.

Gaius made one final adjustment to the rudder as the two galleys converged at attack speed. He gripped the worn timber of the tiller firmly in his hands as he held the course true, bracing his legs to cope with the anticipated command. The galleys were now only ten yards apart.

'Loose!' Septimus roared.

At almost point-blank range, all twenty *hastati* shot their *pila* into the massed ranks of Carthaginians on the foredeck of the *Elissar*. Each spear was eight feet long, with an iron shank that gave the weapon a fearsome penetrating power. As each spear struck its target, its shank broke off from the handle, rendering the weapon useless. The unexpected volley of javelins wrought tremendous carnage amongst the Carthaginians, breaking up the enemy formation that was poised to board the *Aquila*.

'Starboard side, withdraw!' Atticus roared, before taking off in a run towards the foredeck.

The order carried clearly to the slave deck and the drum master repeated the order to the starboard-side rowers. The slaves immediately stopped their stroke and pulled the oars in hand over hand. Within an instant the oars were withdrawn, with only their two-foot-long blades exposed outside the hull.

Gaius leaned the rudder slightly over to converge the two ships and the cutwater of the *Aquila*'s prow tore into the extended starboard-side oars of the *Elissar*. The rowers of the *Elissar* were thrown from their positions like rag dolls as the fifteen-foot oars they manned were struck with the force of the seventy-ton Roman trireme travelling at eleven knots. Many of the oars splintered, while some held together to strike the slave at the handle end of the oar. In the confined space of the slave deck, with the men chained to their positions, there was nowhere to run to, and by the time the *Aquila* had run the length of the *Elissar*, the starboard-side slave deck of the Carthaginian galley was strewn with broken bodies.

'Grappling hooks!' Septimus ordered as the *Aquila*'s fore-deck came in line with the enemy's aft. Immediately three of his men threw the four-pronged hooks across the narrow gap between the galleys. As the hooks found purchase on the *Elissar*'s deck, the marines clambered to grab hold of the attached ropes and pull with all their might. The gap was closed to less than six feet. Septimus ran forward and jumped on the starboard rail, balancing easily with his *gladius* in one hand and rounded *hoplon* shield in the other.

'Men of the *Aquila*, to me,' he shouted, and jumped the gaping void beneath the two galleys, landing solidly on the aft-deck of the Carthaginian ship.

The marines roared as the blood lust of battle overwhelmed them and they followed the centurion without hesitation over the rails of the enemy ship, clamouring to be the first to draw Carthaginian blood. Septimus barged straight at the man nearest him and struck him squarely with his shield, using his momentum to knock the man off his feet, sending him reeling into someone behind. The few Carthaginians remaining on the aft-deck fled before the charge. Behind the marines, Atticus and Lucius jumped onto the deck of the Carthaginian galley, axes in their hands. Their task would take only minutes, time Septimus and his men would have to buy with their blood.

The war cries of the marines spilling over the rail of the *Elissar* fuelled the frustration within Gisco at the sudden reversal. The air around him was filled with the screams of injured and dying men while beneath his feet the deck still reeled from the impact of the Roman trireme's run against the starboard-side oars of his galley. The ranks of his men had disintegrated under the hammer blows of the *pila* volley, and they were in chaos, with neither focus nor formation.

'Men of the *Elissar* to me!' Gisco bellowed as he charged from the foredeck. The veteran soldiers reacted more swiftly than the untested, and so the line of attack was ragged and uncoordinated, but their ferocity bore them on in a headlong rush along the length of the *Elissar*. They struck the line of Romans at full tilt, their momentum checked within a stride by the near-solid wall of shields.

Gisco sidestepped a thrust from a Roman marine before countering the stroke with a slash to the Roman's thigh. The man yelled in pain as the sword bit deeply into the flesh, but before the admiral could deliver the killing blow his sword was stayed by another Roman, who followed the parry with a vicious attack. Gisco immediately realized that although each of the Romans fought as one man, they also fought as a team, overlapping their attacks, their coordination sapping the strength of the Carthaginians' original charge. Gisco renewed the surge of the counterattack, urging his men on through the ferocity of his own charge. The *Elissar* would not fall easily.

The Carthaginian war cries reached a new high as another lunge was made in an effort to break the Roman line of battle. The sound spurred on Atticus and Lucius and sweat streamed from their bodies as they redoubled their efforts to sever the tiller from the rudder. The weathered toughened timber was as hard as iron, but with each axe blow small chips flew away and already they were halfway through the four-inch-diameter section.

On the main deck, Septimus saw a breach developing and immediately fed his best fighters into the gap. Within the space of two vicious minutes the gap was sealed once more and the tide of Carthaginians checked. The last of the reserves were now engaged. The next breach could not be held. If the Carthaginians broke through, the fight would become chaotic and all chance of a withdrawal would be lost.

The tiller finally parted under the blows of Atticus and Lucius. Now, even if the Carthaginian galley managed to get back under way, the loss of her rudder would render her useless.

'Septimus!' Atticus roared. 'Withdraw!'

Septimus heard the signal. 'Fighting withdrawal!' he roared, his men instantly stepping back towards the aft-deck.

The sudden break-off in resistance threw the Carthaginian attack and a gap opened between the lines.

The twenty *triarii* who had remained on the *Aquila* now

loosed volleys of spears into the flank of the Carthaginian forces, checking their advance, allowing the marines vital seconds to mount the aft-deck rails and recross onto the *Aquila*. Within moments the bulk of the marines were aboard, with just a small knot remaining, Septimus amongst them. Under an almost constant volley of spears, the Carthaginians reared up in attack again, their centre driven by a demonic commander, rage emanating from his frame as he tried to cut off the remaining marines. The lines of the grappling hooks were severed as Septimus jumped across the opening gap, the last man to do so.

Gisco could only look on in futile rage as the Roman galley re-engaged her oars, hastening her escape. The Carthaginian fleet was still two thousand yards away, too far behind to stop the Romans reaching the mouth of the strait. All around him his men stood at the side rail of the aft-deck, shouting defiance and insults of cowardice at the Romans. Gisco remained silent, his eyes searching the rails of the enemy ship. The two men he sought were on the foredeck, standing side by side, the taller man, the marine centurion, recognizable from the fight. They were the commanders and he instantly saw they were watching him intently. Gisco burned the images of their faces into his mind. As the gap opened to one hundred yards the Roman galley began to come about to resume her course northwards.

'*Aquila*,' Gisco read on the stern of the galley.

Gisco made a silent promise to the gods that one day he would hunt down that ship and have his revenge on all who sailed on her.

CHAPTER TWO

The sail billowed out with a crack as the trailing wind filled the broad canvas sheet, the running rigging straining against the pull. Within an instant the *Aquila* was propelled to fifteen knots, its cutwater tearing through the sea, throwing a spray of water across the foredeck. The running of a galley required immense skill and concentration, and Atticus noticed the iron look on Gaius's face as he fought to keep the helm true. One slip and the galley's stern would swing through the line of the wind. The sail would be exposed to unequal stresses, instantly snapping the rigging and collapsing the canvas. Worse still, if the rigging held, the galley would capsize under the press of wind.

Atticus watched in silence as the experienced helmsman struck a delicate balance between the prevailing wind and the ship, making the two connect until the galley perfectly matched the wind's speed and direction. Confident that Gaius had the ship in hand, Atticus looked out over the stern rail to confirm the Carthaginians were not in pursuit. The *Aquila* was now four hundred yards clear of the headland at the northeastern tip of Sicily. The Punici had not followed beyond the strait.

Atticus was in turmoil as he realized his ship had escaped. Although he had known the only choice had been to flee from the enemy fleet, the retreat from the Carthaginian galley marked the first time in his whole life that he had run from an enemy. The empty sea behind the *Aquila* mocked the captain for its absence of an enemy and Atticus slammed his fist onto the stern rail. Knowing he had made the right decision was not enough to assuage the dishonour he felt at having fled.

Septimus stood silently by Atticus's side. Eight marines were unaccounted for from the fight on board the enemy galley, six of them *hastati*, junior soldiers, many of them in their first battle. He could only pray that all had died under the sword and that none had been left injured on the enemy's deck. If taken alive their fate would be horrific. The *Aquila* had been saved because of the sacrifice of those men. Septimus recounted their names silently in his mind.

'Where are we sailing to?' he asked finally.

'To the only port Rome holds on the north coast. To Brolium.'

Septimus nodded, looking ahead over the bow. During his time on the *Aquila* he had come to accept that the unfamiliar seas around him held many enemies, as had the unfamiliar terrain of Sicily when he had served in the legions. As a legionary he was always confident that he served in the best land army in the world. The sight of the Carthaginian fleet had made him realize that Rome did not enjoy that same superiority and confidence at sea.

Eight hours later the *Aquila* rounded the eastern headland guarding the approaches to the Roman-held port of Brolium. Atticus stood alone on the bow, preferring solitude as the hours had sped past and league after league fell under the galley's wake. His thoughts had ranged over every detail of the Carthaginian ships they had fought, every difference, however minute, between them and the vessel under his feet, his mind slowly forming a model of the heavier, stronger galleys that would soon plague the waters off northern Sicily.

A sudden change in the tilt of the deck broke Atticus's thoughts as Gaius lined up the *Aquila* to strike the very centre of the hectic waters ahead, crammed with transport barges awaiting a chance to disgorge their contents onto the already crowded docks of the once-quiet fishing town. Even from this distance out, the air around Atticus was filled with the hum of voices from the multitude at work, broken occasionally by the sound of a whip crack as a driver spurred his team of oxen to advance, signalling the departure of yet another fully loaded wagon along the road south to the fortified legion encampment hidden beyond the town.

The scene of docking and departing barges, of unloading and reloading supplies, of man and beast struggling for space on the congested docks seemed completely chaotic, and yet Atticus could sense the underlying order that permeated the entire operation as no voice was raised in anger and everywhere men moved with purpose and intent. The Roman legions had never fought a campaign off the mainland before Sicily, and yet, within a matter of months, the Romans' ability to bring order and discipline to all endeavours ensured that the legions were operating as if they were but a mile from the city of Rome itself. Atticus could only wonder if any natural barrier would ever exist that could protect a people against the seemingly relentless advance of Rome.

Lucius's sharp commands cut through the cacophony as the sail was collapsed and made secure and the oars were engaged in the rapidly dwindling sea room of the inner harbour. Again Gaius's incredible skill was called upon as barge after barge was avoided, their crews shouting warnings and curses as each near collision with the slow, ponderous vessels was averted. Atticus's gaze swept the dock, searching for an opportunity.

He quickly saw one and calculated the angles. It would be tight.

'Three points starboard!' he roared, his voice acknowledged by Gaius sixty yards away with a nod and a nimble touch on the tiller as Atticus ran to the main deck to prepare to disembark.

The *Aquila* aligned her bow with an emerging gap as a barge began to cast off, her now empty hull turning towards the mid-channel. Voices and hands were raised on the docks, calling forward the next waiting barge into the valuable space before one of the taskmasters noticed the *Aquila*'s intercept course, his realization causing a minor panic as the galley's unerring intent became apparent. Lucius roared for the barge to give way, his command instinctively followed by the merchantmen of the transport vessel who feared the *Aquila*'s four-foot bronze ram, and the galley swung deftly into the gap left by the departing barge.

Atticus, Septimus and a detachment of six legionaries ran down the gangway the moment it touched the dock, their determined arrival forestalling any protest from the irate taskmaster.

'Stand by on station,' Atticus called to Lucius, who saluted and immediately ordered the gangway raised and the galley to push off from the dock. The six legionaries fell in pairs behind the captain and centurion and together they marched towards the end of the dock, heading to the town beyond. The slave labourers crowding the wharf moved back to allow the armed men to pass; as a knot of them dispersed, Atticus spotted an officer approaching at the head of a *contubernia* of ten soldiers. He was a tall, gaunt man, determination in his step, his face a mask of fury. Atticus recognized him immediately. He was Aulus, the Brolium harbour master.

'Who the hell do you think you are?' Aulus yelled as he

moved around the gangway of an unloading barge, shoving his way through the queue of bearers that cut across his path. He checked his step as he recognized the approaching captain, ordering his squad of ten men to halt.

'Atticus, you Greek dog!' he smiled. 'By Jupiter's balls! What madness is this?'

The two men shook hands, Roman style, each grasping the other's arm below the elbow.

'I should have known it was the *Aquila*; only Gaius could pull off a manoeuvre like that. And Septimus,' Aulus exclaimed over the captain's shoulder, 'still alive, I see.'

Septimus allowed himself a smile at the friendly gibe, knowing Aulus's dislike of legionaries.

'We couldn't wait for clearance, Aulus. We need to see the port commander immediately.'

Aulus was disturbed by the captain's infectious agitation, something he had never before seen in the young man.

'Atticus, in Pluto's name, what's going on?' he asked, all trace of humour now gone.

'Carthaginians, Aulus, a whole fleet of them. At least fifty ships. Bearing north through the Strait of Messina.'

'A Carthaginian fleet? In these waters? By the gods . . .'

Instinctively Aulus looked around at the assembled fleet of barges. These vessels and their ability to ply goods between the mainland and Sicily were the key to the entire Roman campaign on the island. But they were slow, ponderous beasts in comparison to galleys. Fifty Carthaginian ships would play merry hell with them.

'Atticus, this news must reach the legion commanders immediately,' Aulus said without looking back at the captain, his focus on the barges around him, his mind already picturing their destruction at the hands of the Punici.

'That's why I need to speak to the port commander

immediately, Aulus. He will be able to speak to the legion commanders directly.'

'Atticus . . . Gnaeus Cornelius Scipio is here, in Brolium itself.'

'The senior consul? Here?' Atticus asked with disbelief. 'What's he doing in Sicily?'

'He's here to inspect the legions before the spring campaign,' Aulus replied. 'He only arrived two days ago. He's staying in the port commander's villa.'

Atticus looked up at the villa overlooking the port. It was fifteen minutes away by foot, four minutes by horseback, but that was on a quiet day, when the streets were all but empty. Today the entire town seemed choked with equipment, slaves and draught oxen. He would need the marine legionaries to beat a path to the consul's door.

'Septimus,' he called over his shoulder, 'we need to get to the villa as quickly as possible.'

'Understood,' Septimus replied, and turned to his six men. 'Squad . . . draw swords!' he ordered, his words followed instantly by the distinctive sound of swords being drawn from their scabbards.

All activity around the soldiers ceased as the sound arrested the movement of every man in earshot. Those within range immediately drew back from the group, fearful of the razor-sharp killing sword of the Roman legions. A ripple ran through the crowd as word was passed quickly along the length of the dock and, like a gust of wind blowing through ripened corn, the crowd began to part in front of the soldiers. Septimus turned and slowly drew his own sword, holding it firmly before him, sensing the familiar weight of the weapon, remembering the last time he had drawn it only hours before.

'Fall in behind,' he said to Atticus as he looked beyond him to the channel opening before them. 'Squad . . . double-quick time.'

The squad took off as one, their pace the ground-eating double-quick time that would get them to their destination, over two miles away, in fifteen minutes. Aulus watched them go until his view of them was lost, the slaves around him returning to work as if nothing had happened. But something had happened, Aulus thought, something had changed. The four legions on Sicily had seemed invincible, unbeatable, the best land army in the world. Now the Carthaginians had begun to exploit their best asset, as masters of the sea, and as surely as death follows life, if the fifty ships of the Punici were not stopped, they would strangle and starve forty thousand of Rome's finest.

Atticus and Septimus mounted the final steps leading to the villa's rooftop garden behind two of the consul's black-cloaked praetorian guards, their long wait before being summoned forward by the guard commander further chafing Atticus's nerves after his earlier angry exchanges with the praetorian commander in the villa's courtyard. The *praetoriani* were notoriously arrogant, their privileged position as the guardsmen of the Senate setting them apart from and above the regular soldiers of the legions, and this particular guard commander, an ex-centurion of the Fourth Legion, had a glaring contempt for all ranks other than his own. He had initially refused the *Aquila*'s officers' request for an audience with the consul out of hand, turning his back on them even as they spoke, as if the very effort of refusal was beneath him, and it was only when Atticus mentioned, with barely contained anger, that the entire campaign was now under threat that the guard commander stopped in his tracks to listen before agreeing to seek the consul's permission for an audience.

Atticus and Septimus stood to attention as the praetorian guards came to a halt just inside the boundary of the garden, their arrival seemingly unnoticed by Gnaeus Cornelius Scipio, senior consul to the Senate of Rome, who was standing with his back to them, slowly and methodically splashing cold water from a basin onto his forearms and face. He reached out for a towel and one was immediately proffered by a large Nubian slave before he turned to face the two officers.

Atticus and Septimus saluted in unison, but the consul did not acknowledge the gesture as he poured himself a glass of wine, the pause giving Atticus a chance to study the man before him. He knew Scipio was a patrician, one of the elite of the Roman Republic, and his bearing showed all the hallmarks of a privileged upbringing. He was not a tall man, maybe two inches shy of six feet, but his stance gave the impression that he stood over everyone around him. He moved like a fighter, with long, slow, fluid movements that belied his obvious strength, and although his eyes were downturned, Atticus had the impression that he was fully aware of everyone around him. The consul looked up to face the two men, his eyes never leaving them as he took a drink from his glass, and both Atticus and Septimus knew that they were being assessed by one of the most powerful men in the Republic.

'Report,' he ordered.

'I am Captain Atticus Milonius Perennis and this is Centurion Septimus Laetonius Capito of the marines. We are the commanding officers of the trireme *Aquila* out of the port of Locri, stationed in the Ionian Sea and Strait of Messina. This morning —'

'Wait,' Scipio interrupted. 'I am familiar with the family name Laetonius,' he said with a nod to Septimus, 'but I have never heard of Milonius. What is the origin of your family?'

'It's Greek,' Atticus replied, somewhat puzzled at the line of questioning, 'from Brutium,' indicating the region occupying the 'toe' of the Italian mainland.

'So what is a Greek doing commanding a Roman vessel?' the consul enquired, trying to gauge the young captain before him. He knew that many of the ships of the Roman navy were provided by provincial cities and so their crews were a mix of personnel from all corners of the Republic, but he had thought all the galleys were commanded by Roman citizens.

'The origin of the name is Greek, but we are of Brutium, and citizens of the Republic. I joined the navy when I was fourteen and worked my way up to the rank of captain.'

Atticus had drawn himself to his full height as he spoke, and Scipio could sense the pride and determination behind the words when he spoke of his citizenship and rank. He recalled that Brutium had once been part of Magna Graecia, Greater Greece, a loose confederation of city-states whose founders had originated from the Greek mainland. Rome had absorbed the entire area less than a generation before as the legions washed the stain of Pyrrhus from the peninsula, and so now former enemies had become fellow citizens.

'Continue with your report, Captain,' Scipio said with a wave of his hand, his mind now tinged with a hint of mistrust as the Greek continued.

Atticus quickly recounted the morning's action, emphasizing the enemy's numbers and course.

Scipio listened while the captain spoke, his expression never changing. The consul was used to hiding his thoughts and emotions from those around him, and he had trained his face to remain impassive no matter what news was delivered. This report of a fleet of Carthaginian galleys shook him to his core, however, as he realized its implications. Scipio lifted his glass to take a drink and noted with satisfaction that his hand was rock steady. He turned to his fellow Roman.

44

'Centurion, do you confirm this report?'

'Yes, Consul, every detail,' Septimus replied without hesitation, sensing his friend Atticus bristle as his honesty was questioned. Scipio continued to hold the gaze of each man, his face a mask of indifference. Atticus immediately mistook his demeanour for a sign that he had missed the point of the report entirely.

'Consul, the fleet was moving north through the strait. Their destination must be Thermae or Panormus further along this coast. From there they could range along the entire northern coast, attacking our transport barges as they cross from the mainland.'

Scipio had looked up the moment Atticus began to speak and he listened intently until the captain finished his sentence. It was only then that his expression changed. Not to one of understanding and concern as Atticus had expected, but to one of rage.

'How dare you speak without permission?' he growled at Atticus. 'Do you think me a fool? Hold your tongue!'

Atticus was stunned by the consul's outburst and silently cursed the manner of the man standing before him. His ship had fought hard to escape the Carthaginian fleet and for the past eight hours he had pushed the trireme to its limits. For him there was not a moment to lose and the unreadable manner of the consul irked him. The port commander at Brolium, the man he had hoped to report to, spoke to his captains as near equals, accepting their opinions and dissent in any private discussions. This man, however, this politician of Rome, kept his own counsel and invited none.

'You men will accompany me to the legion encampment immediately,' he said brusquely to Atticus and Septimus. 'Wait for me in the courtyard.'

The two men saluted and turned on their heels. The consul's

personal guard quickly formed up around them and they were escorted from the rooftop.

Scipio walked to the rail and looked out over the docks below. The tempo of the labour there had not abated throughout the afternoon, but it now seemed that they had broken the back of the task of unloading the fleet of barges. With a new threat emerging in the waters beyond the harbour, Scipio wondered briefly if these would be the last supplies for the fighting legions on Sicily.

Hannibal Gisco sat in his cabin on the flagship *Melqart*, drinking wine from a golden goblet. The goblet had once belonged to the prefect of Agrigentum, the city Gisco had captured over a year before. Along with the entire city Council, the prefect had been stoned to death, punishment for closing the city gates against the Carthaginians' initial advance. The man had not died well. In the corner of the cabin, reclined on a couch, Hamilcar Barca sat watching the admiral in silence. He noticed the slight smile on Gisco's face, wondering what thought had prompted the smile, an expression so different from the frustration Gisco had displayed an hour before when he had first returned to the flagship.

Hamilcar had listened then as Gisco outlined the escape of a Roman trireme, concealing his shock at the anger that seemed to emanate from every pore of the admiral's body. The slaves had worked with practised speed as Gisco talked, stripping the admiral of his armour and tunic, bathing his skin with scented water before massaging oil into the obviously tensed muscles of his upper body and shoulders. The familiar routine had gone some way to assuage Gisco's frustration, but only now, as a lingering smile remained on the admiral's face, did Hamilcar judge the moment right to discuss the implications of the Roman ship's escape.

46

'You said she was a coastal galley?' Hamilcar asked, keeping his voice even, suppressing all elements of judgement.

'Yes, lighter than one of our own. Probably a pirate hunter.'

Hamilcar nodded, allowing a silence to develop once more, his experience in the Council chamber of Carthage dictating his line of questioning.

'She will flee along the northern coast of Sicily then?'

Gisco grunted a reply, disliking the young man and his presence on board the flagship. The Council's interference in military affairs had reached new depths with the appointment of Barca, the Council's 'envoy', an advisory observer who shadowed Gisco's command.

'No doubt to the nearest Roman port, where she will give advance warning to all that our fleet has entered these waters . . .' Hamilcar persisted, trying to get Gisco to reveal his thoughts on the change in circumstances.

'It is of little consequence, Barca, the Romans would have found out soon enough,' Gisco replied, avoiding any admission that his failure to capture the Roman trireme was in any way significant.

A sudden knock on the door interrupted their conversation.

'Come,' Gisco ordered.

The commander of his personal guard, Cronus, entered. He snapped to attention.

'Captain Maghreb of the *Hermes* reporting as ordered, Admiral.'

'Good, show him in, Cronus.'

Gisco rose from his chair. He leaned over his desk, strewn with Carthaginian maps of the waters around the eastern and northern coasts of Sicily. Maghreb entered, led by the guard commander and flanked by four more soldiers. His sword and dagger had been removed. He stood to attention and saluted.

'Reporting as ordered, Admiral,' he said, trying to hide the tension in his voice. He failed. Gisco could sense the captain's fear.

'Captain,' the admiral began, 'I have studied all our maps and charts of these waters. I can find no reference to the whirlpool we encountered this morning. The Romans tricked us using superior local knowledge. We could not have been aware of their plans.'

Maghreb visibly relaxed and, although he still stood to attention, Gisco noticed that the tension had gone out of his shoulders and he was no longer holding his breath.

'They will not escape the next time they cross our path,' Maghreb added, sensing the admiral's mood.

'No, Captain, they will not,' Gisco replied, his voice cold.

The two men stood facing each other in silence and Maghreb felt uncomfortable once more under Gisco's gaze. The admiral's expression was impossible to read, but the captain sensed that he would evade blame for the escape of the Roman galley.

He was wrong.

'Guard commander!' Gisco suddenly ordered, breaking the heavy silence. 'This man disobeyed my orders, he must be punished. Seize him.'

Cronus looked at two of the guards and jerked his head towards the captain. They immediately rushed forward and grabbed his arms. Maghreb's initial shock at the admiral's words gave way to fear and he struggled against the men holding him.

'But . . .' he pleaded, fear consuming him, his mind unable to comprehend the admiral's actions, 'you said yourself, I couldn't have known of the Romans' trap. We were taken by surprise. We —'

'Enough!' Gisco bellowed, cutting across the captain's pleas. 'You were ordered to continue your pursuit of the Roman vessel. You did not and they escaped. There are no excuses.'

48

'But . . .' Maghreb began again, hopelessness overwhelming him.

'Take him away, Commander,' Gisco ordered. 'Have him straddle the ram.'

The pronounced sentence instantly silenced Maghreb, an overwhelming wave of terror engulfing him. Cronus saluted and led the condemned man from the cabin.

Hamilcar had watched the entire exchange with disbelief. In the two months since being appointed to shadow Gisco, he had become increasingly aware of the man's serpentine nature. Hamilcar had witnessed scenes like this before and as always his honour was offended by Gisco's methods. The admiral always lulled an enemy before striking and Hamilcar knew it served no purpose other than to satisfy Gisco's ego.

The admiral noticed Hamilcar's expression as he sat back down behind his desk. The captain's renewed cries for mercy could be heard through the cabin door as he was dragged up onto the deck above and brought forward to meet his fate.

'You disapprove, Barca?'

Hamilcar kept his peace, sensing Gisco's dislike for his position, knowing the admiral wanted to provoke a confrontation to justify his actions.

'Let me tell you something, young man,' Gisco began, his voice patronizing. 'Fear is what drives men. Fear of failure. Fear of retribution. Fear of —'

'Hannibal Gisco?' Hamilcar interrupted, his own censure evident in every word.

'Yes,' Gisco replied, as if trying to explain his reasoning to an obtuse child, 'fear of Hannibal Gisco. Maghreb was ordered to hunt down the Roman galley and he failed. Now he will pay for that failure with his life.'

Hamilcar bit back his retort, knowing the futility of arguing against a man such as Gisco. The man had no honour, no sense of the true motivation of men, the drive that inspires them to create and control an empire. He got up slowly from the couch, sensing the admiral's dismissive gaze as he moved towards the door. He walked out without a word, glad to be out of Gisco's company.

Hamilcar reached the deck as Cronus and two others were climbing back over the forerail. Hamilcar walked down the length of the galley, ignoring the guard commander as they passed each other amidships. By the time he reached the fore-deck, Cronus had issued the order for the *Melqart* to get back under way. Hamilcar looked over the forerail to the figure of Maghreb below. He was tied in a supine position, face up, over the six-foot ram of the galley. With the ship at rest, half of his body was submerged under the water; however, as the quin-quereme picked up speed to reach standard, the waves began to crash over him. Maghreb would drown slowly. Very slowly.

Hamilcar watched in dread fascination as Maghreb tried to draw breath between waves. An errant crest filled his mouth with water and he coughed and spluttered to clear his tortured lungs. He gained a moment's respite but within a minute he was caught again. Maghreb threw his face up and Hamilcar was given a vision of pure terror. A cry of anguish was cut short by the cold sea, her unending current oblivious to the fate of the terrified captain. Maghreb cleared his throat again but all the while his lungs continued to fill with water.

At standard speed, in calm coastal waters, Hamilcar esti-mated it would take at least thirty minutes for Maghreb to drown. The *Melqart* was flanked on both sides by other galleys, many of their crew lining the rails to witness the captain's punishment. Hamilcar could see from their expressions that Gisco was achieving his aim of inspiring fear in the heart of each man. Maghreb was silent, his thrashing arms and manic face the only testament to his futile struggle against the sea.

Hamilcar stepped back from the forerail, hiding the captain from his line of sight.

Hamilcar had spent the first ten years of his military career in Iberia, stationed in Malaka on the southern coast. It was the frontier of the Carthaginian empire, a new expansion being forged from the lands of the Celts who had formerly controlled the isolated peninsula. Hamilcar had made his name and cemented his standing amongst the ancestors of his ancient line in that campaign. The fight had been brutal, the territory hard fought and won. Hamilcar had led many men to their deaths, had ruthlessly thrown them against the relentless attacks of the Celts in an effort to secure victory. But always with honour, always with the strength of his men harnessed through loyalty to Carthage and their commander.

Hamilcar had yet to meet the Romans in battle. Years before, Carthage and Rome had fought together as allies against Pyrrhus of Epirus. It was an alliance that precipitated the current conflict, a once-honourable union that Rome had established to save her lands before turning the allied victory into a dishonourable invasion of Sicily on a pretext of saving the people of Messina from the armies of Syracuse, an invasion that threatened Carthage's extensive commercial interests on the island.

The die was now cast. The Roman trireme had escaped and so it was only a matter of time before Hamilcar would face the enemy in battle. His gaze hardened at the thought, savouring the anticipation of expelling the Romans from Sicily, re-establishing the supremacy of his people as masters of the Mediterranean.

A guard detail of sixty legionaries, half a full maniple, stood in formation in the courtyard of the villa with a centurion walking up and down the ranks inspecting the men. A signifer stood at the head of the formation, holding aloft the maniple's standard. The gentle offshore breeze ruffled the cloth of the standard, the gold discs hanging beneath clinking against each other like wind chimes. Septimus studied it and saw the symbol of a bull, marking it as a maniple of the Second legion, one of the four now campaigning in Sicily. Septimus had belonged to the Ninth Legion, encamped with the Second just beyond the town of Brolium. The other two legions, the Sixth and Seventh, were stationed further south, near the border with Syracuse, a politically motivated location meant to keep Hiero II, the king of Syracuse, bottled up. Their static location meant the two legions at Brolium would bear the brunt of the spring campaign.

The inspecting centurion looked past his men to the entrance of the courtyard, spotting Septimus and Atticus. He approached them with the confident, measured stride of a manipular centurion, a man totally at ease with his command and certain of his place in life.

'Identify yourselves!' he demanded of the two men.

'Captain Perennis of the trireme *Aquila*, and Centurion Capito of the marines,' Septimus announced, 'reporting as ordered by the senior consul.'

The centurion grunted, his opinion of sailors and marines clearly written across his face. Septimus ignored the implied slur, although he marked the centurion's face in his mind.

'Fall into the front rank,' the legionary commanded. 'The consul is on his way.'

Atticus and Septimus walked forward and took their place in the formation of soldiers. The centurion took one last look at his assembled men before standing to the fore of the group, the signifer behind and to his left. All waited motionless for the consul to appear.

Scipio arrived five minutes later. He was followed by his

guard commander and the twelve men of his personal guard, the *praetoriani*. Their distinctive black travelling cloaks billowed around them as they marched in step behind their master. The consul flicked his hand upwards and the guard commander called the soldiers to a halt, the hobnails of their sandals reverberating in the quiet of the afternoon air. Scipio walked on alone to inspect the demi-maniple of legionaries. He sensed and relished the stillness of the troops before him, their discipline and uniformity evoking memories of his own time in the legions, a simpler time when rules and orders dictated all his actions, just as they did for the men before him. He noticed the two commanders from the *Aquila* in the front rank of the formation, noticed that they were still in full battle armour. They kept and wore their armour well, although both showed signs of battles fought.

The sound of a horse's snort caused Scipio to turn. A stable lad was leading a grey-white stallion across the courtyard to the assembled men. The horse was Andalusian, a Spanish horse, sixteen hands high. He had been warmed up and groomed and he scraped the flagstones with his right hoof, his body a mass of restrained energy. Scipio walked over to the horse and patted his crest and throat, talking gently to the stallion in the practised tone of a seasoned horseman.

'A magnificent beast,' he said to no one in particular before mounting.

The senior consul settled himself comfortably in the saddle and turned the horse around to face the demi-maniple. He noticed immediately that his mount was a warhorse, the animal responding to movements in Scipio's legs and shifts in his body weight. In battle, the rider would be free to wield weapons in both hands, the horse not relying on the reins for guidance.

'Form up!' Scipio ordered the centurion, before wheeling the horse around.

'Marching column!' the centurion roared, and the demi-maniple transformed itself into twenty rows of three men abreast. Atticus and Septimus were in the front row, the naval captain thankful that he didn't have to move for the column to form up, unfamiliar as he was with the finer points of legionary drill manoeuvres.

The consul's guard led the march out through the double doors of the courtyard, followed by Scipio, who needed to duck beneath the overhead arch of the gateway. The demi-maniple of the Second followed, wheeling right as they left the courtyard to take the winding road down to the docks two miles away. The streets were empty before them, doors and shutters closed to hide the inhabitants within. The towns-people were used to seeing Roman soldiers in Brolium; however, the menacing sight of the black-cloaked guard of the *praetoriani* and the obvious importance of the Roman they escorted prompted the people to hide in trepidation.

The column wound its way out of the town of Brolium and set out on the road south to the encampment. The road was busy, with the constant flow of traders moving between the port town and the lucrative opportunities of the legions' base camp. All stepped aside as the marching column of soldiers approached, many manhandling their carts from the ten-foot-wide dust road into the fields on either side. They stared in awe at the sight of Scipio riding gloriously in the evening sun, his bearing and perfect features heralding his wealth and stature, while the size of his escort announced his importance for all the world to see.

The Roman encampment was located a mile south of Brolium. The camp was the Second and Ninth legions' *castra hiberna*, their winter camp, and was a semi-permanent structure suitable for the soldiers' extended stay in the cold months. Even now the weather heralded the arrival of spring, when Ceres's vibrant touch would transform nature in celebration of Proserpina's return to the world from her winter exile in Hades. The arrival of spring would also herald the beginning of the legions' campaign season, and soon the Romans would march away from Brolium to carry the fight to the Carthaginians holding the western half of Sicily. If they were successful they would not return and a new *castra hiberna* would be constructed deep in what was now enemy territory.

As the column approached the encampment, they passed the advanced stations of the legions. These guard posts were located two hundred yards from the camp on each approach road and were manned by four legionaries. Septimus could see that they had been forewarned of the consul's possible arrival, as all four soldiers stood to attention outside the guard hut where normally one would stand while the other three rested inside. They did not challenge the column but let it pass in silence, their eyes looking straight ahead, not daring to look up at Scipio for fear of drawing his attention.

The main camp was rectangular in shape, built of two squares, one for each legion, and the long axis of the camp ran parallel to the road. The whole area was surrounded by a deep trench, fifteen feet across and five deep with the excavated earth thrown inward to form a formidable rampart, on top of which stood the wall. Near the main gate, the Porta Praetoria, the wall had been reinforced with stone; however, the majority of the palisade was constructed from wooden stakes cut from young oak trees. The branches of the stakes had been sharpened and interwoven with each other to form a near-impenetrable obstacle, and at each corner of the rectangle a twenty-foot-high watchtower stood, giving the sentries advance warning of any approaching force on the uninterrupted surface of the valley floor.

The column passed through the open gates of the camp, again without challenge or check, to be confronted, immediately inside the walls, by the massed ranks of the Second and Ninth legions. They had been drawn up in manipular formation; a legion stood on each side of the road running directly down the centre of the camp to the officers' quarters in the centre. As Scipio rode under the archway of the gate, the legionaries roared with one voice:

'Rome Victorious!'

Scipio rode on at the measured pace of the march, never looking left or right. A man born to command, the blood rushed in his veins at the sound of twenty thousand shouting in his honour. His expression was imperial, a look of fraternal pride, as if each man before him was a younger brother, a brother of Rome. Drawn up across the road before him were the senior officers of the legions. The commander of the *praetoriani* called a halt to the column and Scipio dismounted, covering the last few steps of the journey on foot.

'Greetings, Senior Consul,' a tall authoritative man at the head of the officers declared. 'Welcome to Sicily.' He was Lucius Postumius Megellus, legate of the Roman legions and a member of the Senate.

'Thank you, Lucius,' Scipio replied, his words genuine. Scipio had spent the past seven years in the Senate, all the while gaining in influence and power. His rise had given him many enemies, and on more than one occasion the man before him had clashed with him, but always honourably, always without subterfuge, and for that Scipio respected him.

Legate Megellus turned to introduce Scipio to the assembled officers. The introductions were brief, the salutes formal and exact.

Septimus ignored the confluence of senior officers before him, his gaze firmly fixed on the banners held aloft over the legion to his left. The preying wolf of the Ninth looked balefully from each linen standard, its eyes locked on a former son of the ranks. Septimus had not seen the Ninth in over a year, his reassignment to the *Aquila* severing his link to the only legion he had ever known. He remembered the moment acutely, the moment of choice so many months before, the decision to accept a promotion to centurion in the marines over remaining as *optio* of the IV maniple. It was a decision he had wrestled over but once made he had never looked back. Until now.

Septimus searched the ranks for the signifer of the IV maniple, suddenly feeling the need to reconnect to his old command and the standard he had fought and lived under for so many years. The order to advance the column was given as he found his mark deep within the ranks, the men beneath the banner of the IV hidden by the mass of soldiers around them.

'How reliable is this man's word?' Legate Megellus asked, his question directed at the port commander.

'Captain Perennis has been in Rome's service for fifteen years. I have personally known him for ten. His word is beyond question,' the commander answered, confidence in his voice as he looked over at the young captain.

Atticus stood motionless beside Septimus in the meeting room of the officers' quarters. His expression never changed at the questioning of his report, although he was glad he could rely on his commander for backup. He had retold the salient parts of his report to the group of officers, paying particular attention to what he had seen of the strength and course of the Carthaginian fleet, sticking only to facts and avoiding subjectivity and opinion.

'So you see, gentlemen,' Scipio said as he scanned the faces of the assembled officers before him, the men still reeling from the news they had just heard, 'the Carthaginians have raised the stakes considerably. At best we are faced with dwindling supplies, at worst we are faced with starvation and ruin.'

Scipio's face remained inscrutable as he spoke, the men waiting for his next words. Megellus smiled to himself. He had seen the senior consul in discussion with other men before, and knew his habit of drawing out a silence, a silence which unnerved some men, especially the younger ones, who felt compelled to fill the void. A junior tribune was the first to break the quiet.

'We must accelerate our campaign and strike while we are still strong!' he blurted.

The words emboldened the other junior tribunes and they echoed this view, calling for immediate action, immediate countermeasures, their thoughts and words directionless, over-lapping.

'Enough!' Megellus ordered above the rising sound.

The silence reasserted itself.

'What are your thoughts, Consul?' he asked Scipio.

The senior consul looked down at the maps and charts on the table before him, studying the outline of the northern coast of Sicily on one in particular. For the past twenty years the Punici had occupied the entire island west of Halaesa, a dividing line some fifty miles west of Brolium. Fifty miles to the east of Brolium was the kingdom of Syracuse, the two territories separated by the natural obstacle of Mount Etna and a mutual agreement of noninterference. The Roman legions had filled that vacuum and so, as yet, their supply hubs were still a closely guarded secret.

'I believe we have time on our side for the moment,' Scipio began, every man now hanging on his words, the same officers nodding agreement who moments ago had advocated haste. 'The Carthaginians hold ports further west of our location,' he continued, pointing to the ports of Thermae and Panormus. 'They will need time to discover and confirm our supply routes. That time will give us the opportunity to implement some minor countermeasures. Measures such as using circuitous routes to port and forming smaller fleets of transport barges to make detection more difficult. It will also give me time to consult the Senate before making my decision on how best to proceed with annihilating this new threat. For now, the legions must act as if nothing has changed. We still have a campaign to win and an enemy to beat.'

The officers voiced their agreement in unison, trusting the senior consul, who seemed completely confident in his assessment of the threat. Scipio raised his hand for silence and looked over at Atticus, who now stood outside the circle of officers around the table. He consciously swept aside his intuitive mistrust of the non-Roman, knowing he had to take advantage of the younger man's experience.

'And you, Captain Perennis,' he asked of Atticus. 'As the only naval commander here, what are your thoughts on the matter?'

All the officers turned around to look at Atticus, many with a look of mild astonishment and disdain that the opinion of a lowly captain was being sought. Once again Atticus had been taken off guard by a question from the consul. He had expected to be dismissed after giving his report and so he and Septimus had drifted back to the periphery of the group. Now he was once again the centre of attention.

'I agree that we may have time on our hands as the Carthaginians organize their blockade of the northern and eastern coasts. However, I would advise against sending supplies once that blockade is in place, even using different routes or smaller fleets as you suggest.' Atticus saw a number of tribunes bristle at this contradiction of the consul's view, but Scipio's expression, as inscrutable as ever, did not show censure.

'I believe the Carthaginians are amongst the best seamen in the world,' he continued, 'master planners in both logistics and naval tactics. Any attempt to outmanoeuvre their blockade will result in failure.'

Again Atticus's remarks drew angry mutterings from some of the tribunes as he openly praised the enemy, but he continued undaunted. 'The only successful strategy will be to defeat them in battle and destroy the blockade,' he concluded, his final opinion greeted with icy silence.

Two of the tribunes snorted in derision and turned their backs on the captain, their focus returning to the consul, waiting for him to aggressively refute Atticus's opinion, but Scipio simply nodded. 'Thank you, Captain,' he said. Scipio addressed his senior officers once more.

'While time may be on our side, the next few weeks are vital if we are to overcome this threat. Any indecisiveness in our actions will be catastrophic. I will therefore leave for Rome now, immediately. Word must reach the Senate and I must be the one to deliver it. As the sea is still the fastest route to Rome, I will trust my life to those who have already bested the Punici. I will travel to Rome on the *Aquila*.'

Both Atticus and Septimus straightened up as once again all eyes in the room turned to them. Their course had been set . . . to Rome, to the centre of the Republic and the civilized world, escorting the most important man of the Republic.

'We leave in one hour,' Scipio said, dismissing the officers of the *Aquila*.

'Marcus! You old bastard,' Septimus called as he and Atticus entered the junior officers' mess, immediately recognizing his old commander from the IV maniple of the Ninth.

60

'Septimus!'

The two men met in the middle of the room and shook hands, smiling happily at each other, their meeting the first since the Battle of Agrigentum over a year before. Marcus was ten years older than Septimus, a tall, thin man and, although he was in the declining years of his prime, he still possessed an iron-hard physique and a will and discipline to match.

'How is Antoninus?' Marcus asked. 'Still the same old tyrant?'

'As hard as ever,' Septimus replied, proud of his father's reputation as one of the toughest centurions who had ever commanded a maniple of the Ninth.

'Marcus,' Septimus continued, turning to Atticus, 'this is Captain Atticus Milonius Perennis of the *Aquila*.'

The centurion was about to proffer his hand but he stayed the gesture, his eyes suddenly unfriendly.

'A Greek? By the gods, Septimus,' he said, turning to the marine, 'I cursed the day you accepted your *promotion* to centurion in the marines, but now I find you command with the very people your father and I fought at Beneventum.'

Atticus stepped forward, incensed by the unwarranted insult, but Septimus stepped into his path, his hand raised across Atticus's sword arm.

'Atticus has fought for the Republic for as long as I have, for as many years as half the men in this room. His loyalty is without question.'

Marcus was about to retort but he held his tongue, recalling the bond of friendship he had with Septimus and what a mentor Septimus's father, Antoninus, had been. He slowly proffered his hand once more, his expression this time unreadable.

Atticus remained motionless, his own gaze hostile.

'Any friend of Septimus's is a comrade of the Ninth,' Marcus prompted.

The words seemed hollow to Atticus; however, he shook the centurion's proffered hand.

'A naval captain, eh?' Marcus asked, measuring him. 'What brings you and this orphan of the Ninth to our camp?'

'Grave news,' Septimus said, recapturing Marcus's attention, all humour now gone from his voice.

Marcus indicated a crowded table with a nod of his head and all three sat down. The other centurions looked on in silence, many leaning in to hear the news that had wrought such a change in the expression of the young marine.

'Go on . . .' Marcus said, prompting Septimus to begin.

'Carthaginians,' he began, 'a whole fleet of them, Marcus. Off the northern coast. We expect a full blockade within weeks.'

'Merciful Jupiter,' Marcus breathed.

The centurion was a keen disciple of logistics, as were all centurions by necessity. The success and readiness of his maniple depended in large part on how well it was supplied. No supplies meant no replacements of armour, weapons, and the myriad simple but necessary items needed to keep a modern, effective army in the field.

'So what's the plan?' Marcus finally asked, breaking the silence, the younger centurions deferring to the most experienced man in the room.

'We sail for Rome . . .' Septimus replied '. . . to escort the senior consul to the Senate.'

'And the legions?'

'Scipio ordered that the legions must act as if nothing has changed,' Septimus said, remembering the senior consul's words in the earlier meeting, 'so the Ninth and Second will march out to battle as planned.'

'We'll march out as planned all right,' Marcus remarked, anger in his voice as forces beyond his control threatened to place a stranglehold on his legion, his maniple, his men, 'but if a blockade is enforced those plans will rapidly change. We'll become survivors not fighters, scavengers of food instead of hunters of men.' The room went quiet again as each man contemplated this change of fortune.

'Septimus,' Marcus said suddenly, a hard edge to his voice, 'Antoninus was like a father to me and to serve as *optio* in his maniple at Beneventum was an honour I was proud to repay when I promoted you to my second-in-command. I know there was another reason behind your acceptance of a promotion out of the Ninth and into the marines after the Battle of Agrigentum, and I also know you are a man like your father, a man of honour.'

Septimus nodded, remembering the strength of the bond between the two senior officers of every maniple.

'As my *optio* I always had your back and you had mine,' Marcus continued. 'I call on that bond again, Septimus. If a blockade develops, you and your captain must break it. Whatever needs to be done, you need to do it. We're facing six months of fighting and I need to know that you have our backs covered, that you'll make sure we can fight on and not be hamstrung by the Carthaginians.'

Marcus stood up as Septimus nodded his assent.

'Do I have your word?' he demanded, his tone that of a maniple centurion, a commander of one hundred and twenty men.

Septimus stood opposite him.

'Yes, Centurion,' he replied, their ranks equal but Marcus's experience commanding and earning Septimus's respect.

Marcus looked to Atticus, noting the hard expression on the younger man's face.

'And you, Greek. Will you fight for the legions?'

Atticus stood up slowly beside his friend.

'I'll fight,' he replied simply after a moment's pause.

'Good,' Marcus said.

Marcus extended his hand and Septimus shook it solemnly. Atticus paused for a heartbeat before following suit, his hesitation raising a sly smile at the edge of Marcus's mouth.

'What's the name of your ship?' Marcus asked.

'The *Aquila*,' Atticus replied, his back straightening.

Marcus nodded, noting the name. 'Good hunting, men of the *Aquila*,' he said.

'Give 'em cold iron, wolves of the Ninth,' Septimus replied, his connection to the legion that forged him giving intensity to his words, and for an instant he yearned to be once more in the ranks of the IV maniple. The strength of his will caused every man in the room to stand without command. Septimus and Atticus saluted them and they returned the salute in unison . . . all except Marcus. For a moment his eyes locked with Septimus's and the marine saw the veteran centurion nod imperceptibly, the gesture a reinforcement of the words spoken moments before. The Second and the Ninth, the Bull and the Wolf, would march from this camp onto the battlefields of Sicily. Two creatures born to battle, these beasts would fight, but they would also consume, their strength drawn from their supplies, without which they would weaken and be overcome by the very prey they sought. Their strength was now the responsibility of Septimus, and he would give his life to protect it: not because the Republic of Rome demanded the sacrifice, but because the men of the legions, men like Marcus, asked for it.

CHAPTER THREE

The returning column from the legion encampment reached the dockside at Brolium an hour before sunset. With a curt command, Scipio dismissed the officers of the *Aquila* with orders to be ready to sail at dawn. He turned his horse in the direction of the villa and continued up the narrow winding streets of the port town, the way ahead deserted as before. Within minutes he was in the courtyard of the villa and Scipio dismounted before dismissing his guard.

The senior consul made his way to his quarters, where he was met by his personal aid, the Nubian slave Khalil, whom Scipio had personally chosen from the slave markets of Rome; he was accompanied by two female slaves carrying fresh towels and warm, scented water. Before his appointment to the Senate, Scipio had been a fighting man by profession. His social position in the patrician class had afforded him the opportunity to join the legions as a tribune, but within ten years, by the time he reached twenty-eight, his aggression and ambition had taken him to the rank of legate, the overall commander of a Roman legion. He had used this position and his influential family connections to enter the Senate, where now, at only thirty-five years old, he held the position of senior consul, the highest elected official of the Republic.

Although the battles he fought in the Senate against the other ambitious men of Rome were as fierce as any he had faced on the battlefield, they lacked the element of physical danger, of pitting one man's strength against another's. It was a sensation he relished, and he now lived it vicariously through the fighting men he trained for the arena. Khalil was one of his current stock, a tall, sinewy, powerfully built Nubian whose eyes, although clear and open, seemed to hide a defiant streak that came from having been taken in slavery and not being born to it. Scipio had bent this man to his will, knew he would now kill at his command, but he also knew that it was dangerous to keep such a man in his household, to turn his back on him, to allow him even to approach while he slept. It was this danger, this element lacking in the Senate, that Scipio found intoxicating. It had driven his career in the legions and it had drawn him now to the battlefields of Sicily, to be once more around the fighting men of Rome.

Scipio allowed Khalil to help him undress and the female slaves washed his body before massaging warm oil into his upper torso. They dressed him in a clean white linen tunic and then stood back against the door, waiting for his next instruction.

His habitual routine complete, Scipio began pacing the room, his mounting excitement at the voyage ahead light in his veins. The thoughts of once more facing mortal danger heightened his anticipation.

'Make ready for my departure for Rome at dawn,' Scipio ordered Khalil, who immediately turned to leave. The two female slaves made to follow him.

'Wait,' Scipio said, causing the three to stop. 'You stay,' he ordered, indicating the second of the two women. The others left, closing the door behind them. The woman stood waiting, the basin of cooling water heavy in her hands. She was Sicilian, tall and dark, with large brown eyes and long hair. Her coltish legs were accentuated by the short *stola* dress she wore, the cord around her waist emphasizing the flair of her hips. Scipio estimated that she was no more than twenty. With a nod of his head he indicated his cot in the corner of the room and she moved towards it, placing the basin on the ground as she went, the simple gesture heightening Scipio's raw desire. Her expression never changed as she acquiesced, her face adopting the servile look of all slaves as she lay down on the bed.

Scipio had called her to his room the night he'd arrived in Brolium, but this time was different. She could see the Roman could barely contain his sudden desire. Scipio never questioned why impending danger had this effect on him, he simply gave vent to his base desires. Tomorrow he would take sail back to Rome and he would need to show the calm exterior of a leader of Rome to all on board the galley. He would need to bury deep the excitement and lust for action threatening to manifest itself in his expression. Only now, in the privacy of his quarters, as he moved slowly towards the woman, could he give in to his emotions, the brief coupling a chance to assuage his exhilaration at the approach of danger.

The sun had become a memory for the men on board the *Aquila* as they continued preparations for the dawn departure. The sky still held the light of the departed star, but it was rapidly losing ground to the approaching night, the headlands at the edge of the harbour mouth becoming mere darkened shadows against the more reflective sea.

Lucius approached Atticus on the foredeck.

'We'll be ready to sail by dawn, Captain. The last of the supplies are just arriving from the port barracks.'

'Very good, Lucius. Have my cabin cleared and made ready for the senior consul.'

'Yes, Captain,' Lucius replied, and was immediately away.

Atticus moved to the starboard rail. All around him the frantic activity of preparation continued. As always the sound most commonly splitting the air was the roar of Lucius's voice, his words a whip crack to a careless or indolent crewman. To Atticus the sound was as much part of the ship as the creak of the deck timbers or the lapping of the tidal waters against the hull ten feet below him. His mind tuned out the sounds as his eyes wandered over the barges spread out across the harbour before him. In the near darkness he could vaguely distinguish their shapes, their hulls swinging slowly against the hold of their anchor lines as the current of the outgoing tide kept their hulls in parallel with each other and perpendicular to the dock. The same current pulled at the hull of the *Aquila*, drawing her away from the dock. She answered in kind, as if eager to sail, a creature born to the sea, pulling gently at the ropes that held her fast.

The words of Septimus's former centurion, Marcus, rang in Atticus's ears: 'Whatever needs to be done, you need to do it,' he had said, and Atticus remembered how Septimus had consented without hesitation, revealing the unbreakable bond between former comrades and fellow Romans.

A descendant of Magna Graecia and a sailor all his life, Atticus had never felt any attachment to the Roman citizens of the land-based legions. His duty had always been to his ship, his crew and the people of the Ionian coast under his protection, not to a Republic that was forged by men who were a breed apart from the people of his home city, Locri.

Atticus's ancestors had migrated from Greece over generations, slowly evolving and adapting the local culture to their own. In contrast, the legions of Rome swept over entire regions in a fraction of a lifetime, transplanting their culture and the ideals of their city as they went, absorbing entire populations into their Republic within a single generation.

Atticus stood on the border of two worlds, his friendship with Septimus drawing him ever closer to Rome and the legions, while men like Scipio and Marcus blocked his path with distrust and age-old animosity. Beneath it all, Atticus could hear his ancestors whisper censure and lament for his association with Rome as they spoke of an ancient loyalty to his people who, for over five hundred years, had made southern Italy their own.

The day dawned with the scent of must in the air, the scent of the dry arid land of northern Sicily. Atticus rose from his cot in one of the smaller aft cabins of the *Aquila* and looked out through the opened hatch to the harbour beyond. From his vantage point he could see that all of the transport barges were preparing for departure, taking advantage of the turn of the tide that would ease their navigation of the harbour mouth.

The barges were lumbering vessels when docked, like beached pilot whales lying on their backs in the sun. Under way, however, with their massive mainsails pushing them through the waters, they were transformed into living, breathing creatures, and Atticus admired the seamanship required to sail these vessels in the open seas. A worry crossed his mind that they were sailing into waters where the Carthaginian hunters would be seeking them, but he quickly dismissed it. The Punici only held the ports of Thermae and Panormus, over one hundred miles further along the coastline, and they would be unaware of the Romans' activities in Brolium. Without local knowledge it would take them weeks to discover that this port was the Romans' supply hub for the entire campaign. Only then would they be able to mount an effective blockade. The departing fleet of barges would be safely home long before that day.

Atticus left the cabin and went on deck. He was immediately beckoned to the aft-deck by Lucius, the second-in-command turning and pointing over the stern rail. A hundred yards away, Scipio was leading a guard detail of *praetoriani* towards the *Aquila*. Their approach was framed by the rapidly rising sun in the eastern sky, the clear blue indicating fine weather ahead and the prospect of a quick sailing. He ordered a runner to go below and tell Septimus that Scipio was arriving and to meet him at the head of the gangway. The senior consul would expect to be welcomed aboard by the senior officers of the ship.

'There, sire,' the man pointed, his hand shaking, 'low on the horizon. That's the headland. Cape Orlando. Brolium is a league west.'

'You're sure?' Gisco asked, his voice threatening the same fate the pirate had seen his crewmates suffer.

'Yes, sire, I swear it,' he whimpered, 'we were in these waters for four weeks. We saw the Roman transport barges ply in and out of Brolium many times, although they were too big a prey for us to take. The latest fleet of over two dozen arrived only three days ago.'

Gisco grunted a reply as he stared through the pre-dawn light to the dark mass of the headland on the horizon.

'Remove this man from my sight,' he ordered, 'throw him over the side.'

The pirate screamed for mercy as the guards lifted him off the deck. In two quick strides they were at the rail and they threw the pirate overboard, his cries cut short as he hit the water ten feet below. Within seconds he was lost beneath the waves.

Gisco smiled. The gods were looking favourably on him this day. The day before, one of the galleys in the rearguard of the fleet had captured a pirate bireme as they moved north through the strait. Many of the crew were instantly put to the sword, the Carthaginians sharing the hatred of pirates that all men of the sea held, but the senior crew had been brought to the flagship where they were tortured for information on Roman naval activity in the area. Gisco's original plan called for an extensive search to find the Romans' supply hub once the fleet had reached Panormus, but fortune had smiled on him and the pirates had now given him the information he needed to carry the battle to the Romans.

'Captain Mago,' Gisco ordered, 'signal to the fleet: the first four squads are to remain on station here with the *Melqart*. The remaining six are to continue to Panormus with all possible speed. Have the squad commanders report to the flagship.'

'Yes, Admiral,' Mago replied, and took off towards the stern to signal Gisco's orders to the ships behind them. Within minutes the four squads of five galleys had broken off from the fleet, each squad comprising a quinquereme leading a group of four triremes. The *Melqart* also broke formation.

Fifteen minutes later the four squad commanders boarded the *Melqart*. Gisco met them on the foredeck.

'The Romans are using the port of Brolium as their supply hub. It is there . . .' Gisco pointed towards the distant coast '. . . two points west of that headland. We will move two leagues north of here and cast our net across their course to the mainland. Deploy with bows forward to the mainland. No sails. I want the profile of your ships to be as small as possible. At that distance out, when we are spotted, the transport barges will be too far from port to run. I want your quinqueremes on the extreme flanks. I will take the centre. Get behind them quickly and push them towards me. We will crush them between us.'

'Yes, Admiral.' The four captains saluted and turned to leave the foredeck.

'One more thing, Captains,' Gisco added, arresting their departure. 'We take no prisoners. Every barge is to be sunk. No exceptions. Understood?'

'Yes, Admiral,' they repeated and left.

'Now,' Gisco thought as he looked up at the rapidly brightening sky, 'let them come.'

Drusus Aquillius Melus, captain of the transport barge *Onus*, was nervous. Word had swept through the port of Brolium that the trireme that had rushed into the harbour the day before had encountered a Carthaginian fleet of galleys. The rumours had been contradictory, with some claiming the fleet was travelling east and others that it was going west, while estimates of its number varied from three to over a hundred. One thing was clear though, and on this all were agreed, their days of shipping supplies from the mainland to Brolium were numbered. Melus hoped that the days of his life were not similarly marked.

The captain looked up at the mainsail and checked its line as his barge moved slowly out of the harbour. His ship was two hundred feet long and thirty feet wide, a behemoth of the sea, as long as a quinquereme, but wider in the beam and over twice as tall from the waterline. The offshore breeze was light and he estimated their best speed once clear of the port would be no more than five knots. At this speed the passage to Naples would take nearly two full days. He looked over his shoulder at the thirty-two other barges making their way ponderously under sail. They would separate out as the day wore on, the new ships outpacing the older, the experienced crews faster than the inexperienced. Each ship had its own pace. Unique.

By nightfall they would aim to have a half-mile between each ship, to avoid collisions in the dark. Now, grouped together, the flotilla of transports seemed to Melus to resemble a flock of sheep, the bellies of their broad white mainsails stretching out across the width of the harbour. A sight to see. He looked up above them to the sky overhead. It was a clear day which promised clear sailing. Perfect weather for navigation. Two days, he repeated to himself, two days and home.

The *Aquila* cast off from the dockside as the last of the transport barges weighed anchor and raised sail. The larger vessels moved slowly under sail and Gaius wove the *Aquila* nimbly through their ranks using the galley's superior manoeuvrability under oars. Scipio stood alone on the aft-deck, watching the action of the crew around him intently, his journey on the *Aquila* marking his first time on a galley. The consul was travelling light in comparison to his arrival three days before on one of the transport barges. The confined and valuable space aboard a fighting vessel meant that his entourage consisted of merely his guard commander and four *praetoriani* with his Nubian slave, Khalil, in attendance. In any other place the reduced guard would be foolhardy, but in the isolation of a galley at sea it seemed almost excessive. The only enemies that threatened him were the Carthaginians and, if the *Aquila* was somehow attacked in strength, the fact that his guard was four instead of twenty-four would make little difference.

Atticus watched the consul surreptitiously as the *Aquila* gained the lead on the fleet of barges. Lucius ordered the sail raised, transferring the exertion of the rowers to the wind. The galley's combination of oars and sail would maintain a slight gap on the barges, keeping her in the van of the flotilla. Septimus joined Atticus on the foredeck.

'Rome!' he smiled, and slapped Atticus's shoulder.

Atticus couldn't help but smile, his friend's good mood at returning to his home city infectious.

As a younger man, with the wanderlust of youth powerful in his veins, Atticus had wanted to travel to Rome and all the great cities of the Republic, and from there beyond to the distant shores of the Mediterranean, the great sea that touched all the coastlines of the known world. That ambition had narrowed with age, tempered by realities and his duty to his ship and crew. But the desire to see Rome had always stayed with him, a desire to see the centre of the Republic, to grasp the atmosphere in the city that inspired men to conquer the world around them.

Captain Melus stared at the galley moving effortlessly through the water. The wind had picked up after leaving port and so now, two hours out from Brolium, the galley was still within a mile of the leading ships on the port side of the fleet. Melus had served twenty years on a trading galley, rising to the rank of boatswain. His share of the profit over those years had provided him with the opportunity to purchase a part share in the *Onus* which, thanks to the campaign on Sicily and the almost constant supply drops, was proving to be a profitable investment. That would all change with the commencement of a blockade and Melus cursed Fortuna for her fickle nature.

Suddenly, as Melus watched, the mainsail of the galley collapsed. Even over the distance of a mile, the captain could see the deck of the galley come alive. Something was wrong.

'Ship ahead!'

Melus turned. The cry had come from the masthead. He looked up to see the lookout pointing directly ahead of their course. An acid feeling of dread filled his stomach as he rushed forward to the foredeck. Peering out over the rail, he waited to see the reported ship, his viewpoint twenty feet below the masthead making him wait before seeing what the lookout had seen.

'There,' his mind screamed, 'dead ahead.'

He blinked his eyes rapidly to clear them and refocused on the unexpected and yet feared sight in front of him. He couldn't make out any details beyond the fact that it was directly facing them, its bow pointing like an arrow at his own. It looked like . . . no, he was certain . . . it was a galley.

'Two more ships ahead! A point off starboard and port!' the lookout called again. Melus could hear fear in the man's voice at the realization of what he was seeing. Within five seconds he could also see the two ships himself, flanking the first. It was an ambush. There was no doubt and there could be no doubt of who they were.

Melus was about to sound the alarm when he heard the resonating sound of a signalling trumpet from the fleet behind him. In foggy weather these trumpets were used to alert other ships to avoid collisions. In clear conditions their repeated blasts meant mortal danger.

'Two more ships ahead!' The lookout's cries were now frantic. 'Two points off starboard and port!'

The captain ignored the cries from above, his mind trying to comprehend the warning sounds he was hearing. They weren't emanating from the ships around him, from those who could also see the ships ahead, but from the rear of the fleet. 'They can't have seen them yet,' his mind was telling him, 'unless . . .' He felt a sharp pain in his lower intestines as terror overtook his emotions.

'Sweet mercy . . .' he whispered at the realization of what was happening. 'They're all around us . . . we're trapped.'

'Prepare for action!' Atticus roared, his orders overlain with the repeated blasts of warning trumpets from the transport fleet behind. Five galleys could be seen on the horizon, with the lookout reporting four more on the flanks. The Romans had sailed into a perfect trap.

'Gaius! Two points to starboard. Prepare to sweep. Lucius, orders to below, attack speed!'

'Hold!'

Atticus turned to see Scipio standing beside him, the consul's face a mask of fury.

'Explain yourself, Captain!'

'I'm going to sweep the portside oars of the outermost galley. If we disable her we'll open a gap in the line to allow some of the transports to escape,' Atticus said quickly.

'To Hades with the transports. Your orders are to escort me safely to Rome!'

'With all due respect, Consul,' Atticus growled, his expression hard, 'we can't abandon the transports to the Punici. Without our assistance they will be slaughtered to a man.'

'I am in command of this galley, Captain, and my safety is paramount!'

Atticus stepped forward and leaned in slightly to respond, an instinctive movement to reinforce his argument.

Scipio's guard commander spotted the move and instantly drew his sword, misreading Atticus's stance as a prelude to attack. Within a heartbeat the four *praetoriani* followed suit. Gaius and Lucius drew their own daggers, their reactions instinctive.

Only Atticus and Scipio remained immobile, their faces inches apart, their expressions unwavering. Atticus could feel the blood thumping in his chest, the adrenaline coursing in his veins, his mind racing, his ears filled with the sound of two conflicting voices screaming within him. One called for caution, knowing that Scipio could kill any who disobeyed without remorse or recourse. The other demanded defiance, the fate of hundreds of men in the transport fleet in the balance. To his left and right Scipio's praetorian guards stood with their swords drawn, outnumbering his crew on the aft-deck, their lives on the brink of forfeiture.

'Gaius! Hard to port!' Atticus shouted. His command was met with silence and he turned to the helmsman. Gaius was tensed, his body coiled to release at the first sign of an attack from the praetorian guard opposite him.

'Now, Gaius!' Atticus roared, breaking the taut spell that held each man ready on the aft-deck. The helmsman instantly obeyed, sheathing his dagger before leaning on the tiller, turning the bow away from the oncoming Carthaginian galley.

Scipio remained rigid, his eyes focused on Atticus before him, anger still threatening to overwhelm him. With immense will he suppressed the urge to order the captain killed, to expunge this questioning of his authority, this affront to his power. He reasserted his reason, knowing that, at least for now, the captain was invaluable.

'Stand down!' he ordered and his guards immediately obeyed.

'Captain?' Scipio said, his voice low and menacing. He drew Atticus over to the side rail.

'This ship belongs to Rome, Captain, and on this ship I am Rome. This crew may look to you for command. But make no mistake, Perennis, I command here. Do not hesitate to follow my orders again.'

'Yes, Consul,' Atticus replied, suppressing the last of his defiance, allowing the consul to bend him to his superior will.

'Attack speed!' Gisco ordered with relish. 'Steer an intercept course for the lead barge.'

The *Melqart* came alive under his feet, its two hundred and seventy rowers on four levels bending their backs to the task of bringing the quinquereme up to attack speed. 'Like sheep to the slaughter,' Gisco thought, with a smile as the rising rhythm of the oar-strokes matched the rising tempo of the blood pumping in his veins. There was no escape for the Romans. By now the other quinqueremes would be closing the trap behind the transport fleet, cutting off their escape back to Brolium. Against unarmed barges the fight would be no more than practice for the helmsman of each galley, a chance to exercise their skill at ramming and withdrawing from enemy ships. Gisco estimated the fleet at well over two dozen barges. Far off to his right a lone galley was preceding the transport fleet, her course set to collide with the far right flank of the Carthaginian attack. Gisco regretted that the Roman galley was not within easy range for his ship but then dismissed the thought. There would be plenty of Roman blood spilled on the waters this day.

'Maintain course!' Melus roared to the aft-deck.

The gap between his barge and the Carthaginian ships ahead was closing rapidly as the *Onus* set her bow against the centre galley. The sound of breaking timbers caused him to tear his eyes from the approaching galleys to the fleet behind him. Two transport barges had collided, their frantic efforts to escape causing them to accidentally turn into each other. They're dead men, Melus thought with finality, knowing that the crew of the *Onus* would surely follow them to Elysium if he could not find a way out of the trap.

Melus's twenty years' experience on trading galleys flashed

through his mind. There was only one chance. The galleys were better armed but the transport barges were bigger, almost twice the size of a quinquereme. Against ships that size, Melus knew the galleys could not ram them head on. They could only attack, and ram, on the flanks. His only chance was to run directly at the ship approaching him and hope that the Carthaginian would turn.

Strange, Gisco thought, noticing the barge his galley was targeting had not turned. She was coming directly for the *Melqart*, the gap down to two hundred yards and closing rapidly. Gisco instinctively braced as he contemplated a head-on collision with the larger ship. The adrenaline in his blood coursed through him, picturing the *Melqart* striking the barge through the bow at ramming speed. The collision would be terrifying, the combined speed of both vessels nearly twenty knots. The *Melqart* would survive, of that Gisco had no doubt, but the damage would be catastrophic and casualties high. But what of the story? he thought. What of the story sweeping through the fleet of how Gisco had faced a ship twice the size of his own and rammed her through the bow? No one would ever doubt the courage of Hannibal Gisco.

'Ramming speed!' Gisco bellowed. 'Prepare for impact!

'Cronus!' Gisco's commander of his personal guard was instantly at his side.

'Commander, station two of your men on the aft-deck. If the helmsman alters course against my orders, run him through!'

'Yes, Admiral,' Cronus replied and was gone.

Gisco's will hardened as the *Melqart* came to her top speed.

The *Aquila* swept across the bow of the Carthaginian galley at a distance of two hundred yards. Atticus waited for the enemy ship to alter her course to intercept, willing the

Carthaginian to turn, to force the engagement, thereby allowing Atticus to circumvent the consul's orders. The Carthaginian vessel stayed unerringly on course, the prospect of so many more vulnerable targets too great a temptation for the Carthaginian commander. Atticus cursed at the clear waters ahead of his galley. Over his shoulder the transport fleet was now in utter chaos, with every barge seeking to escape the Carthaginians' trap. Lacking the speed and manoeuvrability of the enemy galleys, their attempts to flee were hopeless.

The Carthaginian galley was not turning. She was not altering her course. Melus replayed his plan in his mind and could find no flaw in his thinking. The Carthaginian should turn. A head-on collision would cause tremendous damage to the galley, damage that could easily be avoided if they turned and pursued.

'She is commanded by a madman,' Melus thought, his shaking hand holding the tiller, doubt and fear assailing him. He measured the distance between the converging ships. The enemy galley was one hundred yards ahead, her bow arrow-like on its determined course.

Eighty yards.

Melus could clearly hear the unchecked drum beat of ramming speed, the sound unnerving, shattering the confidence of his earlier conviction.

Sixty yards.

A sudden urge to turn and run tore through Melus and he closed his eyes to suppress it, clinging to the belief that there was still a chance the Carthaginian would flinch.

Forty yards.

Melus opened his eyes. The prow of the Carthaginian galley filled his vision, its insistent course unerring. His breath froze in his throat as his nerve collapsed, his wits fleeing before the sight in his mind of the destruction of the *Onus* and her crew, a fate that could not be endured, a fate that could yet be avoided if he turned . . .

Melus threw his whole weight behind the tiller, heeling the *Onus* hard over to port. With the wind dead astern, the barge reacted instantly, her bow swinging quickly across the course of the approaching galley. The captain braced himself against the tiller, willing his ship to respond faster. His eyes remained locked on the Carthaginian galley, on the six-foot bronze ram screaming towards them at wave height, praying she would remain on her original course, the sight of so many other targets too great a temptation.

The voice in his head roared in rage and fear, 'Take them, not me. Kill them but spare me —'

His silent cries were cut short by the sight of the ram swinging around to centre itself on the exposed hull of the *Onus*.

Gisco cursed as the Roman barge broke off her line to a head-on collision. He was standing firm on the aft-deck of the *Melqart*, his whole body tensed in anticipation, his mind locked on the thought of the bronze ram sinking deep into the bow of the transport barge, a near-suicidal blow that would rock both ships to their cores. He took precious seconds to react to the unexpected reprieve before his mind roared at him to take action.

'Hard to starboard! Ram amidships!'

The *Melqart* swung immediately onto its final course, the oncoming wind-driven waves breaking over the ram.

The quinquereme struck the transport barge at a speed of thirteen knots, the six-inch squared blunt nose of the bronze ram splintering the oaken hull of the barge, the momentum of the ninety-ton galley driving the point deeply into the bowels of the larger ship. The force of the impact was absorbed by the keel of the galley, but the sudden loss of speed caused the rowers to lose all coordination and the *Melqart* came to a complete stop.

'Archers!' Gisco roared, and immediately ignited, resin-soaked arrows flew from the main deck of the galley to target the enormous mainsail of the stricken barge. For a second nothing happened, the arrows seemingly ineffective, then small flames appeared as if from nowhere on the huge canvas of sail. The flames held and then exploded as they began to consume the sail.

'Withdraw!'

The orders to the slave deck were concise and well practised and the *Melqart* slowly reversed, her ram withdrawing from the mortally wounded ship, the water rushing past it into the gaping hole below the waterline.

'Cut her down! . . . For the love of Fortuna cut her down before it spreads!' Melus roared as he watched the fire grow from the corner of the great sail. Within seconds it began to engulf the entire canvas, the flames licking and then igniting the running rigging and mainmast. The crew of the *Onus* had been drilled many times in the training that now controlled their actions, their fear of fire fuelling their haste, their bare feet running along the timber deck that the fire above them so desperately craved.

The fire continued to consume the sail, its appetite fed by the trailing wind and, even as Melus watched, the first fiery sections began to fall to the deck. The men attacked the fallen canvas with fanatic hostility, beating the flames with water-soaked cloths. One man screamed as a burning section of canvas fell on him, igniting his hair and clothes, and he ran aimlessly across the deck before falling over the side rail.

The deck heeled violently as the Carthaginian galley withdrew her ram and many men fell on the inclined main deck. The entire sail was now aflame and the falling burning pieces overwhelmed the futile efforts of the crew. Melus looked past the burning main deck to the Carthaginian galley. She was resuming her course to the remaining transport barges behind the *Onus*, her crew cheering at the sight of the sinking Roman ship.

Melus held on to the tiller tightly as the deck continued to heel over under his feet, the *Onus* sinking rapidly by the bow. Bitter tears ran freely down his face as shame consumed him, shame for his cowardice, of calling down damnation on his fellow sailors in a bid to save his own life. A rage of frustration and regret overwhelmed him, for he knew he should have stayed on his collision course. The result would have been the complete destruction of the *Onus*, but Melus now realized their fate had been sealed the moment they sailed from Brolium only hours before. By turning his ship he had lost his only chance to exact some revenge from the Carthaginians for the destruction of his ship and crew, his only chance to send some of the enemy ahead of him to Hades.

The *Melqart* increased to attack speed as the helmsman sought out another target. Gisco looked around him at the carnage wrought by his fleet of twenty galleys. Some of his galleys were chasing barges as they attempted to break from the pack and escape, while others had sailed directly into the centre of the transport fleet, causing panic and collisions as they snapped at the heels of the larger vessels.

Gisco saw a knot of men in the sea ahead: Romans who had jumped from a burning vessel. They were keeping together, helping each other as their ship slipped beneath the waves not twenty feet away.

'Helm, one point to starboard!' Gisco ordered, the helmsman immediately seeing the intended target. He lined up the *Melqart* perfectly.

The ninety-ton galley bore down on the knot of men, one of their number suddenly seeing the approaching galley, his cries alerting the others. Hamilcar watched the enfolding scene without comment, despising the brutality of targeting helpless men in the water. Like all on board he had cheered as the *Melqart* had made her first kill, revelling in the destruction of the enemy fleet, praising Tanit, the Phoenician goddess of fortune, for the incredible stroke of fate that had delivered the Roman fleet into their hands.

The frantic pleas of the Romans were cut off as the *Melqart* struck, many of the archers on the aft-deck running to the stern rail, hoping for survivors. There were none. Hamilcar found himself watching Gisco as the admiral stared at the broken bodies of the Romans in the wake of his ship. He marvelled at the duality of the commander. He was an incredible seaman, the perfection of his trap and his ability to understand and outwit the Roman enemy testament to his skill. But he was also capable of incredible brutality, a burning, insatiable blood lust that demanded a heavy price from the enemy.

Hamilcar recalled the brief of his appointment, a shadow to extend the reach of the Council of Carthage to ensure there was no repeat of Gisco's ignominious defeat at Agrigentum. It was a course that Hamilcar had often secretly questioned, wondering why Gisco had been allowed to retain his command. Only now, in the heat of battle, did he fully understand the Council's logic. If Rome was to be defeated in Sicily, men with Gisco's ruthlessness would be needed in every battle. In all its five-hundred-year history, Carthage had never relinquished a dominion to any enemy. Sicily could not become an exception.

Gisco turned as the Roman sailors slipped beneath the waves, immediately noticing Hamilcar's gaze. The younger man continued to stare, a new commitment to forge a unified command welling up within him. Gisco noted the expression and mistook it for a shared satisfaction over the death of the helpless Roman sailors.

'This will send a message to Rome and her legions,' Gisco said, the fire of victory in his words. 'From this moment, from this day, the seas belong to Carthage.'

Hamilcar nodded, bridging the gulf of honour between them with the common belief in their cause.

'We have become messengers of Mot, the god of death. His message is: Death to the Romans.'

Hamilcar's expression remained hard as he absorbed the words, the finality and the determination of the battle-hardened man before him. Gisco fought out of hatred for the enemy, Hamilcar because of his belief in Carthage. In the end their objective was the same, a connection forged as Hamilcar repeated Gisco's vow.

'Death to the Romans!'

The *Aquila* swept northwards through empty seas, her sail raised at the end of a long day, the slaves below deck resting at their posts, their bodies draped over the oars that defined their existence. Atticus stood on the aft-deck, staring out at the rapidly descending sun in the western sky. He was joined there by Septimus, the two men talking silently, their thoughts with the transport fleet lost over the horizon.

The sky was burnt red by the fading sun's light, the sight a fitting backdrop to the day's slaughter, as if the gods were accepting the souls of the dead, their passage to Elysium marked by the bloodstained sky. Atticus had watched the earlier battle for as long as possible, the details rapidly blurring as the

Aquila escaped unopposed, until all that remained in view was a huge pall of black smoke. It was a sight that shamed him and the centurion who had stood beside him in silence.

The breeze was light in Atticus's face as he turned away from the sunset to look out over the quiet deck of his ship. He had been on the aft-deck all day, over fourteen hours in total. Throughout the day his stamina had been fuelled by anger, by bitter frustration at his inability to wield the fearsome weapon under his feet in defence of his countrymen who were dying in their droves just beyond his reach. That stamina was now waning, the battle already becoming a single entity in his mind rather than a series of individual horrors.

Scipio had gone below as soon as the *Aquila* had secured her escape, Atticus noticing that the senior consul had never once looked back at the condemned fleet. He replayed in his mind his earlier confrontation with the consul and, although he realized his challenge to Scipio's authority had been foolhardy, Atticus was also convinced his argument had been just and honourable. The thought of Scipio's cold detachment from the fate of the transport fleet reignited Atticus's latent anger and he cast aside his unease at the repercussions of challenging the consul's order.

Atticus's thoughts turned to the Punici. Their blockade had not been expected to materialize for weeks, but somehow they had located the Romans' supply hub and had caught the Romans unawares, driving a wedge between Sicily and the mainland, a separation which spelled death for forty thousand Roman legionaries.

Atticus re-examined their trap, the sky darkening around him. It had been perfect, a true mark of their incredible seamanship. Coupled with this deadly skill, the Carthaginians, having built their empire on the back of their fleet, had scores of galleys in addition to the fifty Atticus had seen. Now, all that naval power was weighted against the dozen triremes of the Roman Republic; lighter smaller galleys designed for coastal patrol and skirmishing. The odds were insurmountable.

As the *Aquila* fled north, the first stars began to appear in the evening sky. Their arrival gave Gaius his first opportunity to accurately set the *Aquila*'s heading, and Atticus felt the deck heel slightly under his feet as the adjustment was made. Their course was now firmly fixed for Rome.

CHAPTER FOUR

Scipio allowed Khalil to massage his shoulders and back as he lay on his cot in the main cabin. He had left the aft-deck hours before, preferring to spend his time in solitude below decks, away from the company of lesser men. His confrontation with the captain remained at the forefront of his mind. The man had challenged him openly, a defiance Scipio would not forget. He regretted his own loss of composure, a slip that exposed his inner thoughts, and for this reason, even more than the blatant insubordination, he cursed the captain for forcing the argument.

In the Senate, appearance and deception were the cornerstones of a man's survival. At all times a politician had to appear calm, never allowing his true emotions to surface and reveal his inner thoughts. Emotions, once mastered, allowed a politician to invoke them at will, a skill that engendered support from the people and fellow senators, a skill that was vital if one was to become a leader.

Beneath the calm exterior lived the art of deception, the ability to dissemble when the situation required it, to allow men false pretences and to be the puppeteer who controlled the lives of lesser mortals to the point where they fought your battles without even realizing it. Scipio was the embodiment of this type of man, his rise to the height of power in Rome a testament to his command of both himself and others. At the centre of this was control of his emotions.

Scipio now used that control to compartmentalize his mind, to push his self-censure to the back of his thoughts. Coupled with Khalil's strong and practised hands, Scipio's self-control helped to ease the tension in his body and he was asleep within minutes, his anger for the captain stored away to be drawn forth when the time was right.

Sensing that his master had drifted off, Khalil eased the pressure of his hands before withdrawing them from the oiled skin. Suddenly and unexpectedly his latent hatred rose in a wave, threatening to consume him, and his arms shook with the force of his restraint. The daily humiliation he felt at serving at another man's whim was a constant open wound to his pride, and the realization that he could kill the Roman easily was like fire in his veins. He breathed deeply, trying to invoke the patience he had acquired in the four years he had been a slave.

Khalil had been seventeen when he was taken captive. His family had chosen to remain at Napata when the Nubian people of the Kush kingdom migrated to Meroë. It was a choice that was to cost them dearly. The city declined and its dwindling power made it a prime target for the Persians, who constantly raided the east coast of Africa. In just one attack the Persians overwhelmed the pitiful defensive forces of the city and took the population into slavery. Khalil had last seen his family in a slave market on the northern shore of Egyptus, his mother and two sisters sold to the whorehouses of Alexandria while his father was sent to the salt mines of Tuzla. Khalil was sent in chains to Rome, the price for his life a mere five sesterces.

Khalil's first two years were spent enduring backbreaking

labour in a fired-brick factory in Tibur, east of Rome. The infernal heat and relentless toil had honed his body and spirit into a rock of strength and had brought him to the attention of his master, who saw in him the opportunity to return a substantial profit on the price he had paid for the pathetic boy of two years before. He was sold into the house of Scipio, a fate that had revealed the duality of every turn in fortune. On the one hand Khalil was taught the deadly art of combat, a skill that spoke to his latent ferocity and burning aggression. On the other, the Roman senator treated Khalil as a plaything, a fighting dog to train and send out against the other trained dogs. The shame of servitude had never diminished in all his four years of slavery and his hatred burned like the furnaces of Tibur.

As a renewed sense of dishonour enveloped his heart, Khalil slowly withdrew his hands from where they were poised over Scipio's neck. If he killed the senator now, he too would be dead within minutes – and Khalil was not ready to die. Patience and fate had taught him that revenge and freedom could be achieved together, that the opportunity would one day present itself and he would be free to find and save his family from the slavery that bound them all. Khalil would wait.

As the Nubian left the cabin, he extinguished the lantern and quietly closed the door to retake his position in the companionway. The slave leaned his massive frame against the bulkhead and lowered his chin onto his chest, relaxing the muscles in the back of his neck. He quelled the anger within him, burying his hatred deep behind defences that would hide his true feelings from his master. His self-control was immense and within five minutes he was calm. Then, like so many others on the now quiet *Aquila*, he slept.

*

The day dawned six hours later to find Atticus and Septimus on the aft-deck of the *Aquila* once more. The captain had awoken just before dawn as always, a habit born during his years as a seaman when the rising of the sun marked the change in the watch. He had dressed quickly and gone on deck to find the marine centurion already there. The two men discussed the events of the past two days but, as if by mutual consent, they avoided discussing the battle, each man having formed his own firm resolutions, inner promises that spoke of retribution and the heavy price to pay.

Septimus paused in the conversation to look around him. The ship was surrounded on all sides by the sea, an unfamiliar sight as the *Aquila* normally spent her time in coastal waters. The course of the ship seemed directionless, as if it were merely passing over the waves without a destination in mind. The thought unnerved him.

'What's our course?' he asked, knowing that in general they were heading to Rome but wanting to hear specifics that would indicate that Atticus knew exactly how they would get there.

'We're travelling due north across the Tyrrhenian Sea, along the trading sea-lane to Naples. We will intercept the coast a little south of that city and then head northwest along the coastline to Rome.'

Septimus noted the easy confidence of the captain.

'I've never been on a ship out of sight of land before,' the centurion added, the featureless sea providing no visible point of reference.

Atticus turned towards the centurion and smiled.

'My first time was when I was eight,' he remarked, 'and I was alone. I was fishing near the shore in my skiff when a storm blew up. It would have taken my sail away but I managed to secure it and weather out the squall until nightfall. By that time I had been carried out to sea.'

'How did you survive?' Septimus asked, trying to remember what it was to be eight.

'I followed the stars home,' Atticus replied matter-of-factly.

The captain smiled inwardly at the easy description of his escape, a contrast to the unmitigated terror he had actually felt at the time.

'Even at eight you could navigate by the stars?' Septimus asked, doubt in his mind that a young child could achieve such a thing.

'Septimus, one of the first things I remember is my grand-father teaching me about the stars. He said they were the fisherman's greatest ally against the fickle nature of the sea. The sea is uncertain, but the stars are constant, and a fish-erman can trust them with his life. I trusted them that night and I survived.'

'Give me land and a solid road under my feet any day,' Septimus said, knowing he would never possess the skill that Atticus had at sea, an ease born out of a lifetime of pitting his wits against the sea and winning through every time.

'And give me a fair wind and a good ship,' Atticus replied.

Septimus smiled at the rebuttal and turned to walk down to the main deck and the assembled troops of his command. The men were subdued, their flight from the previous day's battle a bitter shame. Septimus sensed the mood, weighing the impact on his men. Routine was a commander's greatest ally and, for Septimus's marines, routine dictated that each day began with combat training. Within thirty minutes they would be sweating heavily under the strain of full combat training, the concentration required clearing their mind of dissension. The men formed ranks and began to warm up. The moves they practised had been performed many times before, but Septimus had taught them that any lesson that might one day save your life was worth learning again and again.

The sweat was streaming down the marine centurion's back by the time he disengaged from the training fight with his *optio*, Quintus. The younger man was also breathing heavily, the sudden burst of speed required to fend off the centurion's attacks sapping him.

'Good,' Septimus said, between breaths, 'very good.'

All around them the men of the marine century were paired up, each group fighting with the heavy wooden training swords that would build the muscle of all and bruise the limbs of the careless. Septimus had them practising a reverse thrust and the men now incorporated that move into their ever-expanding range of skills.

'Take over, Quintus,' Septimus said, before bending down to pick up his tunic, the garment discarded an hour before when the sun was two hours above the horizon. As he walked towards the aft-deck, the cooling sea breeze felt fresh over his toned body, his mood light after the morning's exercise.

The consul was standing to one side on the aft-deck, two of his guards and the tall Nubian slave in attendance. As Septimus crossed the main deck he felt Scipio's scrutiny, and the consul turned and spoke a few words to the unmoving Nubian beside him. The slave nodded, his eyes never leaving Septimus. The centurion mounted the aft-deck and walked towards Atticus at the ship's rudder. The captain was issuing orders to a group of crewmen and, as Septimus approached, the sailors dispersed, fanning out over the ship as each went to the task assigned to him. Atticus looked up at the broad sail, an almost instinctive repetitive look to check and recheck the line of the sail, the angle of the wind, the tension in the running rigging and

all the other myriad of minutiae that occurred simultaneously as a ship sped over the water.

'How long has the consul been there?' Septimus asked.

'About half an hour. He's been watching your men train.
Seems to be discussing the training with his slave.'

Septimus nodded, knowing a summons was coming before
the words were spoken.

'Centurion!' he heard, and spun around to see the consul
beckoning him with a raised hand.

Septimus crossed the aft-deck and stood to attention before
Scipio.

'Your men are impressive, you train them well,' the consul
said coolly. Septimus could sense the undertone of challenge.

'Thank you, Consul.'

Scipio seemed to study the centurion before him, weighing
some unknown factors in his mind.

'I would like you to fight my slave. He is a gladiator from
my own school and would relish the challenge.'

'I would welcome the opportunity, Consul,' Septimus
replied, and once more saluted Scipio before leading Khalil
to the main deck. He caught the eye of Atticus as he went.
Atticus had trained Septimus in one-to-one combat when the
centurion had first come aboard the *Aquila*, but within three
months the former legionary's natural swordsmanship had
surpassed Atticus's median skills. It had been some time since
Atticus had seen Septimus bested in a fight. He smiled broadly
in anticipation.

The marines ceased training as they noticed the pair
approaching, their purpose obvious as Septimus once more
removed his tunic and began to limber up. They quickly
formed a semicircle at the fore end so all could see the
impending fight, the whispered bets and calls of encouragement steadily growing in intensity as Khalil removed his own

tunic to expose his massive frame. Odds were renegotiated as the slave picked up a wooden training sword, his obvious comfort with the weapon a sign that he was familiar with it. All activity on the ship seemed to cease as the two men came toe to toe.

'What's your name, slave?' Septimus asked, the last word spat in derision to raise the ire of his opponent.

'Khalil.'

'Well, Khalil, I will teach you a lesson or two today,' Septimus taunted as he began sidestepping to his right, opening a circle of two arms' length.

'Not before I shame you in front of your men, Roman,' Khalil replied, menace in his voice.

Septimus was shocked by the threat, the audacity of the slave to speak so aggressively to a freeman.

Khalil registered the surprise on the centurion's face and used the moment to attack. Septimus was caught off guard and was forced to backstep as the Nubian's blows came in fast and high. The centurion cursed himself for the momentary lapse in concentration; the simple trick of the Nubian had broken his thoughts and exposed him to the incisive attack.

Septimus counterattacked, parrying the Nubian's blade before striking low, aiming to unbalance his opponent and go on the offensive. Within seconds he knew he was evenly matched. Septimus had years more experience with a sword, but much of that was in the legions, with only ten months of one-on-one combat training. Khalil had over twice that amount in single-combat training, his tutors the best gladiatorial trainers that Scipio's money could buy. Septimus had balance and timing on his side, Khalil had practised technique – and each man tried to force the fight into their realm of strength.

Septimus stepped back again as Khalil flowed into a twelve-

stroke sequence, a seamless series of blows that twice pene-
trated Septimus's defence on the torso and upper thigh.
Septimus grunted as each blow struck, the heavy wooden
sword raising the purple hue of bruising under the skin.
Septimus counterattacked with a series of his own; the strokes
were less defined than Khalil's, but the Nubian was forced to
react quickly to avoid injury. Septimus kept the pressure up,
never allowing the Nubian to pause between attack and counterattack. The unrelenting pace began to take its toll and Khalil
grunted heavily as Septimus punched the hilt of his sword
into his stomach. The gladiator roared in anger as he attacked
again, but Septimus used his superior balance as a defence,
causing Khalil to overreach on the final strike, opening the
opportunity for Septimus to immediately go on the offensive.

Atticus watched in silence from the forward rail of the aft-
deck. At the beginning of the fight he had cheered Septimus
along with the rest of the crew, but now he watched in avid
fascination as the fight developed. The balance between the
two men was incredible. After nearly ten minutes of fighting,
Khalil was clearly feeling the effects of the extended fight in
his sword arm. His strikes were not as fast as before; however,
the sequencing was every bit as deadly, and Septimus was
struggling to fight off another attack.

Both men fought on, sweat streaming from every pore,
every strike now accompanied by a grunt of exertion from
attacker and defender. A killer blow was yet to be struck, but
both showed signs on their bodies of where defences had been
overcome and their flesh had suffered the lash.

'Enough!'

All eyes turned to the source of command; all except the
two fighters, who backed off imperceptibly, their gazes locked,
their chests heaving in unison. Scipio descended to the main
deck and approached the fighters. He eyed them both slowly,

as if balancing them in his mind, his thoughts advancing the fight to an unseen conclusion.

Before the fight, Scipio had been sure of Khalil's superior skills. Within seconds of the beginning, however, his keen eye had discovered the gladiator's obvious disadvantage. Gladiatorial fights were rarely to the death, and rarer still for fighters of Khalil's calibre, when swordsmanship was the attraction of the contest. The centurion, on the other hand, had fought many times when death was in the offing and knew of no other way to fight. For the centurion it was kill or be killed; for the gladiator it was draw first blood and claim victory. Without that exposure to mortal danger, Khalil would never be the centurion's equal. Scipio was sure, however, that in a fight to the death Khalil's steely ferocity would adapt, and no man, certainly not a brute centurion of the marines, would stand against him.

'You fight well, Centurion,' Scipio said, his voice betraying the hollow words.

'Thank you, Consul,' Septimus replied, drawing himself to attention.

Scipio nodded his head curtly to Khalil and turned towards the hatchway to the cabins below. He descended without another word, his personal guard and the Nubian slave following. Only when they were gone did the marines break the silence, the abrupt end to the fight sparking immediate arguments as to the victor and how the bets would be settled.

Septimus let them argue, his eyes never leaving his assailant, even when all that remained was an empty hatchway. He had never fought a man of such ability, and he rolled his shoulder instinctively against the sharp pain of a heavy bruise on his upper arm. Throughout the rest of the day he waited for the slave to return from the decks below so he could discuss the fight and the incredible sequence of strikes that seemed so effortless. He waited in vain, for neither Khalil nor the consul re-emerged.

Atticus could scarcely believe the sight before him. Everywhere he looked the sea was filled with all manner of ships, from the smallest skiffs, through merchant galleys, to the massive transport barges of the grain trade. Atticus felt an overwhelming sense of movement, of constant frenzied activity as ships travelled in all directions, their courses crisscrossing each other, with some setting sail for distant ports while others were reaching their journey's end here, in Ostia, the port town of the city of Rome.

The *Aquila* had sighted land at dusk the evening before and had turned its bow northwest along the ragged coastline of the Italian peninsula. During the night they had passed Naples on their right, its lights scattered over the shoreline of the crescent bay and on into the hills beyond, the individual lights in the dark a mirror of the heavens above. The offshore breeze blowing from the city had filled the air with the smell of wood smoke from countless cooking fires, and underneath the musky scent of humanity from the tightly packed confines of the hidden city.

After the multitudinous lights of the city, only solitary pockets of light around small fishing villages remained. The mainland became dark once more, its existence off the starboard rail of the galley marked by a brooding presence that all aboard could feel, an unnamable sensation that constantly drew the eyes of those on board towards the shadowy features of Italia.

As the night wore on, the *Aquila* found company in the water from other vessels travelling the same route to Rome, the number increasing until finally at dawn, with the galley still some ten miles from Ostia, the brightening vista exposed a multitude of craft in the surrounding sea, a host that was compressed in the mouth of the harbour where the *Aquila* now lay.

The smaller craft in the water gave way to the galley, her bronze ram a deterrent that forged a path through the throng of lesser vessels. Further in, Gaius wove the galley around the larger transport barges, the *Aquila*, a more nimble ship under oar, giving way to the less manoeuvrable sailing ships in the time-honoured courtesy observed by all capable sailors.

Ostia, at the mouth of the river Tiber, had been founded by Ancus Marcius, the fourth king of Rome, over three hundred years before, and its growth and prosperity was intimately tied to Rome, a symbiotic relationship that had seen the once-small fishing village become the trade gateway to the greatest city in the world. Now the *Aquila* carried one of the most valuable cargos that had ever entered the port, a vital message to the Senate borne by the leader of Rome itself, a message that held the fate of the forty thousand fighting men of the legions on Sicily.

Lucius stood on the aft-deck beside the helmsman setting his course into the harbour. Years before, as a boatswain, the second-in-command had been stationed in the waters surrounding this port, and he intimately knew its harbour and the layout of the docks. He was guiding the galley to the *castrum*, the military camp that also served as the docking port for the Roman military galleys that patrolled the nearby sea-lanes.

Atticus stood beside the two men, listening as Lucius pointed out the swarm of nationalities represented by the trading vessels surrounding the galley. The ships had come from the four corners of the Mediterranean, from Gaul and Iberia, from Illyricum on the shores of the Mare Superum across from the eastern shores of the Italian peninsula, and from Greece and Egyptus. These were the places that Atticus had dreamed of visiting when he was a boy, and now the very proximity of the people of these lands filled his imagination with wonder. As his eyes swept back and forward, from port to starboard, he suddenly noticed the consul approaching him across the aft-deck.

'Captain Perennis,' Scipio began, his expression cold, 'once we dock, you and Centurion Capito will accompany me to the city. You will stay there until I personally give you leave to depart.'

'Yes, Consul,' Atticus replied, wondering why their presence was so necessary, knowing that he dare not ask the consul.

Scipio turned on his heel and proceeded to the main deck, where his guard and personal slave were waiting.

Septimus mounted the aft-deck from the other side and walked over to Atticus.

'You've heard then,' he said, indicating the consul's departure with a nod of his head.

'Yes, I have,' Atticus replied, his mind still pondering the reason.

'Why do you think he wants us in the city, Septimus?'

'I'm not sure, Atticus. But this is certain. We're now firmly in his grasp. You heard his order: we can't leave until he *personally* gives us the order.'

'I noticed that,' Atticus said, realizing that the simple request to accompany the consul was in reality anything but simple. Atticus had only known the senior consul for three days and yet he already knew for certain that Scipio never took a step without knowing its consequences three steps down the line.

'Never mind,' Septimus said suddenly with a smile, picking up on Atticus's preoccupation. 'Now I'm guaranteed the opportunity to show you the sights of Rome.'

Atticus shrugged off his sense of unease and smiled, slapping Septimus on the shoulder.

'You'd better be right about Rome,' he said. 'I've waited too long to see this city to be disappointed.'

'Disappointed?' Septimus said with false amazement. 'Atticus, my friend, by the time we're finished you'll bless the day you met the consul.'

Atticus laughed at the centurion's infectious anticipation. He had a feeling that the vision he had in his head of the city, a vision of magnificent temples and grand piazzas, was very different from the city that Septimus would show him.

The *castrum* was located at the extreme northern end of the busy harbour. It was home to the largest single detachment of Roman military vessels, six out of the entire fleet of twelve galleys of the Republic. These six ships constantly patrolled the sea-lanes surrounding Rome, ensuring an uninterrupted flow of trade that was so necessary for the city's growth. More importantly they provided escorts for the large grain transports, as the enormous barges ferried the vital lifeblood of Rome from Campania, over two days' sailing to the southeast.

As the *Aquila* approached, Atticus could see that all but two of Ostia's galleys were at sea; the remaining triremes, the *Libertas* and the *Tigris*, were tied up neatly against the dock. The *Aquila* slowed under the expert hand of Gaius, and lines were thrown from fore and aft to the waiting slaves on land, who quickly tethered the ropes to the dock posts. The order was given to withdraw all oars, both port and starboard, and the sailors on deck began to haul in the ropes, hand over hand, until the *Aquila* moored precisely parallel to the dock. The gangway was lowered and Scipio and his retinue immediately disembarked, closely followed by Atticus and Septimus.

The sight of the *praetoriani* arrested the movement of everyone on the dock, and they backed off to leave a path clear from the *Aquila* to the barracks, unsure of the unexpected visit of a senior member of the Senate aboard a never-before-seen Roman trireme that was not of the Ostia fleet.

As the group approached the two-storey barracks, the port commander emerged from the entrance archway leading to the courtyard within. He was followed by a *contubernia* of ten soldiers, and his determined stride to investigate the unannounced arrival of a galley at his port mirrored the approach of Scipio, whose equally confident pace closed the gap between the two groups in seconds. Scipio noticed that the port commander's pace lessened slightly as he tried to recognize the figure coming towards him, the consul's importance obvious from the black-cloaked guard that attended him. The commander called a halt to his *contubernia* ten paces short and ordered his men to stand to attention, knowing that, whoever it was, the man approaching at the head of a detachment of *praetoriani* outranked him. Scipio raised his hand in the air two paces short of the commander, and his own guard immediately came to a stop.

'Commander, I am Senior Consul Gnaeus Cornelius Scipio. I need eight of your finest mounts immediately to bear us to Rome. My slave and our baggage are to be escorted in our wake.'

'Yes, Consul,' the port commander replied, his mind racing to understand the sudden presence of the most powerful man in Rome in the military camp of Ostia.

'Now!' Scipio shouted, the momentary pause of the commander fuelling his impatience to be in Rome.

The effect on the commander was immediate and he quickly turned and ordered his men to run to the stables to assemble and prepare the necessary mounts. He turned again to face the consul, but Scipio was already brushing past him, striding off in the direction of the entrance to the courtyard that would lead to the stables. The port commander was left standing in their wake before his wits returned once again and he took off in pursuit.

The barracks at Ostia were almost identical to those at Brolium on the northern coast of Sicily. Both, like all others in the Republic, were based on a standard design, a two-storey quadrangle with an archway in the centre of each side leading into the central courtyard. The stables were beyond the eastern archway and it was through this that the *contubernia* now led eight horses of the light cavalry. They were Maremmano, a breed of horse from the plains of Tuscany. The horses were unattractive beasts in comparison to other breeds and, although they were not fleet of foot, they were strong and hardworking, a perfect match for the harsh life of the legions.

Scipio, his four guards and guard commander, and the two men of the *Aquila*, mounted together and rode out through the southern archway, swinging left to travel east along the busy harbour road that led to the city. As they rode along by the water's edge, Atticus's senses were again overwhelmed by the sights and smells in the maelstrom of the busy port. The transport barges, recently arrived from all the ports of the known world, were disgorging their wares onto the dock, with the city traders standing ready to strike a deal with a returning regular or an inexperienced beginner. Gold quickly changed hands as bargains were struck and goods were hauled off by the army of slaves who stood poised behind every trader. Atticus had never seen such a wealth of goods, such a display of appetite, as the voracious city traders insatiably devoured each new barge-load of cargo. Within the space of the first quarter-mile of the dock, he had seen bolts of silk so numerous as could clothe an entire legion, exotic animals that clawed and snarled at the slaves who nimbly handled their cages, birds of every size and hue, the air filling with their song, and, everywhere in between, countless amphorae of wine and baskets of food. It seemed an impossibility that any one city could consume such an abundance, and yet Atticus got the impression that what he was witnessing occurred every day, that the city's hunger would devour the cornucopia before him and then return tomorrow for more.

Atticus felt a tug on his arm and he dragged his attention away from the seemingly chaotic scene to answer the summons. Septimus nodded his head to the left, indicating the sudden change in course of the mounted party, and Atticus wheeled his horse to follow the others as they turned away from the docks and headed into the port town. Here, as before, the streets were crammed with all manner of goods, this time on the move inland towards the city over twelve miles away. The horsemen wove their way around the multitude of slaves and bearers, slowing their progress until they emerged beyond the confines of the town into the open countryside. Within half a dozen miles they reached Via Aurelia, the recently constructed road that ran northwards along the coastline from Rome. They turned south and within ten minutes were crossing the Tiber over the Pons Aemilius, a magnificent stone-pillared bridge with a wooden superstructure of five arches effortlessly spanning the one-hundred-yard-wide stretch of water. Atticus could only marvel at the engineering feat beneath him and he leaned out of his saddle to peer over the thirty-foot drop to the fast-flowing waters below.

'You haven't seen anything yet,' Septimus smiled as he noticed his friend's eyes take in every detail of the bridge. Atticus looked up and Septimus nodded his head to the road before them, to the sight that was opening before them: Rome.

The horsemen entered the city through Porta Flumentana,

one of twelve gates in the Servian Wall, which ran nearly seven miles around the entire city. Built by the sixth king of Rome, the wall was twelve feet thick and twenty high, a mammoth defensive barrier built as a reaction to the sacking of the city over one hundred and thirty years before by the seventy-thousand-strong Gaulish army of Brennus. As the group passed under the great arch of the gate, inscribed with the omnipresent SPQR denoting *Senatus Populusque Romanus*, 'the Senate and the People of Rome', Atticus's eyes were drawn upwards to the height of the Palatine Hill, soaring two hundred feet above the level of the valley floor, upon which the foundation stones of Rome had been laid nearly five hundred years before by the demigod Romulus.

The group wound its way through the bustling streets, swinging north of the Palatine Hill into the valley formed with the Capitoline Hill, itself dominated by the Capitolium Temple dedicated to the three supreme deities, Jupiter, Mars and Quirinus. Atticus had never seen such a multitude of people before. Having spent his whole adult life at sea, he had quickly become accustomed to living in close proximity with others, the limited space of a floating galley isolated at sea creating a claustrophobic and intrusive atmosphere on board. In comparison to the press of the streets and buildings surrounding him, however, the galley seemed capacious. The *insulae*, the apartment blocks on all sides of the narrow streets, rose five or more storeys high, with balconies reaching out to form a near roof that robbed the street of much of its daylight. Atticus felt an undeniable sensation of oppression in the enclosed corridor, and he inwardly sighed in relief as he noticed an end to the street ahead, a brighter, more open space beyond.

Atticus was the trailing member of the group and so was the last to breach the confines of the narrow street out into the Forum Magnum, the central plaza of the sprawling city.

His heart soared as he gazed upon the imperial heart of the Republic. When Atticus was young, his grandfather had regaled him with stories of the great city of Athens, a city his ancestors had called home before the Milonius clan fled before Alexander of Macedon and settled in southern Italia. The tales told of soaring temples and godlike statues, of civilization's birthplace and home, a city that only the Greeks in their power could create. As a child, Atticus had let his imagination fashion a city of incredible presence, a vision he had often dismissed in his adult years, the boasts of an old man longing for his homeland. Now, standing on the cusp of the magnificent Forum Magnum, Atticus was presented with the very visions of his youth transplanted to another city, a city that surely exceeded all others in splendour and power.

Septimus reined in his horse and brought himself back alongside his open-mouthed friend.

'Well?' Septimus asked. 'What do you think?' he added with a smile.

'By the gods, Septimus, I never believed it would be so . . . so . . .'

'Big?' the marine offered.

'I was going to say amazing,' Atticus replied, instantly understanding how the city before him could be the focal point for the power it held over the whole peninsula.

'My father's father spat on the name of Rome when the legions came to Locri, believing them and the city that bore their citizenship to be inferior to any in Greece,' Atticus continued, shaking his head in silent criticism of the belief his grandfather had held.

Septimus began to name the sights of the Forum as they passed through the expansive and busy commercial and governmental centre. To their left was the Temple of Vesta, a towering circular shrine dedicated to the virgin goddess of home and family. Within, Septimus explained, the untouchable Vestal Virgins tended the eternal flame of Vesta, a symbol of the very source of life, the flame connected through the eastern opening of the temple to the ultimate source, the sun. The Virgins, once the daughters of the king of Rome, were now the daughters of the most important Roman families, and their thirty-year vow of chastity and acceptance into the only order of priestesses in Roman religion brought them and their families great honour and prestige.

Standing next to the temple was the Regia. Originally it had served as the centre for the kings of Rome, but now, with power residing in the Senate, the building was home to a spiritually more impressive figure, the *pontifex maximus*, the high priest of the Republic. The imposing rectangular temple housed the shield and lance of the war god, Mars, and it was with these symbols that the high priest administered the divine laws of Rome and kept the 'Peace of the Gods'. Atticus listened in silent awe as Septimus explained that the lance held within the walls of the temple would vibrate in perilous times, a warning sign to the populace from Mars himself that Rome was under threat.

The two men swung their mounts left in pursuit of the senior consul as the group passed diagonally across the Forum. They passed the Umbilicus Urbi, the official centre of the city from which all distances, both within the city and the entire Republic, were measured. It was an isolated, unassuming marble obelisk, six feet high and five in diameter, and yet Atticus sensed the very fact that it was so humble, in such exalted surroundings, merely added to its significance as the marker point of the centre of the known world.

Septimus pointed out their destination in the northwest corner of the Forum, the Curia Hostilia, the court where the Senate met and the centre of all political activity in the Republic.

The building was elevated above the level of the surrounding buildings, its striking façade dominating the northern end of the Forum, a symbol of strength and order. Atticus took his eyes off the impressive sight to look at the senior consul leading them, expecting the order to halt and dismount to come at any moment before they took the final steps of their journey up to the columned entrance of the Curia.

Scipio surreptitiously eyed the steps of the Curia as they approached the Senate building. His own house was a mere half-mile beyond the Forum, around the northern side of the Capitoline Hill that rose up on their left, and it was this destination that the consul now steered towards. As senators on the steps of the Curia recognized him, many of the junior members ran down to question his sudden appearance, while others – men Scipio knew were allied to his enemies – ran up to the entrance to warn those adversaries of the senior consul's presence. As his horse drew parallel to the foot of the steps, he was surrounded by half a dozen men, each wearing the standard woollen toga of the Senate, although all could afford much finer cloth.

'Senior Consul,' one began, 'we were not expecting you for at least another week. What news?'

'Patience, Fabius,' Scipio said with a smile, 'I have travelled far these past two days and I wish to bathe and change before speaking to the Senate on a matter of grave import. Please inform those available that I will return in the afternoon,' he added, knowing that everyone would ensure they were available to hear any news first hand.

'Yes, Senior Consul,' Fabius replied, the junior senator, a recently elected magistrate, barely able to contain his curiosity.

Fabius and the others turned away from the senior consul and began to climb the steps of the Curia, Scipio noting with satisfaction that they were already in deep conversation as to the nature of the 'matter of grave import' that he had alluded to. He knew it was only a matter of time before the whole Senate would be discussing the yet-to-be-disclosed news, their curiosity fermenting within the confines of the Senate building. Scipio would delay his return to the Curia until the last possible moment, allowing the tension to mount to the tautness of a legionary's bow. Only then would he announce the news of the Carthaginian blockade and the threat to the Sicilian campaign. The timing would be perfect for declaring his proposal, presenting the senators with the only possible solution, his solution, without affording his enemies the opportunity to determine a counterproposal. It would be yet another one of his triumphs.

Gaius Duilius, junior consul of the Roman Senate, sat comfortably in the first row of the three-tiered inner chamber of the Curia. He was a *novus homo*, a new man, the first in his family line to be elected to the Senate. It was an achievement of which Duilius was extremely proud – and with good reason, for he was a self-made man who, from humble beginnings fifteen years before, had risen to the second most powerful position in Rome. When Duilius was nineteen, his parents and two younger sisters had succumbed to one of the many plagues that frequently swept the countryside around Rome, and he found himself the sole surviving inhabitant of the modest family villa that sat astride the Via Appia. This vital artery, the main road to the distant city of Brindisi, in the southeast of the country, was a thriving thoroughfare with a constant flow of traders passing the estate entrance on their way to the capital four miles beyond.

Duilius became master of his own estate and, free to make his own decisions, he gambled everything in a bid to capitalize on the estate's ideal location. Using his land as collateral, he borrowed heavily from the usurers of Rome, who were only too eager to deal with him, confident that the young man would quickly default on the loans, allowing them to seize the estate. Duilius used the money to buy slaves and seed and quickly turned every arable inch of his land over to the growing of fresh produce. The markets of Rome had always been supplied by the outlying farmers, small land-holders, many of whom concentrated on individual seasonal crops; although the farmers worked in isolation, they were also careful not to directly compete with their neighbours. For years prices had remained relatively stable with little in the way of competition. Duilius planned to change that system.

In his first season, by using his entire estate, including the landscaped gardens that had been his mother's pride, Duilius had more land under tillage than four average-size farms. He disregarded the delicate balance maintained by the other farmers and planted every commercial crop he could, utilizing a two-tier crop-rotation method that ensured his land was constantly producing. As his first crop was being harvested, Duilius propositioned every passing trader with an offer they could not decline. He sold them fresh produce below market price, taking advantage of the larger volumes he could command, leaving the traders free to transport the produce the mere four miles to the city, where they were free to profit from the margin in the city markets.

Within the first year Duilius was able to purchase his own wagons to transport his produce to the city, and within two more he had paid off his debts in full. Not content with the success of his own estate, he quickly borrowed even greater amounts and bought the two estates adjoining his own, paying the owners above market value, once again turning every inch of arable land over to production. It was then that Duilius got his first taste of the power that money could wield.

With the price of fresh produce falling in the market due to the unexpected competition, the farmers fought back by banding together to lobby the Senate to re-establish the status quo. Duilius had used his new-found wealth to ensure the ensuing vote in the Senate went in his favour, learning two valuable lessons in the process that had stayed with him ever since. The first was the power of money in guaranteeing the loyalty of unscrupulous men. The second was the value of information. Before the vote ever took place, Duilius knew exactly who he controlled, who he did not but, more importantly, who he could not control and who he dared not approach. Over time Duilius refined the dual revelations into one principle: 'Money is only the method, information is the true wealth.'

Now, fifteen years after the death of his parents, Duilius owned the largest single tract of land straddling the city. Many other estates had tried to reproduce his methodology and achievements, but few had succeeded, and none to the same degree. Produce from his estates supplied the city with eighty per cent of its fresh vegetables and fruit, with all of the small farmers driven out of business by the cutthroat competition. These men had seen their livelihoods disappear almost overnight, and the cries of their hungry children had driven their attempts to assassinate Duilius on three occasions over the years. Each failed attempt brought terrible retribution from the Senate where Duilius held a seat, his position easily obtained years before from the votes of a grateful populace of Rome who craved the lower prices in the markets. The senator had used each occasion to further crush the farmers, and both guilty and innocent were forced off their land as punishment in the name of the State, their lands immediately put on the open market where Duilius snatched them up for half their true value.

Six months before, using the fortune that had propelled him into the realms of Rome's elite, he had engineered a nomination to the position of senior consul from one of the sycophantic junior members of the Senate. The vote had been close and costly, but in the end he had been narrowly defeated by Gnaeus Cornelius Scipio, one of the wealthiest men in Rome and one whom Duilius knew he could never control. The defeat had been bitter for Duilius, his first setback since setting out over fifteen years before, and the enmity between the two men had now divided the Senate into three segments: those firmly for Duilius, those firmly for Scipio, and a malleable majority in the centre whose votes were surreptitiously sold to the highest bidder.

Lucius Manlius Vulso Longus, a recently elected senator, quickly adjusted his gaze to the gloomy interior and rapidly searched the room for the man whose acceptance he craved more than anything in the world. He spotted Duilius and crossed the floor, his appearance putting an end to the honeyed words that Duilius had been speaking to a senator beside him, a senator whose vote Duilius had purchased many times. The junior consul looked up irritably.

'What is it, Longus?' he asked brusquely.

'Scipio has returned!' the young man said, his impatience to be the first to inform Duilius causing him to blurt out the words.

'What . . . ? When?' Duilius said, standing, his voice loud in the muted chamber, the seated senator beside him forgotten.

'Just now. I saw him crossing the Forum.'

Duilius's mind raced to understand the reason behind the senior consul's sudden reappearance. Why over a week early?

And why unannounced? As he contemplated the answers his thoughts were interrupted by the sound of the speaker's gavel being struck on the marble lectern in the centre of the chamber. He looked up to see one of Scipio's brats with the gavel in his hand.

'The senior consul has returned from Sicily to inform us of a matter of grave import,' he announced, his words holding everyone's attention.

'What matter?' Duilius asked in the silent pause, his question drawing the speaker's ire at the interruption.

'I know not, Consul,' Fabius replied, relishing Scipio's adversary's ignorance. 'The senior consul will return to the Curia in the afternoon to speak in person to those members of the Senate who are available.'

Fabius left the lectern, to be immediately surrounded by Scipio's allies who bombarded him with questions, none of which he had the answer to.

Senator Duilius looked around the chamber to see the eyes of his own allies looking to him for guidance, their faces blank, their minds filled with the same questions as everyone else's.

Fools, Duilius thought, *don't they understand? There is only one step that must now be taken.*

With a determined stride, the junior consul walked out of the inner chamber, his departure marked by silence as all watched him leave.

CHAPTER FIVE

A tticus and Septimus followed Scipio and his guard into
the courtyard of the senior consul's Roman residence.
The house was on the lower slopes of the northern side of
the Capitoline Hill, an elevated site that afforded the resi-
dents an uninterrupted view of the expansive flood plains
of the Tiber beyond the Servian Wall. The air at this height
was fresher than that of the confined streets of the *insulae*,
and Atticus breathed the earth-scented breeze deeply. Both
men dismounted and followed Scipio into the house, hearing
the heavy wooden courtyard gate closing firmly behind
them, locking the world outside. The trio entered the atrium
of the house, a large open-centred square surrounded by
high-ceilinged porticoes on all sides, the roofs of which
sloped inwards to collect rainwater in the shallow pool
dominating the space. Although Septimus knew of such
senatorial residences, he had never set foot inside a house
such as Scipio's. For Atticus, the house represented the individual version of the opulent wealth that he had witnessed
in the Forum. The air inside the atrium was still and near
silent, the hustle and bustle of the streets outside forgotten,
the house seemingly deserted. The side of the atrium opposite the entrance was opened, leading further into the recesses

114

of the building. The consul walked towards it with the others following in awed silence before he suddenly stopped and turned.

'Wait here,' he ordered; 'my servants will attend you and bring you to one of the bathing rooms. After that, report to the guards' quarters and await my orders.'

'Yes, Consul,' both men answered in unison, the senator already striding out of the atrium to the room beyond.

Septimus whistled tonelessly as he looked around the atrium. The area was sparsely furnished to give the impression of space, but the few items in view spoke of the wealth of the master of the house, from exquisitely carved marble busts of the Scipio family to gold inlaid mosaics on the walls. Moments later a slave arrived. Without comment he led them into the recesses of the enormous house.

Scipio lowered himself slowly into the near-scalding water. The steam in the room had already brought sweat from his every pore and, although the moist air had raised his body temperature, his mind protested at the additional intensity of the water in the mosaic-covered bath. Scipio fought the intense heat until his body temperature adjusted to match its surroundings, and he lay back to allow his mind to clear. There was much to think about, but he had always found that following the simple rituals of life, such as bathing, was a powerful method for ordering his thoughts. The first step in that process was to allow the ritual routine to become his focus. Only then would he experience the calm that was necessary to see the hidden solutions for every problem.

'More heat,' he murmured, and his mind registered the slap of bare feet as a slave scuttled to attend to his command, adding fuel to the fire that fed the underfloor heating of the large *caldarium* bath. Once again his body registered the change as heat built upon heat and his heart rate increased, giving him a light-headed, euphoric feeling.

When Scipio reached the edge of his level of endurance he signalled his attendant slaves to lift him from the bath. Two muscular slaves, sweating stoically in the heated chamber, rushed forward and lifted the near-limp senator over to a marble, towel-covered table. A female slave rubbed perfumed oil into every supple, heated muscle before removing the oil with a strigil, a curved metal tool that scraped off the dirt that had risen from the open pores. Scipio, feeling clean for the first time in many days, made his way into the *tepidarium*, the lukewarm bath in the adjoining room, and once again plunged himself into the crystal-clear waters, taken directly from the aquifer beneath the bathhouse. The water in this bath was a mere two degrees above body temperature, and Scipio lay back in the silence of the chamber, the only other presence an attendant male slave who stood ever ready for an immediate summons. Scipio totally ignored the man, considering the slave to be merely part of the surroundings in his private bathhouse; after the confines of the galley that had transported him here from Sicily, he relished the solitude.

A gentle knock on the door of the *tepidarium* chamber disrupted his thoughts, and he opened his eyes to look to the door, knowing who stood on the other side, smiling at the thought of seeing the familiar face.

He paused for a heartbeat, prolonging the sensation of anticipation.

'Enter,' he said.

The door opened inwards and a woman entered. She moved with a practised ease born of her privileged upbringing and social status, her bearing making her look taller than her average height. She was classically beautiful with dark brown eyes and long auburn hair, her mouth slightly open in a half-smile. She took a seat near the edge of the bath, facing her husband.

'Welcome home, Gnaeus,' she said, her voice sweet in the once-quiet chamber.

'It's good to be home, Fabiola,' Scipio replied, his joy at seeing his wife and the truth of his statement evident in his voice.

Fabiola was wearing an elegant light woollen *stola*, parted slightly above her knee, and the hint of the fine line of her inner thigh caused Scipio to stir slightly in the bath, his loins remembering past nights in the privacy of their bedroom. She noticed the change in her husband and smiled inwardly, drawing pleasure from arousing the most powerful man in Rome.

'I wasn't expecting you home so soon,' she said, concern in her voice at his sudden return.

'Things have turned against the army's favour in Sicily,' Scipio replied. 'The Carthaginians have blockaded the coast and cut our supply lines. If the situation isn't remedied, our army there will not last the campaign season.'

The senior consul watched his wife intently, waiting for her reaction. She was a highly intelligent woman, and Scipio often used her as a sounding board for his ideas. Her thoughts and judgements on any matter were always of value, and he had found that her reaction to his ideas was always in line with his own views.

'This is an opportunity,' she said after a full minute, 'an opportunity for you, Gnaeus.'

Scipio nodded. 'My thoughts exactly,' he replied. 'The Punici have already been beaten on land by our forces. Given time we would push them back into the sea from whence they came. Another victory for the legions. Another province for the Republic. Nothing new and exciting for the populace of Rome.'

'But now the Carthaginians have raised the stakes,' Fabiola added, prompting the continuation of Scipio's thoughts, knowing his idea's end.

'Yes,' Scipio said, 'they have raised the stakes, and they have changed the rules of the game. Our legions have never before faced such a challenge. This threat will fire the imagination and excitement of the plebeians. Their attention will be drawn to the previously insignificant campaign on Sicily by the new struggle developing.'

'And you will save the legions,' Fabiola said with a smile, her own body tingling with the excitement of her husband deciding the fate of so many.

'I will save the legions,' Scipio agreed. 'I will create the navy that will defeat the Carthaginians and the people will cheer this new show of strength, this new extension of our power.'

'They will love you and demand you break tradition and stay to serve another year,' she said, speaking of the prize they had often discussed.

'And I will finally break the asinine rules that bound my term as senior consul and extend my power into another year,' Scipio said with a triumphant smile.

Fabiola suddenly stood up, her eyes locked to those of her husband, the power emanating from him intoxicating, charging the air in the room with an unseen energy that drew her towards him. Her body ached to feed off that power, to draw directly from its source.

'Leave us,' she commanded the attendant slave, and he instantly vanished.

She stepped to the side of the bath and unbuckled the

shoulder straps of her *stola*, allowing the outer dress to fall around her ankles, revealing the thigh-length silk *tunica intima* beneath. Fabiola slowly lowered herself down the marble steps of the bath into the waist-deep warm water. Standing directly opposite her husband, she bent her knees and immersed herself completely beneath the surface before standing once more.

The silken slip clung to her body as she rose out of the water, the feminine swell of her breasts accentuated by the slow deep breathing of her anticipation, her arousal obvious by the darkened circles of her nipples under her *tunica*.

Scipio sat straighter on the underwater shelf of the *tepidarium* bath as his wife slowly approached, his eyes watching her hands grasp the bottom of her slip as she raised it slowly to reveal her sex. As Fabiola reached him, Scipio extended his arms and supported her climb to place a knee on each side of his waist before sitting into his embrace. The heat between them deepened as their movements intensified, their mingled cries echoing off the marbled walls of the private chamber, the power play that aroused them driving their passion.

Amaury, Scipio's bath attendant, listened silently on the other side of the *tepidarium* chamber's door. His dismissal moments before had been unexpected but he dared not let the opportunity pass. The cries of his master and mistress could be heard faintly through the thick oak timbers of the door and he knew that time was now against him. There were few secrets in a home full of slaves, and the consul and his wife's intimate couplings were always juicy conversation for the slave women of the house. This time would be like all others, aggressive, passionate but, more importantly, short-lived. Soon the consul's wife would leave him and his summons for Amaury would immediately follow. He had to be quick. Dropping the linen towels he carried to the floor, Amaury turned and ran to the slave quarters at the rear of the house, praying that Tiago, the stable lad, could be found in time.

'Towels!' Scipio called impatiently, this second call louder than the unanswered first. After Fabiola had left, he had lain back in the water once more, his confidence in his plan renewed by his wife's tacit acceptance of the plan's main tenets, the never-before-encountered threat, the mortal peril of the legions, Scipio's central role in the rescue of the soldiers of Rome. Handled properly, the conquering of Sicily would give the senior consul the power and immortality he craved. He was sure of that now more than ever.

Scipio raised his head and turned towards the door that had earlier been exited by the attendant slave. He was not used to asking twice for anything, from anyone, least of all a slave, and he vowed the man would be severely punished if it was found that he had left him unattended.

'Towels!' he roared, and began to raise himself out of the water when the door burst open as the slave reappeared.

'What is the meaning of this delay?' Scipio asked furiously as the slave ran to proffer a towel to him.

'A thousand apologies, master,' Amaury said with his head bowed, his voice servile in the presence of the man who could, at a whim, have him executed. 'I could not hear your summons through the heavy oak door.'

Scipio looked down on the man before him. The slave was breathing heavily, as if from exertion, but more likely from fear. It hardly seemed probable that the slave had left him waiting on purpose.

Scipio whipped the towel out of the slave's hand and brushed past him into the outer corridor, calling for the slave master of the house. He arrived immediately.

'Six lashes for this man,' Scipio ordered, and the slave master moved into the *tepidarium* chamber to take hold of the slave. Next time he would be more attentive, Scipio thought with a careless attitude, and strode into the *frigidarium* chamber, the final room and the cold bath that would end the ritual.

Out of the corner of his eye, Amaury watched the senior consul leave. He kept his head low and his face impassive but inside he smiled. Six lashes, he thought: a small price to pay for the silver he would receive from his real master.

Scipio strode out into the courtyard of his home as the sun was beginning to descend into the western hills of the Roman countryside. With spring in the offing, these cool afternoons would soon give way to the warmer winds of the new season, when the air would be filled with the scent of blossoms from the manicured gardens surrounding the house. He inhaled deeply and held his breath for a heartbeat, feeling an enormous sense of wellbeing. It had been less than ninety minutes since he had passed the Curia, but the brief interlude, the bath, a light meal, the time spent with his wife, had recharged him to the point that his confidence felt unassailable.

Scipio noted that the two officers of the *Aquila* were waiting, as ordered, with his personal guard. The senior consul nodded to the guard commander and the main gate of the courtyard out to the street beyond was opened. Scipio fell in behind four of his guards with six more trailing, and the troop began the brief journey that would take them back to the Forum Magnum. Scipio always felt a deep sense of satisfaction and importance as he strode through the streets of his city. People all around would stop and stare at the passing senator, many pointing out to strangers the distinctive figure of the senior consul, the most powerful man in Rome.

The group wound its way into the shade of the eastern side

of the Capitoline Hill. On the left Scipio noticed the intense flurried activity of the Forum Holitorium, a section of the mercantile food market that dealt solely with fruit, vegetables and oil. He smiled inwardly at the sight, the source of his rival's wealth. Scipio was a direct descendant of one of the original *patricii*, the founding fathers of the Roman Senate, which had been established nearly three hundred years before. As such he was a member of the patrician class, the Roman elite of upper-class families who continued to make up the majority of the Senate. His rival Duilius, however, was a member of the equestrian middle class; he had clawed his way up using 'new money', wielding his wealth like a blunt instrument as he shamelessly bought his way into power. The irony of the accusation was not lost on Scipio, who also used his wealth, and the power it conferred, to achieve his ends. Scipio believed, however, that his was a more subtle, refined and delicate approach that spoke to his better breeding.

Scipio felt the tension and excitement rise within him as he turned the final corner into the Forum Magnum, the hub of the city, still bathed in the afternoon's sunlight. The Curia Hostilia rose above him to his right and the *praetoriani* guard wheeled neatly towards the base of the steps leading to the Senate. The senior consul's thoughts still dwelt on his junior counterpart and he revelled in the triumph of stealing a march on his rival. As junior consul this year, Duilius was in a prime position to attain the full title next year. But it was not to be, Scipio thought. The Carthaginians had seen to that. They had given Scipio a chance to write his name into history, and to write Duilius out. As the senior consul began to climb the steps that led to the very heart of the Republic, his eyes wandered upwards to the porticoes flanking the entrance into the inner chamber. He noted with pride that a junior senator was stationed at the top of the steps to watch for his arrival.

As the man recognized the approach of the leader of Rome, he spun on his heels and ran into the interior beyond to announce that Gnaeus Cornelius Scipio had arrived.

Atticus squinted towards the evening sun as he gazed out over the inner courtyard adjacent to the guards' quarters of Scipio's house, his thoughts ranging over the events of the previous days. He turned to face Septimus, the centurion lying supine on his cot in the sparsely furnished quarters, taking advantage of the forced inactivity as they waited for the consul's orders.

'Back in Brolium, Marcus said that under blockade the legions would become "survivors not fighters, scavengers of food instead of hunters of men",' Atticus said. 'What did he mean exactly? How quickly will the legions lose their ability to fight effectively?'

Septimus paused for a moment before replying.

'Cut off from resupply, once the Second and Ninth exhaust the supplies they carry with them, they'll be faced with three shortages, two of which they can survive.'

Atticus walked over to his own cot and sat down.

'Which two are those?' he asked.

'Food and equipment,' Septimus replied, sitting up to face Atticus. 'The first is always an issue for every army. A hot meal in a soldier's belly lifts his strength and morale. An empty belly fuels discontentment. If the food supplies that the legions carry are consumed, the men will go hungry, but they won't starve. Once in enemy territory the army will be free to forage, stripping passing farms of their livestock and grain, leaving famine in their wake but keeping the men of the Second and Ninth marching.'

'Marcus called it scavenging,' Atticus remarked, 'and he didn't relish the prospect.'

Septimus nodded, his face grave. 'It's a precarious practice, with foraging teams open to ambush from the enemy; and should the army pass through more barren mountain land, their foraging would become more desperate and widespread.'

Atticus nodded, slowly understanding the difficult challenges faced by a campaigning army. 'You said equipment was also a surmountable problem,' he prompted.

Again Septimus nodded. 'After the stocks of replacements are exhausted, the men will switch to patching up their existing kit. There's countless ways to keep a legionary's kit functional, although the end result might not pass a parade-ground inspection. The only vital pieces of equipment are a soldier's weaponry, his short sword, javelins and a shield. His armour takes second place to these essentials, although men fight more aggressively when they have the protection of segmented armour over their chest and a helmet on their heads. Either way, though, the legions will go into battle and the fallen will provide replacement equipment for the survivors.'

Atticus nodded his understanding. Now only one problem remained.

'So what's the third shortage?' Atticus asked. 'The one the legions can't do without?'

'The most essential supply for any army, Atticus. The supply of men.'

'But between them the Second and Ninth encompass nearly twenty thousand men. Surely it will be months before any loss will become so significant as to affect the ability of the legions as a whole?' Atticus countered.

Septimus shook his head. 'The total might number twenty thousand, but a legion's strength is not in its sheer numbers but in the individual formations within its ranks.'

Atticus's puzzled expression prompted Septimus to continue. 'A maniple consists of one hundred and twenty men.

At any one time there are always at least a half-dozen excused duty because of illness. Once the enemy is engaged, the problem intensifies, as the injured swell the ranks of those unfit for duty. A campaign like this one will be riddled with minor engagements, each one sapping the strength of each fighting maniple. With no supply of replacements getting through from the mainland, maniple after maniple will be struck off the fighting roster and, before long, individual commands will disappear as maniples are cannabilized to provide replacements for others. Mark my words, Atticus, this natural attrition of the army's most basic raw material, through illness, battle injuries and death, and the inability to resupply that raw material to the front line, will destroy the Second and Ninth within a matter of a couple of months.'

Atticus drew in a slow breath as he absorbed Septimus's words, the centurion's explanation painting a vivid picture of the Roman army's demise. The army was like an individual soldier, its loss of men like the flesh wounds sustained in battle, injuries that healed as new men were fed in to fill the breach, the residual scar tissue hardening the man beneath. Without the ability to renew itself, the army, like the individual soldier, would fall from its wounds, its lifeblood soaking into the arid soil of Sicily.

'Senators!' Scipio began, his voice holding the absolute attention of the three hundred men who represented the political power of the Republic. The senior consul was standing tall at the lectern positioned at the centre of the semicircle of three tiers of seating in the inner chamber of the Curia. Only moments before, his arrival had been announced by the *princeps senatus*, the leader of the house, a ceremonial, almost powerless position granted to one of the senior, long-standing senators. Scipio had swept into the chamber with a determined stride, the senators rising as one as a mark of respect to his rank; he had noted with satisfaction that nearly all were in attendance, including Duilius.

Scipio paused before continuing.

'Senators, I come with grave news from our campaign to remove the Carthaginian horde from the shores of our beloved Sicily. I have come in great haste, enduring great personal risk, to deliver this message to you. You men of courage and intellect hold the key to saving the brave men of the legions now fighting overseas.'

Duilius could sense the charged atmosphere of the Senate as they hung on every word Scipio uttered. Although the junior consul knew what was to be announced, he couldn't suppress the tingle of anticipation at Scipio's words, admiring his eloquence and ability to control the mob that was the Senate. Duilius smiled inwardly at the choice of words: 'you men of courage and intellect'. He knew that Scipio, like himself, had little respect for the other senators of the chamber, and yet so powerful was Scipio's ability to control the crowd that those same men firmly believed the senior consul's description of them was fully warranted, believed that both individually and collectively they held the power of Rome in their hands – while in reality it rested neatly on the shoulders of men like Scipio and Duilius alone.

When Duilius had stalked out of the Curia on receiving the news of Scipio's return, he had known there was only one course of action open to him. With the long-before-learnt lesson on the value of information dictating his movements, he had rushed to his town house behind the Forum Holitorium. He had immediately called for Appius, his senior servant, a freedman who ostensibly ran the affairs of the junior consul's town house, but who in reality was the head of a network of agents spread throughout the homes of the senior men of the Senate. Included in their number were four men in Scipio's household, all freedmen who were sold into the house as slaves to spy on Duilius's most powerful rival. The junior consul had impatiently paced the four corridors of the atrium of his home for nearly an hour before, finally, Appius had reappeared with the much sought-after news. Duilius had listened in silence to the report before brushing past the man and returning to the Senate.

Now, as Duilius sat in the Curia watching Scipio's speech, his mind was at peace, the precious time to prepare that had been given to him by his spies allowing him to plan a rebuttal to Scipio's course. As the senior consul sped towards the pinnacle of his speech, the announcement of the Carthaginian threat, Duilius looked from the corner of his eye to the anxious figure of Longus, a junior senator whom Duilius had enlisted to help carry out his plan. Duilius could only hope the young fop was up to the challenge.

'And so my fellow senators,' Scipio was concluding, 'it is with trepidation in my heart that I tell you that the Carthaginians have blockaded the northern coastline of Sicily and effectively cut off our gallant legions from resupply. The Punici have placed a stranglehold on our campaign and, if it is not released, it will surely destroy our army in Sicily, placing the enemy in a position to strike at the very centre of the Republic: Rome itself!'

There was an audible gasp from the entire chamber, followed by a moment's silence before a cacophony of sound erupted, the senators giving full vent to their fears and anxieties. Many men wailed in voices of doom and defeat, Scipio's final words mentioning a threat to Rome itself fuelling their concerns and heightening their apprehension. Scipio scanned the room slowly, his eyes passing over the sea of worried faces. He did not believe there was any immediate or even medium-term threat to Rome itself, but he knew that many of the senators had not served in the legions and did not fully understand the threat that a severed supply line meant to an army. He had needed to make the threat of the Carthaginians more personal to the rich, complacent, isolated men of the Senate. He had needed to formulate a threat to the city of Rome. As his eyes came to the position of Gaius Duilius, he was surprised to see the man calmly surveying the room himself, his face expressionless, as if Scipio had merely announced the yearly crop figures of grain from Campania. Scipio admired the man's self-control and was about to move on, when Duilius suddenly turned and looked his way. Their eyes locked for a heartbeat, and Scipio thought he read a message in his rival's eyes before their gaze was broken. Scipio picked up the gavel and began to pound it on the lectern, the chamber slowly coming back to order.

'My fellow senators,' he began, his voice now authoritative where before it had been conciliatory, 'my fellow senators, Rome must counter this threat. We must defeat the Punici and wipe them from our seas.'

'How?' a voice called, the question echoed by a dozen others.

'By building our own fleet!' Scipio shouted, his voice rising above the questions. 'By harnessing the power of the Republic to create a fleet that will overcome their blockade and sweep their galleys before us. By defeating them as we have every enemy who dared to challenge the might of Rome. By allowing me, your leader, Gnaeus Cornelius Scipio, to lead the fleet into battle for the glory of the Republic!'

The chamber erupted in cheers as the senators clung to the line of hope and victory offered to them by Scipio. They were a mob, completely swayed by the play of their emotions. The senior consul had driven them down with the news of the seemingly unconquerable threat of the Carthaginians before suddenly raising them high with the hope of victory. The cheering lasted for five full minutes while Scipio stood motionless at the lectern, his expression imperious, his stature imposing, exuding strength and purpose. As the noise began to subside, Scipio prepared for the decisive moment of his strategy, when the entire Senate would vote overwhelmingly in favour of his plan and for him to assume the position of commander of the new fleet. As he raised his gavel to finally silence the crowd, a single voice caught his and everyone else's attention.

'My fellow senators,' Longus announced, a slight tremor in his voice as the entire Senate fell silent, 'we are blessed by the goddess Minerva, the wisest of all, to have as our leader the man standing before us, Gnaeus Cornelius Scipio.'

Voices were raised in agreement from across the Senate, and Scipio nodded in gratitude, a sentiment he did not feel as his mind raced to understand the reason behind Longus's speech, knowing he was a pawn of Duilius's. The young senator raised his voice to overcome the noise.

'Truly our senior consul has shown us the way to defeat the Punici. His intellect, guided by the goddess, has unlocked the solution that will save the legions and the fate of Rome itself. He is our leader and the centre of our power.'

Longus paused once more as voices echoed his words. He waited for silence to reassert itself before continuing the scripted words that Duilius had given him prior to Scipio's arrival, the rehearsed speech dictating his words.

'It is precisely why Gnaeus Cornelius Scipio is our leader and our greatest senator that I fear the precarious position he would be put in should he lead the fleet into battle against the unknown strength of the Carthaginians. Without his mighty presence to lead the Senate, we would be surely lost against this new and powerful enemy. I therefore put it to you, my fellow senators, that the senior consul should indeed lead our naval campaign against the Punici, but he should do so from here, the Senate, the centre of Rome's power. Command of the fleet should be delegated to the junior consul, Gaius Duilius.'

The abrupt end to Longus's speech was followed by a moment's silence before, once again, the chamber was filled with raised voices, many debating Longus's speech. Scipio tore his furious eyes from the young senator and whipped them around to Duilius who, as before, sat impassively in the centre of the lower tier, directly opposite the lectern. His gaze was on Longus, and the junior consul nodded slightly before turning to see Scipio watching him. A slight smile formed on his lips as the voices in the chamber called for Duilius to speak. He stood slowly to address the frenzied chamber.

'I concur with the words of the senator and I humbly accept his proposal for me to lead the fleet into battle.'

Duilius sat down once more, his simple statement reigniting the debate raging across the chamber. Scipio pounded his gavel on the lectern to try to regain control of the Senate, but he already knew that his moment of victory had been snatched by the junior senator's unexpected speech. His mind reached back to the knowing look that Duilius had given him at the announcement of the Carthaginian blockade, and he now recognized it for what it was: a look of defiant triumph. He had been outmanoeuvred and the realization made his anger flare up to an intensity that caused him to viciously hammer the gavel on the lectern even as the last voice was silenced by the aggressive blows.

'My fellow senators,' Scipio shouted, his raised voice unnecessary in the silence. He heard the pitch of his own words and immediately fought to bring his emotions under control. He paused and drew a deep breath before continuing.

'My fellow senators. I am humbled by your concern for my safety and the safety of my position as leader of this chamber. But I say to you, the real power of this Senate lies with each individual member. As senior consul I will lead the fleet, knowing that the power of Rome is safe within your hands.'

Scipio watched as many heads shook in disagreement. He gambled one last time, praying that the residual confidence in his proposal would carry the day.

'I therefore call for a vote on my proposal, confident in your sound judgement,' Scipio continued with all the conviction he could muster. 'I put it to the floor that we build the fleet and I command her into battle.'

Whereas before, when Scipio had first announced his intention to lead the fleet, he had been cheered in universal support, now only a smattering of debate could be heard. Within a minute voices were raised in conflict and the Senate stood divided. Scipio's faction followed their leader, as did Duilius's. The undecided majority wavered between the two, the indecisive calling for more debate, unsure of which proposal to accept. Their voices prevailed and the vote was postponed, Scipio's moment swept away to be replaced with the tedious slog of debate. The senior consul surrendered his place at the lectern to the *princeps senatus*, who would head the discussion. It took all Scipio's willpower to contain his rage and walk steadily back to his position amongst the senators.

CHAPTER SIX

Septimus was awakened from his light doze by the approaching steps of a guard detail. The familiar sound and unfamiliar surroundings meant he was instantly awake and on guard. Atticus was already standing in the middle of their quarters, his eyes locked on the door. He had never relaxed. The door was flung open and Scipio's guard commander was framed in the entrance. He looked from one man to the other.

'You are free to go but I need to know your whereabouts should the consul need to summon you.'

His abrupt statement caught the two men off guard and Septimus took a second to form his reply.

'We will be at the Capito house, my family home, in the Caelian quarter,' he said.

'Or at the *castrum* in Ostia with our ship,' Atticus added.

The guard commander nodded and stepped back from the door before leading the guard detail away.

'So!' Atticus said as he turned to face Septimus, happy at the order of release, 'we're going to your family home?'

'Yes,' replied Septimus with a smile, 'just as soon as I've shown you some of the sights of Rome.'

The centurion stood up and began to walk out into the late evening sunshine.

'And if the consul comes looking for us while we're out seeing the sights?' the captain asked.

'There's no way he'll look for us tonight; not if he's just ordered us away.'

'So we'll be at your family home tomorrow. Will that leave us enough time to see the sights?'

'Trust me, Atticus: when it comes to the sights I'm going to show you, one night is never enough – but one night is all most men can handle.'

Scipio stormed into the *tablinum*, the master bedroom of his home, ripping off his toga as he went. He roared for wine to be brought and an instant later a slave entered and proffered the senator a golden goblet. Scipio snatched the drink and downed it in one, the tannic acidity of the wine only exacerbating the burning sensation of rage in his chest. The slave held up the amphora to refill the goblet, but Scipio grabbed the flask himself and ordered the slave to be gone. As the slave left the room, Scipio's wife, Fabiola, entered. Her face was a mask of concern at the sight of her enraged husband. Scipio wheeled around and saw her standing by the now-closed door.

'Fools!' he spat. 'Feeble-minded, incompetent fools.'

Fabiola knew better than to question the source of his rage. She had seen this before, although never so intense. Everyone who was aware of the intimate workings of the Senate knew it to be a ponderous, frustratingly conservative beast. With three hundred of the city's greatest egos confined within one chamber, it was common for the plans of one man, or even one group of men, however well-meaning or well thought out, to be thwarted by the sheer verbosity and squabbling of the Senate. It was plainly obvious that the plans they had earlier discussed had been undone. To question the reason would only give Scipio a focus for his rage and, although he had never struck her, Fabiola had long since realized that her husband had a barely contained violent streak.

'Three hours!' he continued. 'Three hours the fools debated. Like a gaggle of chattering slave women in the market. Three hours and they failed to even vote on the creation of a fleet, never mind its commander.'

Scipio emptied another goblet of wine, again in one swallow. It did nothing to calm his emotions.

'That bastard Duilius. It was his doing. He had one of his pups question my proposal. Just a simple question. But a perfect blow. It was almost as if he had prepared in advance; as if he knew about the blockade before I announced it. His little thrust exposed a chink, just a tiny chink.'

Scipio continued pacing, his fist clenched by his side, his knuckles white from the pressure. 'But it was enough. Enough for the indecisive old men to pause and debate. Before long they weren't even sure if a fleet was necessary, and if it was they debated over who would bear the cost. Now it will be a week before we go to vote. A week instead of a minute – all because of Gaius Duilius.'

Fabiola, her mind agitated by the mood of her husband, could only watch Scipio vent his rage. As he raved, her mind picked up something he had said: something about it seeming that Duilius had known what Scipio was going to announce before he did. She calmed her emotions and partially faded out the voice of her husband in order to think the point through.

The more she considered the possibility, the more she believed it to be true. Someone must have informed Duilius. But who? And when? Of course the galley that had escorted Scipio from Sicily was full of people who knew of the blockade, but it was docked in the *castrum* in Ostia, a twenty-five-mile round trip on busy roads, and not an easy place for a civilian to enter. She discounted that and focused on the more obvious sources: Scipio's *praetoriani* guard, the captain and centurion of the galley, and the household slaves. It became more and more obvious that the leak had come from among their number.

She continued to watch her husband in silence, waiting for him to calm down. Only then would she approach him and offer her advice and comfort. When he was soothed and once more himself, perhaps tomorrow she thought, she would inform him of her suspicions. If there was a spy within the walls of her husband's house, Fabiola was sure that, once found, she would witness the full fury of the violence she always suspected her husband was capable of.

Septimus led Atticus to a bathhouse as the dying sun in the western sky was touching the taller buildings of Rome. The bathhouse was no more than a hundred yards off the main piazza of the Forum Magnum, and yet Atticus was struck by how different the surrounding area was from the vaulted temples and soaring statues of the city's central forum. Here the streets were narrow and the apartment buildings towered eight storeys high, while underfoot the laneways of the plebeian quarter were strewn with human and animal filth, creating a stench that rose to infuse the very walls of the surrounding houses.

Atticus's mind was instantly transported back to the city of Locri and the backstreets he had called home for the first fourteen years of his life; the long summer days when he fished with his father and his stomach was full, and the hard, cold winters when the storms kept the fleet bottled up and the poorer inhabitants of Locri teetered on the brink of starvation. On those dark winter days, Atticus would escape the hovel he shared with his family and spend his days scavenging on streets no different from those that now surrounded him, and he marked the distance he had travelled since his child-hood.

'After dark I wouldn't march a squad of ten legionaries through these streets,' Septimus remarked with a wry smile, and Atticus caught a hint of disdain in the centurion's voice.

The main door of the bathhouse was flanked by two large thuggish men, but they allowed Septimus and Atticus to pass unchallenged while inside Septimus was immediately recognized by an older woman who greeted patrons as they entered.

'My older brothers, Tiberius and Claudius, first brought me here on my sixteenth birthday,' Septimus explained with a smile, 'and I've come back at least once a year since then.'

Septimus produced the requisite amount of silver and both men were ushered into an antechamber, where slaves quickly stripped them of their kit before they were led to the *caldarium*, a large tiled room dominated by a central bath of steaming, scented water. Atticus groaned loudly in content as he slipped into the bath, the hot water quickly infusing his muscles pleasurably and chasing all tension from his limbs. The sensation was amazing, and he sweated stoically before the near-unbearable heat forced him to rise. He was immediately led to a low table where a female slave rubbed oil into his skin before removing it with a strigil and, with a sense of cleanliness Atticus had never felt before, he was shown to the *tepidarium* chamber, where Septimus was already immersed in the lukewarm bath. Again Atticus groaned as he entered the water and Septimus laughed loudly.

'Well,' he asked, 'what do you think?'

'By the gods, Septimus, this is the way to live,' Atticus laughed as two beautiful young women entered, carrying trays of food and a large amphora of wine. Septimus followed his friend's gaze.

'There are many bathhouses in Rome, my friend, but this

particular one offers one other additional service.' Septimus smiled as a goblet of wine was placed in his hand.

The two women moved quickly and efficiently around the room, bringing food and wine at every summons, and their light and carefree conversation instantly put the men at ease. Within thirty minutes Atticus was consumed by an overwhelming sense of wellbeing and his mind, fogged by the numbing effect of wine, drank in the hushed feminine tones that seemed to fill the air. He raised his goblet to have it refilled, but this time it was taken from him and he was led from the bath by one of the young women to a small room off the *tepidarium* chamber. She quietly closed the door and turned to Atticus, slipping off her tunic as she did so. Atticus gasped involuntarily, her beauty and the potent aphrodisiac of youth combining to stir his desire. He became awkward in his haste, but the experienced young woman immediately took the lead and she guided him to a low cot in the corner of the room. She stroked his upper body and wound her fingers through the dense hair of his chest, skilfully controlling his desire before laying him down and straddling him, allowing him to relax completely, her movements slow and hypnotic.

Afterwards the two lay entwined on the cot, her hands once more gently caressing his body with languid strokes. Atticus had never felt so sated and he drifted off into a deep sleep, every outside thought banished from his mind and the world beyond the walls of the bathhouse forgotten for the night.

Septimus arched his back to stretch the muscles in his spine as he walked through the busy streets of Rome. They had both risen at dawn, both finding themselves alone in their respective rooms in the bathhouse. After dressing, Septimus had bidden a farewell to the woman who had first greeted them – with promises of a return – and they had walked, once more, out onto the bustling streets. Atticus could scarcely believe that the serene world of the bathhouse existed behind the walls of the building he had just left, so different from the dilapidated, frantic streets surrounding it, and the thought sobered him as they walked the short distance to the Forum Magnum, stopping a street vendor to buy some food, their appetites sharpened by the remains of the wine in their stomachs. They continued on in silence, each lost in his own thoughts.

'Just beyond this next street . . .' Septimus said, suddenly breaking the quiet between them, returning their attention to the bustling activity all around.

'What?' Atticus replied, dragging his thoughts back to the moment.

'. . . My home,' Septimus smiled. 'It's just beyond this next street.'

Atticus noticed his friend's pace increase at the mention of his home and he adjusted his stride to match. The equestrian middle-class Caelian quarter was a world apart from the narrow streets and soaring apartment blocks of the poorer quarter and Atticus couldn't help marking the differences in his mind.

'Who'll be home?' he asked, realizing that in the ten months he had known Septimus they had never before discussed his family.

'As far as I know, everyone, although I haven't been home in over two years, so my parents and two older brothers will be there . . . and my younger sister will probably be at home.'

Atticus noticed that Septimus's face became solemn at the mention of his sister before his smile returned anew, and Atticus was left wondering what the family would look like: the women probably dark-featured like Septimus, and the men older versions of him.

The streets passed quickly under their feet and before long they reached the entrance to the house, a modest stout wooden gate set into the whitewashed stone wall that ran along both sides of the residential area. A small tablet beside the door was marked with the family name 'Capito'. Septimus banged on the door and stood back to wait. He was about to knock again when the gate opened abruptly and the arched entrance was framed by a man who stood with arms akimbo, his gaze intense, his chin thrust forward at the sight of unexpected visitors. The moment of recognition was marked by the man's arms falling to his side and his face bursting into a happy smile.

'By the gods . . . Septimus!'

'Domitian,' Septimus smiled, glad to see the senior servant of the house, a man he had known since childhood.

The servant stood for a second before turning to run into the house to announce the unexpected return.

As Septimus led them into the small courtyard, Atticus surveyed the simple, unadorned whitewashed walls of the interior building. To the left stood a small stable-house and two-storey barn, its open doors revealing the heaped straw and bags of grain within. Directly in front of them was the main family residence, again two storeys tall with shuttered windows opened across its broad front. In the centre stood the main door and, as they approached, Atticus could hear the shouts of delight within the house as news of Septimus's return spread.

Suddenly an older woman rushed out through the door towards them. She was tall and slim and her features were high, almost regal. She was dark, as Atticus had suspected, with large hazel eyes and black flowing hair. The woman wrapped her arms around Septimus and kissed him on the cheek, her delight at the return of her youngest son evident in the tears forming at the edges of her eyes.

'Oh Septimus,' she said, close to tears, 'welcome home. Welcome home.'

Septimus broke the embrace, embarrassed by the overt display of affection in front of Atticus. The captain could only smile. Beyond the trio, an older man appeared, and Atticus instantly knew it was his friend's father. The resemblance was striking, the same broad build, the same unruly black hair, but Septimus's father also had a vicious scar on the left side of his face, running from his forehead to his cheek, cutting through the eye, which had turned opaque and milky white. But for the injury, he was Septimus in twenty years' time.

Septimus shook his father's hand warmly, legionary style, with hands gripping forearms.

'Welcome home, son,' the older man said, his voice deep and hoarse.

'It's good to be home, father,' Septimus replied, standing tall before his father as he would before a senior officer.

'Those markings on your armour,' his father continued, his hand touching Septimus's breast-plate, 'are those the insignia of the marines?'

'Of a marine centurion,' Septimus replied proudly, this visit marking the first time he had stood before his father as a centurion, the same rank his father had achieved in the Ninth.

'A marine centurion,' the older man said dismissively, as if the first word sullied the second. 'Better an *optio* in the Ninth where your rank commanded some respect.'

'There is no dishonour in commanding the marines,' Septimus countered, but his father ended the argument with a wave, his attention turning to Atticus, leaving Septimus with no choice but to introduce his friend.

'Father, mother, this is the captain of the *Aquila*, Atticus Milonius Perennis, and Atticus, this is Antoninus and Salonina,' Septimus said, indicating in turn his father and mother.

Atticus nodded a greeting to Salonina before shaking Antoninus's hand. The grip was hard and firm, the underlying strength of the man evident in the simple gesture.

'Milonius . . . Greek?' Antoninus asked, his expression inscrutable.

'Yes,' Atticus answered warily, 'from Locri.'

Antoninus nodded slowly, maintaining his grip on Atticus's arm, his gaze penetrating, the handshake only breaking when Salonina turned and beckoned them all to follow through the main door. Beyond was the atrium, similar in design to the one at Scipio's house, but more basic, the surrounding pillars plain and unembellished, the central pool simple and untiled. The group walked around the atrium and entered the room beyond, the *triclinium*, the main dining room of the house. A table stood in the centre of the room, flanked by three couches; the fourth side opened towards the kitchen door, through which slaves were ferrying fresh fruit and bread. The group sat down, with the father taking the head of the table with his wife to his right and Atticus and Septimus occupying the third couch.

'So where are Tiberius and Claudius?' Septimus asked, enquiring after his brothers, 'and Hadria? Is she home?'

Antoninus shook his head.

'Your brothers are in the south on a trade journey with their partner Nerva from the house of Carantus. Hadria is in the city at your aunt's house in the Viminal quarter.'

'Does she still speak of Valerius?' Septimus asked, looking to his mother.

'No,' Salonina answered softly. 'She deeply mourned his loss but I believe her heart is free again.'

'So soon?' Septimus said, a sharp edge to his voice.

'It's been nearly a year since his death, Septimus,' Salonina replied, 'and at twenty she cannot remain a widow for much longer.'

'You know Rome's law, Septimus,' Antoninus added, 'she must remarry within two years to settle Valerius's estate. His father Casca is already stopping me in the forum and asking if I have found any suitors.'

Septimus was about to speak but he held his tongue, his mind flooded with memories of the friend he had lost.

'Domitian!' Antoninus called, his summons answered instantly. 'Send a messenger to Hadria with word that Septimus has returned.' The senior servant nodded and left immediately.

Septimus began to fill his parents in on the details of his life over the past two years. Many things had happened and many things had changed. Two hours later, when the bell rang for the forenoon meal, he was only just beginning to relate the events of the previous four days.

'They march, Admiral,' the man announced as permission to speak was granted.

'When and to where?'

'Yesterday at dawn. They are heading west.'

Hannibal Gisco nodded and dismissed the messenger. He rose from his seated position behind the marble-topped table and walked through the windblown cotton drapes out onto the top-floor balcony beyond. The building was three storeys tall and stood directly on the dock of the port town of Panormus, a magnificent natural harbour that now sheltered the growing Carthaginian fleet. Gisco watched with satisfaction as the remnants of the sixty-ship-strong second fleet dropped anchor two hundred yards from shore. The fleet had sailed up the west coast of Sicily, with orders to set up a blockade around the Roman-held city of Agrigentum. The remainder would add its precious cargo of soldiers to Gisco's command, swelling his army to twenty-five thousand.

As Gisco surveyed the busy harbour, he calculated the rate of advance of the Roman legions, confident that the enemy were unaware of his knowledge of their movements. Over the winter months, the Roman encampment had been under constant surveillance, from both the nearby hills and from bribed local merchants who had given the Carthaginians detailed descriptions of the size and strength of the army within the walled camp. The reports to Panormus had come regularly by an ingenious method stolen from the Persians a generation before: carrier pigeon. These winged messengers gave the Carthaginians an incredible advantage against an enemy who had not yet discovered the birds' unique abilities and so, not thirty-six hours after the Romans had marched, Gisco had been handed the chance to get one step ahead of his foe.

Gisco thought back to the messenger's words. The Romans had left their winter encampment yesterday, marching west. Gisco knew their destination was undoubtedly the cities of Segeste and Makella to the south of Panormus. These two city-states had defiantly sided with the Romans immediately after their victory at Agrigentum, although they were deep within Carthaginian territory. Gisco had ordered the cities besieged and was confident that, given time, they would once more fall under his control. He had already decided the fate of the inhabitants of the cities, a fate that would act as a deterrent to any other city-states within his territory that were considering defecting to the Roman cause. His private promise of retribution could only be carried out if he stalled or, better yet, stopped the Roman advance.

Gisco immediately discounted the option of a direct assault. The Roman legion's fighting abilities on land far exceeded his own army's, a fact demonstrated by the Carthaginian defeat at Agrigentum. If he was to defeat the enemy he would need to extend his strategy of strangling the Romans into submission.

The legions were no more than a week's march from the territorial dividing line, a demarcation running south from the coastal town of Caronia on the northern coast that had indicated the furthest advance of the Romans in the previous year's campaign season. That line was almost exactly halfway between their start point at the winter encampment and the Carthaginians' base camp in Panormus, and so if Gisco was going to slow their advance he realized he would have to reach the line first. The admiral turned abruptly from the balcony and called for his aide. The man entered immediately.

'Assemble the section commanders in the main hall immediately for a briefing and send orders to the cavalry to make ready to advance before the day's end.'

'Yes, Admiral,' the aide replied and left.

Gisco walked over to the table and surveyed the detailed map of Sicily. The first Roman soldiers had landed on the island only four years before. At first the Carthaginians had viewed their arrival as a mere annoyance and had not even opposed their landing at Messina, confident that they could and would defeat them at the time of their choosing. They had been wrong, Gisco thought with frustration. The Romans had proved to be better than the Carthaginians on land and now controlled the entire eastern half of the island. Gisco would redress the error of not exploiting the Romans' vulnerability at sea. As a combined force on land and sea, the Carthaginians were more than a match for the enemy. He would make the two sides of the same coin work in unison to isolate and destroy the Romans. No army could stand alone. Gisco would make sure the Romans learnt that lesson well.

*

Atticus listened in silence as Septimus and his father discussed the threat the legions faced in Sicily. The remains of the forenoon meal had been removed from the table only moments before, the servants moving in silence, Atticus noticing that many had their ears cocked at the incredible news that Septimus was relaying. At times Septimus looked to Atticus for confirmation or agreement on a point, but Atticus noticed that Antoninus never looked his way, the older man unconsciously touching his scar as he spoke to his son about his old legion.

Suddenly Atticus's drifting thoughts were shattered by a scream, a shriek of delight that caused all heads to turn to the dining-room entrance and, as he watched spellbound, a young woman bolted into the room and threw herself into Septimus's arms. Atticus had never seen anyone so beautiful in all his life.

Hadria wore a simple white *stola*, secured around the middle with a thin braided leather belt. She was not tall, her head only reaching to Septimus's chest, but her legs were long and tanned and she danced in her sandals an inch off the ground. Her whole body seemed to radiate vitality and health and her face was a picture of happiness as she laughed up at her older brother, her open mouth sensuous. Hadria did not have Septimus's dark complexion. She was fair, with flawless skin that spoke of her youth. Her shoulder-length light-brown hair had elements of blonde where the sun had bleached the strands and the colour set off the light in her sea-grey eyes. Atticus had never seen such emotion expressed in anyone's face before, and the affection she held for her brother was there for all to behold.

Septimus laughed at the infectious happiness of his sister and it was a full minute before their embrace was relaxed. Only then did Septimus turn to his friend.

'Atticus,' he began, 'I would like to introduce you to my sister, Hadria.'

'It's a pleasure to meet you, Hadria,' Atticus said, captivated by her.

'And you,' Hadria replied demurely, her gaze penetrating, unnerving.

She broke the link and danced around to sit beside her mother as all retook their seats, the mood lifted further by her presence.

Within half an hour the conversation turned trivial, the topics lighthearted as Septimus regaled his sister with tales from his time away. Hadria sat with rapt attention as her brother spoke, her gaze never leaving his, her questions infrequent yet incisive, the perfect listener. Septimus held her gaze and the two-way link allowed Atticus to watch Hadria surreptitiously from the corner of his eye. He studied her closely, his eyes picking up every detail of her profile, his senses overwhelmed by her beauty. The thread of lighter conversation brought Atticus back into the group and the discussion drifted on into the late afternoon.

The evening ended with Salonina announcing the lateness of the hour, her hand held out to Hadria as a gesture for her daughter to accompany her from the room. Hadria groaned playfully and jumped off the couch in one fluid movement. She kissed her father and brother on the cheek before bidding goodnight to Atticus, the simple politeness accompanied by a broad smile.

Atticus returned the pleasantry and watched Hadria leave the room. As he turned back, Septimus and Antoninus began to talk once more of the legions in Sicily, the older man expanding on a thought he had developed over the previous hours.

*

Atticus rose early the following morning and walked through the atrium of the house into the main dining room for breakfast. The four members of the Capito family were already there talking animatedly in a tight circle around the low table. They did not immediately notice Atticus's arrival and so he was free to observe them unawares. For a family that spent a considerable time apart they were very close and, judging from the occasional laughter and the smiling expressions of all, Atticus suspected that the conversation between them was light and inconsequential, typical family talk that touched on the details of their daily lives.

Atticus's eyes rested on Hadria in the group before him. She was wearing a pale blue *stola* that set off the colour in her eyes perfectly and seemed to accentuate the fairness of her skin. She was listening to a story being told by her father and she laughed and clapped at his punch-lines, her joy infectious, her parents laughing with her.

'Atticus!' she called, noticing her observer for the first time. 'We've been waiting for you.'

For a heartbeat Atticus noticed an intriguing look behind Hadria's radiant smile, a lingering touch to her gaze that spoke of something beyond affection, a look that heightened his awareness of the most beautiful woman he had ever met.

CHAPTER SEVEN

'And so, my esteemed colleagues of the Senate, I now call for a vote on my revised proposal, I call for a division of the house to settle the matter.'

Scipio sat down and surveyed the crowded chamber with inner disgust. The senators were having mumbled conversations with those around them at this new call to vote. Scipio had estimated that it would take a week for the Senate to decide on a course of action to defeat the Carthaginian blockade. He had been wrong. The debate was now in its tenth day and the seemingly endless rounds of debate and voting, over ridiculously minor points, had frayed his patience to a thread. On the fifth day the Senate had finally decided that a fleet was needed. The following two days had been taken up with a decision on the size of the fleet and two days after that on how the fleet would be financed. Only now were the senators debating the command of the campaign.

The leader of the house banged his gavel on the lectern and called the assembly to order.

'Following the senior consul's submission and the aforementioned views of the junior consul, we will now divide the house. All those in favour please move to the eastern wall, those against to the western.'

Scipio remained seated in the front tier, his position in front of the eastern wall a call to all his supporters to rally to his side. Scipio inwardly scoffed at the term 'supporters'. He had spent the past ten days cajoling and subtly bribing half of them in an effort to gain their backing. Only a tiny minority of them actually voted in line with the conviction that their actions were in Rome's best interest. Only a tiny minority of them had that courage. The rest of them needed to be led like cattle.

In the centre of the chamber, Gaius Duilius stood abruptly. Scipio watched him like a hawk. Of the three hundred individual votes of the Senate, only two really counted in this debate, Scipio's and Duilius's. The direction of the junior consul's turn would decide the matter, one way or the other. Scipio watched the man's calm exterior, hating him anew. Duilius had thwarted his proposals at every turn, but always through intermediaries and always with a subtle, clever approach that never really jeopardized any proposal as a whole. In this way important decisions like the one to build the fleet were made, but Duilius had chipped away at Scipio's propositions, undermining his authority at every turn. Scipio had needed to give ground each time, including this last proposal on leadership, and so he watched with the bile of hatred rising ever further in his throat as he waited for Duilius to react, unsure if he would be able to control his actions should the junior consul vote against him this one last time.

As the tension in the chamber reached breaking point, Gaius Duilius turned.

From the beginning of the debate ten days earlier, Duilius had believed in the fundamentals of Scipio's approach. The fleet was needed, of that there was no doubt. Given the Carthaginians' superiority in naval skills, the fleet would need to outnumber

149

any force the Punici could put to sea. Simple logic that needed no debate. The city would need to fund the building of the fleet from the public coffers, and taxes would need to be levied to make up any shortfall. Again this fact was irrefutable. And yet Duilius had challenged Scipio on each occasion.

The exercise had been expensive, but necessary. Duilius needed to show Scipio that he could hold up his ambitions indefinitely in the senatorial quagmire if he did not give ground on the most important proposal, that of leadership of the fleet. The debates had been taxing and the individual votes tedious but now, as the members of the house stood up to vote, Duilius felt real power surround him. He had always known the motivation behind Scipio's proposals, the thirst for power that drove his actions – as it did Duilius's; and, as the entire Senate chamber looked to see which way the junior consul would turn, Duilius felt the power of Rome in his hand.

Scipio had amended his proposal on leadership. He had had to. Scipio would indeed go to sea with the fleet and he would be the overall commander, but Duilius would sail too. The junior consul would take the vanguard and would be tactical commander of the fleet, while Scipio would have strategic command, the senior consul's position in the rear of the fleet giving the illusion of safety that the Senate demanded. Duilius had engineered the debate to highlight this compromise to Scipio and the senior consul had accepted, each man knowing that once the fleet was out of sight of Rome and beyond the Senate's gaze, the power struggle would start afresh. But now, on this day and at this time, Duilius was ruler of Rome and he savoured the sensation.

Duilius turned and walked towards the eastern wall, his supporters immediately following to leave a forlorn minority of twenty senators on the other side of the chamber. The men of the Senate cheered at this final decision, this conclusion to their debate, the tension of the previous ten days released in a moment of shared relief. Scipio stood and was surrounded by senators who slapped congratulatory hands on his shoulders and back, as they did for Duilius, the two men seen together as the joint saviours of the Sicilian campaign, an accolade Scipio had planned as his own. The senior consul walked towards Duilius through the press of cheering senators and magnanimously offered his hand in a show of shared responsibility for the battles ahead that would be faced together. Duilius took the hand and the crowd cheered anew. The expressions of both men were expansive, both reflecting the thrill of the moment and atmosphere of the crowd. Both expressions were only skin deep. As their eyes locked only an astute observer would have seen the momentary exchange. For Scipio and Duilius the surface solidarity hid the challenge that had been thrown down and accepted. From here on the glory of Rome would take second place to the power struggle that the Carthaginian blockade had ignited between them. Both men knew that there could be only one ruler of Rome.

'No, no, no, Gaius,' Lucius argued, 'we can't rely on every helmsman having your skill. Any new ships built will be sailed by, at best, fishermen and traders.'

'Even so,' Gaius countered, 'the ram is still the best way for a raw crew to defeat an experienced one. There's no way we can teach the legionaries to board properly within a reasonable time!'

Atticus looked on in silence, allowing the argument to draw out the full opinion of both men, their knowledge and experience vital if a solution was to be found. The three men sat in the enclosed main cabin of the *Aquila*, the trireme resting against her ropes at the dockside of Ostia.

Atticus had remained at the Capito home for three days in total, his own departure coming two days after Hadria's, the insistent calls from her aunt compelling her to return to her house in the Viminal quarter. The lack of news or orders from the Senate had chafed Atticus's patience and he had arisen on the third day with an overwhelming urge to see his ship. On arriving at Ostia he had put every waking hour and all his energy into the *Aquila*. The entire running rigging had now been replaced, as had the mainsail, the replacements drawn from the extensive stores of the military camp that serviced the dozen ships of the Ostia fleet. The rowers had been brought up and housed in the slave compound behind the *castrum* and the slave decks had been thoroughly cleaned. Even now slaves were diving beneath the galley, removing barnacles and limpets from the hull. Once cleaned, the galley would be a half-knot faster at her top stroke.

The three senior sailors of the *Aquila* had been discussing possible tactics for over an hour, the captain playing devil's advocate to the second-in-command and the helmsman. Each time the two men agreed on a point, Atticus would counter their solution, finding a chink in their logic that would set the two men talking again. They had discussed every possible approach and how the Carthaginians might respond to any move. Having seen the Punici in action twice, the three men had little doubt of the calibre and resolve of their foe. Every possible scenario finished with the same conclusion, the same imbalance: experience.

A new Roman fleet would be crewed by inexperienced men, civilian sailors and legionaries used to fighting on land. Inexperienced sailors meant that ramming would be a near-impossible tactic, the manoeuvring skills required taking months to perfect, the combination of angle and speed needing to be precise. This was especially pertinent since the Roman craft were of a lighter design and would be unsure of penetration if the angle was off by more than ten degrees. Over ten degrees it was likely that the ram would simply deflect off the heavier Carthaginian hull. The call for ramming speed also needed to be exact. Too late and the ship would lack the necessary momentum; too soon and the galley slaves would be spent after the first couple of encounters; it was likely that any large-scale confrontation would last for hours.

The ability to manoeuvre alongside for boarding took considerably less skill: the angle less important, the speed only needing to be sufficient to overtake the opponent. The three men had all agreed that traders, and even fishermen, could be taught enough to master the simple manoeuvre within a week at most. The problem of inexperience now shifted to the legionaries. To train them as marines would take several months, the ability to board successfully and in sufficient numbers vital in the first minutes of any attack. Once on board, they would be without their favoured four-foot *scutum* shields and their years of training as land-based fighting units would count for naught, armed as they would be with a *hoplon* shield along with their *gladius*.

'Gaius, Lucius,' Atticus interrupted, trying to bring the discussion back to its centre, needing to forge ahead, 'we're all agreed that the sailing crews can be taught how to manoeuvre for boarding but not for ramming in the time we have.'

'Yes,' both men replied.

'And we're also agreed that our legionaries cannot be taught to board and fight using the traditional methods in the time we have.'

'Yes,' both men said again, this time Lucius sighing as the discussion circled around the obstacle.

'Right. We need to concentrate on solving one of the

problems only. I think the solution to the sailing problem will be harder to find, so I suggest we concentrate on the boarding issue. We need to find a way of getting our troops onto the enemy decks in sufficient numbers and with their *scutum* shields. Once there they'll be unstoppable.'

'Once there . . .' Gaius said, as he put his mind to the task. The cabin became silent again as all three men applied themselves to the problem. They were still without a solution an hour later when a messenger knocked on the cabin door.

'Messenger approaching,' Domitian called from the courtyard. The senior servant turned from the main gate and ran into the atrium of the Capito estate, repeating his call as he ran. Septimus heard the call in the smaller enclosed courtyard at the rear of the compound, where he had been practising his swordplay. He threw the wooden sword to the ground and strode through the house, meeting Domitian halfway.

'Messenger approaching on horseback,' the foreman said.

Septimus nodded and brushed past him. As he exited the front door of the house, the mounted praetorian guard entered through the main gate. He spotted Septimus and cantered towards him.

'I have a message for Centurion Capito and Captain Perennis of the *Aquila*,' he announced.

'I am Centurion Capito. Captain Perennis is at the *castrum* of Ostia,' Septimus replied.

The praetorian guard nodded. The other messenger, sent directly to Ostia, would find the captain. The mounted soldier looked Septimus up and down, the man before him wearing a sweat-stained tunic, the black dishevelled hair giving him a wild, untamed look. He didn't look much like a centurion. Bloody marines, the guard thought.

'My master, Senior Consul Scipio, orders —'

'Get off your horse and deliver your message properly,' Septimus interrupted, his voice hard, having noticed the unconscious look of disdain creep onto the guard's face before he spoke. The guard hesitated, but only for a heartbeat, the underlying menace of the command triggering his instinct as a soldier. He dismounted.

'My master —'

'Properly!' Septimus interrupted again, his tone like iron. 'You're addressing a superior officer, soldier. I'll give you one last chance to get it right.'

Septimus drew himself to his full height. At six foot four inches he stood half a head above the guard. The praetorian fully believed that he was in mortal danger, even though he was armed and the centurion before him was not.

He adroitly stood to attention and saluted, slamming his bunched fist against his metal breast-plate, his eyes now fixed dead ahead in regulation fashion.

'Beg to report,' he began. 'My master, Senior Consul Scipio, orders you to attend his town house immediately.'

Septimus waited a moment in silence, a part of him still debating whether or not he should strike the guard for insubordination. The praetorian seemed to sense the centurion's thoughts and instinctively braced himself for the blow.

'Very well,' Septimus said suddenly. 'You're dismissed,' he added, realizing that it would be best not to send the guard back to Scipio with a black eye.

The praetorian saluted again and remounted his horse. He wheeled around and galloped off.

'Domitian!'

'Yes, Septimus,' the foreman replied as he stepped out from inside the main door from where he had witnessed the exchange.

'Order my personal aide to lay out my kit and have one of the stable lads ready a mount.'

Domitian acknowledged the command and was gone. Septimus strode to the main gate and watched the messenger weave his way through the throng of people on the street. He turned and entered the house and within minutes re-emerged in full dress uniform. He mounted the horse held by the stable lad and cantered out through the main gate.

Atticus approached the town house of the senior consul slowly, the winding streets keeping his mount down to a trot. He had followed the praetorian messenger from Ostia, relying on the guard to guide him to the city and to the senator's house within. Atticus was a creature of the wide open expanses of the sea; whereas he could plot any course on the featureless water using the sun and stars, his sense of direction failed him completely in the enclosed streets of Rome. As he turned into the walled courtyard of Scipio's town house he saw Septimus standing near the entranceway into the atrium beyond.

'About time,' Septimus called up. 'I've had to wait here until you arrived.'

Atticus nodded a smile, knowing that the centurion was probably burning with the same curiosity as he was.

'Any idea why we've been called now?' he asked as he dismounted beside Septimus.

'No. I only know from the news I heard on the street when I passed through the Forum Magnum that the Senate has approved the building of a fleet and both Scipio and Duilius will command it.'

'Duilius?' Atticus asked as both men passed under the entrance into the serenity of the atrium.

'This year's junior consul. Owns half of the land straddling the city and stocks most of the markets from his fields.'

Atticus nodded, realizing that he knew very little about the most important citizens of the city and the main players in the Senate.

The praetorian guard commander was waiting for them inside.

'Come with me,' he ordered brusquely, although his rank was no higher than the captain or centurion's.

'Friendly as ever,' Septimus murmured.

The commander led them through a series of rooms, some obviously for entertaining guests and dining, and others that seemed to serve no visible purpose other than to display the artwork and statues adorning the space. The house was expansive, the simple courtyard and atrium deceptively small given the depth of the house. They came upon Scipio under the shade of an awning in an inner courtyard. He was sitting alone, apparently deep in thought. He did not look up as the three men entered.

The guard commander peeled off and the men of the *Aquila* approached alone.

'Captain Perennis and Centurion Capito reporting as ordered,' Atticus announced as both men snapped to attention.

'Ah yes,' Scipio said, looking up as if noticing them for the first time.

'The Senate has decided to build a fleet of one hundred and fifty triremes. You are to report to Publius Cornelius Lentulus, the master shipbuilder in Ostia, and assist him in this task, specifically to relate to him your experience of the enemy and their capabilities.'

'Yes, Consul,' both men replied.

They waited for a further command but none was forthcoming. Scipio looked back down at his notes, seeming to forget the two officers. A full minute passed.

'You're dismissed!' the senior consul finally said, and Atticus and Septimus turned on their heels and left.

The two men retraced their steps through the house back to the main courtyard where a stable lad held the reins of their horses.

'By the gods, Septimus . . .' Atticus breathed, his face a mask of astonishment. 'One hundred and fifty galleys. It's a mammoth task. It'll take six months at least and then they'll have to find men to crew them all.'

'Atticus, Atticus . . .' Septimus chided with a smile, amused by his friend's astonishment. 'Look around you, man. Look at the city that has been built here. Built by Scipio and others like him in the Senate. If they have decided that one hundred and fifty galleys are to be built, then built they shall be – and not within six months either. They know the threat is more imminent and the ships will be needed sooner. I'll bet the deadline is half that time and the crews are already being levied as we speak.'

Atticus shook his head, disbelieving. Surely the Senate had set too big a task for Rome to complete.

Septimus looked up at the sun. It was an hour after midday.

'We still have time to meet this master shipbuilder today,' he said as he mounted. Atticus nodded and mounted his own horse, wheeling it around to follow Septimus out through the main gate. In his mind's eye he tried to picture such a massive armada. He could not. His logical mind told him it wasn't possible in the time they had. In six months the campaign season would be over and Sicily would be strewn with the starved bodies of the Second and Ninth legions. At best they had three months to break the blockade.

Septimus's words echoed in his ears as he rode back towards the Forum Magnum and his eyes were drawn up to the magnificent buildings that surrounded the central plaza. They were truly the work of great men; determined men who set themselves a task and followed through regardless of the cost or consequences. Perhaps his friend was right; perhaps the Senate had set Rome the task knowing she could respond in kind. As his mind debated the mission ahead he subconsciously spurred his horse to a greater speed; his innate impatience to get started drove him on and he brushed past Septimus to take the lead. By the time they cleared the Porta Flumentana on the road to Ostia, their horses were galloping at full tilt.

'Here they come again!'

Marcus Fabius Buteo spun around in the direction of the shouted warning in time to see yet another cavalry charge from the woods to the left of the marching column.

'Form up!' the centurion roared, and ran to position himself at the head of the lead transport wagon, the maniple's signifer running behind him, the standard becoming the pivot point of the formation.

As Marcus ran, a Roman cavalry unit tore through a gap in the supply train, the riders' heads low in an attempt to gain every ounce of speed from their mounts. The Carthaginian cavalry were over three hundred yards away. At full gallop they would cover the distance in less than twenty seconds. The Roman cavalry had to engage them fast and as far away from the valuable supplies as they could and so they rode like men possessed, the seemingly endless attacks pumping adrenaline through their veins to overcome the fatigue in both horse and rider.

'Stand the line!' Marcus shouted as the maniple formed around him. Every soldier heard the command and braced himself forward against the coming onslaught. The command meant no fall-back, no reserve rally point. There would be no further order to manoeuvre and they would fight where they stood, each man knowing the reason. They could not leave the supplies undefended.

The attacks had begun five days ago, before the legions had even crossed the territorial dividing line. The first surprise strike had been the most devastating. Although the maniples guarding the supplies, including the IV of the Ninth commanded by Marcus, reacted instantly to the cavalry charge, they were no match for the swift and manoeuvrable mounted enemy. Without the support of their own cavalry units, who were dispersed along the entire length of the three-mile-long marching column, the infantry soldiers could do little but hold their ground and defend themselves. It was at the point of impact in that first attack that Marcus realized the true target of the enemy. While small detachments peeled off the main cavalry charge to keep the infantry tied down, they made no attempt to push home their attack or penetrate the defensive shield walls of the legionaries. Instead their focus had been the supply wagons. Dozens of fire arrows had been loosed into the heaped wagons while spearmen targeted the tethered oxen. The result had been catastrophic. The Carthaginians had disengaged after only five frenzied minutes, leaving the supply train in chaos. Marcus, like the other centurions, had ordered the men to douse the flames while frantic appeals for support were sent up the line to the legion commanders. That first attack had cost them a tenth of their entire supplies.

The legions had camped that first night on the very spot of the attack, the engineers hastily erecting the protective palisade of a marching legion in enemy territory. The attack had been dissected in detail, the legions' commanders quizzing the centurions who had witnessed the coordinated ambush. Changes were made. Defences were strengthened. Counter measures were deployed, including cavalry and a fire guard with responsibility for protecting the combustible supplies.

The ambushes had reached their peak on the third day when a combined force of enemy infantry and cavalry attacked at a river ford. The Romans had been quick to respond and the enemy had been severely bruised and routed, their foolhardy infantry suffering the most against the determined legionaries. The Carthaginians had switched back to exclusively mounted attacks after the minor setback and so now, on the fifth day, an hour after midday, Marcus and his men were forced to respond to yet another strike, the fourth that day.

From one hundred and fifty yards away, Marcus heard the crunch of steel, bone, man and horse as the two cavalry forces collided. The collision was vicious, the naked belligerence of both sides turning the fight into brutal combat where no quarter was asked or given. The men of the IV maniple could only watch in silence, their teeth bared in hatred at the enemy out of their reach. All eyes were on the chaotic mêlée.

'On the flank!'

Marcus saw the danger immediately as he reacted to the cry. Another enemy cavalry unit of fifty mounted men had broken from the cover of the woods and were bearing directly down on his maniple's position, bypassing the engaged Roman cavalry, heading straight for the supply train. The order went out for the Roman reserve cavalry to counter this second thrust, but Marcus knew they would not arrive in time, positioned as they were at the very rear of the supply train.

'Charge weapons,' the centurion shouted, and the men of his maniple roared a defiant primal scream as they thrust out their *pila* between their shields, presenting a wall of deadly steel to the approaching horsemen. The oxen behind the men bellowed in terror at the confused scene around them, the sound mixing with the war cries of the fast-approaching Punici. Marcus leaned forward into his shield and braced his left foot behind, steadying himself against the wave of man and beast approaching at the terrifying speed of thirty miles per hour. The ground beneath him trembled with the force of the charge.

'*Hastati!*' he shouted, the enemy now one hundred yards away.

'Loose!'

The whooshing sound of forty *pila* released together filled the air above the shield wall as the *hastati* of the IV put their might behind the throw of their javelins, their craving to bring death to the enemy fuelling their effort. The javelins seemed to hang in the air for a heartbeat before falling into the oncoming charge. Man and horse buckled and fell under the deadly shower but the charge was barely checked and the Carthaginians came on over their fallen comrades with renewed hatred and drive.

'Steady, boys!' Marcus shouted, his men taking strength from the calmness of the command.

The cavalry charge turned at the last possible second, sweeping down the line of the shield wall, the deadly points of the bared *pila* forcing the turn. The Carthaginians hurled both fire arrows and spears into the supplies behind the wall of legionaries, striking blow after deadly blow against the precious supplies. One rider was slow to turn and his mount crashed straight into the braced, interlocked shields at the head of the maniple. The one-thousand-pound horse tore through the wall, catapulting two soldiers into the oxen and wagons behind, killing them instantly. The horse slammed directly against the six-foot-high wagon wheel with a sickening crunch. The Carthaginian rider was thrown and landed deep within the ranks of the legionaries where he was instantly dispatched under the blows of half a dozen blades.

As the last of the riders swept past Marcus, the centurion ordered a second volley of *pila*, this time into the undefended rear of the charge. Again the missiles had a deadly effect on their targets but again the charge did not waver. As the Carthaginians exhausted all their arrows and spears they peeled off and began their retreat to the woods, the lead rider sounding a horn that signalled to the Carthaginian cavalry engaged with the Romans that it should break off and retreat. Within an instant the field before the defending Romans was clear once again. The attack had lasted no more than four minutes.

Marcus ordered his maniple to regroup while he surveyed the aftermath. The enemy had left maybe a dozen or more of their number dead or dying on the field, while the Roman casualties were perhaps half that number amongst the cavalry, plus the two legionaries who had been crushed by the Carthaginian horse. Smoke was once again rising over four of the twenty laden supply wagons, but the fire guard was working efficiently and the threat was soon extinguished. The centurion counted eight oxen dead in their traces, the equivalent of an entire team for one wagon.

In the five days of attacks, Marcus estimated they had lost nearly twenty-five per cent of their entire supply train. They were ten days out from the *castra hiberna* at Floresta, which meant they were approximately four days short of the first besieged city of Makella. Four days, Marcus thought; four days before they could set up a more permanent defensive palisade as they worked to lift the siege of Makella. Four more days of attacks on the supplies before they could be properly protected. If things continued as they were, they would arrive at their first destination with half the supplies they had set out with. They would be able to resupply from the city once the siege was lifted, but only in terms of food and some basic equipment. Everything else was lost for good – irreplaceable until the blockade was lifted.

'Form up!' he commanded, echoing a similar command up

and down the line as the last of the fires was extinguished and the depleted oxen were once again redistributed by their drivers. The IV maniple formed up behind the standard held high by the signifer. It had been singed in an attack two days before and the sight of the battered standard brought pride to Marcus's chest, a fitting symbol of the fighting men of his command and a defiant reminder of the nine men he had lost over the previous five days.

The legions would reach Makella, of that there was no doubt, but the cost was high. The enemy knew where to hit them and how. They had attacked suddenly, with a ferocity born from sensing the closeness of the kill, the scent of a weakened and desperate enemy cut off from home. The legions would reach Makella but Marcus suspected they would go no further, the open marching column too easy a target for the focused attacks. At Makella they would make their stand, lifting the siege while being besieged themselves. Not by a visible enemy who offered battle, but by an unseen foe who snapped at their heels and sapped their strength.

'March,' Marcus shouted, his subconscious mind picking up the ripple of command as it fed down the line, his thoughts on the dark future ahead of them. His attention was brought back to the moment by the whip crack of the ox drivers. The men around them involuntarily started at the loud crack, their nerves strained to breaking point as they waited for the next cry of attack, knowing that the day was far from over.

'Come.'

Atticus opened the door and entered the small office in the north wing of the *castrum* at Ostia. He was followed by Septimus, and the presence of the two men made the enclosed space seem claustrophobic. Publius Cornelius Lentulus, master shipbuilder of the Roman fleet, sat behind the desk poring over a scale model of a trireme made from light balsam timber. Parchments were strewn all around him, covering the desk and the wall-mounted shelves, many lying on the floor where they had fallen from the overloaded spaces. The master ship-builder was an older man with thinning hair and a greying beard. He glanced up with a mild look of surprise on his face, as if he seldom received visitors in his office.

'Yes?'

'Captain Perennis and Centurion Capito of the *Aquila*,' Atticus said by way of introduction.

'Ah yes,' Lentulus said genially as he stood up to greet the men, 'my Carthaginian experts.'

Atticus smiled at the description. 'Experts' was stretching the description of their knowledge a little too far.

Lentulus led them out of his small office into a larger room down the corridor. This room also seemed to be in chaos, but the disorder was confined to a large table in the centre of the room. The table was surrounded on all sides by chairs, four of which were occupied by Lentulus's team of junior craftsmen, each one an apprentice of the master. They stood as Lentulus entered but he signalled them to be seated with an impatient wave of his hand, as if the courtesy was not sought.

'This is Captain Perennis and Centurion Capito of the *Aquila*,' he announced. The four apprentices looked at the officers with intense interest. They had never seen a Carthaginian warship, and their natural curiosity for all things nautical fuelled their interest in the men; they would normally have considered them to be mere ballast on the magnificent ships they designed.

Lentulus chaired the conversation but he allowed his apprentices to ask the majority of the questions. Atticus described the ships he had encountered in detail, from their speed and manoeuvrability, to their size and draught. Septimus offered confirmation of the enemy's deck layout and hatch placement from his memory of the fight aboard the Carthaginian galley, the upper features of the deck giving some indication of the hidden framework beneath. The questions were thorough, and in many cases Atticus did not have the answer the craftsmen sought, his knowledge limited to the sailing capabilities and his thoughts on the design merely subjective. Any unanswered questions sparked fierce debate amongst the competitive apprentices, and on two occasions the debate nearly erupted into blows before Lentulus intervened and brought the discussion back to order.

The interview lasted over two hours, and when Atticus and Septimus finally emerged from the room the sun had slipped below the western horizon. They walked to the *Aquila* in silence, both drained from the intense conversation. Atticus had not been given the opportunity to ask any questions of his own, particularly about what kind of schedule Lentulus envisioned for the completion of the fleet, although the master shipbuilder and his team didn't seem to be wasting any time. Design and concepts were one thing, he thought; it was a whole other problem to implement those ideas and actually build a vessel.

The following morning Atticus woke as usual just before dawn. He dressed in a light tunic and went on deck. The morning was crisp with a cool breeze that held no cold and a promise of warmer spring weather as the sun rose in the eastern sky. The trading docks beyond the *castrum* were already busy, the half-light of the pre-dawn sufficient for the ships to manoeuvre to the dockside to begin the process of unloading, the shouted calls of their commanders muted as the sound carried over the harbour. Atticus ordered one of the crew to bring him some food, and he settled down on the aft-deck to eat.

Septimus joined him half an hour after sunrise and they set off to Lentulus's office once more.

They arrived there to find the master shipbuilder packing some of his hurried designs and supply manifests into a shoulder bag. He escorted the two officers to a coastal barge that was preparing to sail, explaining that they were heading to the coastal town of Fiumicino, two miles north of Ostia at the mouth of a small river that gave the town its name. The three men boarded and the barge immediately shoved off, passing the *Aquila* as she went, the trireme now the only galley tethered to the docks. The news of the Carthaginian fleet in the south had spread throughout Ostia and Rome and the traders had frantically called for extra escorts, the hidden danger beyond the horizon made terrible by wild rumour. The Senate had immediately agreed, fearful of a panic that would drive the traders from Rome's shores, and so the entire Ostia fleet was now constantly at sea.

The coastal barge cleared the harbour with ease, the sea-lanes relatively quiet in the dawn light. Lentulus quizzed Atticus on some of the finer details of his experience with the Carthaginians, the master shipbuilder having been up for most of the night with his apprentices and having discovered further unknowns in the Carthaginian design. Atticus answered what questions he could. The two men were still deep in conversation when the barge came in sight of Fiumicino.

The coastal town was small and unremarkable, a fishing village that had changed little over the generations, its proximity to the centre of a mighty republic having little effect as the trade routes, on both land and sea, simply passed by on either side, the village a tiny island in the middle of a fast-flowing river of humanity. The beach stretched flat and wide north and south from the village, the sand an unusual black from the high level of ferrous deposits on the shoreline. There were two large trading barges beached on the shore immediately north of the mouth of the small river. Atticus counted four more holding station half a mile offshore.

As the coastal barge drew level with the beached traders, Atticus noted the frenzied activity on board and around the slightly tilted vessels, their broad, almost flat keels resting on the compacted sand. The ships were unloading timber, huge logs of oak and pine, which were being lowered onto waiting wagons to be hauled and pushed above the high-tide mark. The barge beached fifty yards beyond the northernmost trader and all disembarked, jumping down the eight feet into the ankle-deep waves. Atticus noticed immediately that the ground beneath his feet was rock solid and, although he had jumped from a height, he left no footprints in the black sand.

The tide was two hours from full and the aft section of the beached traders was already under three feet of water, the slaves and crew of the ship working frantically to unload the last remaining timbers. At high tide the vessel would float once more, the added buoyancy of an empty hull assisting the re-launch. Once away their place would be taken by the four traders waiting offshore.

The unloaded timbers were being sorted on the beach, the slaves' activities commanded by two of Lentulus's apprentices. One was working with the stockpile, separating oak from pine and further separating these in terms of length, girth and approximate age. The other apprentice was meticulously checking each timber, looking for signs of rot or fungal infection, rejecting even vaguely suspicious timbers to leave only the solid. For ones so young they worked with confidence and efficiency, their entire adolescent lives having been dedicated to their craft.

The men of the *Aquila* followed Lentulus above the beach, cresting a wind-formed dune to view the flatlands beyond.

Both Atticus and Septimus stopped at the sight before them. A veritable city of tents had been erected directly behind the drift line of the dunes, the white canvas peaks stretching a mile northwards from the fishing village on their right. Everywhere men moved with purpose between the tents, many carrying the tools of their trade: carpenters, ironmongers, ship-wrights and more. How long had it been, Atticus wondered in awe, forty-eight hours? Two days since the Senate formally announced the decision to build the fleet? The city had moved with incredible speed, the logistics seemingly effortless for a society as ordered as that of Rome. For the first time Atticus felt a creeping confidence about the task ahead.

CHAPTER EIGHT

Hannibal Gisco watched the Romans' activity from the heights above the city of Makella, having arrived from Panormus two days before, covering the twenty miles in one ride. He had witnessed the last of the attacks on the Romans' supply train as they completed the remaining miles of their march. The ambushes were near ineffectual in themselves, the Romans' anticipatory preparations and defence blunting the cavalry charge. And yet Gisco had noted minor damage to the supply column, a fallen ox, a burning wagon, as his cavalry retreated to the safety of the surrounding hills. When the Romans had resumed their march they had left a small pile of smouldering supplies in their wake, a mere drop of blood from a wounded beast, but when taken in combination with all the attacks of the past days, Gisco was sure those same wounds ran deep.

Gisco was joined on the summit ridge by Hamilcar, the initial uneasy truce between the two men having now developed into a more tactical alliance. Gisco, an admiral by rank and a sailor by nature, relied on Hamilcar's greater experience on land and he had learned to trust the younger man's instincts. Gisco also saw an advantage in forging a friendship with the heir of the Barca family, an ancient line that claimed a direct link to Queen Dido herself, the legendary founder of Carthage. The Barca clan had a permanent seat on the Council of Carthage, a seat now occupied by Hamilcar's father, and Hamilcar often alluded to the close relationship he enjoyed with his father, a relationship Gisco planned to use to his own ends.

'Prisoners in charge of their own prison.' Hamilcar smiled at the sight of the last of the column unwinding into the rectangular palisade.

Gisco smiled in return at the description. It wasn't far from the mark. Hamilcar had persuaded Gisco to abandon the siege of the city below, arguing that the prize was no longer necessary. The Romans were welcome to Makella, and Hamilcar was sure that the price they had exacted for the city's freedom was more than the Romans had bargained for.

Marcus's maniple was one of the last to ford the River Eleuterio before climbing the gentle slope into the palisade beyond. The countryside around him was quiet, the terraced vineyards unattended, the walled city of Makella – less than half a mile away – tranquil in the late evening light. The centurion's eyes were drawn upwards to the surrounding hills, the tallest rising a thousand feet to the north. He was sure the enemy were somewhere nearby, watching their every move, and he hated the sensation.

The IV of the Ninth was no longer a frontline maniple, not on paper at least. The last nine days had cost Marcus fifteen dead and twenty-six wounded, fifteen of whom were walking and in the ranks. The other eleven were buried somewhere in the supply train on a wagon. Marcus had personally checked on the wounded men himself that very morning and he had come away bitter and angry, knowing he was going to lose at least four more before the day was out, their wounds mortal.

The maniple would be stood down until replacements could be found, replacements that Marcus knew would never come, not from Rome at least. Now one of two scenarios would unfold: either another maniple would fold before his and he would be given the remnants, or his maniple would be broken up to feed others. For a proud fighting man it was a bitter coin toss.

From his tent in the centre of the encampment, Lucius Postumius Megellus, commander of the Second and Ninth, heard the shouted order for the gate to be closed. The sound gave him a profound sense of relief and he immediately chastised himself for the feeling, cursing the Carthaginians who had hounded his column for the past nine days and chased them like wolves until, now, Megellus only felt safe within the confines of a perimeter wall.

The camp was temporary only, built with the six-foot-long pointed oak *sudis* stakes that travelled with the column. The lead maniples had begun the camp three hours before dusk, laying out the boundaries of the rectangular encampment before beginning the digging of a trench, ten foot wide by five deep, the earth thrown inwards to form a rampart, on top of which the *sudes* were implanted and intertwined with lighter oak branches. The camp had been built each night on the march and dismantled each morning with an efficiency born out of repetition and training, the hard labour of construction forgotten each new day as the column marched onwards.

Megellus would now change the nature of the camp. He would order it transformed into a *castra stativa*, a standing camp. The walls would be made more solid. Stone would be gathered from the nearby river and added to the vulnerable points of the wall around the gates. Towers would be built on the four corners of the *castrum* to warn of any approach by the enemy.

The legate bit back the bile of disappointment that had emerged so soon in the campaign. Scouts had returned from the city with reports that the enemy had fled at the sight of the advancing column, although Megellus suspected they had simply withdrawn rather than offer combat to an enemy that would be defeated in time anyway, and with a lot less Carthaginian blood spilt.

The legate would confirm the reports in the morning by sending ten maniples to the city gates. The show of force would impress the Council of Makella and imbue in them a sense of victory, justifying their decision to support Rome and not Carthage. Megellus would then split his command and send the Second forward to cover the three days' march to the city of Segeste, again to lift the siege that the legate was sure would be already lifted when they arrived. The enemy would attack their supplies on the march and again there would be losses, the quartermaster estimating that already nearly half of their original equipment was gone.

The Second would take Segeste but would go no further. They would build a second standing camp, a second island in a sea of hostility. The campaign would grind to a halt, the army forced onto the defensive in an effort to protect and hoard its valuable, now irreplaceable supplies. This was no way to fight a war, Megellus thought bitterly, a man used to fighting aggressively and offensively.

The legate walked out of his tent and observed the hurried activity around him as the army prepared to bed down for the night. It was becoming dark and Megellus watched the *vigilae*, the night guard, take their posts on the walls, their eyes searching the darkened surrounding countryside for the unseen enemy. There will be no attacks this night, Megellus thought sarcastically, for why would the Carthaginians attack the now inert Roman army. Only two weeks before Megellus had informed his men that the campaign would continue as before, as if the blockade did not exist, but the Carthaginians' tactic of specifically targeting the supplies had thwarted the legate's intentions. The Punici had drawn their blades and used them to deadly effect. The legions were now hamstrung, crippled and cut off from home.

At the forefront of Megellus's thoughts were the vital questions of how long the legions could now hold out in hostile territory, for without resupply they would eventually have to turn back – and how far they would need to withdraw. On the first question, only time would tell. The second? If the legions did finally withdraw, the Carthaginians would pursue them, of that there was no doubt, the enemy gaining strength and confidence as the legions bled those same resources into the sand. With a dread feeling Megellus answered this second question in his mind. If the tables were turned he knew what he would do. He would pursue the enemy to the bitter end. The Punici would employ the same determination they had shown over the previous nine days. The legions would be pursued past the territorial dividing line of the last campaign. They would be pursued past their winter camp and, finally, if the Carthaginians were not checked, the Second and Ninth would be pushed into the sea itself.

Atticus crouched down and scooped a handful of seawater from the shallow surf, splashing the water onto his face in an effort to clear the exhaustion from his mind. One hundred yards away the *Aquila* rested gently against her anchor line, the setting sun reflected in the wave tops thrown up as the shifting current broke against her hull. Atticus stood up and turned his back on the shoreline, walking slowly up the gentle slope of the beach at Fiumicino, arching his back as he went to stretch his tired muscles. He glanced over his shoulder one last time to see the two crewmen who had rowed him ashore already asleep in the bottom of the small skiff. After another sixteen-hour day training raw recruits, Atticus couldn't begrudge them the rest, and he silently cursed the late hour of the summons from the camp prefect which kept him from his own cabin.

Atticus had asked to see Tuditanus five days before, the same day the training schedules had been issued to the galleys, the *Aquila* amongst them, tasked with training the new sailing crews arriving daily at Fiumicino. Atticus had instantly come ashore to see the camp prefect but his request for a meeting had been denied, as had every repeated request since. Until now.

Walking up the beach, Atticus was once more struck with awe by the activity surrounding him. For the past week he had watched as barge after barge, marching column after marching column arrived at the coastal village, to fill the beach with raw materials and the tented city with sailors and soldiers. Fiumicino was now home to some ten thousand people, half of them craftsmen, who laboured every daylight hour to turn rough raw timber into graceful spars and frames for the developing fleet, and so now, as Atticus crested the dunes at the head of the beach, the skeletal frames of twenty triremes stood tall on the sand above the high-water mark.

The camp prefect's tented quarters stood apart from the main camp, enclosed within a palisade on a patch of raised ground overlooking the village of Fiumicino. Atticus identified himself at the gate before being ushered in, his arrival expected by the guards. He ducked under the awning of the tent and stood to attention, his eyes rapidly adjusting to the gloom of the interior. Tuditanus sat silently behind his desk poring over a series of scrolls, murmuring quietly to himself before he raised his head to acknowledge Atticus. A former manipular centurion and veteran of the Pyrrhic War, Tuditanus now held the highest rank an equestrian could achieve in the legions, and his attitude was one of a man completely at ease with his station in life.

He held Atticus's gaze for a full minute before standing up and circling around to the front of his desk.

'You asked to see me, Captain Perennis?' Tuditanus said impatiently.

Atticus instantly bit back the words that rushed to his lips. 'Yes, Camp Prefect,' he answered evenly. 'It's about the training schedule issued to the galleys.'

'Go on . . .' Tuditanus said slowly, irritation in his voice.

'I believe the approach ordered is wrong,' Atticus said in a rush, his course set. 'The new crews can't be trained to ram in the time we have. We need to teach the crews how to steer a galley for boarding and make that our priority.'

'You believe a Roman sailor cannot be taught how to ram?'

'No, Camp Prefect, not in the time we have.'

'The time *we* have?'

'The time the legions in Sicily have.'

Tuditanus nodded, although Atticus could clearly see it was not in agreement.

'You're Greek, are you not, Captain?'

'Yes, but I don't see —'

'And you believe the orders of your Roman commander are ill-advised?' Tuditanus asked, cutting Atticus short.

Once again Atticus held his words, anger flaring in him as he was confronted anew by Roman arrogance. He breathed deeply, his mind searching for a way to persuade the camp prefect that the orders were wrong without saying as much.

'I know Lentulus chose a traditional design to speed up construction because his apprentices and many of the craftsmen have built identical galleys in the past. But I also know that the Carthaginian galleys are stronger than our own and their crews more skilled – and we can't be guaranteed victory if we rely on the ram.'

Tuditanus circled and stood once more behind his desk, bunching his fists as he leaned forward.

'You Greeks are all the same. You underestimate Rome, Perennis, with the same arrogance your ancestors did.'

Atticus made to protest again but Tuditanus silenced him with a raised hand. 'Now let me be very clear on this,' he continued, his gaze piercing, 'the sailing crews will be trained how to ram and you will make that your priority. If I hear that you are doing otherwise, I'll have you and your crew flogged before the entire camp. Now get out of my sight.'

Atticus saluted and turned on his heel, the acid rising in his stomach as he fought to suppress his anger. Minutes later he was back at the water's edge, kicking the hull of the skiff to waken the two crewmen who were instantly at the oars, their captain's dark mood quickening their oar-strokes as they skulled through the darkness.

Scipio crested the windblown dune at the head of the beach south of Fiumicino and paused, allowing his stallion to breathe easy after the twelve-mile gallop from the city. His guard detail of four mounted *praetoriani* halted ten paces behind him. The senior consul had left his town house in the half-light an hour before dawn, and now, forty minutes later, it was as if he had travelled to the shore of a distant land. The southern beach before him was deserted and seemed unworldly after the enclosed, cramped streets of the capital and the busy northern trade road, the Via Aurelia, five miles inland. Scipio breathed deeply, the cleansing, salt-laden onshore breeze fresh in his face.

The final decisions on the fleet had been made over a week before, and since then he had been working tirelessly on the organizational elements of the plan, his position as fleet commander giving him overall responsibility for the task. With the full support and power of the Senate behind him, Scipio had issued a number of sweeping decrees which immeasurably speeded up the process. Entire crews were drafted from the trading populace of Ostia. An army of slaves had been commandeered from the surrounding estates and towns to provide labour. Their combined strength would be used to construct the fleet and then it would be harnessed to propel the ships through the water as each slave would be sent to man the oars of the very ships they built. Fleets of transport barges had also been requisitioned and the vital raw materials they carried seized by order of the Senate. The decrees had been brutal. Scipio had no doubt that many traders had already lost their livelihood as a result of the enforced orders and yet he felt no remorse. Rome was threatened, therefore Rome must react. If individuals had to be sacrificed for the greater good then so be it. History would remember men like Scipio and the glory of Rome. No one would remember the casualties.

The senior consul swept his eyes northwards, to the beach on the other side of the small fishing village that straddled the mouth of the river. The area was beginning to come alive, the sun's imminent arrival signalling the start of the working day. Scipio spurred his horse and trotted down onto the almost stone-hard sand. His guard followed. The group crossed the river at the edge of its mouth, where the ground met the incoming tidal waves. The dual action created a natural ford and the shallow water splashed high as the horses' hooves cut its surface. Once on the other side the group turned up the beach, passing the frame of a partially constructed trireme as they did so. This was the first time Scipio had been to the site and his eyes swept over every detail before him, the endless lists he had reviewed in Rome made real on the beach at Fiumicino. The galley frame was almost lost in a forest of supports and yet Scipio could make out the sharp lines of the vessel beneath. Even now, although it was only partly built and was caged by scaffolding, the galley looked as if it would soar over the water, and Scipio felt a surge of admiration for the craftsmanship of his fellow Romans.

Scipio counted twenty frames in number, the exact total he had seen on an obscure list a week before. When the decision had been made to build the fleet, there had only been sufficient material and skilled labour available in the immediate vicinity of Rome to construct these twenty ships. Even now supplies were arriving and being distributed that would fuel the construction of a further one hundred and thirty galleys, but the twenty before him would put to sea first. Scipio entered the tented city and headed for the camp prefect's quarters. A lantern was lit inside, the occupant already working diligently. Scipio had chosen Tuditanus personally, his choice based on two facts. The first, that Tuditanus was a hard taskmaster and would stick rigorously to any schedule, and the second, that Tuditanus was in Scipio's employ and, while on the surface he might report to the Senate, in reality he answered only to the senior consul.

Septimus woke thirty minutes before dawn, his mind surfacing through a groggy fog of fatigue. As he rose he looked across the dark cabin to the sleeping figure of Atticus, his friend laid out as if he had been knocked unconscious. He crept from the cabin, gathering up his sword and shield as he did and climbed the aft-gangway to the deck above. The mood up top was subdued, the men on duty coming to the end of their watch as dawn approached. Septimus ordered one of them below to get him food while he washed his face with water in a futile attempt to refresh himself. Atticus emerged five minutes later, Septimus noticing that under the dark lines of fatigue on his face the captain was seething with anger.

'I take it your meeting with Tuditanus didn't go well?' he prompted as Atticus took the basin of water and poured the contents over his head. A week before, Atticus had outlined his fears to Septimus, the centurion immediately deferring to his friend's experience, sharing his impatience as they waited for Tuditanus's summons.

'The bastard completely ignored me. He said I was under-estimating the Romans,' Atticus replied, slamming his fist onto the railing as he looked out over the beach.

'Maybe he has a point, Atticus,' Septimus said. 'Lentulus is a clever man and Tuditanus is no fool.'

'So you think because I'm not Roman I'm wrong?' Atticus countered, his anger rising anew.

'That's not what I said,' Septimus replied, keeping his tone even, sensing that Atticus was close to losing his temper.

Atticus curbed his anger, knowing it was misplaced when directed at his friend.

'So what now?' Septimus asked.

'Now I need your help,' Atticus replied. 'I can't risk training the recruits yet on boarding manoeuvres, but we've got to give the legionaries a fighting chance. Can you train them on some of the techniques for boarding?'

'My own orders call for me to demonstrate our knowledge of Carthaginian tactics, but I think I've enough scope to teach them some of the basics,' Septimus smiled, liking the idea of circumventing the camp prefect's orders.

Atticus nodded his thanks as he noticed a number of skiffs

disembarking from the beach, each one filled with the sailing recruits who would spend their day on the *Aquila*. The sight prompted Septimus to make his way to the main deck before climbing over the side and down a rope ladder into the small skiff tethered to the galley. A crewman of the *Aquila* was waiting there for him, the week-old daily routine dictating the steps of both men. As Septimus sat down, the crewman pushed off and started to row towards the shore.

Septimus jumped out of the skiff into the ankle-deep water and walked up onto the beach. All around him the area was coming to life as drowsy men walked off their weariness and stretched tired muscles. A long day ahead. He crested the dune at the top of the beach and walked onto the flat coastal plateau behind, heading towards the hastily erected training camp at the northern end of the tented city, an expansive square of land that housed the legionaries of the Fourth, the Roman legion that had arrived at the beginning of the week. Septimus had been tasked with instructing one of the maniples on the fighting skills of the Carthaginians, specifically on how men trained in one-to-one encounters.

The centurion was challenged at the gate of the camp by two of the *vigilae*, the night guard, who, although three hours into their watch, stood alert and ready. A tightly run legion, Septimus thought, as he identified himself. He passed through and headed for the quarters of his own men, spotting Quintus, his *optio*, standing beside a fire with two of the twenty *principes* of the *Aquila*'s half-century. They were having a murmured conversation, keeping their voices low in the quiet time before dawn.

The *optio* spotted his commander approaching and broke away from the two men.

'Good morning, Centurion.'

'Morning, Quintus . . . all quiet?'

'As a grave. With the work we have those legionaries doing, they're sleeping like babies.'

Septimus smiled at the description. The men of the Fourth were anything but babies. As one of the legions of the northern army, the Fourth had historically been at the centre of all of the major conflicts as Rome expanded her borders northwards. Their symbol was the boar, and it was a suitable emblem, for the soldiers were both vicious and stubborn. Septimus realized that the latter quality would make the task ahead more difficult.

Septimus turned to his *optio* as a trumpet sounded for roll call.

'Quintus, I want to shift the focus of training and teach the legionaries some of the basics of boarding.'

'Yes, Centurion,' Quintus replied, Septimus noticing the underlying scepticism in his *optio*'s voice. Having gone through the training only ten months before, the techniques and steps were fresh in Septimus's mind; however, he would let Quintus, a marine with two full years' experience, take the lead on the agenda.

'So, what do you think is the best way to proceed?'

'We introduce them to the *hoplon*.'

Septimus nodded, knowing that that portion of the training was especially difficult for men used to handling the four-foot *scutum* shields of the legions.

'We have to start somewhere, and the sooner the legionaries realize that they don't have a shield that will defend their torso and legs at the same time, the better,' Quintus added.

'Agreed,' Septimus said, as the men of the V maniple of the Fourth formed up in the training square. Their centurion, Marcus Junius Silanus, approached and Septimus groaned inwardly. Silanus had absolutely no respect for marines, an opinion he constantly expressed both to Septimus and to the men of his own maniple.

'What's on today's agenda, marine?' he asked, his tone laced with condescension.

Septimus drew himself up to his full height, a good two inches taller than Silanus, the centurion's tone goading him.

'More of the same, Silanus,' Septimus replied, 'just teaching your boys how to fight.'

Silanus bristled at the slight against his maniple.

'Look, marine,' Silanus growled, 'orders are orders – which means my maniple has to sit here and watch your men dance around all day, but don't think for one second you can teach the V anything about real fighting.' He turned on his heel and marched back to his men. Septimus watched him go, angry at himself for allowing Silanus to incite him into another round of insults. If he was going to prepare the legionaries for naval warfare, he needed to get Silanus on side.

An hour later, Quintus finished his demonstration to the assembled maniple of the Fourth. Septimus called for questions but none was forthcoming; he knew the silence was not because the men completely understood the techniques of fighting with a rounded *hoplon* shield, but rather because of the contempt the legionaries felt for the foreign shield. At the eye of that contempt was Silanus, the centurion providing a focal point of disdain for the marines and their method of fighting, and by extension the Carthaginians. Septimus caught the centurion's eye and held his gaze. If the men of the V maniple were going to be trained, Septimus knew that Silanus would have to be taught first.

Lucius Fulfidias reached out from his position at the front of the small skiff and grasped the rope ladder. With a single fluid movement he swung his feet onto the rungs and quickly climbed onto the deck of the *Aquila*. The four other men in his skiff followed suit. He was the captain of the newly formed command crew, chosen because of his experience commanding trading galleys, while the other four men were his second-in-command, helmsman, boatswain and drum master. Four other skiffs were quickly alongside, each one containing the five men of a command crew. Once on board, Fulfidias followed the other trainee captains to the aft-deck where the young commander of the military trireme stood confidently beside his helmsman. Fulfidias sneered inwardly at the sight, disliking the man and what he represented, a servitude enforced by Rome – and the young pup wasn't even Roman himself, he was a bloody Greek. Who in Hades was he to command a galley of the Republic?

Fulfidias was a trader from Naples, his ship a nimble bireme named the *Sol*. She was a small vessel, her cargo hold tiny in comparison to the gigantic trading barges, but she was fast and the shallow draught allowed her to berth at any port. It was this flexibility and speed that had given Fulfidias a niche in the markets of Ostia and Rome. For over ten years he had built a reputation of being the first to market with the pick of every season's first crop. It was not a commodity for the common man, but one for the affluent of Rome who, as a sign of their status and wealth, liked to be the first to serve each new season's bounty at their table when entertaining guests. Fulfidias traded primarily in new-season wines from the Gaulish coast, and first spring lambs and suckling pigs from Campania. It was a lucrative business, with the rich paying exorbitant prices to have goods merely weeks before their social peers.

Two weeks before, when the Roman military had begun trawling the port of Ostia for crews to man their new fleet, the *Sol* had been in dry dock, her hull undergoing repairs to damage caused by the odious shipworm that had dug deep into the timbers of the bireme. With his ship temporarily out of action, Fulfidias had been left with nowhere to go to, and he had been indentured into military service at the Senate's pleasure.

As Fulfidias waited on the aft-deck for the remaining crews to come on board the *Aquila*, his thoughts strayed to his own ship. She would be afloat by now, the repairs only three days short of completion when he had been drafted into service. She would be sitting at the dockside in Ostia instead of heading south under a favourable wind to Campania, where the approach of spring heralded the birthing season for sheep. In another week Fulfidias knew it would be too late for him to set sail and another trader would beat him to market with the prized lambs. The market of Ostia had no loyalty, no honour if those virtues stood in the way of profit, and so the men who regularly dealt with Fulfidias would immediately deal with the new supplier. The contacts and negotiating terms carefully built up by Fulfidias over ten years would be wiped away in one season.

As the trireme got under way, the young military commander began explaining the training that the teams would be undergoing that day. Fulfidias was not listening. He had sailed on trading galleys for over thirty years and he firmly believed there was nothing the young pup could teach him that he didn't already know. The captain of the *Sol* raged internally at the injustice of life. The injustice of a system that robbed him of his livelihood with impunity. He had been forced into service, knowing that a refusal would result in banishment from the sea-lanes of Rome, and so he had acquiesced, but only to the point of being present. For Fulfidias that presence fulfilled his portion of the unfair contract.

*

Atticus finished his description of the day's training ahead to the assembled captains and helmsmen on the aft-deck as the *Aquila* headed for the open sea. Of the ten men present, a half-dozen or so seemed to be giving the discussion their full attention, the number an increase on the day before. The others were distant, while two had expressions of open hostility. Atticus could understand their frustration and anger. He had chosen the life he led, a life dedicated to the navy. The men around him had also chosen their own path, until Rome had decided that they would follow her whim.

Atticus did his best to inject respect into his instructions, knowing that some of the men had greater experience of seamanship than he, albeit on non-military vessels. Many of the helmsmen and captains had sailed on galleys before and had a firm grasp of the basics, but they lacked the tactical thinking and fast decision-making skills required of a military commander. At sea and in battle, the line between victory and defeat was often drawn between men who commanded the events of the battle and men who simply reacted to the attacks of others. To be victorious at sea a captain needed to take the fight to the enemy.

As the *Aquila* sailed directly away from the shore she passed through the busy north–south sea-lane. The trireme was under oar power and so Gaius deferred to the sail-propelled vessels as he nimbly negotiated the crossing. Atticus looked over his shoulder at the receding shoreline. Against the black sands of Fiumicino, the polished skeletal frames of the new triremes stood out like ivory on black marble, their purpose evident even to an untrained eye. The spread of news in Ostia, Rome – in fact the whole Republic – was the result of the interconnected threads of the trading routes. That Rome could not keep anything secret was simply an unavoidable side effect of trade. The problem could not have been avoided, even if the camp had been placed away from a trading route. From the ships supplying raw materials to the merchants supplying the camp, there were simply too many people interacting with the site. It was only a matter of time before the Punici knew every detail there was to know about Rome's new fleet.

Atticus cursed inwardly as he counted the odds stacked against them. Currently the Romans had no advantages over the Carthaginians. News of the new fleet would spread south eventually and the element of surprise would be lost. The enemy ships were heavier and crewed by more experienced sailors, highly skilled in ramming, while the newly recruited Roman crews were hopelessly unskilled. The Roman legionaries were certainly a match for the Carthaginians but, because of Tuditanus, they lacked the skills necessary for boarding and so could not carry the fight to the deck of an enemy galley.

As the *Aquila* cleared the last vessels of the sea-lane, Atticus turned once more to his trainees. It was time to begin. The training schedule was tedious and unrelenting and the recruits far from ready for battle. He could teach them the basics of every manoeuvre but in the end it was experience that counted. He could only hope they would have enough time.

CHAPTER NINE

'How old is this report?' Gisco roared. 'Ten days at least,' the messenger said, cringing from the admiral's furious gaze.

'*Ten days!* Ten days and it's only reaching me *now?*'

Gisco stormed forward with the parchment crushed in his balled fist. He raised his arm and made to strike the messenger. The man drew back and threw his arm up to protect himself, knowing that the admiral's fury would make any defence useless. Gisco stopped short and looked upon the cowering man with disgust.

'Get out!' he shouted, and the messenger fled.

The admiral turned and walked over to the desk in the centre of his tent high in the hills overlooking Makella.

The past five days had been quiet, the Romans now firmly ensconced in their camp beside the city walls below. The Romans had marched half their forces west to the city of Segeste two days after their arrival at Makella, their goal to once again lift a siege that Gisco had already lifted. The admiral had accompanied Hamilcar on the three-day shadow column that harassed and attacked the marching Romans' supplies, and had personally directed two of the ambushes. As before, their attacks, when viewed individually, had been relatively ineffective, but taken as a whole, they had inflicted significant losses on the Romans' irreplaceable provisions. The two weeks of fighting had cost Gisco over four hundred cavalry, but he had robbed the Roman legions of their manoeuvrability. It had been an uneven trade in his favour and he had been satisfied with the deal.

Until now. The news on the document in his hand changed everything. At first he had looked at it with incomprehension. It had only been a few weeks – four at most – since the blockade had been imposed, and yet, if the report was to be believed, the Romans were already building a fleet to challenge his own. How could they have moved so fast? And with such aggression? The Roman military's prowess on land was well established and was such that Gisco was unwilling to attack them until the odds were heavily in his favour. Their navy, however, had always been inconsequential when compared to that of the Carthaginians. Their galleys were light and fast, but they were weak-hulled and no match for his own.

Gisco had one hundred and ten galleys in the waters around the west and north coast of Sicily. Surely the Romans could not dare to hope to overcome them? And yet the admiral knew from experience that the Romans did not do anything by half. The report was based on two things: one fact and the other rumour. The fact was the location of the new fleet, two miles north of Ostia on the Roman coast. The rumour was its size, and was stated as 'in excess of one hundred'. This second part of the report would have to be verified. Gisco called for his aide and issued instructions for his horse to be prepared. He would leave for Panormus on the coast immediately. One thing was certain, one thing the report did not state but which was true nonetheless: the Romans were taking the fight to the Carthaginians. 'Good,' Gisco thought, buckling his scabbard, 'we'll be ready for them.'

*

'So when will they be ready to sail?' Scipio asked.

This was his second day at the camp and by now the senior consul was fully informed of almost every aspect of the operation. Only this one crucial question remained to be answered.

'In four days,' Tuditanus replied.

'You're sure?'

'Yes, the hulls were completed on the twenty galleys yesterday. All that remains is the inner works, which have been immeasurably simplified to suit the task.'

'Simplified how?' Scipio asked, his natural curiosity aroused.

'We have stripped out everything bar the bulkheads and the upper and lower decks. There will be no cabins, storage decks or sleeping quarters.'

Scipio nodded, understanding the logic of the decision. The fleet was being built for battle, a confrontation that would occur sooner rather than later. At this point in time there was no need to look at the functionality of the ships beyond the oncoming clash, the future beyond the battle still shrouded in uncertainty.

'Do not tell the Senate of this schedule. If asked, your answer is six days. I want no one to know the ships will be ready in four.'

'Yes, Consul,' Tuditanus answered, never questioning the senior consul's motives, Scipio's gold being sufficient to command his allegiance.

Scipio dismissed Tuditanus and sat back on the couch in the expansive tent. In four days the first twenty galleys of the new fleet would be ready to sail. The Senate's decision on command would be followed, but on the senior consul's terms. He would take charge of these first twenty ships. What was important now was to take the initiative. The people of Rome were anxious to hear about the new fleet, anxious to know that the threat of the Carthaginians was being dealt with. The man who commanded the first fleet to sea would be the man they would remember. Scipio would be that man. He would sail the twenty new galleys into the port of Ostia and step triumphantly onto the dock, the backdrop of new triremes a show of force that would for ever after be associated with Scipio. In his mind's eye he pictured every detail of the event. It would be perfect.

Septimus felt an incredible sense of freedom well up within him as he galloped along the Via Aurelia towards Rome. He glanced over his shoulder and spied Atticus hard on his heels, the captain's expression mirroring his own, the unexpected furlough giving both men the opportunity to escape the confines of Fiumicino for twenty-four hours. Both men were acutely aware that this was going to be their last leave before sailing south again, and so Septimus had decided to visit his family home one last time. Atticus, a stranger in the city, had asked to accompany him and Septimus had quickly agreed.

An hour after leaving the camp at Fiumicino, Atticus and Septimus arrived at the Capito home. As before, and aware that her son was visiting for perhaps the last time, Salonina sent a messenger for her daughter. Hadria arrived in time for the evening meal and the family sat down together, the probable finality of the occasion neither acknowledged nor discussed.

The meal lasted three hours; however, when Salonina finally announced her intention to retire, Atticus was filled with disappointment at the shortness of the evening. Her husband Antoninus rose with her and both took their leave of the group before departing. The table before them was clear except for wine goblets and a half-filled amphora, the servants having cleared away all traces of the meal. Atticus, Hadria and

Septimus sat in silence. Atticus leaned forward and picked up his wine, his smile returned by Hadria. He willed Septimus to go, to leave him and Hadria alone, although he was unsure what he would do if such an opportunity presented itself. The silence dragged on.

Hadria felt lightheaded. The pleasure of the evening combined with the wine she had drunk filled her with an enormous sense of wellbeing and she smiled unabashedly. She had noticed Atticus look at her again during the evening, his gaze intense and searching. Hadria recalled her first impressions of Atticus weeks before, how handsome he was, his dark Grecian complexion made striking by his green eyes. She also remembered becoming acutely aware of Atticus's sidelong glances at her that evening and the touch of his gaze had sent shivers down her spine. For days afterwards she had been plagued by guilt, her attraction to Atticus feeling like a betrayal of Valerius; but now – as before – she did not want the night to end, and so she waited, content to know that Atticus was near her.

Septimus fought hard to suppress his growing disquiet at what he was witnessing, all the while wondering if he was misjudging the looks being exchanged between Atticus and his sister. His boyhood friend Valerius had been dead less than a year and, although his mother had said that Hadria's heart was free, Septimus felt it was wrong for his friend and sister to share any feelings of attraction.

'Atticus?' Hadria asked, her voice finally breaking the silence. 'Tell me about your ship. Why is she called the *Aquila*?'

'She is named after the star constellation,' Atticus answered, and began to describe the positions of the five major stars that formed the figure in the night sky. Hadria leaned in close to follow his every word.

'Aquila was a faithful servant of Jupiter, the king of the gods,'

Atticus explained. 'During the king's war with the Titans on earth the eagle carried Jupiter's lightning bolts from the heavens to strike the Titans. After the war was won, Jupiter immortalized Aquila in the stars as a reward for his loyalty.'

Hadria noticed that Atticus spoke in hushed tones, his deep, sonorous voice giving passion to the ancient story, a passion that reflected his obvious bond to his ship.

'Loyalty . . .' Septimus said suddenly, breaking the spell around Hadria, 'the cornerstone of any friendship. Wouldn't you agree, Atticus?'

'What?' he said, looking over at Septimus, the centurion's expression unreadable.

Hadria was also unable to read Septimus's face, but she knew the tone of his voice, knew its portent with the absolute certainty of a sibling. The underlying menace was undeniable. Her mind raced to understand its cause until she suddenly realized the reason for Septimus's animosity. Valerius.

'Septimus,' Hadria said, cutting off her brother's repetition of his question, 'it's late and I'm tired. Would you kindly escort me to my room?'

The suddenness of the request and the sweetness of the tone in which it was made arrested Septimus's comment. Hadria stood up and made to leave the room, her brother falling in beside her. She glanced over her shoulder at Atticus who looked confused by the sudden turn of events.

'Goodnight, Atticus,' she said, trying to make her voice sound dispassionate.

'Goodnight, Hadria. Goodnight, Septimus.'

The centurion did not return the platitude and the brother and sister left the room.

The abrupt end to the night and Hadria's hasty departure had caught Atticus off guard. He had been acutely disappointed when Septimus had not left after the meal, but he had still held out hope that he would be able to engineer a moment alone with Hadria. Despite his frustration he smiled to himself. Perhaps there would be another chance.

Hadria turned at her door to say goodnight to her brother. He still looked slightly aggravated but she pretended not to notice and kissed him lightly on the cheek. The intimate gesture returned a slight smile to his face.

'Goodnight, Septimus,' she said.

'Hadria?' Septimus said, catching his sister lightly by the forearm, arresting her departure. 'Do you no longer mourn for Valerius?'

Hadria sighed, her expression kind, sensing the question had been on her brother's mind.

'I think about him every day, Septimus, but I have learned to live without him in my heart.'

Septimus nodded, his gaze somewhere in the middle distance, his memory on the Battle of Agrigentum a year before, standing shoulder to shoulder with Valerius in the centre of the line as the final assault of the Carthaginian heavy infantry rushed towards them.

'So you will marry again?' he asked softly.

'I have little choice, brother, but yes, I will marry again. I can only hope to someone worthy of Valerius's memory.'

Again Septimus nodded, this time his eyes looking to Hadria's.

'And I hope you will never feel that pain of loss again,' he replied, gently squeezing his sister's forearm in affection. 'Goodnight, Hadria,' he smiled.

Hadria returned his smile before closing her door. She stood in the darkness of her room, listening to the receding sound of her brother's footsteps, remembering his parting words, sensing that his hope encompassed them both. It was only then that she recalled the lie she had just told her brother. There had been many days over the previous weeks that she had not thought of Valerius; she had thought only of another man, a man who had crept into her feelings and into her heart.

'Well, where in Hades are they?' Marcus cursed, his hand instinctively going for the hilt of his *gladius* as his eyes scanned the near-impenetrable line of trees.

'I don't know, Centurion. They followed a deer into that copse about ten minutes ago,' Corin, the *optio*, replied, indicating the island of dense woodland at the top of the rise.

'Just the two of them?'

'Yes, Centurion. Legionaries Gratian and Nerva.'

Marcus immediately pictured the two men in his mind.

'I left strict standing orders that no group smaller than a *contubernia* was to detach from the maniple.'

'Yes, Centurion,' Corin replied, knowing that terse answers and complete agreement was always the safest option when addressing a superior officer, especially an officer with Marcus's reputation for discipline.

Marcus cursed again and walked forward towards the copse, his shield raised slightly to cover his flank. He searched the line of trees again, suppressing the urge to call out the men's names. With the Roman encampment at Makella three miles behind him, his maniple was deep in enemy territory, and any overt betrayal of their position could be fatal.

Marcus unconsciously flexed the muscles of his sword arm, the cramps becoming more frequent as his body reacted to the lack of salt in his system. The ration had been halted more than a week before and so now Marcus, like every other legionary of the Ninth, was experiencing the onset of salt deprivation. The movement of his arm relaxed the tortured muscle, allowing Marcus's mind to fixate once again on the ever-present ache in his stomach.

The food supplies of the legion were near exhaustion and, with the camp and the adjoining city both effectively under siege, the legions had been forced to engage in foraging. It was a normal practice for a fighting army in the field, but one that carried significant risks. The Carthaginians knew how tenuous the Romans' supply situation was, and so their attacks on the foraging parties were marked by their intensity and ferocity. Legate Megellus was forced to send units no smaller than a maniple into the surrounding countryside and the parties had to range further and further in an effort to keep the camp supplied.

The IV of the Ninth had left camp at dawn to forage in the valley to the north of the encampment. Marcus's maniple was once again near full strength, the death of Centurion Valerius of the VII resulting in the cannibalization of his maniple to feed and replenish others. The resulting influx of men from the VII, proud men who resented the break-up of their maniple, had infused Marcus's command with a miasma of anger and isolation that had badly affected morale.

Marcus glanced over his shoulder at his assembled men. To a man their expressions were grim and angry. When facing the enemy those expressions signified the ferocity of a fighting legion. Now, those same expressions represented the low morale and simmering discontentment of hungry men. After three hours of foraging, the wagon accompanying them held only wild game and fowl, barely enough to feed the maniple itself. The Carthaginians had swept the countryside of live-stock and grain stores, creating an island of hungry men in a sea of ravaged farmland, and the desperation of his men was palpable, a desperation that fuelled their indiscipline and the reckless action of Gratian and Nerva.

Marcus turned once more to the tree-line and spat in anger. When the two legionaries returned Marcus knew he would have to order a harsh punishment for their insubordination. He could only hope they would return empty-handed. If they carried a deer on their shoulders the men would cheer their return, a cheer that would instantly turn to resentment when Marcus had the men flogged for disobeying the standing order. It was brutal discipline but entirely necessary if the men were to be kept in check. With their backs to the wall, any lapse in the rule of command would result in anarchy.

Marcus tensed as he caught a flicker of movement within the copse. 'About bloody time,' he cursed as he hardened his expression. Out of the corner of his eye he caught another disturbance, the second fifty yards from the first. He reacted before his mind could fathom their cause.

'Shields up!' Marcus roared before the first flight of arrows darted from the undergrowth.

The legionaries moved with lightning speed, their previous indolence forgotten as training took over their actions.

Marcus felt the arrows slam against his own shield, their flat trajectory driving the arrowheads deep into the leather. An arrow tore past his shield and struck him in the upper arm, the punch of iron knocking him off balance. Behind him the arrows struck the wall of shields as one, negating the killing power of the surprise attack.

'Form up on the centurion!' the *optio* called. The maniple moved forward as one, their line enveloping Marcus and coalescing around his position.

Marcus grunted as he caught the shaft of the arrow embedded in his upper arm. The wound felt numb, a feeling Marcus knew would not last, and he fought to break the arrow before the pain arrived. The shaft snapped at the instant a second wave of arrows struck. The Carthaginians were steadying their aim after the first rush of attack and Marcus heard the cries of his men as they fell under the onslaught.

'*Testudo!*'

The flanks instantly folded and the maniple deployed into two lines, the second holding their shields aloft at a forward angle to complete the tortoiseshell of protection. As quickly as it began the rain of arrows ceased, the tree-line once more becoming still.

'Steady men, wait for the command,' Marcus shouted to his men, their swords drawn behind the wall of shields, their eyes fixed dead ahead.

The copse seemed to exhale a breath of aggression as the legionaries waited in silence. Suddenly a lone war cry was heard, the noise a low growl, its source undefined in the undergrowth. Within a heartbeat it multiplied and reached a crescendo, and the Carthaginians surged out of the woods.

'*Orbis!*' Marcus roared above the sound of fury.

The legionaries moved instantly, the command expected, and before the Carthaginians had covered half the distance the IV had formed into a defensive circle. The Carthaginian front line struck the solid line of shields with all the momentum of their downhill run, their shoulders bunched into the charge in an effort to breach the armoured wall and expose the flesh beneath.

The Roman wall bowed under the pressure before legs made strong from endless marches began to push the formation back into shape, the Carthaginians forced to spill around the edges.

'Give 'em iron!'

The legionaries roared in attack as they began the rhythmical series of strikes made efficient through years of training. Marcus bunched his shoulder behind his shield and heaved forward against the press of the enemy. The surge opened a small gap between his shield and the next, a gap large enough for his *gladius* to seek out flesh and bone. The sword struck home and Marcus withdrew the bloodied blade, allowing the gap to close again as he readied himself for the next lunge.

The wall buckled to Marcus's left as a legionary fell, the flanks moving to close the gap and re-form the line. The Punic and Roman war cries were now mixed with the common cries of wounded men as the bloody slaughter continued, the Carthaginians maintaining the pressure of attack in a bid to break the back of the Roman defence. As commander Marcus detached his mind from the sound of battle to seek out signs of weakness or panic. All around him men were falling, Roman and Carthaginian, but neither side was giving quarter. Marcus knew he had to force the issue if a break was to be made.

'Maniple! Prepare to manoeuvre!'

Every Roman heard the command, their bodies tensing in anticipation of the change in formation.

'Wedge!'

Again the legionaries moved as if guided by an unseen hand, forming a wedge with the centre of the front line as its point. The Carthaginians were caught off guard by the sudden change in formation, their flanks left with a vacuum of enemy before them as the centre of their line now took the full brunt of the Roman attack.

'Advance!' Marcus shouted, pressing forward at the head of the wedge.

The enemy line staggered under the hammer blow, its shallow depth unable to stem the press of Roman shields before suddenly collapsing under the onslaught, which split the Punic line and annihilated the cohesion of the formation.

Marcus felt the pressure against his shield lift as the enemy turned, his *gladius* automatically striking out at the exposed lower back of a Carthaginian, the black blood of his kidney running down the blade of Marcus's sword. A surge went through the Roman formation as the enemy fled, their blood lust aroused, calling for slaughter, the sudden release from imminent death provoking them to slay all before the line.

'Hold!' Marcus roared, his voice like a whiplash to break the spell of pursuit.

The legionaries halted at the order, their ingrained obedience to a centurion's command transforming their thirst for retribution into shouts of challenge and insult at the retreating enemy.

'*Testudo!*' Marcus commanded, the legionaries once more forming a protective barrier as the last of the enemy re-entered the copse at the top of the rise. Within seconds the Carthaginian archers recommenced their deadly barrage, their aim steadied by their desire for revenge.

'Sound the advance?' Corin asked.

As Marcus considered the question he saw two Carthaginian runners break from the edge of the copse and run headlong down the far side of the rise. Messengers, he realized.

'No, we withdraw. Out here in the open our tactics are superior. In enclosed woods it would be every man for himself. We need to withdraw to Makella before reinforcements are brought up and the Punici recover their nerve.'

A cry to their left caused both officers to turn. Another legionary had been hit, the arrow finding the break in armour between breast and neck. The men around the fallen soldier bristled with anger at the sight, their exposed position offering no chance to repay the enemy in blood. Instinctively they took a step forward towards the copse, each man yearning for the command to advance and charge the Carthaginian position.

Marcus sensed their mood and reasserted his command,

dispatching men to cover the horses of the wagon fifty yards behind. The tortoise formation withdrew slowly, gathering up their wounded as they did, using upturned *scutum* shields as stretchers for those who couldn't stand. The rain of arrows continued to punish any man left exposed in the formation. The maniple formed around the wagon, the meagre catch of dead animals thrown away to make room for the wounded. Men of the IV lay with soldiers of the VII, the shared fight and blood spilt casting aside previous loyalties to form new bonds.

The maniple moved off slowly, their shields constantly charged against the threat of arrows or a renewed attack. Marcus ran his gaze over the rise before him, his sword sheathed, his hand pressed against his shoulder to stanch the flow of his blood. Romans and Carthaginians lay dead together, their over-lapping corpses mocked by Pluto, who respected neither rank nor race, the god of the underworld counting them only as dead men for his charge. Marcus counted over a dozen fallen Roman warriors, men who had stood where others might have fled. The wagon to his back contained a dozen more, the boards of the wagon already soaked with their blood, a steady stream that marked their passage over the road to Makella.

Once out of range of the copse, Marcus ordered the maniple to increase to double-quick time, the intensified pace chewing up the ground beneath their feet. The road behind them remained empty, Marcus knowing that pursuit was unneces-sary. The enemy had made their point. The area around Makella was Carthaginian territory and a Roman maniple alone outside the encampment was no longer safe. From here on the Ninth Legion had two choices. Either stay in the camp and starve or come out in full force. There was no middle ground.

CHAPTER TEN

Septimus walked out into the sunlit courtyard half an hour after dawn to find his mother, father and Atticus already there. The captain was mounted on one of the mares from the newly formed barracks at Fiumicino. She had all the hall-marks of a military horse, broad in the chest and barrel with a servile expression that bore witness to the hard life she led. Septimus paused and took a moment to study his friend closely, unsure of how he now felt. His sister's abrupt end to the evening had left his challenge to Atticus unsaid, and now as they waited for Hadria he found himself re-examining the lingering gazes he had witnessed between them, the memory making him uneasy.

Hadria appeared at the door a moment later and paused before walking out into the courtyard. Her gaze was on Septimus as she walked towards him, her emotions in turmoil at the imminent departure. From the corner of her eye she sensed Atticus staring at her intently, and she struggled not to return his gaze, knowing that to do so would reveal her heart to her brother. She reached for Septimus and hugged him tightly, her eyes welling with tears, a silent prayer passing through her mind for his safe return and for that of the man she could not hold. As she broke her embrace she sensed

Septimus's eyes searching her own and resolutely returned his gaze although her heart called out for one last look at Atticus.

Salonina suddenly began to wail, her fears for her son surfacing in a wave of emotion, and Septimus turned to her. She hugged her son ardently, whispering a hope for him to be safe, and Hadria noticed that Septimus's complete attention was on his mother. She seized her chance and turned her head towards Atticus. For a heartbeat their eyes locked and passion swept between them. Hadria silently mouthed a message, unseen by all except Atticus, before she whipped her head around as Septimus broke his mother's embrace. He shook his father's hand once more and mounted his horse.

Atticus spurred his horse and rode out into the busy street, his eyes locked forward, not daring to look over his shoulder as he heard Septimus fall in behind him. The horses quickly settled into an easy gait, Atticus unconsciously steering his mount through the growing throng as the city came to life. His mind was flooded by visions of Hadria and what he had just witnessed in the courtyard. The confusion he had felt the evening before when she abruptly retired to bed was swept away by the message she had mouthed, a message so fleeting that he had almost missed it. But now, as he replayed the moment in his mind, he was sure not only of what she had said but of how she felt, for her message was, 'I must see you again.'

Thirty minutes later the two riders were once more on the Via Aurelia heading northwards towards Fiumicino. Atticus was anxious to learn more about Hadria; as the previous confines of the city had kept them riding in single file, making conversation impossible, he now let the pace of his horse fall off, allowing Septimus to catch up and ride abreast.

'We should be back in camp within twenty minutes,' Atticus began, breaking the silence, wanting to broach the subject of Hadria indirectly.

Septimus nodded, his own thoughts guarded, but also on Hadria. He had decided during the thirty-minute ride through the city that he needed to confront Atticus, to forestall any intentions he might have regarding Hadria.

'Atticus, by law Hadria must remarry within the year,' he said bluntly, turning in his saddle so he could face his friend.

'I know, Septimus, your father mentioned it on my last visit,' Atticus answered warily, taken aback by Septimus's unexpected comment.

'Then you realize she cannot entertain advances from anyone other than a suitor.'

'What are you saying?' Atticus asked angrily, knowing the answer implied in Septimus's comment.

'I saw the way you were looking at her,' Septimus shot back, his gaze hostile as he reined in his horse, 'and I'm telling you to stay away from her.'

'And why couldn't I be a suitor?' Atticus stormed, bringing his own mount to a halt.

Septimus was on the cusp of revealing the reason behind his demand when he realized how weak and pathetic his motive was. He was suddenly overwhelmed with shame and his pride made him angry at Atticus for putting him in this situation.

'You could never marry her, Atticus,' he spat.

'Why?'

'Because you're not suitable,' Septimus shouted, his words now twisted to suit his purpose.

There was a moment's silence as Atticus recoiled. 'Why?' he shouted again, his horse shifting restlessly as he leaned out of his saddle, his face inches from Septimus's.

'Because you're not Roman,' Septimus countered, his own anger rising uncontrollably. 'Hadria must marry someone of her class, an equestrian from a Roman family.'

'Maybe Hadria should decide that for herself,' Atticus said.

Septimus wheeled his horse to separate the two mounts before turning one last time to face Atticus.

'I wanted to ask you, Atticus, but now I'm telling you,' he said, his face a mask of determination. 'Stay away from Hadria!'

Septimus spurred his horse and he galloped away, barging past slower travellers on the busy road, their irate shouts ignored.

Atticus could only watch him leave, his anger washing over him at what had just occurred, at how foolish he had been to think that Septimus was different from the arrogant Romans who believed they were above all others.

'We need to lure them out, make them commit some of their fleet to an opportunity they cannot refuse.'

'And then?' Gisco asked.

'Then we take them. We capture their force and learn their true strength.'

The admiral nodded, agreeing with Hamilcar's logic. What they needed now, needed most of all, was information. The enemy were building a fleet, that much was known. What was unknown was what type of ship the Romans would deploy, when they would launch and how many there would be.

Gisco knew the Romans were aware of his fifty ships, the galley that escaped them in the Strait of Messina having surely reported their strength, with the loss of their transport fleet confirming that presence. He was confident that they did not know of the second fleet of sixty that had sailed up the west coast, but he could not be sure and he had learned early in his military career that – when making plans – it was best to assume the worst. He would assume they did know. The final piece, a piece he was sure no one knew, was that he had persuaded Hamilcar to return to Carthage to call up a third fleet, the home fleet of the sacred city of Carthage herself.

Gisco closed his eyes and pictured the Roman galley he had seen in the Strait of Messina. The sight before him made him clench his teeth in anger, but he swept the emotion aside and concentrated on the details. She had been a fast ship, faster than any trireme in the Carthaginian fleet, although she would be no match for a quinquereme, whose fourth row of oarsmen would give her enough speed to overtake any smaller vessel. Was she typical of the Roman fleet? Did they possess any quinqueremes of their own? Would the new fleet be a mix of the two? Her design had been lighter than his own vessels, the reduction in weight and smaller draught making her faster over the waves. Would the Romans use a heavier design to better match his ships? Had they found out the secrets of the Carthaginian design, the new concepts employed by the master craftsmen of the Punic empire that had allowed the Carthaginians to combine strength and speed? If they had captured any of his ships then those secrets would be laid bare before any trained eye. The fleet had lost four ships since arriving in northern Sicily, three in a squall while travelling from Panormus to the blockade, and Boodes had reported the loss of a galley sent on patrol a week before. Had she also been lost to bad weather or had the Romans captured her? There were too many unanswered questions and the frustration of uncertainty caused Gisco to stand up and begin pacing the room.

Hamilcar watched him pace, studying him anew. Three days before he had agreed, at Gisco's persistent request, to sail to Carthage to commandeer the home fleet. It was a request that only a Council member like his father could grant, and Hamilcar was acutely aware that Gisco was attempting to use Hamilcar's contacts on the Council to serve himself. By personally requesting the fleet on Gisco's behalf, Hamilcar also knew he was tying his fate to that of the admiral's. He had initially resisted, reluctant to intertwine his destiny with Gisco's, but had finally relented when he realized that Gisco's request served the greater needs of Carthage. The Carthaginians were a maritime people, a nation at home on the water. The navy was the strength and backbone of that empire and Hamilcar realized it was time for the city to flex that power.

'So how do we lure them out?' Gisco asked suddenly, turning towards the seated Hamilcar to find the man already staring at him.

'We use the same tactic our forefathers used against Agathocles, the tyrant of Syracuse. We offer them a city,' Hamilcar replied, the idea having been formed, developed and tested in his own mind over the past few days.

Gisco smiled at the simplicity of the idea, a tactic that had worked against a different enemy over forty years before. Agathocles, then ruler of Syracuse in the southwestern corner of Sicily, had broken the uneasy truce of the time by attacking and taking the Carthaginian stronghold of Messina. The Carthaginians held only one other stronghold on the island, the city of Agrigentum in the west. The Carthaginian leader Maharbal did not have sufficient forces to fight his way across the entire island of Sicily to regain Messina, and so he devised a plan to make the enemy come to him. He offered Agathocles the city of Agrigentum.

One of the city councillors had presented himself before Agathocles, claiming the inhabitants were ready to rise up against their Carthaginian oppressors. The leader of Syracuse had immediately taken the bait and led his army across the island to liberate Agrigentum, only to find the gates locked against him. In his anger he besieged the city, even though he was over a hundred miles from the safety of his own territory. It was the mistake Maharbal had hoped for. The Carthaginian leader swooped down with his army to surround the enemy, trapping them between his forces and the hostile city.

The resulting battle had been a disaster for Agathocles, undone by his own greed and recklessness. Gisco was confident the Romans had the first trait in abundance, for why else would they have built their Republic if not to satisfy their appetite for the lands and wealth of others. But were they reckless? Gisco ran through the list of Carthaginian-held cities in his mind. He smiled as the perfect match for his purpose presented itself. Gisco would not need to rely on the Romans being reckless, for the city he chose would appear easily within their grasp. It was a city located on an island off the northern coast of Sicily, an island far removed from the blockade and any visible threat from the Carthaginian navy. It was the city of Lipara.

Gaius Duilius sat patiently as the camp prefect of Fiumicino made his report to the Senate. The battle-worn ex-centurion looked oddly out of place in the hallowed inner chamber of the Curia; however, he showed no sign of being intimidated by the surrounding senators. Duilius surmised that Tuditanus had faced more menacing foes over the course of his military career than this group of languid old men.

The junior consul's mind wandered as the prefect outlined the progress of the fleet's construction. Duilius already knew the main details of the report. Not by virtue of having seen Tuditanus's written work, but from the reports of half a dozen spies in the camp who fed him updates both day and night. For that reason Duilius had not been to the camp, although he was fully aware of Scipio's visit the day before and the thought made him turn to the senior consul now seated in the centre of the bottom tier of the semicircular rows. His attention returned to the present as he picked up an in-accuracy in the report.

'Prefect,' Duilius said, his interruption stopping Tuditanus in his tracks, 'did you say the first batch of twenty galleys will be ready in six days?'

'Yes, Senator,' Tuditanus replied, his voice confident.

'No sooner?' Duilius asked, with an implied disbelief hidden beneath the seemingly innocent question.

'No, Senator. Six days.'

Tuditanus held the junior consul's gaze. He had been warned by Scipio to expect the question, the senior consul knowing that in a camp the size of Fiumicino there would be few secrets, and certainly none that would escape Duilius.

'I see,' Duilius said finally. He stood up.

'Senators,' he announced, 'I humbly ask the senior consul, in your presence, to allow me to take the fleet to sea once it is ready.'

A light applause followed the submission. Scipio rose to reply.

'The junior consul may personally take the fleet to sea in *six* days,' Scipio said, his words neatly avoiding the trap that Duilius had set. More applause was heard and Duilius nodded a thank-you at Scipio, both men knowing that the gesture was not one of gratitude.

Duilius retook his seat. His spies had told him three days, four at the most, and the galleys would be ready to sail. He was acutely aware of the opportunity that would be afforded the first man to command the fleet to sea, even if the journey was from the construction site to the *castrum* in Ostia. It was an opportunity to stamp their command of the fleet in the minds of men, an opportunity that would negate any agreement made in the Senate. The rule of Rome was the rule of the mob. If the people chose Scipio as the fleet's leader, there was little Duilius could do to point out the joint leadership agreement. The mob would only remember one name. Duilius needed to find a way of making sure that name would be his.

Atticus marvelled at the gleaming hulls of the twenty triremes beached just above the high-water mark of the beach. He and Septimus had arrived back in Fiumicino two days before and had immediately recommenced their training routines, although Septimus now spent all his time in the camp of the Fourth. Anger flared up within Atticus as he recalled their sudden argument on the ride back from Rome and Septimus's demand to stay away from Hadria, and he consciously swept the memory from his mind, concentrating instead on the *Aquila* as the galley slipped her mooring and the order was given to get under way.

Training the new recruits on how to ram when all his reason demanded he should train them for boarding had frustrated Atticus, but at least on this day he knew he would be teaching them a lesson that was vital, regardless of the galley's method of attack. All of the trainees under his tutelage were already skilled sailors, and so in many cases it was simply a matter of adapting their skills, teaching them how best to manoeuvre a galley while choosing the most appropriate oar-stroke. Today's lesson would concentrate on that second element.

The *Aquila* moved away from the beach at two knots, steerage speed. Her pace was not dictated by the nearest of the sea-lanes running perpendicular to her course, as Gaius could easily negotiate the tricky passage at standard speed, but by the need to conserve the strength of the rowers for the lesson ahead, a lesson that would be learnt at their expense. Atticus had kept this lesson until last, knowing it to be the most important for any command crew of a galley. When the assembled men on the main deck took to their own galleys in the near future, they would remember this day well.

Once the *Aquila* cleared the sea-lane, Atticus ordered all twenty-five trainees below to the slave deck. As they descended, he ordered the slaves to be chained to their oars, knowing that what he was about to do would endanger the trainees crowded on the narrow walkway along the length of the deck. He re-examined his decision on the method he had chosen to teach this all-important lesson and satisfied himself that there was no alternative, not if he wanted the lesson to be remembered.

With an additional twenty-five men below decks, the area was claustrophobic and, for some of the trainees, frightening. Many had never been on a slave deck before and the sight of two hundred near-naked men chained to their fifteen-foot oars struck dread into their hearts. The slaves' expressions were unmoving and yet the trainees could feel the open hostility in the confined space. The slaves were men like the Romans who stood over them, the difference in their circumstances dictated only by the ever-fickle fate that controlled all their lives.

'Men,' Atticus shouted, his voice muted by the press of bodies and the surrounding timbers, 'this deck represents the strength of your ship. These men, although slaves, are part of your crew. You must treat them accordingly. To abuse them is to sap your own strength.'

Atticus watched as the message was absorbed by those men who had never owned slaves and had never become callous in their treatment of them. Others, Fulfidias among them, had slaves of their own and had worked with them all their lives. For men like this, Atticus's words sounded weak, unbecoming for the master of a ship.

'In battle,' Atticus continued, 'you will face many challenges. The principal one will be your ability to know and understand your own ship and its capabilities. Of all your ship's capabilities, one of the most important is the strength of the slaves at your oars. These men give you the ability to out-manoeuvre your enemy and escape or close in for attack. The crucial thing you must know is that their strength is finite. Once it is spent your ship is lost.'

The trainees listened in silence and then looked around them at the chained men an arm's length away. A shouted command shocked them back to attention.

'Battle speed!' Atticus roared.

The two hundred oars of the *Aquila* increased with the command of the drum beat to battle speed, seven knots.

'The galley slaves of the *Aquila* can row at battle speed for two hours. During that time the forty reserve rowers will also be used to keep that pace.'

Atticus let them row for thirty minutes. At that point the first few reserves were called up to replace the weaker rowers of the crew. The trainees in the centre of the walkways were pushed aside as the hatchway to the lower deck was opened and some of them were given a brief glance of the twilight hell beneath them; the stench of the bilges combined with the foul smell of the confined quarters of the reserve rowers rose up through the open hatchway.

The rowing continued on at battle speed, the only sound being the beat of the drum keeping time on the crowded deck. As the sweat began to increase on the backs of the slaves and their breathing became more laboured, many of the trainees began to form an understanding of what Atticus had spoken about.

'Attack speed!'

Again the order had come as a surprise to many and again they turned their attention to Atticus.

'At attack speed the *Aquila* is moving at eleven knots.'

Many of the trainees, some of whom had never been on a galley before their indentured service, marvelled at the incredible speed. For a sailing ship it was the equivalent of running before a strong wind, a tricky manoeuvre that was rarely attempted.

'The rowers of the *Aquila* can maintain this speed for fifteen minutes. It is only three knots faster than battle speed, but the extra effort required cuts their ability to an eighth of the time.'

Again the trainees looked around them. Many now began to count the minutes. Ten passed.

'Ramming speed!'

The drum master of the *Aquila* repeated the order and increased his beat. The slaves redoubled their efforts, many grunting through the pain of the backbreaking pull. Others cried out as cramped muscles gave way under the strain.

'At ramming speed, even the best rowers will collapse after five minutes!' Atticus shouted over the cries of pain and suffering. He secretly gritted his teeth to force his will to continue.

The first rower collapsed after two minutes.

Within another sixty seconds twenty more were down.

'All stop!' Atticus shouted, putting an end to the enforced barbarity of the lesson. He spat the bile of self-shame from his mouth at the sight of the near-broken men, many at the end of their strength, while others who had gone beyond their limit lay prone under their oars. One did not rise again, his heart broken from the effort.

Atticus never flinched from pushing his galley slaves to their limits when the situation required it. To show compassion and spare the slaves could mean endangering a ship, and so Atticus had long ago hardened his heart to the fate of the men below decks. Even so, he believed in treating the slaves well, not just because healthy slaves rowed better, but because, like all sailors, he knew that one day the tables might be turned and in defeat Atticus could find himself chained to an oar. By treating his slaves well he hoped that Fortuna, the goddess of fate, would place him under a similar master if his time ever came.

Atticus ordered the oars to be withdrawn and the sail raised. For the next hour the *Aquila* would have to make do with canvas only. He ordered the trainees back onto the main deck and then, standing on the aft, he addressed them once more.

'We do not know what lies ahead for our fleet. At the very least we will be called upon to raise a blockade. We might even meet the Carthaginian fleet in battle. In either case you will need all your resources to stay alive and in the fight. The *Aquila* has three hundred and thirty men on board, two hundred and forty rowers, thirty sailors and sixty marines. She has fought in many battles and has survived them all. That is because I know that each man on board is valuable in the fight. To ignore any part of your crew is to doom your ship. The lesson is this . . . Know your ship. Know your crew. Know your strength.'

Septimus woke at the sound of the clarion call announcing the start of a new day. He sat up on the cot in the cramped tent and reached out for the water basin on the ground. It was half full and he emptied the contents over his head, the cold water barely penetrating the deep fatigue he felt. Over the past two days he had had fewer than four hours' sleep each night. Silanus continued to frustrate his attempts to properly prepare the legionaries of the V maniple, and so Septimus had stepped up the hours of training in an effort to force the issue. It was not working, and Septimus had realized during the night that he would have to confront Silanus once and for all.

As Septimus walked out into the dawn light, the V maniple were forming on the training square for roll call, the procedure carried out with practised efficiency before the men were released for breakfast. Each *contubernia* of soldiers shared a single tent and the men ate in their groups, the arrangement more efficient in a temporary camp. Septimus noticed Silanus walking towards his own tent and moved to intercept him.

'Silanus!'

The centurion turned to the call and his expression immediately became dismissive as Septimus approached him.

'We need to talk,' he said.

'Really,' Silanus replied with a sneer, 'about what, marine?' Again the last word was spat out, but Septimus ignored the gibe.

'About the training, about how your men aren't ready for battle, not against an enemy trained on the deck of a galley where a legion's formations count for naught.'

'So you say, marine. I say my men are unmatched in combat and no matter how differently the Carthaginians fight, even one to one, my men won't be beaten.'

Septimus smiled, although the smile did not reach his eyes. Silanus had taken the bait.

'Would you be willing to test that assertion in single combat?' Septimus asked. 'You against me?'

'Gladly,' Silanus nodded, returning Septimus's smile with the same underlying enmity. He made to turn but Septimus grabbed his sword arm, arresting him.

'But if I win,' Septimus continued, 'I want your word that you and your men will submit to the training.'

Silanus looked wary. 'And if I win?' he replied.

'Then I'll back down and concede that your men are without equal.'

Again Silanus nodded, jerking his arm to release Septimus's grip, a malicious grin once more on his face, and walked away.

Septimus watched him go before turning to find Quintus standing behind him. His *optio* moved forward.

'Your orders, Centurion?' he asked.

'Form up the men around the training square, Quintus,' Septimus said with a smile. 'I'll be teaching the first lesson today.'

Fifteen minutes later the legionaries of the V were formed

on three sides of the square with the *Aquila*'s twenty marines occupying the fourth side. The shouts of encouragement were sporadic as bets were exchanged between the marines and the legionaries, the odds agreed as even. Septimus and Silanus stood at the centre of the square, six feet apart as each limbered up, their heavy wooden training swords swinging with ever-increasing speed as the tempo of calls from the crowd increased. Quintus stepped forward between the two fighters and drew his sword, holding it straight out between them until both were ready. With a flash he dropped his blade and withdrew, the shouts from the crowd reaching a crescendo as the fight began.

Septimus studied Silanus's movements as the two began to circle, noticing immediately that although he was right-handed, his body was finely balanced, the natural weakness of his left trained out of him many years before. Silanus moved with practised ease, confident of his ability and yet not rushing his attack, sizing up Septimus with every turn, weaving his sword from side to side to distract the marine. The two men continued to circle.

'The Fourth Legion, the boars – right, Silanus?' Septimus said, his words breaking the silence between the men although they were surrounded by a wall of sound.

'What?' Silanus said after a moment, his face betraying the break in his concentration.

'You're a man of the Fourth? A boar. One of the boars of Rome?'

'Yes, I am,' Silanus replied, the need to do so automatic.

'Then what does that make your mother?' Septimus said, loudly enough only for the centurion to hear.

Silanus's face was mottled with anger as he tore into the fight, the words striking rage into his heart. Septimus had been ready for the strike but he was shocked by the sheer speed of the movement, his anticipation of the style of attack saving him, giving his reactions the extra time needed to counter the lunge. Silanus had attacked in the manner of the legions, albeit in a stylized way born out of adaptation to one-to-one combat. He had feigned to his left, where training dictated he lunge with his shield, before following through with the sword in his right hand. Septimus countered the stroke before backing off, the centurion following him step for step, keeping the pressure up, raining blow after blow on the marine.

The cheers from the legionaries of the Fourth becoming ever more strident as Silanus moved in for the kill, Septimus continuing to give ground before the furious centurion, waiting for the perfect time to counterattack. The moment came without warning and Septimus shifted the balance of his stance as he made ready. Where before Silanus had randomized his strikes, the sustained attack on Septimus had made his movements rhythmical, the years of training overcoming his individual style to reassert itself over his actions. It was the failure of all men of the legions in one-to-one combat and was the first lesson Atticus had taught Septimus on the *Aquila*. In one-to-one combat, predictability was death.

Septimus allowed the centurion one more strike, his mind predicting the blow long before it began. Then he counter attacked.

Septimus sidestepped the next expected strike and parried Silanus's blade, breaking the centurion's rhythm. He immediately followed with a thrust to the centurion's groin, a killing blow that forced Silanus to react swiftly, his body turned off balance. Septimus reversed the strike at the last moment and brought the blade higher to the centurion's stomach, again forcing Silanus to further shift off balance to counter the stroke, the original feint slowing his reactions. Silanus's twisted torso exposed his kidneys and Septimus struck beneath the centurion's extended sword at his lower back. The centurion grunted loudly as the tip of the heavy wooden sword struck his kidneys, driving a sharp pain into his stomach and chest. He immediately withdrew, pain etched on his face.

Now the men of the *Aquila* were cheering with blood lust as Septimus pressed home his attack, this time Silanus giving ground as the marine rained unpredictable blows on him. Septimus's training on the *Aquila* came to the fore as the marine gave full vent to the conditioning of his combat instincts, while Silanus's reactions became erratic as desperation crept into his defence as he fought to break the cycle of attack. Septimus feigned a strike to the centurion's lower left side and suddenly thrust his sword upwards, the point driving towards Silanus's face. The centurion reacted instinctively, without thought to the consequences, and whipped his sword up, swiping Septimus's blade away but leaving his entire torso exposed. Septimus circled his blade around the sideswipe and brought the blade under Silanus's arm, turning his body around as he did to put maximum momentum behind what he knew would be the last strike. The flat blade of the wooden sword slammed into Silanus's stomach with a force that drove the wind from his lungs, and he pitched forward over the sword, falling heavily on all fours, his own sword thrown from his hand by the strength of the impact.

Septimus stepped back from the defeated centurion and turned to his men, holding his sword aloft in victory. He made to walk over to them when a hand on his shoulder arrested him. He turned to find Silanus facing him, the centurion still hunched forward with his hand over his stomach.

'By the gods, Septimus, you fight like Pluto, like the lord of the underworld himself,' Silanus gasped as he drew himself to his full height, proffering his hand as he did so.

'The same way the Carthaginians fight,' Septimus said, accepting Silanus's hand, noting for the first time a look of respect on the centurion's face.

Silanus nodded and turned towards his men, barking orders at them to form up and prepare for the day's training.

Septimus smiled as Quintus came up and slapped him on the shoulder. The twenty galleys would be ready to sail within days and the rumour around the camp was that the senior consul was taking the galleys to the *castrum* at Ostia where they would make a great show of arriving and disembarking. If Ostia was to become the new home for the V maniple of the Fourth, Septimus would arrange for his *optio*, Quintus, to accompany them to continue the training, safe in the knowledge that finally he had an ally in Silanus. With the completion of the entire fleet still weeks away, time was on their side, time enough to teach the legionaries of the Fourth the vital skills they would need to survive the treacherous decks of a Carthaginian galley.

Gaius Duilius rose from his bed at the sound of the incessant knocking on his bedroom door.

'Who is it?' he shouted irritably, trying to judge the time from the light in the room. It was just after dawn.

The door burst open and his senior servant, Appius, entered, followed by one of his spies from the camp, a carpenter named Calvus. Duilius rose as they rushed across the floor, their agitation obvious.

'They sail today, my lord,' Calvus said, his anxiety etched on his face.

'*Today?*' Duilius replied. 'All reports said *tomorrow*, the *fourth* day!'

'That was the plan as everyone knew it, the schedule that Tuditanus had kept us to and swore us not to reveal to anyone

– lest the enemy become aware of our plans,' Calvus explained, 'but last evening as we prepared to end our day, Tuditanus himself ordered the work to continue overnight. We were ordered to stay at our posts and finish the work by firelight.'

'Why was I not informed of this?' Duilius asked, turning to Appius. 'Why didn't one of the other spies report this?'

Appius was speechless.

'We were all ordered to remain in camp last night on pain of death,' Calvus interjected, 'so none could spread the news beyond Fiumicino. I was only allowed to leave when the work was completed.'

Duilius swore at the simplicity of the plan that had thwarted him. By forcing the craftsmen and slaves to work overnight they had pushed the schedule forward twenty-four hours. Twenty-four hours that Duilius had been planning on using to arrange a 'surprise' inspection by him and some of the senior senators. Once at camp the next day, the fourth day, they would all see the fleet was indeed ready to sail and Duilius would pursue the offer Scipio had made in the Senate to allow Duilius to sail with the fleet when she first put to sea. That plan was now frustrated, ruined by Scipio's simple change in the schedule. Duilius cursed his lack of foresight.

'Shall I saddle your horse?' Appius asked.

At first Duilius did not hear the question, furious as he was at being outmanoeuvred.

'What?' he asked, his mind still not in the moment.

Appius repeated the question.

'No,' Duilius said, realizing that to turn up in Fiumicino alone without senatorial backup would be useless, his rank as junior consul second to Scipio's.

Duilius dismissed the two men and began pacing his room. He forced his mind to quiet so he could examine the problem from every angle. There was no solution; nothing to stop

Scipio making his triumphant entrance into Ostia. Duilius might have won the first round in the Senate when he forced Scipio to back down over the command of the fleet, but the senior consul had won the second, a round that would give Scipio the backing of the people of Rome.

'Today?' Lucius said, disbelieving. He had been about to get the *Aquila* under way when his captain had came up to him on the aft-deck, his expression uneasy.

'Yes, today,' Atticus repeated, 'I've just received the orders.'

'But why the haste?' Lucius asked.

'Who knows?' Atticus replied. 'All I can be sure of is that the trainees aren't ready. I'm going to have to confront Tuditanus again – at least make him agree to continue the training at Ostia.'

'I'll row you ashore,' Lucius offered, and both men strode to the main deck and climbed down to a tethered skiff. Within minutes they were on the beach.

The activity around them seemed chaotic as the two men ascended the beach towards the camp prefect's tent. Sailors clambered over the decks of the twenty galleys to install the running rigging of each, and the voices of the boatswains so recently taught on the *Aquila* could be heard shouting orders to the men who scrambled to obey. Atticus surveyed the ship closest to him and studied the near-finished arrangement of ropes. The rigging, to a casual eye, looked perfect, but Atticus quickly spotted a mistake, one that would only become apparent when the crew tried to raise sail. The boatswain had used the wrong sequence in completing the rigging and the lifting yard would foul the instant the crew tried to raise it aloft. He shook his head at the sight. The crews were simply not ready yet.

The activity around the boat explained the sailors' haste. In front of each galley, slaves were laying out cylindrical logs on the hard-packed sand. The logs stretched out a hundred yards in front of each ship and led down to the water line, now at low tide. The galleys were suspended two feet off the ground on a timber frame that had supported the hull during construction, and logs were now placed in the gap beneath, leaving a space of six inches. As the last logs were put in place in front of the ship nearest to Atticus and Lucius, whip cracks filled the air and the slaves, at least three hundred in total, took the strain of the ropes tethered to the galley. With a mighty effort the ship was pulled forward on her frame, the action snapping the timbers of the frame until the galley crashed the six inches onto the logs underneath. More slaves rushed forward to clear the majority of the debris, even as the galley lurched forward on its way to the water line, the gentle slope of the beach aiding its progress. Atticus could see that within the hour all twenty galleys would be at the lower end of the beach, awaiting the tide that would free them from the land.

The two sailors of the *Aquila* were so engrossed by the unfolding scene that they did not notice the horsemen stationed fifty yards beyond them, the group also watching the galleys being made ready. Scipio turned to Tuditanus.

'You've done well, Prefect.'

Tuditanus's eyebrow raised at the rare compliment, although he was sure not to let the senior consul see the gesture.

'Thank you, Senior Consul. I have sent word to the legion's camp to have the men made ready. The tide rises rapidly in this area, so the galleys will be afloat within three hours.'

'Good,' Scipio replied, his voice and expressions once more minimal. He calculated the time in his mind. All being well, he would be rounding the headland at Ostia before noon.

Demades stood to attention as his task was dictated to him. He was not a military man – in fact he had never held a weapon in his hand in all his forty years; however, the stance seemed appropriate given the rank of the man speaking to him. The Carthaginian admiral had arrived unexpectedly an hour before, compelling Demades to race from his residence to the Council chamber, all the while fearing the worst, unable to think of a reason why Hannibal Gisco would want to visit the tiny island.

Lipara, which was also the name of the only city on the island, was located twenty-four miles off the northern coast of Sicily and was the largest of a group of eight islands. The island had been occupied since ancient times, primarily because of the hard black volcanic glass, obsidian, which was abundant under the soil. Its cutting edge had been prized by the inhabitants of the mainland, and the trade had made the otherwise insignificant island an important centre for commerce. The coming of iron had eradicated the trade in obsidian, but the islanders had adapted and now sold volcanic pumice to the rich inhabitants of the Roman Republic.

The arrival of the Carthaginians two years before had originally caused great consternation to the inhabitants of Lipara, not least to their senior councillor, Demades, who saw their coming as the death knell for their trade and for the Council that controlled both the trade and government of the island. In the event, the Carthaginians had had little impact on the lives of the ordinary people, who simply switched their trading routes to serve the empire of Carthage. Never before, however, had a senior Carthaginian figure been in the city, least of all the supreme commander of their entire army and navy. It was for that reason that Demades had attended Gisco personally, one leader to another. Demades had tried to take the upper hand in the meeting – after all, Lipara was his city and he was the senior councillor – however, within a heartbeat, Gisco's overpowering will had cowed him and thereafter he listened in silence.

'I beg your pardon, Admiral, but you want me to do what?' Demades asked as Gisco got to the crux of his plan.

'I want you to travel to Rome and announce to their Senate that Lipara wishes to switch allegiance to the Roman cause,' Gisco repeated, annoyed with the awkward fool before him.

Gisco had met many like Demades before, and all had proved to be the same, big fish in small ponds. It was only when a bigger fish arrived that men like Demades realized that their power over a small city was naught when compared to the military might of an empire such as Carthage's. Even in the face of this reality, however, Gisco had always noticed that these men still clung to the opinion that they were somehow equal to him. They were not, and in the past Gisco had been forced to draw blood to prove the point. It was only because Demades had been to Rome before and his face was known to all the traders that Gisco did not kill him now and replace him with an imposter. The traders would testify to the legitimacy of his claim to be the senior councillor of Lipara, a legitimacy that was required if the Senate was to be won over.

'But, Admiral, Lipara has always been loyal to Carthage. We have never given the governor cause for concern. I don't understand,' Demades said.

'You don't need to understand,' Gisco snarled. 'You will ask the Senate to send a force to free your city, telling them that we, the Carthaginians, have strangled your trade and your people are prisoners on the island.'

'But . . . but . . . that's not so, Admiral. Our trade has flourished under your benevolent rule and our city has prospered. We have no wish to become a Roman possession, I assure you.'

Demades began to panic. He desperately wanted to obey the admiral, but he couldn't understand what was being asked of him. Were the Carthaginians really going to abandon his island? If so, why would they want the Romans to take possession of Lipara? Why not just sail away?

'You're a fool, Demades,' Gisco spat, losing his patience. 'You will travel to Rome and deliver the message I have given you.'

Demades nodded, a look of puzzlement still on his face.

'Cronus!' Gisco shouted to the door behind Demades. The admiral's guard commander entered and stood to attention.

'Demades,' Gisco continued, 'this is Cronus. He will travel with you to Rome along with four of my personal guard. They will travel disguised as your personal guard and will be with you at all times.'

Demades looked to the towering figure of Cronus, his eyes moving from the expressionless face to the sword hanging loosely by his side. At Gisco's words he returned his gaze to the admiral.

'If you so much as breathe a word beyond telling the Senate the message I have outlined, Cronus will kill you, but not before he sends word to me of your betrayal. If I receive such a message, I will personally take the lives of your wife and two daughters.'

Gisco's eyes swore the truth of the threat and Demades nearly lost control of his bladder as terror threatened to unman him. He nodded to indicate his understanding, not trusting his voice.

'Take him away,' Gisco ordered, and Cronus manhandled the councillor from the room.

The guard commander escorted Demades the short distance through the streets to the dockside. A trading barge was making ready to sail and Demades was bustled on board.

'I can't go now,' he protested. 'What of my family? I must speak with them.'

'Take him below,' was the only reply from Cronus, an order that signalled rough hands to take Demades to the main cabin.

The barge pushed off from the quayside, the helmsman setting a course that would take her north to Rome.

'A sight to see,' Atticus remarked to himself as the first of the twenty galleys made her way awkwardly through the breaking surf to the calmer waters beyond. It was hard to believe that it had only been two and a half weeks since construction of the fleet had begun on the once-empty beach. One by one the ships floated in the gentle swell of the tide before the oars were dropped into the shallow water and orders were issued to get under way. Given that the slaves on board had never manned oars, it was an impressive feat, and Atticus was proud of the drum masters, who had to create order from the probable chaos below decks. The successful launch of each ship was met by a cheer both from men on the beach and those on deck, and it was impossible not to feel overwhelmed at what had been achieved in so little time.

Septimus stood apart from Atticus on the aft-deck. He was dressed, as were all the marines now stationed on the galleys, in full battle gear, a show of force for the traders of Ostia. The necessities of their shared command demanded his return to the galley, and so an uneasy truce had been established between them, their argument not discussed but not forgotten either.

Atticus looked beyond the completed galleys to the beach sweeping north and a three-mile stretch of coastline where the construction frames for the next batch of fifty galleys were being completed. The number of people in the camp had exploded over the past week, and so now the fishing village of Fiumicino boasted a population greater than most cities. Atticus estimated that in less than three weeks the sea would be home to fifty more Roman galleys, all of which would need to be manned by capable crews.

As the galleys got under way, the *Aquila* slipped into formation, as did two galleys of the Ostia fleet, the *Neptunus* and the *Asclepius*. All three deferred to the *Mars*, the first ship launched and the designated flagship of the fleet. It was upon this ship that Scipio himself sailed, his statuesque figure on the foredeck visible to all those on the ships flanking the vanguard. Atticus smiled at the sight, knowing that if the *Mars* were to encounter a Carthaginian galley today, Scipio would immediately be knocked off his perch.

Fortuna must be smiling, Fulfidias thought, feeling favoured as his galley prepared to make the turn south to the port of Ostia. Only hours before, his dismal outlook had been as unchanged as it had been over the previous two weeks. He had stood on the aft-deck of his beached galley that morning and barked orders at his new crew, his tongue lashing all who came within range of his foul humour. That attitude had changed the moment he had answered a summons to the prefect's tent.

He had never spoken to Tuditanus before then, but all knew of his fearsome reputation, and Fulfidias was apprehensive as to why he was being sent for. That apprehension had increased at the sight of the senior consul, Scipio himself, in attendance. They had asked him many questions, mainly about his previous sailing experience on trading galleys and the legitimacy of his business dealings in Rome. On both counts Fulfidias had spoken with pride and confidence. It was then that Scipio had announced that Fulfidias's galley, the *Salvia*, would be renamed the *Mars* and would become the flagship of the new fleet.

Fulfidias now looked down the length of his new galley to the figure of Scipio standing alone on the foredeck. He had debated whether or not he should join the senior consul on the bow of the ship but had decided against it, remembering the cold manner that Scipio had exhibited since coming on board. Never mind, Fulfidias thought, there would be plenty of time to build a relationship with the most powerful man in the Republic. Fulfidias knew that Scipio would open new doors for him, doors that would surely reveal incredible opportunities for profit. In his mind he distinctly heard the click of Fortuna's wheel as it turned in his favour.

Scipio ignored the light spray of water on his face and the feel of his damp toga where it was pressed against his skin by the oncoming warm breeze. He had been told the journey to Ostia would take no more than thirty minutes, and so he had decided to spend the entire time on the foredeck of the lead ship, the most prominent point in the newly formed fleet.

The sight of twenty-three galleys in the busy sea-lane drew astonished looks from the crews and passengers of other ships, and all noticed the seemingly sculpted figure of the Roman on the lead galley. Scipio knew it was only a foretaste of what he would encounter in the busy port ahead. He glanced over his shoulder at the triremes formed up behind him. They were indeed an impressive sight, one that he had never seen the like of before, and certainly one that would suggest power to all in Ostia and Rome beyond.

Scipio also noticed the three galleys of the regular fleet. They were in mid-formation, in a solid line of three abreast, their arrangement exact and controlled. Their precision was in marked contrast to the ships ahead and behind them which, it seemed, were struggling to maintain a semblance of the same order. He had earlier debated whether he should make one of the experienced galleys his flagship, but had dismissed the idea. The 'old' fleet was a familiar sight to the world, a fleet built by obscure and forgotten men. The new fleet was Scipio's and, if he was going to stamp his authority and ownership on its galleys, he needed to mark them as such. Making one of the new ships his flagship was the first step in achieving his aim.

The fleet rounded the northern headland of the port of Ostia as the day reached its zenith, the springtime sun shining white from a cloudless sky, reflecting a million shards of light in the rippling waters of the bay. As more and more galleys appeared, the immediate reaction on the dockside was one of fear. The weeks of circulated rumours about the Punici horde had struck terror in the hearts of the traders, and now it seemed the enemy were striking at the very heart of the Republic.

The initial fear and consternation slowly gave way to jubilation as Roman banners flying from mastheads were recognized and all realized that the galleys approaching were not harbingers of ruin but the promised saviours that would sweep the seas for Rome. Word quickly spread, and soon almost the entire population of Ostia lined the quayside, cheering and waving the return of safety and security.

The ships fanned out as they approached the dock to create an illusion of greater numbers, so spectators on land had to turn their heads to take in the full spectacle. Two hundred yards from shore, the galleys stopped in line abreast and only the centre ship, the one that had been in the lead, continued on. While some had already noticed the tall, lone figure on the bow of the trireme, now all eyes fell on the sight as the ship made the final approach. The cheering continued, but now with a renewed focus, as the leader was identified, the man that personified the mighty strength of the assembled galleys.

With yards to go, the *Mars* heeled over hard to come parallel to the dock, a fluid movement belying a complex manoeuvre that the experienced galley captain made look effortless. Lines were thrown to shore and eager hands took hold to haul the ship in, the oars withdrawing to allow the ship to rest four feet from the dock. The gangway was quickly lowered and ten black-cloaked *praetoriani* rushed down to push the crowd back, their efforts creating a semicircular space at the foot of the gangway. Only then did Scipio appear at the head of the gangway. He paused there, taking in the frenzied cheers and shouted accolades. As the voices began to wane, he spread out his arms to call for quiet. The multitude leaned forward.

'Citizens of Rome!' Scipio shouted, his words carrying easily over the heads of the quieted crowd. 'Our forefathers conceived an ambition. A hope! To spread the light of democracy from the centre of Rome to the corners of the world so all could live in peace and prosperity.

'For hundreds of years, each generation in its turn has stepped forward to carry that torch onwards. Each generation taking its turn to expand the frontiers of the Republic. Now it is our turn, our responsibility.'

The crowd leaned ever forward, hanging on the spoken words.

'It is not a task that promises victories or guarantees success. It is a task that requires sacrifice, and hardship, and perhaps death itself to those who carry that torch beyond the borders of our Republic.'

The crowd listened in complete silence, the only sound the lapping of the water against the dock and the cries of solitary seagulls overhead. Some recognized Scipio for who he was; most did not know his face.

'A month ago a new kind of enemy appeared to threaten our Republic and our way of life. A savage, brutal enemy who moved with lightning speed to cut off the valiant men who carry the torch of Rome to the oppressed people of Sicily. It is a merciless enemy that, if not stopped, will surely carry the war to the gates of Rome itself!'

The crowd moaned in dismay at the thought, many recalling the terrible fear they had felt only moments before.

'But fear not, my fellow citizens! The Senate has heard your cries and has responded. I have heard your cries and I have responded. I stand before you now on the very threshold of a new era for our glorious Republic. An era of renewed expansion and prosperity. With the fleet gathered before you, and the scores of galleys being built, I will sweep the enemy from our shores and from our seas.

'I will free the island of Sicily and open her ports to Rome.

'I will expand the frontiers of the Republic.

'I, Gnaeus Cornelius Scipio, will make you, the citizens of Rome, masters of the sea!'

The crowd erupted in a tremendous roar as the words struck their hearts. A wave of sound crashed over Scipio and his own heart soared as thousands of voices were lifted in his name. He raised his clenched fist in triumph, the classic pose of the victorious, and the noise increased, the blood lust of the crowd now whipped up by the prospect of carrying the fight to the enemy.

Scipio let them cheer. His face was a mask of imperious strength as befitting his power, but inside he laughed at their gullibility. They were a mob, a mindless mob. He had called them fellow citizens but he felt completely detached from them. They were beneath him, and he resented the very fact that he was forced to breathe the same air as them.

Scipio knew, however, that he needed to harness their power – and to do so meant speaking on their level, a level that spoke of shared wealth and prosperity, of bright futures and security. He had hired half a dozen Greek rhetoricians, the best that his silver could buy, to speak on his behalf in every forum in Rome. They would reiterate Scipio's promise to keep Rome free from the enemy threat, and ensure that his name was on every street corner in the city, on every man's lips and in every man's mind.

By the time the full fleet was ready, all of Rome would know who commanded the might of the Republic. Duilius would sail with the fleet but none would know his name. Only Scipio would be remembered. He would lead the fleet south and destroy the outnumbered Carthaginians. Then he would complete the conquest of Sicily.

As the crowd cheered, Scipio imagined the same sound multiplied a hundredfold. He imagined the streets of Rome lined with adoring crowds as his victorious triumph wound its way to the Curia. He imagined being given the *corona graminea*, the grass crown, the highest military honour the Republic could bestow, reserved only for those who rescued a beleaguered army.

Scipio looked out over the upturned faces of the cheering crowd. The people loved him as a leader because he offered them the world. In the future, when he delivered it, they would worship him as a god.

CHAPTER ELEVEN

From where he sat in the main cabin, Demades clearly heard the call from the masthead. Ostia had been sighted. He crossed the cabin to the starboard side and lifted the hatch to peer out over the busy waterways around the Roman port. The bright sunshine caused his eyes to water and he blinked against the discomfort. He had not seen the sun since the ship set sail from Lipara two days before.

Demades had passed the entire journey in his cabin. At first the confinement was imposed and his demands for his release had gone unanswered through the bolted cabin door. Hours out of port, Cronus had finally opened the door. Demades had immediately renewed his protests, calling for the ship to return to Lipara, but the guard commander had simply ignored him. Without a word he had walked away, leaving the door open. On a hostile galley, isolated at sea, a locked door was pointless. Demades had slammed the door shut in defiance and it had remained that way for the rest of the journey.

Demades's initial thoughts had dwelt on the injustice of his plight. His bitterness and sense of hopelessness soon gave way to fear, not only of Cronus and the words Gisco had spoken, but also fear of the Romans. He realized the Carthaginians were setting some kind of trap for the Romans and, although he had no idea what form that trap would take, he knew that his city was the bait. As the presenter of that lure, Demades's involvement would be synonymous with the trap. He was caught between the two opposing forces and the realization made him sick to his stomach. Whichever course he took, if he betrayed the Carthaginians to the Romans or the Romans to the Carthaginians, his life and the lives of his family would be forfeit if he did not find a way to avoid his fate.

Atticus watched Gaius swing the rudder to port and the *Aquila* turned neatly around the headland into the harbour at Ostia. The helmsman straightened the tiller and adjusted the ship's trim to line her up with the *castrum*, now crowded with the twenty galleys of the newly formed *Classis Romanus*, the Fleet of Rome.

The activity of the traders and merchants of the port seemed reinvigorated at the sight of the anchored fleet, as if its very presence had eradicated the Carthaginian threat in the south, and ships sailed purposefully and confidently out under the offshore breeze for the far-flung ports of the Mediterranean. The *Aquila*'s course took her through some of the busiest parts of the harbour, but rather than before when the *Aquila* had had to weave her way between ships, those same ships now changed their course to make way for the military galley.

Atticus had been ordered to Ostia by Tuditanus to further the training of the command crews of the new fleet, a task he did not relish given that those same trainees were now captains in their own right and not subject to Atticus's orders. He had a feeling they would not be as responsive as they had been before and, given that some had been blatantly unco-operative in the first place, their further training relied almost completely on any respect they had for his experience, a respect he knew in some cases did not exist.

Septimus was also in Ostia, having joined his *optio*, Quintus, the day before and, as the *Aquila* approached the dockside, Atticus could see the familiar figure of the centurion standing beside his opposite number from the V maniple of the Fourth.

The day's training would involve teaching boarding techniques to the legionaries under the guise of demonstrating how the Carthaginians boarded enemy galleys. It would be the legionaries' first taste of boarding, albeit in calm waters and without heavy battle armour, but it would be realistic, and the hope was that this realism would speed the training process. As the *Aquila* docked, the gangway was lowered to allow the men on board. They tramped up the gangway in single file. None seemed enthusiastic about the day ahead.

One hundred yards away, the ship bearing the men from Lipara reached the crowded docks. Cronus stood at the head of the gangway with the barge's captain.

'If we do not return you are to sail directly to Lipara and inform the admiral that we have been betrayed.'

The captain nodded as Cronus turned to Demades. 'Remember, Demades, that although you will have the opportunity to betray us once we are in the city, you will not be able to stop this barge from sailing with news of that betrayal. If the admiral receives such a message, your family will be immediately killed.'

Demades nodded, his fear and understanding evident. Cronus disembarked, followed by the sullen and silent Demades and then four of Gisco's, now Demades's, personal guard. Once they were ashore, the gangway was raised and the ship shoved off from the busy quayside to allow another ship to moor in her place.

'Wait here,' Cronus ordered, and strode off alone towards a livery to hire horses for the journey to Rome.

Demades stood in the centre of the four men, cut off from the frantic world around him by the constantly vigilant guards. As his eyes roamed over the teeming waters, he caught sight of a galley sailing apace into the *castrum*. His breath caught in his throat at the sight, his heart rate increasing as he recognized the pennant flying at the masthead. It was an eagle in flight, the namesake of the galley it soared above.

'The *Aquila*,' he breathed to himself, his mind racing, scarcely believing what he was seeing. Demades had not seen the galley in over two years, ever since Lipara had fallen into Carthaginian hands. The city had always been a prime target for the pirates who sailed the northern shores of Sicily, and so the *Aquila* had always been a welcome sight in the city's harbour, so much so that Demades knew the captain of the *Aquila* well.

'Let's go.'

The abrupt command broke into Demades's thoughts and he turned to see Cronus tower over him again. The Carthaginian grabbed the councillor by the arm and led him through the crowd towards the livery. Demades was forced to walk briskly to keep up with the taller man's stride; although the pace made it difficult for him to look back over his shoulder, Demades could not resist the temptation. The sight of the galley produced a tiny flicker of hope in him, a flame he nursed on the headlong gallop to Rome.

Scipio sat in silence as Duilius made his rebuttal. He was impressed with the junior consul, an emotion he rarely felt, but one he believed was warranted given the item being debated. Scipio was not involved in the debate itself, but he had surreptitiously engineered its acceptance on the agenda, something he was very pleased with given the awkward position it put Duilius in.

The Senate was debating the levying of taxes to fund the construction of the new fleet, specifically, in this case, the application of a new tax on produce sold in the markets. If effected, it would be diplomatically called the 'rescue tax', in reference to the legions trapped behind the blockade in Sicily, a name the Senate hoped would make the tax more palatable to the populace. It would be a tax that would be borne in part by the buyer and in part by the vendor. As Duilius was the largest merchant in the city, he stood to lose a great deal of money if the tax was passed, especially if the vendor was chosen to pay the greater part. This put Duilius in a no-win situation. If he opposed the tax he would be seen as unpatriotic. If he let it pass without conditions he would end up paying a huge portion of the costs of the new fleet. To watch the political balancing act that Duilius was now forced to perform gave Scipio immense satisfaction.

As the junior consul retook his seat, another senator stood to address the chamber and the debate continued. It was then that Scipio's eye caught Longus moving across the chamber towards a man who had just appeared at the entrance to the Curia. Scipio watched the two in conversation, remembering the junior senator well and the contrived speech he had given that had started the ten-day-long debate on the decision to build the fleet.

'Councillor Demades?' Longus said as he approached the man, confirming his recognition of the familiar figure he had spied from across the chamber.

'Senator Longus,' Demades replied, relieved to see a familiar face.

On the one occasion Demades had addressed the Senate, Longus had been present as a member of the Senate committee responsible for trade with the Aeolian Islands, of which Lipara was one. The junior senator had taken the responsibility very seriously, an attitude reflected in the councillor from Lipara, and the two men had formed a connection. It was this familiarity that Demades now clung to as he tried to control his nerve.

'I need to speak with the senior consul immediately,' Demades said, before looking over his shoulder at Cronus standing outside the columned entrance.

Like the other armed men of the personal guard, Cronus was barred from entering the chamber by the senatorial guard. The brief seconds out of their presence had emboldened Demades, and he had considered the idea of alerting Longus to their true identity – but the almost imperceptible shake of the head that Cronus had given him, as if he could read his thoughts, banished the idea from his mind, and he committed himself once more to this part of the Carthaginians' plan. The safety of himself and his family was paramount.

'What is it?' Longus asked, sensing Demades's trepidation, suspicious of a man who before had been an ally but now came from an island under the enemy's control.

'Lipara wishes to form an alliance with Rome,' Demades said in a rush.

'What?' Longus said, incredulous. 'You're sure?'

'Yes, of course I'm sure,' Demades replied forcefully, his fear making him irrational.

Longus was taken aback by the unusual intensity of the man, but he instantly dismissed it as irrelevant. If what he said was true then Rome was poised to make a huge strategic gain over the enemy. The councillor had asked for the senior consul, but Longus had no intention of informing Scipio. His first loyalty was to Duilius.

'Wait here,' Longus said and he turned to re-enter the chamber. As he did so he collided with Scipio, who suddenly came out from behind a pillar.

'No need to find me, Longus,' Scipio said, his caustic voice signifying his belief that the junior senator had not been going to deliver the message directly to its intended source, at least not until after Duilius had heard it.

'Come with me, Councillor,' Scipio said, and brushed past Longus, leading Demades through a small archway to an antechamber beyond. Longus could only look on in exasperation as the councillor was led away. Only when the two men were out of sight did his wits return and he ran into the crowded chamber.

'Why?' Scipio asked, trying to keep his expression neutral, struggling to keep his mounting excitement under control.

He listened as Demades outlined the reasons that Gisco had told him to recite. They were plausible in themselves, although Scipio would have been content if no reasons for defection had been forthcoming. For him the mere chance of glory was proving too great a temptation, and he had to force himself to think about the proposal rationally.

The opportunity was almost too good to be true. According to Demades, the island was there for the taking, with only a small Carthaginian garrison in the city itself and no naval presence in the area. It would be the new fleet's first victory, minor given the odds, but major given the island's strategic location as a naval base off the northern coast of Sicily. More importantly, it would be Scipio's first victory, and the first step on his road to absolute power. It might even help the legions, he thought sardonically.

His thoughts were interrupted by the arrival of Duilius in the antechamber, flanked by a small number of senators, Longus amongst them.

'Senior Consul,' Duilius began, 'I just heard the news.'

'Yes, Senator,' Scipio replied. 'Given the importance of the city, I plan on sailing immediately with the twenty galleys of the new fleet to take possession of the island.'

'Senator,' Duilius replied, thinking fast, 'the situation is too dangerous for you to expose yourself. As per the Senate's resolution, I must be the one to command the expedition.'

'I see no danger, Duilius,' Scipio replied confidently. 'The island is undefended and is willing to defect. Councillor Demades will testify to the fact that there is no Carthaginian naval presence in the area. Taking the island under our protection will be a mere formality.'

'We must put the decision to the Senate,' Duilius said, knowing he had a chance of reversing Scipio's decision in the chamber.

'No!' Scipio said, suddenly angry. 'There will be no debate. You forget yourself, Duilius. As strategic commander of the fleet I am in charge here and I have determined there is no danger. Therefore I will sail at once.'

'I must protest, Scipio,' Duilius said.

'Protest as you wish, Duilius. In fact I give you leave to debate my decision in the Senate. While you are discussing my actions, I will be on my way to free the people of Lipara.'

With that, Scipio strode past the hamstrung Duilius, pushing his way through the knot of senators behind the junior consul. Demades watched him go. He had set the trap and the Romans had fallen prey. Now it was time to save himself.

'You surely don't need a personal guard in Rome,' Longus said, half looking over his shoulder at the five men following himself and Demades.

'One never knows,' Demades said, thinking fast. 'The news I carried from Lipara would be seen as a betrayal by the Carthaginians. I need protection from assassins.'

Longus laughed at the suggestion, confident that there were no Carthaginians in Rome.

Earlier Longus had watched Duilius storm out of the Senate and head towards his own town house. He was furious at the defeat of his mentor at the hands of the senior consul and was still wondering how he could reverse Scipio's decision to sail to Lipara. He realized all he could do was wait for Duilius to summon him to his aid and hope that when the time came he could be of service. As the antechamber had emptied, Longus had noticed the lone figure of Demades, his presence forgotten by all in the heat of the moment. Demades had immediately approached the senator and asked him for his assistance, although at the time he would not say what assistance was required. Longus agreed and now led the councillor to his modest town house at the foot of the Palatine Hill.

On their arrival, Longus summoned a servant to show Demades to the guest quarters, with instructions thereafter to show the personal guard to the servants' quarters.

'I will accompany you into your room,' Demades's guard commander said suddenly.

'You will hold your tongue,' Longus stormed, amazed at the blatant insubordination.

'It's all right, Senator Longus,' Demades blurted, stepping forward, his voice nervous, 'the commander only fears for my safety.'

'You are entirely safe within these walls,' Longus retorted, insulted by the insinuation that his house was not safe, and taken aback by Demades's defence of the errant officer.

'Yes, of course,' Demades replied, again caught between conflicting forces. One look at Cronus confirmed the course he had to take.

'But, Longus, I promised my wife that I would keep a guard with me at all times. I do not wish to break my word.'

Longus paused for a moment, ashamed by Demades's obvious

trepidation, embarrassed that the man was so concerned about the good graces of his wife. Demades noted the disgust on Longus's face and bit back the feeling of humiliation.

'So be it,' Longus said. 'Please join me in the main dining room when you are refreshed,' he added before stalking off, musing all the while on how much Demades had changed since their last encounter.

Cronus waited until the Roman left before escorting Demades into his quarters.

'Curse you, Demades, why are we here?' he hissed, pressing the councillor against the wall as he held his neck firm in his hand.

'I had to come,' Demades spluttered, the pressure on his throat frightening. 'Longus insisted I accept his hospitality before making the return voyage to Lipara. To refuse would have been seen as an insult.'

Cronus snarled at the explanation, searching Demades's voice for signs of deception. He heard only fear. With one last squeeze of pressure he released the councillor. Demades fell to the ground, his hand massaging his damaged throat. He kept his eyes low, trying to hide the myriad of emotions he knew must be written on his face. If Cronus gained any inkling of what Demades was planning, he knew he would be dead in a heartbeat.

Septimus's face remained grim as yet another man failed to make the jump between the two galleys. The legionary's clambering hands on the side rail drew cheers from some of the men on the foredeck of the *Aquila* before he fell the ten feet to the water below.

'At least this one can swim,' Septimus muttered to himself as he watched the man make his way over to a waiting rope ladder. They had almost lost one of the men earlier, who had fallen like others before him to the cheers of all, but had not risen immediately after sinking below the water. Two sailors had been quick to realize that the man couldn't swim and they had dived in to rescue him. It had never occurred to Septimus that most of the men couldn't swim, a skill he took for granted having learned it in his childhood in the river Tiber.

The training was, as expected, proving to be slow and gruelling. The men were jumping without sword or shield or the extra weight of body armour, and yet many could not make the jump. They were brave soldiers, of that Septimus was sure, for the Fourth had a fearsome reputation; but like all men when faced with an unfamiliar danger, they lacked confidence. Even those who made the other side landed off balance, and in a fight would be easy prey for a defender. It was going to take a number of days at least until all would be able to make the jump with ease. Then Septimus would have to move on to the more difficult task of teaching the legionaries the vital tactics needed for the first frenzied moments of any boarding.

As the cheers died away and the next man prepared to make the jump, Septimus heard the loud call to order and all on deck immediately snapped to attention. Without moving his head he looked towards the gangway, which was now flanked by the familiar and unwelcome sight of the *praetoriani*. They stepped aside as Scipio came on board. The senior consul surveyed the assembled men.

'Soldiers of Rome,' he shouted so all could hear, 'we sail within the hour. Prepare to depart.'

Silanus saluted and ordered his men ashore. As one they obeyed and made their way onto the main deck and down the gangway to the dockside. They were followed by the command crews of the galleys, who had been under Atticus's tutelage on the main deck. Septimus strode to the dockside rail and looked along the quay. Black-cloaked *praetoriani* were fanning out along the docks, each one carrying the same message to the sailing crews as ship after ship came alive with activity. He was joined at the rail by Atticus.

'What do you think?' Atticus asked, puzzled by the order.

'I don't know,' Septimus replied, although he felt uneasy owing to the presence of Scipio himself.

Atticus turned to Lucius. 'Prepare to get under way.'

'Hold!' a voice said unexpectedly. It was Scipio, the overheard order causing him to stop halfway down the gangplank and spin around. His expression was hostile as he made his way back to the main deck.

'This galley is not part of the *Classis Romanus*, Perennis,' he spat. 'That honour is reserved for the new fleet only. I need men who will follow my every command without question; men who are loyal to Rome and the Senate. You and your crew are to remain in Ostia.'

'As you wish, Consul,' Atticus replied, struggling to keep his voice even.

Scipio turned and walked off the *Aquila* without another word.

Atticus and Septimus watched from the foredeck of the *Aquila* as the *Classis Romanus* raised sail and set course for the mouth of the harbour. The ships were moving in a loose formation, the more efficient crews outstripping others, although none dared to overtake the *Mars*, commanded by Scipio, at the head of the fleet. Septimus spotted Silanus on the main deck of the flagship with half of his maniple assembled behind him. He saluted the centurion and Silanus returned the gesture with a nod before turning away from the rail. The sight of the fleet under way had brought cheers from both the dockside and crews of the trading ships in the harbour, and the crews of the galleys had returned the gesture, even though they were unaware of their destination.

For security reasons the galley captains had simply been told to make ready to depart. No further details were made available and none would be forthcoming until the fleet was safely at sea. Only then would the crews learn of their mission. What they did know, however, was that the ships were now stocked with two days' worth of provisions. This was not unusual in itself – military galleys always carried a week's provisions as a matter of course – but this was the first time the fleet had taken on supplies, as before the men were fed in the mess halls of the *castrum*. If the fleet was only sailing to Fiumicino, as the men suspected, then why the need for supplies?

From Atticus's vantage point the course and position of the lead ships were lost in the confusion of galleys in formation, but he estimated they would be making the turn to starboard, and Fiumicino in the north, within minutes. The shape of the formation changed as the course correction was made, the galleys turning onto their new heading. Atticus could scarcely believe what he was seeing.

'Come about south,' Scipio ordered as the *Mars* cleared the mouth of Ostia harbour. Fulfidias issued the orders to his crew before turning to ensure the ships behind were matching his course.

'Southerly course as ordered, Consul.'

Scipio nodded, never taking his eyes off the fleet behind him. His chest seemed to fill with pride at the sight.

'Set course for the Aeolian Islands, Captain,' Scipio said as he left the aft-deck.

Fulfidias's mind raced as the last command sank in. The Aeolian Islands. Enemy territory. Only an hour before he had watched with amusement from the main deck of the *Aquila* as the legionaries of the Fourth made their first disastrous attempts at boarding. Now, as the fleet sailed into possibly hostile waters, Fulfidias wished he had not witnessed the training. Given time, he knew the legionaries would prove to be very capable at fighting in naval battles, but if they encountered the enemy on this voyage the time needed would never materialize. Fulfidias realized that if the fleet did encounter the Carthaginians, their only hope for survival would be to turn and run.

Gaius Duilius strode alone around the four sides of the atrium of his town house, his mind a whirl of thoughts as he tried in vain to find a way to turn the tide of battle once more in his favour. If round one had been his Senate victory, and round two Scipio's triumphal entrance into Ostia, then this was certainly round three, and once again Scipio was heading for victory. Duilius cursed the system that now held him fast, the very system he had so artfully controlled many times before but which now seemed intractable.

The Senate was unlikely to revoke Scipio's decision to sail to Lipara and, even if Duilius managed to raise the issue in debate, Scipio would have arrived at the island, liberated its people, set up a garrison and returned home in triumph before the senators of Rome were even ready to vote on the matter.

He had reviewed the idea of sailing with the fleet but, being second-in-command, and out of sight of the Senate where he enjoyed support, Duilius knew that Scipio would humiliate him by giving him command of the rear-guard, or a scouting vessel. Either way, without the certainty of battle on the horizon, Duilius would be unable to push his claim to be in

246

the vanguard of any action. As he walked, Duilius cursed the goddess of fortune for her fickle nature.

'One hour, Demades,' Cronus said, his voice agitated by the unwanted confinement within the senator's house, 'do you understand? One hour and then you make your excuses. Tell the Roman we will leave at dawn.'

Demades nodded, not trusting his voice. One hour was more than enough. What he had to say to Longus would take minutes only.

'And remember,' Cronus added, 'not a word to anyone, especially this senator. It may seem you are safe when not in my presence, Demades, but it only seems that way. If we do not return to Lipara safely, your family will be slaughtered.'

Demades left the Carthaginian alone in his room without another word and walked out to the atrium. He centred all his attention on keeping a measured stride, fearful that if he looked over his shoulder he would see Cronus watching his every move. As Demades entered the main dining room, he saw Longus, as protocol demanded, already waiting there to receive his guest. Demades forced a smile onto his face and Longus returned the gesture, although his face also showed a look of puzzlement at the councillor's obvious discomfort. As Demades sat down he looked towards the arched exit back to his quarters, his eyes lingering on the opening, trying to ascertain if Cronus had indeed followed him.

'I hope you find the guest accommodation to your satisfaction, Demades,' Longus said lightly.

Demades spun around, his face a mask of fear. 'I'm in mortal danger, Longus,' he exclaimed.

Longus was immediately taken aback. 'That's ridiculous, Demades,' he said. 'Get a hold of yourself, man. You are safely within my house. Apart from your own guard, I have twenty men stationed within the walls. You are untouchable while in my presence.'

Demades had turned to look at the entranceway again as the senator spoke and immediately shot around as Longus finished speaking.

'It is my guard who imperil me,' he explained to Longus's look of disbelief. 'They're not mine, they're Carthaginian!'

Longus was speechless, his mind trying to fully comprehend Demades's words.

'But how . . . ?'

'I was ordered here by the Carthaginian admiral, a man named Gisco, to tell the Senate that Lipara was willing to defect,' Demades explained, keeping his voice low, fearing Cronus's appearance.

'By the gods,' Longus exclaimed as the realization struck him. 'Then that means . . .'

'Your fleet is sailing into a trap,' Demades said, his voice broken under the admission.

Longus immediately shot up from his seat.

'Guards! Guards! To me!' he yelled.

'No!' Demades shouted, fear coursing through him. 'My guards will hear.'

'To Hades with you and your guards,' Longus said as the approaching sound of running feet could be heard beyond the room.

From the guest quarters, Cronus clearly heard the cry of alarm from within the depths of the house. Instinct immediately took over his actions as he drew his sword and ran to the door of the room. He opened the door in time to see two of the house guards rush through the atrium to the dining room beyond, their destination, the source of the call to arms. Demades had betrayed them, there was no other explanation.

As Cronus slipped out of the room he cursed his own stupidity for allowing the councillor out of his sight. He had thought Demades a fool, a coward who was subdued to the point of total obedience; however, he had been wrong. Cronus knew he would pay for his mistake with his life, surrounded as he was on all sides by hostile forces. With a warrior's cold detachment he accepted his fate, muttering a brief homage to Mot, the god of death in whose presence he would soon be. As he slipped into the atrium, his mind listening to the heated voices in the main dining room, he whispered a second prayer to Tanit, the Punic goddess of fortune. His words to her were not a plea for his own safety, but rather a request to grant him the opportunity to have revenge on the man who had sealed his fate.

'You and you,' Longus ordered, 'guard this man.'

Two of the Roman guards stepped forward and stood on both sides of Demades.

The councillor protested, begging Longus for understanding and mercy, but the senator's ears were deaf to his words. More guards were arriving by the second, the alarm now spreading to the entire house. Longus ordered men to secure the room while others were dispatched to the guardhouse and guest quarters to apprehend the Carthaginians in their midst. The senator's final orders put steel and determination into the soldiers' actions. No quarter was to be given.

Cronus heard the heavy footfalls of running men as at least four passed the doorway behind which he was hidden. He opened the door a crack to see the four men charge open the door to Demades's room, roaring a battle cry as they did so to steel their nerves. Cronus knew it would take vital seconds before they realized their prey had fled. He shot out of the room and headed straight to the dining area not twenty yards away. The Roman guard stationed at the entrance was looking into the room, his back turned to Cronus, his attention drawn to a conversation in the room. The Carthaginian thanked Tanit for the opportunity he had prayed for.

'Don't you understand, Longus?' Demades pleaded. 'I had to do it. They would have killed me and my entire family if I had refused.'

'You are nothing,' Longus spat, 'your family are nothing.'

The senator paced the room, waiting for the cries of all-clear from the detachments sent to kill the Carthaginians. He turned back to Demades.

'You will accompany me to the house of Gaius Duilius. There you will tell him everything you know. Everything! If you try to deceive us again I will have you flayed alive.'

Demades ignored the threat, his mind past fearing the danger that surrounded him on all sides. What mattered now was making the Romans understand that he was on their side and that his family were in danger. Somewhere in his tormented mind he was sure the Romans would listen to reason.

As Cronus ran the last few yards towards the Roman guard, his left hand slipped a dagger from a sheath in the small of his back, rotating it until he held it overhand. At full tilt he plunged the knife down into the back of the Roman's neck, instantly severing the spinal column, the guard dead before he hit the floor. Cronus ran unchecked into the room beyond, his eyes taking in the details before him.

The room seemed full of Roman guards, his momentary glance insufficient to count them individually. His mind registered them as a group, his fighting instincts receiving the threat and calculating the odds. He had time for one sword thrust, one victim, knowing that by the time he withdrew and recovered he would be overwhelmed. He could take only one man with him beyond the gates of Hades. The choice was simple.

Demades spun around at the shout of warning from the main entranceway. His mind registered the oncoming man, Cronus's face a mask of rage and insanity, and the detail of Demades's surroundings seemed to fade as his entire being focused on the sight. His mind cleared, the pervasive fear he had felt dissipated in the certain knowledge that death was a heartbeat away.

Longus could only look on in horror as his guards continued to rain blows on the lifeless body of the Carthaginian. He had appeared out of nowhere, crossing the room in seconds, driving his sword to the hilt into Demades. The momentum of the charge had taken the councillor off his feet, carrying them both along until the Carthaginian fell onto his victim. The Carthaginian had made no effort to rise after the fall but had leaned into Demades and whispered something unintelligible. Only then did the Roman guards react, the first blows from their swords killing the Carthaginian instantly, the shock of the attack causing them to continue striking the inert body.

'Enough!' Longus shouted, his words bringing an end to the butchery.

'Senator!' a voice called, and Longus spun around to its source.

'The four Carthaginians in the guardroom have been killed, Senator,' the guard reported.

'Very well,' Longus announced, struggling to regain his composure after the incredible savagery he had just witnessed.

He cursed the death of Demades. Not because he believed

he deserved to live, but because he had value as a source of information regarding the Carthaginian plans in Lipara.

Longus began to stride from the room, a guard falling in behind him as he went. He dismissed his concern for the loss of Demades. It was true that he might have had some more use, but the reality was that he had delivered the most important piece of information at the outset. The Roman fleet was sailing into a trap.

Scipio stared at the sea opened out before him, the waters sparkling in the late-afternoon sun. He was alone on the foredeck, a position he had made his own on the ship, with orders to the *praetoriani* guarding the approach to the deck to let none pass without his express permission.

The senior consul held out his wine goblet and immediately a slave rushed forward with an amphora of wine to recharge his drink. He brought the goblet up to his mouth and took in the rich smell of the wine, a vintage from one of his own land-holdings north of Rome. Scipio's thoughts ran to the days ahead, days that would be filled with glory and personal success. Already he knew his consulship would be marked in history as one that witnessed tremendous adversity, adversity that he had and would overcome with fortitude and bravery. His immortality was already being assured, and Scipio would seize any chance to enhance the living legend being created. He knew that Sicily would give him that chance.

The Carthaginian invasion was a gift from the gods, an opportunity for Scipio to write his name into history. His father before him, Lucius Cornelius Scipio, had gone down in the annals as a great general, victor at the Battle of Volaterrae, conqueror of the Etruscans, a champion of Rome. He had been given the cognomen, Barbatus, conqueror of the Barbarians, and it was against this benchmark that the young consul now set his ambition. His position as senior consul gave him a guiding hand on the direction of his beloved Rome, a hand he fully intended to use to his own ends.

The arrival of a Carthaginian fleet off the northern coast of Sicily had thrown up a barrier to victory, but Scipio was unconcerned. He had faced many challenges in his life and had overcome them all. He was wholly confident that he could overcome the enemy fleet. He would bring order to Sicily and cast out the Carthaginian hordes. History would remember him as the conqueror of the Punici, founder of the Roman province of Sicily. Gnaeus Cornelius Scipio Sicilianus, he thought, testing an imagined cognomen. He liked it. Smiling, he raised his glass to make a silent toast to the future, and his destiny.

As he heard the shout, Gaius Duilius looked up from the table in his study, his shallow attention easily broken from the half-hearted attempt to immerse himself in matters other than the departure of the new fleet under Scipio's command. He listened intently, waiting with his breath held until he heard the call again. It was someone shouting his name. Duilius rose from behind his desk and walked out into the peristyle, the small, colonnaded garden at the back of his town house. From his position he looked down the long axis of the house through the main dining room and the atrium beyond. As his eyes focused on the distant point, he heard the call again, and then watched as a servant opened the main door of the house. Duilius immediately recognized Longus.

The junior senator pushed his way past the servant and entered the atrium, renewing his calls. Duilius frowned at the discourteous interruption. Longus was a useful ally, one that had proved resourceful in the past, but he was also sycophantic, a fawning, immature man who constantly looked to the junior consul for guidance. Duilius recalled that when he was Longus's age he was already a self-made man and owner of the largest estate in Rome.

Duilius walked into the main dining room to intercept the young senator. He moved in silence, refusing to raise his voice in an uncivil manner even as Longus destroyed the tranquillity of his house. Longus spotted him from the atrium and made towards him, his face a mask of concern mixed with relief at having found his mentor.

'Thank the gods you are here, Consul,' he began.

'What is it, Longus?' Duilius cut across irritably.

'The fleet are sailing into a trap.'

For a second Duilius did not register the words, their meaning seemingly impossible.

'A trap?'

'Yes, Consul. The councillor from Lipara, Demades, informed me.'

Again Duilius paused. 'Where is this councillor now?'

'Dead. Killed by his own guard. They were Carthaginians.'

Duilius absorbed the information, his mind dismissing impractical questions, searching as always for the crux of the problem. There was a trap. The fleet were unaware. Time was against him. He instantly decided which problem needed to be tackled first. Time.

'Saddle two of my fastest horses,' he shouted to an attendant nearby. The man rushed away, the urgency of the order infectious.

'Longus, you and I will ride to Ostia. With luck there will be a galley there to take us south in pursuit of the fleet. As they are unaware, they will not be rushed. We may yet catch them.'

Duilius walked out into the atrium and looked up into the afternoon sky. Scipio had left Rome hours before. Even

254

allowing for time to prepare the fleet, the head start seemed insurmountable.

Atticus looked out over the now unfamiliar sight of the empty *castrum* dock at Ostia. It was an hour before sunset and the crew of the *Aquila* were using the last of the day's light to make final preparations for the galley's planned return to Fiumicino at dawn. Atticus's eyes ranged over their activities without absorbing the detail, his mind firmly fixed on the sudden departure and unknown course of the *Classis Romanus*.

His thoughts were interrupted by the sound of approaching horses and he turned to see two men arrive at speed. They were experienced horsemen, weaving their mounts along the approach paths to the docks, avoiding the stockpiles of military supplies that littered the whole area. Atticus walked from the foredeck to the head of the gangway in anticipation of their arrival. The horsemen stopped directly beside the *Aquila* and both men dismounted.

'Sailor,' the older of the two shouted, 'where is the captain of this vessel?'

'I'm the captain,' Atticus replied, 'Captain Perennis.'

The older man nodded and strode up the gangway, ignoring the protocol that dictated that all should first ask for permission before boarding. Atticus backed away from the head of the gangway, giving the approaching men room to come onto the main deck. Both wore senatorial robes, although it was obvious that the younger man deferred to the older.

'Captain Perennis,' the older man began, 'when can you be ready to sail?'

'On whose orders?' Atticus replied, asserting his authority as captain.

'On mine, Gaius Duilius, junior consul of the Senate of Rome.'

Atticus immediately noted the unyielding, authoritative voice and bearing.

'Within thirty minutes, Consul,' he replied.

'Very well, Captain, make it so.'

Atticus turned and issued curt orders to his ever-attentive second-in-command. The crew redoubled their efforts to finish preparing the galley, the imminent departure changing nothing except their pace. A runner was sent below to find Septimus.

'What is our destination, Senator?' Atticus asked as the activity intensified around him.

Duilius turned and weighed the question, determining how much the captain needed to know at this stage. The young man before him seemed competent, his position as captain of one of Rome's military vessels a testament to his unseen abilities. He judged him to be in his early thirties, maybe a year or two younger than he was. Duilius had himself risen to the heights of his own world at that age. The man before him had done the same. If achievements mark the man, then the captain could be trusted.

The junior consul nodded towards the aft-deck and led Atticus and Longus to a quiet spot by the starboard rail.

'I need you to sail with all possible speed in pursuit of the new fleet, Captain,' Duilius began. 'We have learned they are sailing into a trap set by the Carthaginians.'

'By the gods,' Atticus whispered, 'what is their destination?'

'Lipara.'

Atticus nodded, his abrupt question and the lack of further unnecessary queries justifying Duilius's judgement of his character.

'If you'll excuse me, Senators, I'll have one of my men show you to the main cabin,' Atticus said, and left the two senators alone on the aft-deck.

256

He went directly to the main deck to coordinate the preparation of the ship, his heart pounding in his chest as his thoughts went to the untried and unaware fleet sailing south.

The *Aquila* shoved off from the Ostia docks twenty minutes later, her full complement of crew and marines on board. The two senators joined Septimus and Atticus on the aft-deck as the galley cleared the busy inner harbour under oar power. Directly ahead the sun was setting rapidly, its golden light causing all to shield their eyes against the glare. Gaius kept both hands steady on the tiller, his eyesight seemingly unaffected as he nimbly wove the galley through the obstacle course of the Republic's busiest port.

As the *Aquila* reached the mouth of the harbour, the protective headland to the north slipped behind them, exposing their beam to the full force of the northerly wind. Atticus called for the oars to be shipped and the mainsail raised as Gaius adjusted his course southwards. The orders were carried out with alacrity, and Duilius noted the efficiency, wondering why Scipio had not taken such an obviously competent crew on his voyage south. The *Aquila* shot ahead under full sail, making twelve knots as her spear-like bow cut through the white horses of the wave tips.

Atticus noted the intense stare of Duilius as he looked ahead to the darkening horizon. Lipara was no more than thirty-six hours to the south. Scipio's considerable head start was now weighed against the experienced crew of the *Aquila*. The galleys themselves were evenly matched, the *Aquila*'s design copied in every hull of the *Classis Romanus*. Only the crews were different, with men new to their galleys set against men such as Gaius and Lucius, who'd spent countless hours minutely adjusting the trim of the *Aquila* to garner every knot of speed from the wind.

Atticus found himself matching the intense stare of the senator as he looked to the horizon ahead. He remained silent, knowing there would be plenty of time to question the consul on what was known of the trap. Right now those questions took second place to the immediate need to ensure that his galley was running at her top speed. Within fifteen minutes the water around them was shrouded in darkness, the night's arrival seemingly portentous, the obscure seascape suppressing the hope of the men standing on the aft-deck of the *Aquila*.

CHAPTER TWELVE

From the main cabin in the *Mars*, Scipio clearly heard the call of land sighted on the port quarter. He consulted the maps laid out before him, his finger running down the line of the ship's course as described by the captain the day before. Fulfidias had estimated that the *Mars* would sight the volcanic island of Stromboli at the beginning of the third day and now, an hour after dawn, the ship was indeed sailing past the island.

Scipio noticed the sulphuric stench infusing the air in the cabin and he went on deck to see the famed island that he had never laid eyes on before. The legendary volcano rose over three thousand feet above the sea, its summit constantly spewing out noxious smoke that seemed to fill the entire eastern sky off the port bow.

Scipio approached Fulfidias.

'Report, Captain.'

'We are an hour short of Lipara, Consul. Our next land sighting will be Euonymos, and immediately after that we will be able to see the island of Lipara.'

Scipio nodded. 'Call me when we pass Euonymos,' he said, and returned to his cabin.

*

'Land ahead, three degrees off the port bow!'

Atticus glanced up at the masthead lookout and followed his pointed hand to the low cloud ahead on the eastern horizon.

Stromboli.

He rubbed his tired eyes with his thumb and forefinger, the morning sun seemingly brighter than usual after the darkness of the pre-dawn.

'Anything?' a voice beside him enquired.

Atticus turned to see Duilius standing beside him, the consul's bloodshot eyes testament to the sleepless night shared by all on board the *Aquila*.

Atticus shook his head before returning his full concentration to the horizon ahead.

Fifteen minutes later the *Aquila* was parallel to Stromboli, the half-mile-high volcano hiding the morning sun and casting a three-mile-long shadow across the sea through which the galley sailed at speed.

'An hour from Lipara,' Atticus thought.

'Lucius, what's our speed?'

The second-in-command signalled the drop of the marker on the foredeck and counted aloud until it passed his position on the aft-deck, one hundred and twenty feet from the start point. He closed his eyes momentarily to calculate.

'A shade over ten knots, Captain.'

'Orders to below, engage oars at attack speed. Once rhythm has been established, accelerate to ramming speed.'

'Yes, Captain,' Lucius replied and went below to the slave deck.

From the aft-deck, Atticus clearly heard the drum master call the slaves to order, making them ready to engage. It was a tricky manoeuvre, one only an experienced crew of oarsmen could accomplish. At attack speed their stroke was eleven knots, one faster than the wind. Their first stroke would have to be perfect, with each oar hitting the water simultaneously, otherwise the current of water flowing past the ship would foul any oar out of sequence. There was no margin for error. Atticus waited for the order to engage to be given, holding his breath until the drum beat started. The order to engage was coupled with the first beat and two hundred oars hit the water as one. The *Aquila* took on the extra knot of speed with ease. Within a minute the order for ramming speed was given and the *Aquila* reached her top speed of thirteen knots.

'How long can your slaves maintain this speed?' Duilius asked, watching the manoeuvre intently.

'Five minutes under normal circumstances,' Atticus began. 'However, with the wind taking the lion's share of ten knots, the rowers only have to make up the additional three. The tempo is as high as ramming speed but the effort is greatly reduced.'

Again Duilius nodded, his face reflecting his admiration and understanding of the skill required for such an operation.

Atticus noted the unspoken compliment. In the brief time he had known Duilius, he had begun to form a very different opinion of senators from the one Scipio had ingrained in him.

The *Aquila* sailed past the island of Euonymos at thirteen knots, her every stroke taking her closer to Lipara. Atticus stood with Septimus and Duilius on the foredeck, the three men searching the sea ahead in silence. Atticus was tempted to increase the oar-stroke to beyond ramming speed, a move made possible given the trailing wind. It was a highly dangerous manoeuvre, though, one he had seen carried out only once before – and that with disastrous consequences. Above ramming speed the individual beats on the drum began to merge and the guiding rhythm, so important in keeping two hundred men working in unison, could be easily lost. Atticus dismissed the idea with reluctance. He would have to rely on their current speed and pray to Fortuna that they would be in time.

'Ships ahead!'

The entire crew looked to the masthead at the call, each man following the line indicated by the lookout to the horizon dead ahead.

'How far?' Atticus called up.

'I estimate five miles, Captain, sailing in line-astern formation, just short of Lipara harbour.'

'*Stercus!*' Atticus spat. 'Too far to signal.'

'We're too late,' Septimus said aloud to himself, speaking the dread words that all felt.

'Maintain course and speed,' Duilius said, 'perhaps the Carthaginian trap is not set to be sprung. We may yet reach them in time.'

Atticus nodded, wanting the possibility to exist.

Scipio surveyed the seemingly quiet city of Lipara from the aft-deck of the *Mars* as the galley entered the crescent-shaped harbour. The city stood in the centre of the bay, the land rising sharply behind to create a series of undulating hills stretching northwards along the spine of the island. What activity there had been on the docks had ceased at the sight of the Roman galleys approaching the mouth of the harbour, and so the trading ships that were moored to the quay stood quiet and forlorn. Scipio smiled as he imagined the panic now unfolding in the Carthaginian garrison somewhere deep within the city.

The *Mars* hove to in the centre of the bay, the other galleys deploying left and right in line-abreast formation. Scipio had personally chosen the formation, remembering the impact the sight had had on the people of Ostia, a sight that would inspire fear in the heart of any enemy standing on the shoreline. The senior consul experienced a feeling of anticlimax at the ease of their approach. Once back in Rome he would need to embellish his report on the capture of the city, if only to satisfy the city's appetite for glory. A victory easily won was not a tale worth telling.

Scipio waited impatiently as the inexperienced crews manoeuvred their galleys in the confines of the harbour. Although the ships were under oar power, their efforts seemed uncoordinated and clumsy. The simple transformation of the fleet from line astern to line abreast was still incomplete when Scipio's patience ended.

'Standard speed!'

The *Mars* got under way, her advance matched by the galleys flanking her position. Scipio adjusted the folds of his toga, readying himself for disembarkation.

Duilius watched in hopeless silence as the last of the *Classis Romanus* breached the harbour mouth four miles ahead. The Roman galleys were moving with intent, but without haste, allowing all on board the *Aquila* to grasp on to the slim hope that the trap could yet be averted.

Atticus, his years at sea compelling him to be ever vigilant, continued to scan the four quarters of the horizon for any sight of an approaching enemy.

'There!' his mind screamed as he caught a flicker of movement off the southernmost tip of the island, a headland less than a mile from the harbour.

'Ships off the port forequarter!' the lookout called, all eyes turning to where Atticus's gaze was already rooted.

'Carthaginians!' Atticus said, the unfurled masthead banners confirming the already realized truth. 'Moving at attack speed.'

Atticus counted ten galleys, with more rounding the head-land with every stroke of their oars. They were led by a quinquereme, an alpha male leading the attack wolves unerr-ingly to their prey.

'All stop!' Duilius said suddenly.

Atticus hesitated for a heartbeat before relaying the order to the crew. The sail was immediately collapsed and the *Aquila*'s oars brought her to a complete stop within three galley-lengths.

'Your orders, Consul?' Atticus asked, urgency in his voice, knowing that every second counted. Septimus stood beside him, his hand holding the grip of his sword tightly, the prox-imity of the enemy heightening his readiness.

'Set course for Rome, Captain,' Duilius answered, his voice laced with futile anger.

Atticus and Septimus made to protest, but Duilius cut them short, anticipating their words.

'I cannot compound Scipio's fate by sailing into Lipara. If both he and I fall into enemy hands the fleet will be leader-less. Our priority is Rome and the legions of Sicily. One extra Roman galley at Lipara will not stave off defeat.'

Atticus had been making ready to retort but he stayed his words, surprised by Duilius's explanation of his decision, the consul's honesty creating trust, the collaborative style of command encouraging compliance.

'That fool Scipio,' Longus spat, 'he deserves the fate his pride has led him to.'

'But the fleet does not,' Duilius cursed, slamming his fist down on the side rail. 'They are Romans. Men who answered the call of their city. They should not die like rats in a trap.'

Atticus nodded imperceptibly at Duilius's words, the under-lying belief striking a chord with his growing connection to Rome.

'Bring her about, Gaius!' he ordered, his faith in the consul's vision enabling his obedience to the command. 'Set course for Rome.'

The *Aquila* swung neatly as her oars engaged, the crew silent as the full realization of their failure to catch the *Classis Romanus* struck home. Behind them the Carthaginian quinquereme rounded the mouth of Lipara, her hull down in the calm waters of the inner harbour.

Atticus and Septimus continued to look over the aft-rail as the *Aquila* retreated northwards under oars, the familiarity of the scene imposing a silence on both men. The faces of the command crews and marine centurions of the *Classis Romanus* swept through their minds, the faces of men already lost, men already mourned. Within minutes the details of the horizon were lost in the distance and the inevitable defeat was accepted.

'Enemy ships astern!'

Scipio spun around at the sound of the strident call. Over three hundred yards away five galleys were rounding the southern headland into the bay, with a dozen more in pursuit. They were led by a colossal ship, a quinquereme that towered over the triremes surrounding her. All were tearing through the water, rounding the headland in the time it took for panic to spread throughout the Roman fleet. Carthaginian war cries split the air and Scipio's stomach tightened at the sound. The veneer of a Roman consul fell away to be replaced with his experience as a legionary commander.

'Captain! Evasive manoeuvres! Centurion! Form ranks, prepare for battle.'

Scipio registered the centurion's salute and affirmation as he responded instantly to the command.

Fulfidias, however, did not respond. Scipio whipped around, taking his eyes off the enemy to find the captain standing motionless, his eyes locked on the approaching Carthaginian galleys, a look of sheer terror on his face. Scipio struck him hard across the face, the open-handed blow knocking Fulfidias off balance. The captain regained his stance and looked at Scipio, his expression of panic unchanged.

'Captain!' Scipio shouted. 'Get control of yourself and this galley or I'll have you thrown over the side.'

Fulfidias reacted. 'Drum master!' Scipio heard him roar above the cacophony of sound enveloping the panicked ship. 'Full ahead. Ramming speed!'

The *Mars* lurched forward as the oars bit into the calm waters of the harbour.

Scipio was given an instant to survey the Roman fleet, expecting to see the other galleys break formation and prepare to engage the enemy. His expectation was wrong.

Gisco bellowed at the top of his voice as he echoed the war cry of the men assembled on the foredeck of the *Melqart*. The sword in his hand felt light and he held it above his head to renew the frenzied cries of his crew, the sound filling his warrior soul. From the moment the lookouts on the heights above Lipara had signalled the arrival of the Roman fleet, Gisco had felt the exhilaration of battle rise within him. The Carthaginian fleet of twenty galleys had been moored in the village of Pianoconte, a mere two miles around the southern-most headland and completely hidden from any vessel entering the harbour of Lipara. When the *Melqart* had rounded the headland, Gisco's heart had soared at the sight of the Roman galleys formed in line abreast, facing away from the mouth of the harbour. The formation seemed an act of madness, an asinine deployment that left the ships entirely vulnerable to the type of attack Gisco was now employing. The arrival of the Carthaginian galleys had transformed the scene into one of sheer chaos.

At the northern end of the fleet a number of Roman galleys were already racing towards the beach, skirting that end of the city in order to beach their ships and escape on land. Gisco had anticipated a possible fight on land and so had deployed two thousand soldiers within the city. With the Romans in disarray, their capture was inevitable. Gisco laughed out loud at the sight of the remaining galleys attempting to turn to engage his own fleet. No more than four ships had got under way in a manner that seemed to suggest competency and, as he watched, one of them endeavoured to ram a Carthaginian trireme one hundred yards off his starboard bow. The Roman's trajectory was hopelessly inaccurate and the ram merely bounced off the heavier hull of the target. Gisco smiled malevolently as the crew of the Carthaginian trireme grappled the Roman ship and boarded her, reversing the attack the Romans had forfeited through their incompetence.

The smile was once more wiped from Gisco's face as his eyes searched for the other three ships that were showing signs of a determined resistance.

'Orders to the helm,' he shouted, 'turn two degrees starboard. Intercept and ram the Roman ship closest to the dock.'

Seconds later, the course of the *Melqart* adjusted under Gisco's feet as the quinquereme pointed her bow at a gap left in the centre of the Roman line by one of the few ships that had had the good sense to break formation and give themselves steerage space. As the galley raced through the gap, Gisco looked left and right to the Roman triremes. The starboard ship was entangled with another, while the port one seemed simply incapacitated by the total panic of her crew.

'Archers!' Gisco shouted, his men immediately loosing volley after volley into the stricken crews, their aim deadly at the short range.

The *Melqart* emerged from the gap at attack speed, her course once again changing as the helmsman bore down on the lone Roman trireme ahead of them. Gisco felt the surge of pace as the galley moved to ramming speed. He looked down at the six-foot bronze ram splitting the wave tops in front of the rushing galley, its squared face racing ahead of the ship in its haste to sink itself into the enemy's hull. Gisco raised his eyes once more to the Roman galley, desperately trying to flee parallel to the shoreline. He sheathed his sword and gripped the rail before him, tensing his body for the impending impact. At fourteen knots the momentum of the ship would drive all six feet of the ram into the Roman galley.

Scipio felt the deck of the *Mars* heel over beneath him as he watched the Carthaginian quinquereme speed through the Roman line. He spun around to look for Fulfidias, enraged that the captain was looking for an avenue of escape when all around them Roman galleys were locked in a chaotic, desperate fight with the Carthaginians. The enemy were spreading out to pick off individual targets and, as Scipio watched, a Carthaginian galley rammed a Roman trireme amidships, the crack of the impact filling the air, the sound immediately followed by the dread cry of the Punici boarding party as they swept onto the stricken ship. Scipio knew that if the *Mars* was to survive she needed to turn into the fight, not flee before it, and his eyes searched the aft-deck for the spineless captain.

The first drop in speed came suddenly, a barely perceptible drain, as if the galley had somehow snagged on an underwater obstacle that was sapping her strength. Scipio immediately noticed the change and he searched for the cause, his mind suddenly registering the ever-increasing whip cracks from the slave decks below as the rowers were whipped to comply with the impossible task of maintaining ramming speed, an order issued by Fulfidias the moment the oars had engaged over five long minutes before. Scipio cursed the idiot, realizing he had expected Fulfidias to be every bit as competent as the captain of the *Aquila*.

'Commander,' Scipio said, his praetorian guard standing by his side with their shields raised, 'form up around me. We are about to be boarded.'

The commander saluted and the ten praetorian guards formed a ring around the consul, their black *scutum* shields creating a fortification against the coming onslaught. Scipio looked to the main deck to see the legionaries of the Fourth formed up ready to repel the enemy. Their faces were set in the legionaries' blank expression of battle, discipline holding them firm, bravery giving them resolve. The senior consul turned again to the enemy ship. It was upon them.

The six-foot ram of the *Melqart* struck the side of the *Mars* with a terrifying crack, its unyielding bronze striking deep in a killer blow that drove to the very core of the smaller ship. The ram split the deck beneath the rowers, crushing the slaves like grain under a millstone, their cries mingling with the tortured sound of the ship. The momentum of the Carthaginian galley drove the trireme up onto the cutwater of the larger ship, the impact throwing all on the deck of the *Mars* off their feet, as if the hammer of Vulcan had fallen amongst them.

Like a dark wave of Hades, the Carthaginians spilled over the forerail of the *Melqart* onto the deck of the Roman galley, their war cries renewed in the battle frenzy of attack. The men of the Fourth were immediately on their feet, but they found themselves instantly overwhelmed, their sixty outmatched by the scores of Punic warriors still pouring from the Carthaginian flagship. Within minutes each legionary was fighting for his life. All sense of order was lost in the Roman ranks as men fought desperately against overpowering odds.

The lone voice of a Roman centurion cut through the air to rally his legionaries into a coherent unit and the men summoned innate battle tactics as they tried to adopt a unified defensive position, their career-long training giving them a moment's respite. It did not last.

The Carthaginians pressed home their attack on the main deck, their superior numbers and ferocity keeping the balance firmly on their side. The Romans struggled to build an effective defensive wall on the confined deck, and time and again their flanks were exposed. The Roman commander's attempt to rally his troops died on the end of a Punic sword and, to the last man, the legionaries of the Fourth fell under the Carthaginian assault.

Scipio took another step backwards as a fresh wave of Carthaginians attacked his small band of *praetoriani*. They had been largely ignored during the Carthaginians' first onslaught, with only individuals or small groups of two and three peeling off from the main attack to seek out other targets on the blood-soaked deck. His guard was down to seven men, a pitiful number that would be instantly overwhelmed the moment the legionaries' defence collapsed on the main deck, freeing the entire Carthaginian horde to seek out new prey. Scipio stumbled over an inert body as he moved towards the stern rail and he looked down to see the captain, Fulfidias, lying supine on the deck, an arrow buried deep in his neck. His face was fixed in a grotesque scream, the expression robbing him of dignity, revealing the terror the man had experienced at the moment of death. Scipio spat on the man, cursing his incompetence.

Another of Scipio's guards fell and a Carthaginian warrior charged through the gap, his sword raised for the killing blow. Scipio deftly sidestepped the swipe and brought his own dagger up in an underhand blow into the lower back of his attacker.

The knife drove deep into the kidneys of the Carthaginian, a gush of dark blood confirming the strike. Scipio twisted the knife and withdrew it, pushing the man aside and readying himself for the next attack. A cheer from the main deck signalled the final defeat of the legionaries and the knot of men on the main deck dispersed to fan out over the ship. Scipio spotted a large group heading for the aft-deck and he bent down to pick up the sword of a fallen praetorian, stepping forward into the line formed by the four remaining guards, ready to die with his men.

'Hold!'

The bellowed order split the air and the Carthaginians checked their attack. Scipio did not understand the shouted order in Punic but he realized its significance and he searched the crowd of blood-soaked warriors for their commander. The Carthaginians parted and a solid bull of a man strode forward, his bearded face matted with sweat. He was older than Scipio, by at least a dozen years, but he carried himself with the bearing of a commander. He stood directly opposite Scipio and looked him up and down, his face fixed in a crooked smile. He turned to his men and issued more orders in incomprehensible Punic. The men rushed forward and struck at the four praetorian guards, taking them by surprise and killing them where they stood. Scipio roared a curse at the Carthaginian commander and readied himself once more. The commander laughed at the defiance.

'Put down your sword, Roman,' the Carthaginian said in fluent Latin.

Scipio did not move, his expression hard. The Carthaginian commander sheathed his own sword and walked forward until he was within range of Scipio's blade.

'I do not wish to kill you, Roman, you wear the robes of a senator. Who are you?'

Scipio drew himself to his full height.

'I am Gnaeus Cornelius Scipio, senior consul of the Roman Republic,' he said, speaking in a tone that reflected his disgust at having to address the Carthaginian commander. In the pause that followed, Scipio studied the man before him, wondering what fate the Carthaginian had in store for him.

The Punic commander smiled, a smile that did not reach his eyes but rather emphasized the loathing that dwelt behind the gaze. For the first time that day, as Scipio gazed upon the hate-filled expression, he felt fear in his heart.

Atticus looked out over the aft-rail of the *Aquila* as the last traces of the volcanic smoke disappeared in the southern sky, the island of Stromboli now twenty miles behind in their wake as the galley sped northwards towards a darkening horizon. The drum beat of standard speed infused the air, but to Atticus the sound went unnoticed, its staccato rhythm blended into the myriad of familiar sounds that he had known half his life. Only unusual sounds alerted his concentration, and so he turned abruptly as he heard Duilius approach. He stiffened to attention in anticipation of an order, but Duilius waved his hand.

'Stand easy, Captain,' he said, his voice lowered so as not to be overheard.

Atticus turned once more to the aft-rail and resumed his vigil. Duilius leaned on the rail beside him. Minutes passed.

'Do you think any will have escaped?' the consul asked.

Atticus simply shook his head, too weary to answer.

'You seem sure,' Duilius said, glancing sideways at Atticus.

Atticus stood upright and faced the consul, Duilius mirroring his stance.

'They never had a chance,' Atticus said, Duilius noting an underlying anger in the captain's voice, 'condemned men from the first day they arrived in Fiumicino.'

Duilius was shocked by the finality of Atticus's answer, and his own anger began to rise.

'Why?' he asked, an edge to his voice.

'Because the Carthaginians outclass us in nearly every way and we don't have the experience to beat them on their terms.'

'So the *Classis Romanus* should never have been born,' Duilius asked angrily, 'is that it? We should abandon Sicily and the legions?'

'No,' Atticus replied, the thought of futilely having to argue his point with another Roman making him angry, 'but I do believe we need to stick to our strengths and challenge the Carthaginians to the only fight we know we can win.'

Duilius was about to rebuke the captain again, but something in his voice made him pause and he realized that what he had thought was defeatism was in fact frustration.

'So what are our strengths?' he asked, his gaze searching.

'Our sailors can't match the Carthaginian crews, but our legionaries far surpass the Carthaginians' best fighters. We need to take the fight to the enemy decks.'

'How?' Duilius asked, realizing at that moment that he knew nothing of naval tactics.

Atticus outlined the sailing skills necessary and the time that would be needed to train the crews. He paused as he decided if he should reveal the whole truth, the gaping problem in the tactics he outlined, the legionaries' inability to board successfully. He recalled the consul's earlier honesty and decided to gamble with the truth.

Duilius absorbed the entire argument, for and against, before replying.

'Why were the sailing crews not taught boarding manoeuvres at Fiumicino?' he asked.

'Because our orders were to train them in ramming

techniques only, the one area the Carthaginians have complete superiority.'

'By whose orders?'

'Tuditanus's,' Atticus replied.

Scipio's man, Duilius thought to himself.

'Do the other galley captains agree with your judgement?' the consul asked aloud.

'The captains of the Ostia fleet are Roman. They follow orders without question,' Atticus said, a hint of disdain in his voice. 'It takes an outsider to see what they cannot.'

Duilius nodded. He had seen it many times himself in the Senate, from the first day he walked in as a *novus homo*, a new man. The senators from the older families were blinkered by tradition and age-old stability, bred from a young age to replace their fathers in the Curia. It was because Duilius was an outsider that he was able to see what they could not, that he had been able to use the system in a way they would never discover, and it was the reason he had risen so far so fast.

Duilius gazed intently at Atticus as his mind weighed the task ahead of him. He was not a military man. In fact, he had never been on board a galley before two days ago. Now, however, he was overall commander of the *Classis Romanus* and he realized in an instant that, if he was going to succeed, he would need the expertise of men like the captain before him, men whose qualities reflected his own.

'Captain Perennis,' he said suddenly, 'I want you to draw up a full training schedule when we return to Fiumicino, one that encompasses both ramming and boarding.'

'Yes, Consul,' Atticus replied, his hand unconsciously gripping the aft-rail as frustration was replaced by anticipation.

'But . . .' Duilius continued '. . . you also need to solve the problem of the legionaries.'

Atticus nodded as he consciously brought the entire argument to the forefront of his mind once more so he could examine it anew.

Duilius studied Atticus's expression and saw that his mind was already at work on the problem. He nodded to himself. The captain was indeed a man like himself, a man who became focused and driven when the odds were stacked against him. He turned once more to peer out over the aft-rail as the last of the day's light fell below the western horizon, his thoughts returning to the day past and the weeks ahead.

CHAPTER THIRTEEN

M arcus read the parchment in silence as the legionary
stood before him in the centurion's tent, the dagger still
in his hand.

'This was hooked to the pommel of the knife,' the soldier
said, holding out his hand to reveal a signet ring.

Marcus took the ring and studied it. It was gold, with an
ingrained symbol on its face. '*SPQR*.' He turned it over slowly
in his hand, his mind reeling from the news on the parchment, news that the Carthaginians had stuck to a tree outside
the main gate during the night using a Roman dagger. It had
been found by the legionary standing before him when the
dawn light revealed its presence.

'Who else knows of this parchment?' Marcus asked abruptly.

'Only the two legionaries from the II maniple. They were
stationed at the gate beneath our watchtower.'

Marcus got up and walked to the entrance to his tent. From
his vantage point he could see the gate sixty yards away. There
was only one guard on duty.

'*Stercus!*'

His eyes whipped across to the tents of the II maniple.
Aelius, the centurion, was striding away from his tent towards
the centre of the encampment, towards the legate's quarters.

Behind him the men of his maniple were talking animatedly in groups, with individuals breaking off to head to other parts of the camp.

'The bloody fool,' Marcus cursed.

'You, come with me!' he ordered, and walked out to intercept Aelius. The legionary followed.

The three men met twenty yards short of the legate's command tent. Aelius saw the parchment in Marcus's hand.

'By the gods, Marcus, we're lost.'

'Get a hold of yourself, Aelius,' Marcus spat. 'Curse it, man, your maniple will spread the news to the whole camp before roll call.'

'I-I-I . . .' Aelius stammered, looking back over his shoulder at the sound of raised voices, realizing his mistake.

Marcus turned abruptly and walked determinately towards the commander's quarters, the legionary following behind again, leaving Aelius standing alone in the middle of the parade ground. They passed the hospital tent and, as they did, both men instinctively covered their mouths with their hands for protection.

The first case of typhus had been confirmed a week before, the legionary collapsing on parade, the telltale rash on his chest only found when he was stripped inside the hospital tent. The word had spread like wildfire, the dread news that plague stalked the encampment driving the last remnants of hope from every soldier of the Ninth Legion. Malnourished as they were, the men were ripe for the scythe of typhus, and the hospital tent was already full, a hellish place where the moans of dying men rent the air.

Two legionaries of the III maniple stood to attention as Marcus reached the entrance of the tent, their fists slamming against their armoured breast-plates in unison. Marcus ignored them and ducked his head under the opening into the outer awning. Without requesting permission he strode into the inner tent. Megellus was seated behind his desk, his expression immediately hostile at the unannounced interruption. He hadn't slept the night before, his mind in turmoil as it fixated on the deteriorating situation of his legions, and his face was drawn and colourless. The admonition he had formed in his mind fled from his lips as he noticed Marcus's uneasy expression.

'What is it, Centurion?'

'Beg to report, Legate, these were stuck to a tree outside the main gate using a Roman knife.'

Megellus stood up to take the proffered parchment and ring. His eyes widened as he immediately recognized the ring. He turned it over to read an inscription on the underside of the face.

'No, it can't be . . .' he muttered, the parchment in his hand forgotten.

'Who found this?' he asked suddenly, his anxious face betraying his mounting apprehension.

'This man,' Marcus replied, stepping aside to allow the legionary to move forward.

'Tell me everything,' Megellus ordered.

The soldier quickly related his discovery of the message. Megellus listened in silence.

'Who knows of this?' he asked as the legionary finished.

'Word is spreading throughout the camp as we speak,' Marcus admitted angrily, silently cursing the centurion of the II maniple for his carelessness.

Megellus cursed as he sat back into his chair, taking up the parchment as he did so, dreading what he would find written by the hand of the enemy.

Marcus watched the legate intently. Megellus's stature seemed to dissipate before his very eyes as he read the Carthaginians' report of their total victory at Lipara. When

278

Marcus had read the report minutes before, his mind had tried to dismiss the words as enemy propaganda, a vicious ploy to eradicate the last vestiges of hope within the Roman encampment. The ring, however, put paid to that hope, although Marcus could not fathom the special significance that Megellus had afforded it, beyond it being crude proof as to the veracity of the report.

As Megellus finished reading the report, he unclasped his right hand to reveal the ring within. Twenty galleys lost, three hundred dead, fifteen hundred in chains. The defeat was absolute. He twisted the metal band in his hand, turning it once more into the light to read the two inscriptions. Megellus had recognized it immediately. He had seen it many times before, each year on the finger of a different man. Each year on the finger of the senior consul of the Senate of Rome.

Megellus's gaze lifted from the ring to the face of the centurion before him. Marcus's face was grim, the cheeks drawn from fatigue and hunger, but Megellus could see that his strength and determination were still intact, elements forged from a life serving in the legions. The legate wondered how long those would last in the face of such adversity.

The remaining meagre supplies of the Ninth were disappearing fast and with the defeat at Lipara, there was now no hope of resupply in the near future. Megellus had lost all contact with the Second at Segeste, the three-day march through enemy territory an unbridgeable gulf. No doubt the camp prefect was reading an identical parchment that very morning, and Megellus could only guess as to what condition the Second was in. If the Ninth was a mirror guide, the camp at Segeste was close to collapse.

Megellus stood up, his will forcing his body to stand erect. His aching muscles protested at the enforced activity and a fleeting fear ran through the legate's mind. He dismissed it brutally, telling himself the ache was from salt deprivation and not the onset of the monstrous disease that had struck down over eighty of his men.

Marcus stood to attention as Megellus addressed him.

'Assemble the men for roll call,' he ordered, his voice controlled and authoritative.

Marcus saluted and left.

The legate adjusted the straps of his armour, conscious of the need to be an example to his men. The forlorn mood in the camp over the past few days had been palpable. With news of the defeat at Lipara spreading like wildfire, it was about to get much worse. The breaking point had not yet been reached but Megellus knew that, once it was upon them, the men of the Ninth, faced with starvation, would be deaf to orders and near impossible to command.

The campaign was only eight weeks old. If relief did not arrive soon, Megellus would be forced to abandon the cities of Makella and Segeste to their fate and march his legions back east to Brolium. The port was ten days' march away, ten days through enemy-held territory, during which the Carthaginians would allow the legions no quarter. It would be a march across the landscape of Hades. Only strength and determination would see them through, two pillars that were crumbling before the legate's eyes under the weight of pestilence and starvation.

Gaius Duilius looked out at the calm waters off Fiumicino to the fifty Roman galleys riding gently against their anchor lines. They had been launched two days before but workmen still clambered over their decks and rigging to complete the final stages of construction. Within twenty-four hours they would sail to Ostia, to join the fifty completed galleys already stationed there, swelling the numbers of the reborn *Classis Romanus*. The men worked with dogged determination, a sense of finality in their efforts as if the very ships they created would lead short, ill-fated lives. A similar emotion was suffusing the sailors and legionaries of the fleet, a dread that sucked the fighting spirit of all and sapped the discipline of the camp.

News of the defeat in Lipara four weeks before had arrived in Ostia via trading ships. The reports had emptied the port, the traders moving north to the coastline of southern Gaul and eastern Iberia. A pervasive fear was stalking the city of Rome, with all eyes turned to the southern horizon and the expected horrific sight of the Carthaginian fleet approaching to sack and enslave the city. A permanently tense atmosphere filled the forums of Rome, as if the populace were living on borrowed time.

Initially the Senate had panicked at the news of the defeat, with many calling for immediate negotiations with the Carthaginians in the hope that Rome could be spared an attack at the price of abandoning the legions in Sicily. Duilius had rounded on the Senate, his fury and passion shaming the lesser men to commit themselves once more to the path of honour they had chosen. Now, four weeks later, that fleet was nearing completion, with a final thirty ships scheduled for launch in two weeks' time.

Atticus watched the wordless labour of the craftsmen as they completed the final stages of rigging the latest batch of fifty galleys. The *Aquila* sailed past the fleet at speed, her course set for one of the newly built wooden piers stretching out from the black sands of Fiumicino. A galley captain waved across the forty-yard gap to Atticus, and he returned the gesture with a nod, recognizing the man as a former trainee, now the captain of his own galley. Atticus was once again filled with disquiet at the thought of these raw crews facing the seemingly invincible Carthaginians. Once at Ostia the crews would undergo further training to ensure that all were familiar with their own ship and its capabilities. Even then they would fall well short of the years of experience the Carthaginians enjoyed.

The order was given for steerage speed and the *Aquila* slowed, the galley rising and falling in the gentle surge of the tide. Lines were thrown from the foredeck and slaves took the strain, their practised efficiency bringing the *Aquila* to a gentle stop. The gangplank was lowered and Atticus walked down it briskly, checking his armour as he went. His meeting with Duilius was at noon and promised, like the others, to last well into the afternoon. Ever since Lipara four weeks before, Duilius had become an avid student of seacraft and naval warfare. He had chosen Atticus as his tutor and they had met as often as the consul's schedule allowed. Duilius was a quick study and was mindful of his inexperience, a fact that made Atticus's task much easier.

The beach was alive with activity, the frames that would house the keels of the final thirty galleys already rising out of the remains of the scaffolds used for the completed galleys in the water. Beyond the noise of the hammering and sawing of timber, Atticus could hear the familiar sound as weighted wooden swords clashed in the legionaries' encampment. He had not seen Septimus over the past few weeks, but it was rumoured that Septimus rarely slept and the legionaries of the Fourth followed his example, their thirst for vengeance over the loss of their comrades fuelling their strength and endurance. For the men of the Fourth, there would be no repeat of Lipara.

Atticus crested the dune at the top of the beach and continued on to the consul's tent, situated where once the prefect's tent had stood. Tuditanus had been taken into custody by Duilius the moment the *Aquila* had returned from Lipara and he had not been seen since. Atticus could only guess at Tuditanus's fate, but he was sure that Duilius had not been lenient.

Duilius's expansive quarters were set aside from the rest of the camp and, although the structures were made of canvas, they looked almost permanent, as if the consul's quarters had stood as long as the village of Fiumicino. The entrance was guarded by *praetoriani*, their faces dour and uninviting. They too felt the shame of the defeat at Lipara. The sworn duty of their unit was the protection of the Senate, in particular the senior members. The loss of the senior consul under their charge was a dishonour to all of them.

Atticus passed through the checkpoint at the main gate, surrendering his weapons on request. He was subjected to two further searches before being admitted to the outer section of the consul's tent. There he was questioned by an *optio*, the junior officer checking the captain's details against the schedule confirmed by the consul's private secretary. Only then did Atticus enter the inner tent, all the while flanked by two praetorian guards.

Duilius was standing with his back to the entrance, his mind focused solely on a canvas map hanging from the wall of the tent. The map depicted the southwestern coast of Italy, from Rome to the city of Righi on the toe. It also included the northern coastline of Sicily. It was this section of the map that held the consul's attention. Duilius turned around as the guard announced Atticus's presence.

'You're dismissed,' Duilius told the guards.

The guards hesitated for a second, their instincts momentarily overriding the order. This was the first time the consul had requested their absence and, although they knew the captain from previous meetings, in the present climate they were trusting no one. Duilius glared at them and they saluted and left.

'Sit down, Captain,' the consul ordered.

Atticus sat in one of the two chairs facing the large central table.

'So, Captain, the deadline approaches for the launch of the

final galleys of the fleet. Have you solved our problem?'

Atticus had known the question was coming, although he didn't think Duilius would open the conversation with it. The direct approach threw him and his carefully prepared answer fled from his mind.

'No, Consul,' he replied after a pause, 'I have discussed it at length with my senior crew and we're still drawing a blank. We cannot think of a way to quickly and safely transfer legionaries from an attacking ship to the deck of another.'

Duilius nodded, his face inscrutable. The consul had hoped for a more positive answer, but all the while he had expected disappointment. Atticus's response was the same answer he had had from every captain he had surreptitiously asked over the previous weeks. Their answers had all been the same. The legionaries could not be made full marines in the time they had.

Septimus staggered down the beach as if drunk, fatigue fogging his mind, his stupor allowing him to ignore the pain of the cramped muscle in his upper arm. The muscle had gone into spasm during a simulated combat exercise, forcing him to throw up his shield to protect his unguarded right, the blow from his opponent coming before the man had time to realize the centurion was in pain. The legionary had instantly disengaged, overcoming the aggressive urge brought on by the close-quarter fight. Septimus had waved away the offers of assistance and simply walked away from the training ground, his destination the cool waters of the sea that had revived him so many times over the preceding weeks.

At the edge of the water, Septimus kicked off his sandals, unbuckling his armour as he did so. The breast- and backplates fell onto the sand and Septimus stepped out of the circle of discarded kit. He walked into the sea, feeling the cold water soak his feet and legs before venturing further in. He stood for a moment in the hip-deep water, waiting for the surge of a wave to reach him before plunging headlong into the wall of water. The noise of the beach was immediately lost under the wave and Septimus struck out hard under the water, watching a maelstrom of tiny bubbles cascade over each other under the turbulence of the surf. He angled his stroke upwards and immediately broke the surface behind a second wave. The water seemed to instantly revive him and he directed his body to the nearest barge, one hundred yards from the shore. His powerful overarm stroke covered the distance in two minutes. He grabbed onto the anchor line of the barge and rested, his breath returning to normal within a minute, his healthy body shrugging off the exertion. Feeling renewed, he turned once more to shore and swam back through the breaking water.

Walking alertly from the sea, Septimus surveyed the frenzied activity on the beach, activity he had ignored on his way down to the water. His eyes scanned left and right, taking in the full vista of the construction site. As his gaze brought him to the south end of the beach, he spied the *Aquila* tethered to one of the wooden piers. As always there was activity on deck and in the rigging. Septimus smiled as he imagined hearing the raised voice of Lucius barking orders to all on board to make perfect the already impeccable galley. Septimus pricked up his ears and tried to single out the voice but it was lost in the cacophony of sound on the beach.

Septimus had noticed the galley on previous occasions, the first time prompting him to run down to meet Atticus and ask him if any news had been received in Ostia regarding the Carthaginians. The camp was all but cut off from the outside world now that security had been increased in the wake of the defeat at Lipara, and Septimus, like everyone, relied on infrequent seaborne news from Ostia.

Strapping his armour back on, Septimus decided he would call on the ship that evening if she were still in port. It would be good to see Atticus again, an opportunity to put their argument behind them over an amphora of wine. He looked forward to spending a night on board the *Aquila* after four weeks of sleeping on land. He smiled at the transformation his predilections had undergone in just under a year. He had always considered himself a land animal. Now, in contrast, he was beginning to think he would never feel at home anywhere except on the deck of a galley.

After a moment's hesitation, Atticus decided he had to try. He quickly turned around and re-entered the consul's tent. The *optio* inside looked up in surprise at the unexpected return.

'I need a gate pass,' Atticus said simply.

The *optio* looked doubtfully at the captain, knowing that passes through the camp's security checkpoints were not given lightly.

'Please wait here, Captain,' he said, and turned to walk into the recesses of the elaborate tent to find the consul's private secretary.

Atticus tapped his feet impatiently as he waited. Duilius had dismissed him only moments before, after six long hours, with orders to return at noon the next day. The unexpected eighteen hours of leave were probably the only opportunity Atticus would get, and so he prayed his request for a pass would be granted. In the time allowed he could have sailed back to Ostia; however, once there, he would be faced with the same security. Given he had just met with the consul in private, Atticus reckoned his odds were higher if he requested a pass now.

The personal secretary, a former centurion and camp prefect, emerged from the rear of the tent. He looked Atticus directly in the eyes, as if he were trying to find some level of subterfuge in the simple request for a pass.

'The consul has agreed to the granting of a pass,' the secretary said, his voice revealing a reluctance to accept Duilius's magnanimous treatment of the young captain. 'I just need to know your destination, for the paperwork.'

Atticus nodded, smiling at the bureaucracy that infused every aspect of military life.

'Rome,' Atticus replied, 'the Viminal quarter.'

The secretary noted the information and handed Atticus a small scroll.

Atticus immediately left the tent and headed for the camp stables. Using the security pass as a mark of urgency and importance, he requisitioned a horse and rode south from the camp, intersecting the Via Aurelia ten miles short of the city.

The evening was drawing in as Atticus breached the Servian Wall surrounding the city. At sundown the gates to the city would be closed and locked until dawn the following morning, the age-old practice a precaution against a surprise night attack. Atticus stopped the first citizen he encountered within the city walls, asking the man for directions to the Viminal quarter. Atticus's route took him through the Forum Magnum, the central plaza still alive with activity even as the sun was sinking into the western sky. The fading light had prompted the lighting of torches in the porticoes of the temples, and the whole area seemed sanctified, a fitting earthly realm for the gods represented in the marble statues that looked down on Atticus as he passed. He paused at a statue of Venus, the goddess of love demurely covering her nakedness behind enfolded arms. Atticus reached out and touched the plinth, his lips forming a silent prayer to the goddess for assistance in his search.

Atticus reached the Viminal quarter as the streets darkened around him. Looking up, he could see the tops of the tallest buildings still bathed in muted sunlight, their walls reflecting slanted rays that temporarily saved the streets from complete darkness. With only the family name of the house to guide him and an entire quarter to search, Atticus sensed the hopelessness of his task. Soon it would be dark; Septimus's earlier warning about night-time predators made its way to the forefront of his thoughts.

The street-side traders were locking up their stalls for the night, their actions rushed after a long day of work, the promise of home spurring their haste. Atticus stopped many in their task as he asked for directions, his questions answered in hurried dismissive tones and gestures. The people moving in the street were becoming mere shadows when Atticus spotted a tavern offering lodgings and a stable for his mount. He walked towards it; the leave had afforded him an unexpected opportunity and he cursed his inability to take advantage of it. As he passed two house servants his mind registered their conversation. The mention of a name caused him to turn around, the sudden movement startling the two women.

'Did you say your mistress was Hadria?' he asked, his looming figure in the dark causing the women to hesitate.

'What of it?' the smaller woman demanded, her voice signifying her advanced age while her tone spoke of a woman who deferred to few.

'I'm looking for the house of Capito, for a woman named Hadria.'

Atticus's entreaty was met with silence, the suspicious expressions of the two women masked by the darkness.

'We are servants in that house,' the woman replied finally, her hand pointing out a doorway not fifty yards from where they stood.

'Can you take a message to your mistress?' Atticus asked, trying to make his voice sound friendly and unthreatening.

'I will pay you for your trouble,' he added, handing a bronze dupondius to the smaller woman, her hand closing on the coin, feeling its weight and shape.

'What message?' she asked.

'Tell your mistress that Captain Perennis awaits her message in that tavern,' he said, indicating the building almost directly across the road from Hadria's aunt's house.

The woman nodded, the gesture almost lost in the nearly pitch-darkness. The two hurried away and Atticus made his way to the tavern. He hoped the message was ambiguous enough to forestall any gossip amongst the servants, knowing that Hadria would want to keep any meeting secret.

Atticus banged on the door and an innkeeper opened a small, face-high hatchway in the stout wooden door. Atticus asked for lodgings and, after a brief moment when the innkeeper looked beyond Atticus into the darkened street, the door was opened. A stable lad was called to take Atticus's mount, and a young boy ran fearlessly out into the street to guide the horse away to a nearby enclosed courtyard. After the darkness of the street, the oil-lamp light of the tavern was warm and inviting. The atmosphere was subdued, with only four other guests in the spacious room. Atticus ordered an amphora of wine and some food and then settled down in a corner to wait. The whole idea had been ambitious, a goal set on the hope that Hadria had returned to her aunt's house in the city, that he would be able to find the house and that she would be willing to see him. He thanked Venus for the good fortune that had carried him thus far.

After thirty minutes, Atticus began to question whether his run of good fortune had ended with the discovery of the house. He anxiously watched the door, willing a knock to be heard that would signal her arrival. Doubts began to fill his thoughts. Perhaps the message had been intercepted by one of her brothers who, unknown to Atticus, had returned and was staying in the same house. Or perhaps the servant had simply pocketed the money and the message had never been delivered. The last reason he had thought of, the one he did not want to contemplate, was that Hadria had received the message but did not want to see him.

A loud knock broke his thoughts. The knock was repeated, louder than before. The innkeeper walked across the room to the door, shouting to the person outside to be patient. As before, he opened the hatchway to peer out at the caller. Words were spoken that Atticus could not hear, although he could tell the person on the other side of the door was a man. The innkeeper turned.

'Is there a Captain Perennis here?' he called.

Atticus stood up to identify himself, his hand automatically going to the hilt of his sword.

'Someone here is looking for you,' the innkeeper explained, his eyes seeing Atticus's guarded gesture. His hand stayed firmly on the iron bolt holding the door closed.

Atticus walked to the door and looked out. A soldier was standing there, a house guard who looked alertly up and down the darkened street.

'I am Captain Perennis,' Atticus said through the hatchway.

The guard turned back to the hatchway.

'The mistress of my house requests you accompany me. She has a message for her brother which she wishes you to bear,' he said, the guarded message revealing nothing of Hadria's identity to the prying ears of the innkeeper.

'Open the door,' Atticus ordered.

'It's not safe out there,' the innkeeper said, 'and you haven't paid for your room or the lodging for your horse.'

Atticus reached into his pocket and withdrew a bronze

290

sestertius. The innkeeper bit the coin before putting it in his pocket. Only then did he draw back the bolt.

Atticus stepped out into the street once more, his hand remaining steadily on his sword. The soldier turned and walked up the street, passing the main doorway the servants had indicated earlier. The street was strangely quiet, the only sounds those of muted conversations and laughter behind the burned brick walls of the houses. The guard made a sudden left turn into a narrow alleyway, the path leading along the north wall of the town house. The soldier's steps took him unerringly to a small wooden door set into the wall. He tapped on the door and it immediately opened, a shadowy figure beyond beckoning them in off the street. The door was immediately closed and barred. Atticus followed the guard across a courtyard bathed in subdued light from second-storey windows. They made their way towards a door, and again the guard had to knock before the sound of a sliding bolt signalled their permission to enter. The opening door threw a long rectangle of light out into the courtyard and Atticus once again experienced the relief of entering a well-lit room.

The guard who had opened the door and the escort left, leaving the young captain alone. Atticus looked around the simple square room, its doorways probably leading to other reception rooms and the atrium, their destinations now hidden from view. A long, low marble bench stood in the middle of the room, minimal furnishing that spoke to the room's use as a waiting area. Atticus could not sit, and he paced the room for what seemed an eternity. Finally a door opened and a woman entered.

In the weeks they had spent apart since their last encounter, Atticus had formed a picture in his mind of Hadria. A simple, unadorned portrait that spoke to her beauty and poise. It had become his icon, the image he evoked when the end of a day allowed him a moment's peace. He could see now that even his elaborate imagination did not do justice to the real vision before him. She literally shone with beauty, the soft light of the room behind her infusing her hair and framing her image in the doorway.

'Hadria,' Atticus whispered, his voice instinctively lowered in the muted space.

She walked forward at his summons, her movements slow and ethereal, her smile suddenly radiant and infectious.

'You kept me waiting,' Atticus said playfully.

'Your message took me completely by surprise,' Hadria countered with a smile. 'First I had to wait until my aunt retired for the evening. Then I had to dismiss all the servants to make sure none would see you enter.'

Atticus smiled at the convoluted arrangements.

'I almost decided you weren't worth the trouble,' Hadria added teasingly.

Atticus smiled but did not reply immediately and a silence began to spin out between them. They both gazed intently at each other, the air around them becoming charged with unspoken emotions before Hadria suddenly rushed the last few yards between them and flung herself into Atticus's arms. He held her tightly, drinking in the smell of her perfumed body, the feel of her against him. They drew slightly apart and kissed, the intimacy of the moment causing them both to catch their breaths.

As Atticus framed Hadria's face in his hands, he noticed tears forming in her eyes and he thought his heart would break at the sight.

'We have so little time,' she explained before he could speak, 'only minutes before the guard commander returns to escort you back to the tavern. I told him that you were going to courier a message for me to my brother in Fiumicino.'

'But I don't understand,' Atticus began, 'I am not expected back at camp until noon tomorrow. There is so much I need to tell you, so much I want to know.'

'We can't be together, Atticus,' Hadria tried to explain, 'not yet.'

'Why?'

'Because of Septimus.'

'Septimus,' Atticus spat as he broke away, striding around the marble bench until it separated him from Hadria, 'I already know what he thinks.'

Hadria's confused look prompted Atticus to continue.

'He thinks I'm not good enough for you. That because I'm Greek, I'm beneath you.'

Hadria's face showed instant shock and she shook her head, her hands outstretched across the bench.

'No, Atticus, that's not true.' She pleaded, 'Whatever Septimus has told you is only a front. Septimus wants us apart because of Valerius.'

'Valerius?'

'Yes, Valerius Cispius Clarus, my first husband.'

'But why . . . ?'

'Valerius was Septimus's best friend,' she explained. 'They grew up together and joined the Ninth Legion together. He took Valerius's death at Agrigentum very hard. I even believe it was one of the reasons why he transferred from the Ninth to the marines.'

Realization began to dawn on Atticus's face and he walked once more around the bench to be by Hadria's side.

'So Septimus is concerned . . .' Atticus began.

'. . . that history could repeat itself,' Hadria concluded.

'So why didn't Septimus tell me this himself?'

'Because he's a proud man, Atticus, and I think he would see his concern as being a weakness.'

293

Atticus instinctively held out his arms again and Hadria moved into his embrace, her worries momentarily forgotten.

'I love you, Atticus. I know that now. But I also know the terrible price that would be paid if Septimus found out we were together before I had a chance to somehow allay his fears.'

Atticus smiled at the loyalty underlying Septimus's concerns.

'Why are you smiling?' Hadria asked.

'He must love you very much,' Atticus said simply.

'Yes . . . he does,' she said, his understanding touching her deeply.

She moved up and kissed him full on the lips, allowing the contact to linger. The sound of approaching footsteps caused Hadria to suddenly break contact. The guard commander was returning.

'Please take care, Atticus . . . Take care until we meet again,' she breathed, her voice cracking with the fear she felt for the man she loved. Atticus embraced her, allowing her to draw strength from him and the intensity of their shared love before she drew away from him again. She turned quickly and rushed towards the door. For a brief second her body was outlined in the dim light from the hallway beyond, and she turned towards him one last time, whispering his name as she did so. Then she was gone.

The activity in the camp was as frenzied as before when Atticus rode through the main gate an hour before noon. His pass was checked one last time and then confiscated to avoid it being used again. Atticus willingly relinquished the document, having no further use for it. He knew he would not get another chance to leave the camp on such an extended leave.

Atticus checked the course of the sun in the clear blue sky. He had more than enough time for a swim and a bite to eat aboard the *Aquila* before his meeting with the consul. He hastened his step and crested the dune separating the camp from the beach. The sight before him caused him to stop. Of the fifty galleys that had been moored off the beach the day before, only a dozen or so remained, and they were in the process of getting under way, their bows pointed south towards the port of Ostia. It was not their progress that drew his gaze, however, it was the twenty huge transport ships that had taken the galleys' place off the beach. They were ganged together in four groups, each one congregated around one of the four wooden piers that stretched far enough out to sea to ensure the barges did not become beached as they unloaded their cargo of humanity. Atticus stopped a soldier who was hurrying past him.

'What legion are they, soldier?'

'They are the Fifth, of Liguria,' the young legionary said before running off again.

Already the beach just above the breakwater was crowded with the disciplined formations of the newly arrived legion. Every few moments a fully formed maniple would begin the march up the beach between the framed workings of the ship-builders. Like the Fourth, which was already encamped in Fiumicino, the Fifth was a garrison legion and therefore consisted of roughly five thousand soldiers in forty maniples. These legions lacked the additional numbers of auxiliaries and mounted cavalry that would swell their size to ten thousand, the complement of a campaigning legion such as those in Sicily. Judging from their regimented ranks and the fact that they were part of the Republic's northern defence, Atticus suspected they were a tough, experienced unit.

Atticus walked down the beach towards the southernmost pier where the *Aquila* had been moored the evening before. Beyond the two barges now moored on the pier he could see his own galley anchored two hundred yards offshore, its position well removed from the cumbersome transports. Atticus walked away from the pier to an isolated spot on the beach and waved to the galley. His wave was returned by Lucius on the aft-deck, who immediately recognized the captain. Atticus watched as a skiff was launched. He pointed towards the end of the pier, indicating where he wanted to be picked up, and then began walking the short distance back to the barges.

The pier was eight feet wide and stretched for one hundred yards into the sea from the high-tide mark of the beach. Atticus walked down the right-hand side of the pier, the stern-faced soldiers marching three abreast coming past him on the other side. As Atticus drew level with the centre of the barge, he paused to look up onto the main deck, his progress temporarily blocked by the unloading of a large crate hanging precariously from a crane.

The rail at the side of the low deck had been removed to allow for the six-foot-wide, twelve-foot-long gangplank to be lowered onto the pier. These massive gangplanks were ubiquitous on all trading barges, their width and sturdiness allowing for everything from livestock to gangs of slaves to be unloaded quickly. The gangplanks normally lay on the main deck and were simply thrown over the side of the ship when in port, their momentum checked at the last moment by guide ropes attached to the deck end. It was a simple yet skilful manoeuvre requiring split-second timing and a firm hand. One slip and the gangplank would fall completely over the side of the barge, an embarrassment often witnessed by Atticus in the busy ports of the Republic.

The legionaries waited patiently at the back of the main deck as the crane, its base attached to the main mast, swung out over the lowered gangplank. A shouted command ordered the gang of sailors controlling it to ease it away, and they slowly lowered the lifting arm until the crate hung over the pier at the foot of the gangplank. A second team of sailors holding the rope attached to the crate fed the line through a pulley at the top of the crane and the cargo dropped gently onto the pier. Men clambered over the crate to untie it and the crane was hoisted away again in search of the next crate. Atticus stepped around the knot of men manhandling the cargo and walked on towards the end of the pier.

Atticus spied the small skiff making its way towards him and he waved a greeting. A sudden thought arrested him and he spun around to look back at the barge. The legionaries had recommenced their disembarkation, their disciplined ranks forming at the head of the gangplank before marching down its twelve-foot length, three abreast. The formation wheeled right at the foot of the gangplank and continued on down the pier towards the beach. Within a minute an entire maniple, twenty rows of three men abreast, had disembarked.

Atticus was dumbstruck by the simplicity of the idea forming in his head. His sceptical side argued against the basic concept, but his logical mind overcame the doubts to once more re-establish the solution firmly in his thoughts. Atticus began to run, his flight drawing puzzled looks from the sailors in the skiff. He passed the legionaries marching along the pier and continued on to the beach. He stopped for a second to get his bearings, his eyes searching the construction site before him, but Lentulus, the master shipbuilder, was nowhere to be seen. Atticus started running again, this time up the beach towards the camp. As he ran his face took on a determined expression, the idea turning over and over in his head.

CHAPTER FOURTEEN

Scipio retched again at the overpowering stench surrounding him in the pitch-black recesses of the bottom deck of the Carthaginian galley. The cramped space of the hold was in marked contrast to where Scipio had spent the first two weeks of his captivity, locked in the fortified garrison at Lipara. From the window of his cell he had been able to look out over the harbour and watch the loss of his *Classis Romanus*, not through destruction but through conversion and amalgamation into the Carthaginian fleet. Sixteen of his original twenty galleys had survived the ambush and their number had swelled the ranks of the enemy in a bitter twist that shamed the once-proud consul. At the end of the two weeks the Carthaginians had made ready to sail again from Lipara. It was then that Scipio had been dragged from his cell and without explanation thrown into the hold where he now languished.

His stomach cramped as he doubled over, its contents long lost, and he fought to catch his breath. The claustrophobic nightmare of the confined space filled his consciousness again and threatened to overwhelm him. He dug deep into his courage to fight the rising panic but found his nerve failing. His legs ached in the confined space, the five-foot headroom forcing him to alternate between squatting and crouching in an effort to keep off the filthy, cockroach- and faeces-infested deck. A bulkhead separated him from the slave quarters and he could hear their moans and wretched coughing through the timbers. It was a sound that chilled his blood.

Scipio was not sure exactly how long he had been in the hold but he estimated it had been at least two weeks. The hatchway above him had opened intermittently during that time, his captors giving him stale bread and brackish water, their offering always accompanied by an insulting remark spoken in their incomprehensible language. During the first week Scipio had done his best to present an outward display of indifference to his predicament, not wanting to give his captors the satisfaction of knowing how much he was suffering. The act had produced a brutal response on two occasions, the second a blow to the head that had knocked him unconscious. The second week had marked the onset of a pervasive fear, a feeling that he would be left to die in the hold, and it was then that all trace of real defiance had fled. As the drum from the slave deck above him continued its unending beat, Scipio felt the final vestiges of his resolve begin to dissipate in the darkness engulfing him.

Hannibal Gisco walked down the length of the rowing deck towards the guarded hatchway that led to the lower hold. He moved silently, his eyes ranging over the rows of chained galley slaves. As the taskmasters patrolling the deck became aware of Gisco's presence, they intensified their whip lashes on the backs of the rowers. Their increased barbarity was not born from zeal but from fear. Gisco noted the change and smiled inwardly to himself. He had been surprised to learn that the Romans used their own sailors as taskmasters on the slave deck. Years before, Gisco had ordered the position filled by slaves taken from the ranks of the rowers themselves.

Gisco's method meant that from the moment those chosen picked up the whip and delivered their first lash, they became enemies of their fellow slaves. Any sign that a taskmaster was sparing his former companions from the lash was instantly punishable by returning that slave to the ranks of the rowers. Once back amongst those men, the former taskmaster's life was measured in hours, their death normally occurring during their first relief break when, along with the men they had recently whipped, they were confined out of sight in the hold beneath the rowing deck. The move had immeasurably enhanced the effectiveness of the taskmasters, causing them to become vicious, almost inhuman in their ferocity, the fear that they might be seen as lenient intensifying their brutality.

Gisco stopped as he came to the hatchway. The soldier posted there saluted and stepped back.

'Find two more men,' Gisco ordered, and the soldier departed.

As the admiral waited, he replayed the information he had already stored in his head. Over the past two weeks, the eighteen Roman captains who had survived the ambush had been systematically tortured for intelligence regarding the new fleet. Some had been tougher than others, some more informed, but all had eventually revealed some fragment of the overall strategy.

The Romans were planning to build one hundred and fifty ships, all of the same class as those taken at Lipara. The initial twenty were now either destroyed or in Carthaginian hands, which meant the bulk of the fleet was yet to be deployed. The timing of their deployment was still unknown but could be readily estimated by the speed at which the Romans had built the initial twenty. When Gisco first heard the reported construction time, he had not believed it. He had personally supervised the interrogation of three captains to confirm the report. The first twenty had been built in a little over two weeks and, on the day they sailed, fifty more keels were being laid down. Given that nearly all the reports stated that Rome was constantly increasing the rate of construction, it was reasonable to assume the fleet was near to completion.

Gisco was also sure that the Romans knew the full details of the trap laid for them at Lipara. His guard commander, Cronus, and the traitor Demades had not returned from Rome. Demades had betrayed him. Before leaving Lipara, Gisco had fulfilled his promise and had put the councillor's family to the sword, but not before the three women had spent a long night in the company of the garrison soldiers.

The only remaining piece of the puzzle was the man who would command the Roman fleet. Many of the captains had spoken of a Roman named Gaius Duilius, the junior consul, as being next in line to command. None of the captains knew anything of the man himself, his background or his abilities. Gisco was sure, however, that the man beneath his feet, the senior consul of Rome, would have the personal information he required to get the measure of the man he would soon face in battle.

The hatchway above Scipio opened suddenly. Rough hands reached down and hauled him up onto the rowing deck of the galley. His legs cramped as he straightened them and he gritted his teeth against the pain. The light was muted below deck but, after the pitch-darkness of the lower hold, Scipio shielded his eyes against its intensity. His hands were instantly pulled down and held behind him.

Scipio looked up to see the face of the Carthaginian commander, the same man he had met in battle on the aft-deck of the *Mars*. Scipio was immediately aware of the contrast between them. The Carthaginian stood tall and proud, his gaze fierce and confident. Scipio, by contrast, could only mimic those same qualities. His toga was filthy and clung to his flesh, his posture stooped and pathetic. Scipio tried to draw himself to his full height but his legs cramped again and so he set his own expression into what he believed was hardened defiance as he looked up at his captor.

The Carthaginian smiled and walked away, the guards forcing Scipio to follow through a series of narrow companionways to the main cabin at the stern of the ship. Once there the Carthaginian commander sat down behind a central desk.

'Remove his toga!' Gisco ordered, his face expressing his disgust at the filth of the robes.

Again Scipio was manhandled roughly as his toga was removed, his tunic underneath equally filthy.

'Leave us,' Gisco commanded the guards.

The two adversaries were left alone.

'I demand to be treated in accordance with my rank,' Scipio said, trying to establish a level of arrogance he did not feel.

'*Vae victis*: "Woe to the vanquished",' Gisco spat, evoking the retort of a Gaulish commander, who had used the phrase more than a hundred years earlier after sacking the city of Rome.

'Sit down, Roman.'

Scipio tried to stand firm.

'Sit down or I will have my men take you back to the hold.'

Scipio flinched at the threat, the thought of returning to the pitch-dark prison sending a spasm through his intestines. He sat down quickly.

Gisco noted the reaction, disgusted at the outward show of fear in one who claimed to be the leader of Rome.

'My name is Hannibal Gisco. I am the overall commander of the Carthaginian forces fighting to free Sicily from Roman tyranny.'

Scipio bit back an instinctive retort, not wanting to antagonize his enemy.

302

'I have "spoken" with the captains of your fleet,' Gisco began. 'It seems their loyalty did not extend beyond saving their own lives. They were very willing to divulge every detail of your new fleet. Its size, complement, class of ship.'

Scipio tried to maintain an expression of indifference, but the Carthaginian's words caused a latent anger to rise within him. *I have been betrayed by everyone,* he thought bitterly.

'There is just one final piece of information I need you to confirm, Roman,' Gisco added.

'I will not betray my city,' Scipio answered feebly, trying to make his voice sound bold and confident. Even in his own ears he heard the hollowness of his words.

Gisco laughed.

'Enough Romans have already done that,' he said dismissively. 'I simply want you to tell me about the man who will command the Roman fleet.'

Scipio sat straighter as his mind pictured the hated face of Duilius.

'If you cooperate I will confine you to a cabin rather than the hold you have just left,' Gisco added.

Scipio could not hide his reaction to the bribe and the opportunity to reach beyond his captivity to have his revenge on Duilius. Gisco noticed the change and smiled inwardly. This was going to be easier than he had anticipated.

'Now,' Gisco said, 'tell me all you know of Gaius Duilius.'

The junior consul looked up from the obviously hurried yet comprehensible sketches laid out before him. The two men at the other side of the table looked confident, as if the idea was a proven strategy, rather than a concept based on an idea formed only an hour before.

'This design is feasible?' Duilius asked the older man.

'Yes, Consul,' Lentulus replied.

...d back down at the drawings once more. On ...esign looked practical, the very solution he had ...er the preceding weeks.

...en can we test it?' the consul asked.

'We can rig the *Aquila* with the new system and be ready ...o test it within forty-eight hours,' Atticus replied.

Duilius nodded. He deliberately overcame the infectious conviction of the two men and looked at the idea rationally. To second Lentulus to the *Aquila* and take him out of the building programme would delay the launch of the final thirty galleys but, if the idea were feasible, it would go a long way towards levelling the odds between them and the Punici. He glanced surreptitiously at Atticus, the captain's gaze firmly on the drawings on the table. It seemed the outsider had found what everyone had been looking for but none could find.

'Make it so,' he replied simply.

The two men stood to leave, the younger man saluting with a clenched fist to his chest. Duilius nodded his dismissal, his expression hiding the eagerness he felt to see the simple line drawings before him turned into reality.

'He is not of noble birth?' Gisco asked, trying to find a trace of guile in the Roman's words. He could find none. The man before him clearly hated Gaius Duilius. Of that there was no doubt, although Gisco could not fathom a reason.

'No, he is not,' Scipio spat. 'He is low-born, the son of a middle-class farmer.'

The monarchy in Carthage had been abolished over fifty years before, but Gisco, like all those in positions of power in both the military and government, could trace their lineage to at least one of the ancient monarchs. The idea that a non-noble could rise to a position of power was foreign to him, and he contemptuously considered Rome's acceptance of such leaders as a further sign of their fallibility.

'So how did he rise to such a position?' Gisco asked.

'Money,' Scipio said disdainfully, as if the very word was vulgar, his mind automatically ignoring the fact that it was the riches of his own ancestors that had ensured their place in the first Senate.

'Has he military experience?'

'He has never known combat and has no military training.'

Again Gisco found the answers hard to believe and he forced himself to think about the Roman's words objectively, to suppress the rising confidence he felt at the failings of his enemy.

'But to rise to such a position he must be resourceful?' Gisco asked, almost to himself.

'Yes, he is resourceful, but only in matters of secrecy and deceit.'

Gisco nodded. He felt nothing but disdain for the man sitting opposite him. The Roman was consumed with hate. It was an emotion Gisco understood well, but Scipio was readily betraying his own city in his pursuit of vengeance against a fellow Roman he considered his enemy. In his quest to destroy this man Duilius, Scipio was willing to forfeit a whole fleet of his own countrymen.

'You have been most helpful,' Gisco remarked.

Scipio smiled in pathetic gratitude.

'I would ask you, Admiral,' Scipio said, his voice filled with a new hope, 'for the opportunity to bathe and put on new clothes before being escorted to my cabin.'

Gisco smiled.

'Guards!' the admiral shouted.

The door was immediately opened and three soldiers stepped into the room.

'Return this filth to the hold,' Gisco ordered.

Scipio's stature seemed to collapse at the command. He began to raise his hands to his face in despair when his arms were grabbed from behind and he was pulled to his feet and dragged from the cabin.

Gisco watched him leave. If Duilius was junior in rank and ability to this broken man, then the Carthaginians were poised to sweep the sea clear of Rome for ever.

'Release!'

For a heartbeat the *corvus* remained motionless as the holding rope went slack. It began to fall, slowly at first, until its own weight caused it to pick up momentum and it slammed down with a shattering crash onto the foredeck of the galley across from the *Aquila*.

'Good,' Lentulus said, as if to himself, one of his apprentices automatically nodding his agreement by his side.

'But too slow,' Atticus added. 'It's got to start falling the instant it's released.'

'I agree,' Lentulus replied thoughtfully. 'I will make some modifications.'

Atticus watched the sailors pull on the rope to raise his invention once more to its position. He had named the new weapon the *corvus*, for the raven was a harbinger of death and Atticus fully intended to make sure the device lived up to its name.

The *corvus* was a combination of a crane and a gangplank, thirty-six feet long and four wide, a massive ramp with its bottom end hinged to a vertical mast installed in the centre of the foredeck. The mast rose forty feet above the deck, allowing for the ramp to be raised to a vertical position and the hinge pivoted through one hundred and eighty degrees, making it possible to deploy the *corvus* on both the starboard and port sides of the galley. In one fell swoop the ramp could be lowered and legionaries rushed across to board an enemy ship. The ramp was big enough to allow the legionaries to carry their full battle kit, including the four-foot *scutum* shield, and in sufficient numbers to ensure a standard battle formation line could be deployed on the enemy's deck within seconds.

Atticus left the craftsmen and walked over to the side rail where Septimus had been watching the latest test, Atticus having asked him on board for his expertise on legionaries' tactics.

'You know,' Atticus smiled, 'if this works, the marines will be out of a job.'

He turned to Septimus but the centurion was not laughing; indeed his expression was troubled.

'I came to the *Aquila* the night before last,' he said unexpectedly, giving voice to the question that had been on his mind since then. 'You weren't on board.'

'No,' Atticus said, his mind racing to cover his absence from the *Aquila* and his trip to Rome. 'I was with Duilius in his quarters and didn't get back until after midnight.'

Septimus nodded, his expression giving nothing away, but inside his anger was building. Atticus was lying to him. Septimus had spent the night on the *Aquila* and he knew that Atticus had never returned. He was about to challenge Atticus on the lie when they were interrupted.

'We're ready to try again,' Lentulus said behind them.

'To speed the fall of the ramp, the *corvus* will no longer rise to the vertical. The angle will put more stress on the mast, but I am confident it will still hold.'

Atticus nodded at the solution and looked over to the sailors who were once more holding the release rope taut.

'Ready?'

The sailors nodded.

'Release!'

This time the *corvus* fell immediately with no hesitation.

'Better,' Atticus remarked.

At that moment a rogue wave struck the *Aquila* and the gap between the two galleys opened wider. Before Gaius could bring the *Aquila* back into position, the far end of the *corvus* slid off the foredeck of the 'enemy' galley.

'That's another problem we have to tackle,' Lentulus said.

Atticus watched the *corvus* being raised again as the *Aquila* was manoeuvred back into place. In battle the only thing holding the two ships together would be grappling hooks. If the enemy reacted quickly and severed the lines, they could easily manoeuvre their galley away. Any boarding party across the *corvus* would be stranded while anyone on the ramp itself when the ships parted would fall into the sea. They had to find a way to make the ramp secure, to lock the ships together.

'I think this raven needs to be given claws,' Atticus said.

Gisco studied the man opposite him with interest. The Nubian stood tall and erect, his balanced stance betraying the slave's obvious fighting abilities. His gaze was arrogant, an emotion Gisco had never encountered in a slave before, and it fascinated him.

The Nubian had been found in the Roman consul's quarters after the ambush at Lipara. Gisco had immediately noticed the stature and bearing of a trained fighter and had arranged for the Nubian to be spared the fate of galley slave reserved for all those taken alive in the ambush. Now, as the Carthaginian fleet approached Panormus, Gisco had finally found the time to study the potential of Scipio's personal servant.

Khalil had outlined his later life and captivity in detail, confirming Gisco's assumption that he was a gladiator. The thought of using the Nubian as a force against the very people who trained him appealed to the admiral's sense of fate. Only the question of Khalil's loyalty remained. Of the hate he felt for the Romans there was no doubt, and Gisco was confident that Khalil would savage any Roman he met in battle. For Gisco to be able to command the Nubian, however, he needed to find an inducement to ensure his loyalty.

'I will need men like you in the battle ahead,' Gisco said.

Khalil remained quiet; however, Gisco noticed the flicker of interest in the Nubian's eyes. The sight convinced him to continue.

'If you fight well against the Romans and obey my every command, I will grant you your freedom when the battle is won.'

Again Khalil remained impassive, the silence irking Gisco.

'Do you agree?' he asked, his anger beginning to flare at the unreadable Nubian.

'My freedom is of no concern until I repay a debt of pride. I want the life of Scipio.'

Gisco smiled at the request, one he would never allow; the consul's life was far too valuable to be thrown away at the behest of a mere slave.

'Agreed,' he lied, noting with satisfaction the savage expression of Khalil as he nodded his assent.

Admiral Gisco stepped off the gangplank of the *Melqart* onto the busy docks of Panormus. He paused as he looked over at the frenzied activity of the port, the preparations for battle already well advanced. By his orders the fleet blockading the western coast of Sicily had been summoned to Panormus, and so the northern port was now home to over one hundred galleys. Gisco had consulted Hamilcar before his departure for Carthage and both were in agreement. Given the detailed reports of the Roman captains, the new Roman fleet would be in the waters of northern Sicily in less than two weeks.

At Lipara, Gisco had closely inspected the new Roman galleys. They had been hastily built of untreated, unweathered timbers. The hulls were too new to the water and the timbers had not bonded completely. Given time they would become hard as iron, but now they lacked significant strength beneath the water line, certainly not enough to stop a six-foot bronze ram.

Hamilcar was due to return in a little over a week with another forty galleys to join the burgeoning Carthaginian fleet in Sicily. Gisco recalled the young man's hesitation when he had first requested the additional ships. It was only after Gisco explained the simple logic behind his demand that Hamilcar agreed. It was not enough to simply defeat the Romans in battle. The Carthaginian fleet needed to wipe out the entire Roman fleet down to its last ship. To accomplish that objective none must escape; Gisco knew only numerical superiority would guarantee him total victory.

Septimus crested the dunes at the top of the beach and headed directly for the consul's quarters, his pace quickened by the limited time available before the sea trials for the new *corvus* would take place and his presence would be required back on board the *Aquila*. A sliver of guilt caused him a heartbeat's hesitation, but he dismissed it quickly, using the lie that Atticus had told him to justify his decision to seek out Lutatius. Septimus knew he had caught Atticus unawares, his decision to spend the night on the *Aquila* unannounced and unexpected and Atticus's equally unplanned absence from the galley too unusual to go unchallenged.

Septimus had been disturbed by the lie, not because he expected complete honesty from his friends, but because his earlier suspicions about a possible involvement with his sister had instantly reared their head. He had therefore decided to confirm his suspicions – at least in part – by calling in an old loyalty.

Septimus reached the consul's quarters and ducked inside. An *optio* was seated behind a desk, its surface covered by neat piles of parchments, the endless lists of a military operation.

'I need to speak with the consul's private secretary,' Septimus announced, his voice and presence causing the *optio* to immediately stand to attention.

'Yes, Centurion. Who shall I say is making the request?'

'Septimus Laetonius Capito of the IV of the Ninth.'

The *optio* nodded and disappeared into the inner room of the tented quarters.

A moment later he reappeared, followed by an older man, the latter with a broad smile on his usually dour face.

'Septimus!' the secretary laughed. 'I see a centurion before me where once stood a boy of Rome.'

'Lutatius,' Septimus replied, stepping forward to shake the hand of the former camp prefect of the Ninth. Lutatius had been a centurion when Septimus joined the Ninth, a training commander who moulded new recruits into fighting legionaries. A veteran of the Third Samnite War, he had been a hard taskmaster, but he had also seen in Septimus the potential that had eventually borne fruit at the Battle of Agrigentum.

'I hear you're training the pups of the Fourth,' Lutatius said. 'Are they as hard to train as you once were?'

Septimus laughed, liking the older man, casting his mind back to his first months in the legions and the endless grinding pace that Lutatius had enforced. The two men continued to reminisce.

'I need a favour . . .' Septimus said finally.

'Name it,' Lutatius replied, noting the sudden seriousness in Septimus's tone.

'I need to know what destination was recorded on a pass given to Captain Perennis of the *Aquila*.'

'Isn't that the galley on which you now serve?' Lutatius replied, the details of every command stored in his sharp mind.

Septimus nodded, revealing nothing that might cause Lutatius to hesitate to reveal the information.

'Wait here,' the secretary said after a moment's pause, and he re-entered the inner tent. He reappeared with a large bound ledger open in his arms, his eyes running down an unseen list of passes approved and issued.

'Here it is,' he said finally. 'Atticus Milonius Perennis . . . eighteen-hour gate pass . . . destination? . . . Rome, the Viminal quarter.'

For an instant Septimus's face revealed the sudden flare-up of anger within him before he wiped the expression from his face. He had expected the information that Lutatius revealed, had even prepared himself for the confirmation of his suspicions, and yet when Atticus's betrayal was spoken out loud, Septimus was almost overwhelmed by the force of his anger. The Viminal quarter, the home of Septimus's aunt and the residence of his sister, Hadria.

'Thanks, Lutatius,' Septimus said abruptly, before striding out of the consul's quarters, automatically setting out for the *Aquila*, his mind clouded by visions of his sister and the man he had come to respect and trust over all others. As he crested the dunes again and made his way down towards the shore-line, his eyes discerned the figure of Atticus standing on the aft-deck of the *Aquila*, the galley tethered to the pier, the gang-plank lowered to receive Duilius and his praetorian guard. Atticus was making ready to sail and Septimus singled out his familiar voice amid the cacophony of sound on the busy beach.

The sight and sound stopped Septimus dead in his tracks and he stood rooted to the spot halfway down the beach, feeling for the first time the tightness of his grip on the handle of his sword. He released the pressure slightly, flexing his fingers, never relinquishing his touch on the moulded grip. Septimus's mind was in utter turmoil, one moment determined to challenge Atticus and an instant later feeling that he should give his friend the benefit of the doubt; after all, the Viminal quarter was vast and he had no proof that Atticus had been visiting Hadria. As if his thoughts were projected to the aft-deck of the *Aquila*, he saw Atticus suddenly turn, the captain's face breaking into an excited smile as he spotted Septimus, his hand raised to beckon the centurion so the sea trials could begin. Septimus automatically stepped forward, his stride once again determined.

By the time Septimus reached the gangplank of the *Aquila*, his mind had chosen a course. He lacked proof but the evidence was damning. When the opportunity presented itself, he would confront Atticus and demand an answer. The decision allowed him to push the impending confrontation to the back of his mind, his focus shifting to the all-important part he would play in proving the worth of the *corvus*. He nodded to Atticus as he reached the main deck, his friend nodding in reply. For an instant Septimus's mind fixed on the one aspect he had not yet faced, the answer to the question of how he would react if Atticus had indeed been with his sister. A renewed flash of anger revealed the only answer he knew was possible.

The *Aquila* cut through the calm water at her attack speed of eleven knots. Duilius gripped the side rail and steadied himself against the swell of the deck, his legs slightly splayed for balance. From his position on the aft-deck the demi-maniple on the foredeck looked like a solid mass, the linked *scutum* shields forming a wall that seemed barely able to restrain the soldiers behind. Beyond the bow of the galley Duilius could see the 'enemy' galley making her way towards their position, the convergent course bridging the gap between the ships at a frightening pace. The galley was one of the new fleet and, as the two ships jostled for position, the disparity in skill level between her helmsman and that of the *Aquila* was obvious even to the untrained eye of the consul. In battle a Carthaginian galley would be harder to engage for the inexperienced crews of the new fleet, but Duilius could see that the manoeuvre was nonetheless achievable.

The 'enemy' galley was trying to gain the broadside of the *Aquila*, a tactic the Carthaginians would use to ram their prey. All the helmsman of the *Aquila* had to do to counter the move was mirror each turn his opponent made, thereby keeping the galleys bow to bow. The gap closed inexorably and at the last turn, when the galleys looked set to simply sweep past each other, the helmsman of the *Aquila* turned her bow into the 'enemy's'. The two ships collided with tremendous force, the reinforced bow of each absorbing the blow and transmitting it down the length of the ship, the reverberation almost throwing Duilius to the deck. The collision robbed both galleys of most of their speed but they continued to slide past each other.

'Now!' Duilius heard, and there was a flurry of activity as grappling hooks were thrown onto the opposing deck.

The ropes were instantly made taut and the two ships came to a stop, their fates now linked together by the precarious threads. Duilius watched as the crew of the other galley attacked the lines with axes, severing the ropes in single blows. Within seconds the two ships would be free once more.

'Release!'

This time Duilius watched in awe as the huge boarding ramp was dropped from the foredeck. The underside of its forward section revealed three vicious foot-long iron spikes that seemed to reach out to the 'enemy' foredeck. As the ramp crashed down, the spikes were hammered home into the deck, locking the two ships together in an inescapable grip. The legionaries instantly surged across the ramp, the first row of three presenting a solid shield wall at the front of the charge. Duilius counted aloud in his head. The entire attacking force of sixty legionaries was across in less than twenty seconds. The demi-maniple now stood together on the foredeck of the 'enemy' galley, their shields linked in a classic battle formation, facing down the length of the opposing galley. There was no enemy to engage on board the allied galley, but Duilius could immediately appreciate the deadly effectiveness of the attack.

'Hold!'

The order was shouted from within the ranks of the legionaries and Duilius watched a centurion disengage from the centre of the line. He was a tall young man, one Duilius recognized from his frequent visits to the training camp at Fiumicino. The centurion recrossed the ramp and made his way up along the galley. He mounted the steps from the main deck and stood beside the captain and shipbuilder who were already standing expectantly in the centre of the aft-deck. The centurion saluted the consul. Duilius looked at the three men.

'How long before these devices can be installed on every galley?' he asked, the question his explicit approval of the tactic.

Lentulus smiled, the other two men suppressing the smile behind cold military expressions.

'A week at most, Consul, in time for the launch of the last batch of thirty galleys.'

'Make it so,' Duilius commanded. 'I want daily progress reports.'

'Yes, Consul.'

Duilius turned his back on the men and walked once more

to the side rail. He watched as the legionaries were ordered to return to the *Aquila* and the *corvus* was once more raised. The galley swung away and turned her bow again to the beach. The sound of the drum signalled the re-engagement of the oars and the deck became alive beneath his feet once more. The sound of the beat allowed Duilius's mind to organize what he would need to achieve in the coming week. He had barely finished the first day in his mind when the galley reached the southernmost wooden pier at Fiumicino.

Atticus watched from the aft-deck as the junior consul disembarked from the *Aquila*. He had noticed the galley had not docked with its usual agility and he turned to see the frowning face of the helmsman, Gaius.

'Something troubles you, Gaius?' Atticus asked as he approached the more experienced sailor.

'It's the *corvus*, Captain,' Gaius replied. He had discovered a distinct disadvantage to the device, something that could jeopardize any vessel on which it was deployed. He understood the importance of the weapon and how it was Atticus's discovery, but he also knew the captain would expect nothing less than an honest appraisal, the safety of the ship paramount.

'The trim of the ship has been severely altered,' he continued. 'With the weight of the *corvus* on the foredeck the *Aquila* is heavy in the bow. It makes little difference in calm waters, but I fear in a storm the galley would be unmanageable.'

Atticus nodded. He admitted to himself that neither he nor Lentulus had considered the impact the heavy ramp would have on the finely balanced galley.

'Unmanageable to what degree?' he asked, knowing that Gaius would not have raised the issue if the problem wasn't significant.

'To the point of being unseaworthy.'

Atticus nodded once again, this time in silence. He would discuss the issue with Lentulus, although he had no doubt that Gaius's prediction was accurate. Ultimately they would have to inform Duilius.

Atticus turned again to the bow and the unfamiliar sight of the *corvus* on the once-empty foredeck. He could not suppress the sense of hope he felt at the sight, even though his mind called for caution. The Carthaginians were far from beaten, but at last Atticus could picture their defeat in his mind's eye. This new device, this *corvus*, had made that possible. The legions of Rome were unequalled in their fighting prowess. With the *corvus*, Rome could carry that killer ability onto the sea itself.

'Ninety-six!'

Marcus repeated the number in his head as the centurion of the IX maniple, the centurion of the watch, prepared to strike again, his expression grim, his bloody work almost done.

'Ninety-seven!'

The sound of the whiplash filled the very air, its strike no longer accompanied by the cries of pain that had struck at the heart of every legionary of the Ninth.

'Ninety-eight!'

The legionary of the VII maniple hung like a butchered carcass across the interlocked *pila* spears, the flesh of his back in tatters, his legs soaked with his own blood.

'Ninety-nine!'

Marcus darted his eyes left to Megellus, the legate standing alone in front of the I maniple, his armour hanging loosely from his shadowed frame, his gaunt face set in a mask of determination.

'One hundred and all done!'

The centurion of the IX stepped back from the stricken

soldier, his own torso and face spattered by the blood of the man he had beaten. The whip hung loosely by his side, its flayed tip dripping flesh and blood into the hard-packed sand of the parade ground. Megellus nodded a dismissal to the centurion before stepping forward.

'Soldiers of the Ninth!' he shouted, his voice carrying easily over the nine thousand men who could still do duty. 'We are soldiers of the Republic, legionaries of the Ninth, the Wolves of Rome. The Ninth will not tolerate insubordination. Rome will not tolerate dereliction of duty!'

Megellus let his words hang in the air for a minute before he gestured to two orderlies to cut the legionary down. They ran forward and quickly cut the bonds that splayed the soldier across the X profile of the two spears, lowering him gently onto a stretcher. One of the orderlies ran his hands deftly over the still body, searching for a sign of life. There was none. He looked at Megellus and shook his head before they lifted the lifeless soldier and removed him from the parade ground. The entire legion followed their progress, ignoring the standing order of eyes front.

Megellus cursed inwardly. One hundred lashes was a brutal punishment, a heavy coin that was warranted for the crime of insubordination, but it was rarely a death sentence and was never envisioned as such. Given the soldier's malnutrition, his chances of survival had always been slim, but regulations were clear and the punishment could not be changed. The legate's gaze ranged over the massed troops before him, sensing their hostile mood, a mood that had turned inward over the previous week to focus on the commanders of the legion, the men they believed were condemning them daily as their comrades fell from typhus, malnutrition and exhaustion.

'Troops dismissed!' Megellus shouted, his order echoed by the centurion of each maniple. Where before the men would snap to attention before dismissal, the majority simply shuf-fled off the parade ground, many glancing back over their shoulders with hooded eyes at the legate.

'Prefect,' Megellus commanded, 'assemble the senior cen-turions in my tent.'

The legate heard the slap of a fist on armour as he strode into his quarters, the camp prefect recalling the manipular commanders.

Five minutes later Megellus's tent was filled with the senior officers of the legion, each one a veteran of more than twenty years, each one acutely aware of the precariousness of their situation.

'Ten days,' Megellus said simply, his face unable to hide the bitter disappointment of this final decision, 'ten days and our final supplies will be exhausted. Ten days and we march, first to Segeste and the Second and then south to Agrigentum.'

Many of the centurions nodded; others, Marcus among them, simply held the legate's gaze.

Ten days, Marcus thought, ten days during which the Ninth could still hold its head high amongst the legions of Rome. After that it would be stained with the mark of utter defeat, and Marcus felt the bitter bile of shame rise in his throat at the thought. For an instant his mind pictured a scene played out between three men nearly three months before at Brolium. He recalled the words vividly, the deal struck between them, the strength of their bond forged over a vow of honour. The memory straightened Marcus's back and he stood tall amongst his commander and comrades. Whatever happened, he would stand tall for ten more days.

CHAPTER FIFTEEN

The light breeze accompanying the rising sun caused the war banners to billow out from the mastheads, the first rays of sunlight stroking their linen cloth. The dawn was heralded by the low baritone call of a sounding horn, its resonance signalling to the fleet to make ready to sail. Gisco gave thanks to Shahar, the god of dawn, for the westerly wind, its sudden arrival a further fortuitous omen for the battle ahead.

As the light strengthened the admiral could see the surrounding ships of the Carthaginian fleet nestled in the harbour of Lipara. Never before had he seen such a confluence of galleys. He held out his right hand and surveyed the calloused skin of his palm. He had heard that the Greeks could see the pattern of a man's life and fortunes in the lines on his palm. Gisco wondered what mark represented his control of the most powerful fleet Carthage had ever assembled. He bunched his fist at the thought, feeling the strength of his grip. He smiled at the prospect of using the fist and the power of the fleet within its lines to hammer his enemies.

Six hours before, in the dead of night, a sentinel galley had returned from the north with news that the Roman fleet was beating southwards towards the northern coast of Sicily, a fleet of war galleys followed behind by transport barges. Their course was set for Brolium and the blockade around it, a formation of galleys that Gisco had already withdrawn into the main fleet two days before to swell his command to one hundred and sixty-one galleys. The fastest route for the Romans would take them between the Aeolian Islands and the Cape of Mylae on the north coast of Sicily, a channel only five miles across. It was there that Gisco would meet the enemy, leaving the Romans no route to circumvent his line of battle.

As the outermost galleys of the fleet raised their sails and began to manoeuvre out of the harbour, Gisco re-examined his battle plan. He could find no flaw in his strategy. His fleet surpassed the Romans' in experience, seamanship, and numbers. If the Romans decided to attack his line head on they would be slaughtered. If they tried to turn and run in the narrow channel they would be slaughtered. There would be no escape and no quarter given. As the *Melqart* got under way beneath him he hammered his fist onto the side rail, feeling his blow connect with the power of his ship. Within minutes the quinquereme's superior speed took her to the vanguard of the fleet, giving Gisco an uninterrupted view of the horizon. His pulse began to rise as he anticipated the sight of the Roman fleet breaching the solid line of the sea ahead. Remembering the complete victory he had accomplished in the harbour of Lipara, he almost regretted the ease with which he knew he would crush the Roman fleet.

'Land ahead!'

Instinctively the three men glanced up to the masthead lookout.

'Sicily,' Atticus remarked to himself, anticipation in his voice.

Duilius turned to the captain by his side, seeing the steady gaze of the younger man, sharing the pent-up expectancy. The junior consul had chosen the *Aquila* as his flagship and so the galley sailed in the vanguard of the fleet. To his left and right the new fleet of galleys spread out in a rough arrow formation, the flanks held by experienced galleys of the Ostia fleet and others requisitioned from Naples and Capua. Duilius could not help feeling immense pride at Rome's achievement, the fleet of one hundred and forty ships, both new and old, testament to the Republic's strength.

Atticus consulted the map spread out on a small table on the aft-deck, briefly consulting with Gaius as each man recognized features of the familiar coast. The captain nodded briefly as agreement was reached and Gaius altered the course of the lead galley to turn the fleet west. Signals were exchanged from the stern rail and Atticus noted with confidence that the captains of the new galleys matched his course while maintaining formation.

'That's the Cape of Mylae,' Atticus explained to Duilius and Septimus as he pointed to a headland five miles ahead off the port quarter. 'And those are the Aeolian Islands,' indicating a darker mass of land on the starboard quarter horizon.

'How far beyond is Brolium?' Duilius asked.

'Roughly twenty-five miles beyond the cape, a little over four hours at our current speed,' Atticus replied automatically, his own thoughts also focused on the distant islands. He wondered if the Carthaginian fleet had left the island or if they were still at the port city. Either way he relished the encounter, and Atticus recited a vow to make them pay a heavy price.

'Enemy galleys dead ahead!'

Gisco reacted instantly to the call.

'Signal all galleys. Enemy sighted. Battle formation!'

The crewmen responded immediately, rushing to transmit the commands to the ships on the left and right flanks.

'Battle speed!' Gisco ordered the helmsman and the *Melqart* sprang forward as the ship's oars were engaged.

The admiral walked calmly to the bow, his unhurried steps in contrast to the frenzied activities of the crew as final preparations for battle were made. As he walked up the steps to the foredeck, he caught sight of the approaching Roman galleys. Their sails were lowered against the oncoming wind, relying solely on oar power to propel them through the channel. Gisco smiled coldly as the order was given for his own sail to be lowered and secured against the lifting yard. The Carthaginian fleet had arrived on station under sail and their rowers would be fresher as battle was joined.

Gisco looked left and right as his fleet moved into formation. His own ship was in the centre of the three-mile line, with the remaining quinqueremes interspersed among the triremes. Boodes, his most trusted squad commander, was anchoring the starboard flank against any attempt to escape to Brolium while the port flank was held by Hamilcar to cut off retreat to the Aeolians.

The admiral stared across the five-mile gap to the Roman galleys, his eyes narrowing in hate as he watched them deploy into a line of battle. Over a year before, Gisco had been forced to abandon the city of Agrigentum in the face of the Roman legions. He had believed his army unbeatable but the Romans had shamed him. He now twisted the bitter memory into pure malice for the enemy. There would be no repeat of his ignominious defeat.

'Damn it, Lucius, signal them to hold the line!'

Atticus continued to look left and right as the *Aquila* reached her full battle speed. Lucius bellowed over the side rail for the order to be passed down the line, the command having an immediate effect on those who heard it directly. The line of battle had been slow to form and was now becoming ragged as the ships increased to battle speed. Each ship was guarding the flanks of her port and starboard cohorts, the very reason for line-of-battle formation. If the Roman line struck the Carthaginians unevenly, many ships would be immediately exposed to the deadly rams of the enemy. The experienced galleys on the flanks worked hard to dress the line and slowly the formation re-established cohesion.

Atticus grunted his satisfaction and turned once more to the approaching enemy ships, now only three miles away. They were in perfect line-of-battle formation, their expert seamanship evident in the quick collapse of their sails and steady spacing between each ship. The Carthaginians would try to run through the line of Roman ships, destroying the formation so that every ship would have to fight as a single entity. The Roman plan was to engage the Carthaginians at the first point of contact, turning their bows into the enemy's and stopping them from breaching the line. It was a tactic never tried before, but Atticus could think of no other that would allow for maximum use of the *corvus*.

As the Roman captain took one more look to his port and starboard, he could see that some galleys were still not fully in line. The air was filled with shouted orders as ships' captains commanded their crews and coordinated with their flanking galleys to keep formation. A sliver of doubt rose in Atticus's thoughts as he recalled the command crews' lack of experience. The final week in Ostia had been consumed in relentless training of the crews on how to use the *corvus*. The first head-on contact was crucial. After that the Carthaginians would have the advantage.

Septimus breathed easily as he looked over the faces of his demi-maniple of the Fourth. Only the faces in the front row were familiar, the remaining six members of his own marine command. The rest of his former command were scattered amongst the legionaries of the new fleet, their fluency in boarding providing each party with a backbone of experience. As Septimus's glance reached the end of the line, he nodded to his new *optio*. Quintus had also been reassigned and was now commanding a demi-maniple of his own, while Septimus had been given a tough second officer of the Fourth. He was an older man of few words, but the men respected him and he would anchor and steady the line on the enemy deck.

Septimus could sense the impatience of the legionaries. They were men of the Fourth, the Boar. Their legion had been dishonourably wounded at Lipara and the loss of twelve hundred of their comrades called for *vindicta*, revenge on the hated Punici. Over the years Septimus had heard many words spoken to troops before battle. In his time as centurion he had given such orations himself, a way to rally his command before battle, the words spoken to whip up the men's fighting frenzy. With cold realization he knew only two words would be needed that day to unleash their fury. As he heard the shouted command for the galley to increase to attack speed, he drew his *gladius*, knowing that the enemy were close. The eyes of sixty men were locked on Septimus, ignoring the approaching enemy over the centurion's shoulders. Septimus raised his sword.

'Avenge Lipara!'

The men roared with demonic blood lust, a roar of pure aggression. Septimus smiled grimly. They were ready.

Atticus felt his mind clear as the *Aquila* moved to attack speed. He instinctively looked left and right at the battle line to watch the other galleys match his speed. They were committed. At attack speed, the final gap of a mile would be closed in less than two minutes. There was no time for final changes, no time for doubts. His whole being became focused on the enemy before him. Over the preceding weeks he had begun to consider the enemy in abstraction, a faceless foe to be outwitted and outmanoeuvred. Now he vividly recalled each encounter, the dishonour of fleeing in the Strait of Messina still sharp, as was the rage he felt at the slaughter of the transport fleet at Brolium.

The Carthaginians were quarter of a mile away, close enough for Atticus to pick out individual details. The centre of their line was held by a quinquereme, a behemoth in comparison to the triremes flanking her hull. Atticus realized it would be the flagship, the head of the serpent. The *Aquila* was on course to strike the Carthaginian line three galleys south of the centre point. He etched every detail of the quinquereme in his mind, marking it as his prey. After the lines collapsed he would hunt her down. For the Romans, the fleet was not the last line of defence, it was the only line. The Punici had to be defeated and their commander struck down. In the centre of the Roman line, Atticus knew only the *Aquila* was equal to the task.

As the gap closed between the lines, Gisco's focus was interrupted by the sight of an unusual structure on the bow of each Roman galley. At one hundred yards his mind had little time to react and he dismissed the sight, concentrating on the gap in the line between the two enemy galleys before him. The *Melqart* would sweep through, her archers raining death as she passed, before turning once more into the rear of the line. The Romans would turn to meet the threat, exposing themselves neatly. With the entire Roman fleet consisting of triremes, Gisco was confident that no enemy ship could match the speed and power of the *Melqart*.

326

He recalled the glory of the day when his ram had claimed four Roman transport ships. At the time he had revelled in the victory, his first chance to repay the hated Romans for his defeat at Agrigentum. Now he was faced with battleships and his endless appetite for revenge was goaded by the increased danger.

'Archers, ignite!' Gisco ordered.

The pitch-soaked tips of two dozen arrows were lit at the shouted command, the archers drawing their bows to ready themselves for the command to release.

Gisco watched as the Roman galley on his port quarter veered into his course, setting her bow against that of the *Melqart*.

Gisco smiled at the idiotic manoeuvre. He would crush them for their recklessness.

'Prepare to withdraw the portside oars,' he commanded.

Gisco allowed himself a quick glance to starboard to see the rest of his line. The *Melqart*'s superior speed had put them a half-ship length beyond the line and so his galley would strike the Roman line first. He turned to the bow as the final yards swept beneath his hull.

'Withdraw!' he roared. 'Helmsman, hard to port!'

The ninety-ton *Melqart* tore into the side of her smaller opponent. The larger galley shook with the impact but Gisco saw the Roman trireme was almost capsized by the blow. Futile grappling hooks were thrown from the Roman deck, but the momentum of the quinquereme was too great and her speed continued almost unchecked. One Roman was plucked from his ship, his hand caught on the line connected to a grappling hook held fast by the *Melqart*. He was thrown into the gap between the grinding hulls, the hook finally releasing as his body was pushed under.

Gisco saw the device he had noticed earlier suddenly fall towards his ship. It was a ramp of some kind, a crude boarding device with massed ranks of legionaries formed behind it.

Gisco watched in fascination as the ramp fell onto the main deck of the *Melqart*, a series of spikes penetrating the timbers of the deck. The quinquereme shuddered at the moment of impact and for a heartbeat the two ships were locked by the inanimate ramp before the momentum of the *Melqart* broke the spell and the ramp was torn apart by the opposing forces on either end of its length. The spikes tore a huge gash along the deck before finally releasing, the ramp buckling under the strain, throwing legionaries from the far end where they had been poised to attack. Gisco roared defiance as he watched the ill-fated tactic thwarted and the quinquereme shrug off the remnants of the boarding ramp.

The cutwater of the *Melqart* tore into the extended port-side oars of the Roman galley, the splintered spars snapping like twigs against the reinforced bow.

'Loose,' Gisco roared above the crashing sounds.

The arrows seemed to dart across the rails of the enemy ship, the point-blank range allowing the archers to keep their trajectories almost horizontal, their precision deadly. Fresh calls of panic rose from the trireme as fire took hold of the deck, the cries mixed with the screams of the dying.

The *Melqart* broke through the back of the Roman line out into an uninterrupted sea. Gisco ordered the portside oars to re-engage before running to the stern rail to witness the devastation his galley had wrought on the Roman ship that had dared to challenge him.

'Come about to re-engage!' he ordered automatically as he continued to scan the back of the Roman line, expecting any minute to see other Carthaginian galleys break through.

'Loose!' Septimus roared.

The twenty *hastati* of his command threw their *pila* spears as one, the volley striking the knot of Carthaginians on the foredeck of the galley directly opposite the *Aquila* in the Carthaginian battle line, the two ships only thirty yards apart and closing. Septimus felt the deck tilt beneath him as the bow of the *Aquila* was aimed at the enemy's bow. He braced himself against the impact, holding the straps of his *scutum* shield tightly.

The collision of the equally matched ships drove the momentum out of both, and for an instant the rowers were thrown from their stations, the rhythm of their stroke shattered. Grappling hooks were thrown and made secure, creating the moment of inertia required.

'Release the *corvus*!' Septimus roared.

The thirty-six-foot ramp crashed down across the gap separating the foredecks, crushing the side rail of the enemy ship, the spikes driving deeply into the weathered timber deck. Septimus was instantly away, the legionaries following behind him at a rush. They roared in attack, the sudden onslaught temporarily stunning the Carthaginians. The Punici rallied into the charge, echoing the Romans' cries with calls to their own god of war.

The legionaries deployed with terse commands, the ingrained training of years taking control of their movements. Within an instant they presented a solid wall of interlocking shields, against which the Carthaginian charge broke in disarray.

'Advance!' Septimus ordered above the clash of battle.

The legionaries began to step forward. At each footfall they shoved their shields forward, the copper boss at the centre striking the enemy and parrying their blows. *Gladii* were punched through the narrow gaps in the wall to wound or kill the faceless enemy beyond, the cries of pain mixed with shouts of futile rage at the pitiless wall of shields. The twenty *principes* made up the first row of attack, their physical strength driving the tide of legionaries forward. Those Carthaginians that fell wounded under the wall were instantly dispatched by the junior *hastati* in the rear, giving no quarter to the desperate enemy. Within five minutes the Romans had cleared the foredeck, leaving a trail of dead behind them, and the enemy were beginning to buckle.

'We have them,' Duilius said with relish as he watched the legionaries' relentless advance from the aft-deck.

Atticus didn't reply, his eyes restless, his sailor's instincts compelling him to continually search the four quarters of the galley. The scene on board the Carthaginian galley captured by the *Aquila* was being repeated on all sides, the *corvus* tipping the odds inexorably in the Romans' favour. Not every Roman galley had met with success the first time and Atticus counted six individual duels developing in the waters behind the Roman line as opponents struggled to manoeuvre to ram or board. Smoke billowed into the sky as a Roman galley burned furiously, the desperate cries of her crew filling the air.

The sound of a tremendous crash caused Atticus to spin around to see a Carthaginian quinquereme drive home her ram into the exposed flank of a Roman galley. The Roman vessel had been stationary in the water, her bow transfixed by her *corvus* as a battle raged on a captured ship. The blow was incredible, the trireme buckling under the strike, the six-foot ram of the quinquereme disappearing into the hull of the smaller ship, pushing the trireme up onto the cutwater of the Carthaginian galley. The trireme was close to capsizing and Atticus watched as sailors were thrown over the side into the maelstrom of the churning sea.

'Consul!' Atticus shouted, immediately recognizing the quinquereme.

Duilius spun around to face the captain.

'That quinquereme is the Carthaginian flagship. We need to take her.'

Duilius looked over the starboard rail across the two-hundred-yard gap to the enemy ship. He considered the position for a mere second.

'Agreed,' he said.

'Lucius, prepare to get under way,' Atticus ordered immediately.

Atticus's order was accompanied by a shout of triumph from the legionaries on the enemy deck. The Carthaginians had finally broken, their nerve shattered by the ruthless advance of the Roman soldiers. Atticus took off at a run, rushing down the length of the galley and across the *corvus*. The enemy deck was slippery with blood, the brutal work of the legionaries. Atticus searched the ranks of the legionaries, instantly recognizing the imposing figure of Septimus. He called the centurion's name, causing Septimus to break off a command to his *optio* in order to turn. He strode back to the foredeck, his sword bloodied by his side, his shield scored and dented.

'We're breaking off the assault, Septimus. The Carthaginian flagship is on our starboard flank. We're going to attack her.'

Septimus nodded, his face grim. He turned to his waiting legionaries. They were still hungry. The remaining Carthaginians of the trireme had gone below decks to make one last stand.

'Drusus!' Septimus called, his *optio* reporting immediately.

'Fire the deck. We're withdrawing.'

The *optio* saluted, his face showing none of the surprise he felt at the decision to abandon the Carthaginian galley at the moment of victory. He ran to complete the order.

The demi-maniple formed up and marched quickly across the *corvus* once more. Atticus led them, making his own way once more to the aft-deck. Septimus watched as Drusus and two legionaries fired the deck, setting the main mast and mainsail alight before finally igniting the tiller. Once they were gone, Septimus had little doubt that the Carthaginians would be able to control the fire, but their ship would be hamstrung and useless. They would be lucky to escape.

The centurion was the last man across the *corvus*, the ramp immediately raised as he once more set foot on the deck of the *Aquila*. The galley was instantly away, swinging her bow to starboard as she came about to face her prey.

'What's the count, Drusus?' Septimus asked.

'Four dead and seven wounded. Two of those won't fight again this day.'

Septimus's face remained grim as he calculated the odds. Septimus had counted approximately fifty warriors on board the Carthaginian trireme they had just taken. The flagship would surely have twice that number. Septimus was left with forty-nine able men and five walking wounded. Good odds, he thought sardonically, the fire of battle still fierce within him. To him, the men of the Fourth had shown their courage. He would lead them again over the *corvus*, confident that they would follow him into the firestorm awaiting them.

The *Aquila* swung around in time to see the *Melqart*'s first attempt to break free of the impaled Roman trireme. The bow of the quinquereme was buried deep within her victim's hull, the untested, untempered timbers giving way completely under the hammer blow of the six-foot bronze ram. It was a killer blow, the water rushing past the ram into the lower decks of the stricken galley. Once the ram had been withdrawn, the trireme would sink like lead, taking two hundred chained slaves with her, and their cries of panic and fear could be heard above the clamour of battle.

Atticus watched the oars of the quinquereme dig deep into the water, the oar shafts straining to extract the ram. The Carthaginian was only vulnerable when stationary. Once free, her speed and power would give her unassailable odds against any Roman galley. The *Aquila* had to strike before she was released from her quarry.

'Ramming speed!' Atticus roared. 'Steer dead amidships!'

The *Aquila* accelerated to thirteen knots, her ram thrusting forward at every oar-stroke. The strike would merely wound the larger ship, but it would also bind the *Aquila* inexorably to her hull, like a bull terrier attacking a wolf, refusing to release the grip of its jaws. The *Aquila* swung onto her final heading, her arrowed bow fixed on course. Atticus whispered a prayer to Jupiter, calling on him to remember the Titans and infuse his Eagle with strength.

'Captain!' Gisco bellowed in rage. 'Get below decks and make sure those slaves are whipped to within an inch of their lives.'

The captain scurried away, fearful of the terrible wrath evident on the face of the admiral. The *Melqart* was stuck fast, the splintered hull of the Roman trireme gripping the bow of the larger ship like teeth. Gisco's fury knew no bounds as he watched the tide of battle turn against the Carthaginians. The ramp he had seen so easily destroyed by the *Melqart* was spewing Roman legionaries onto the decks of the Carthaginian triremes, the deadly effect of the new tactic fully realized on the more evenly matched ships. All around him, Roman formations were sweeping his men from the decks of their own ships, slaughtering them with cold efficiency.

Every minute spent attempting to extract the ram from the Roman ship robbed Gisco of the chance to assuage his anger and satisfy his lust for vengeance. From the corner of his eye he saw an approaching galley on a collision course. He spun round to see her, watching in satisfied anger as the trireme advanced at ramming speed, willing the battle to come to him. As his gaze swept the galley, he caught sight of the name on the bow, *Aquila*. His hatred threatened to overwhelm him and he squeezed his hand until the nails dug into the flesh of his palm. Here was a focus for his revenge. The *Aquila*, the galley that had escaped him in the Strait of Messina.

'Prepare to repel!' he roared from his position on the aft-deck.

The bulk of his men were on the main and foredecks, the archers selecting targets on the deck of the trireme impaled on the ram. The order was lost in the noise of battle. Gisco turned to Khalil, the man's massive frame tensed under the leather-bound chest-plate.

'The Romans depend on discipline and command,' Gisco snarled. 'Bring me the head of the Roman centurion and I will grant you your wish.'

'Yes, Admiral,' Khalil replied, his mind already picturing the Roman consul he had once called master under his blade. The sight hardened his resolve and hatred for the Romans. Gisco sensed the hatred, smiling to himself. He too would have a target in the fight to follow, the captain of the *Aquila*. The man had disgraced him in the Strait of Messina, dishonouring him before his own fleet. Now he would extract the price of that humiliation in blood.

Gisco drew his sword, his personal guard following suit. He turned and marched quickly across the aft-deck, his eyes never leaving the approaching galley. He roared his order again, this time his command heard by many on the main deck. They turned into the sight of the Roman galley, their faces first registering shock and then cool determination as they formed up to receive the oncoming assault, eager to bloody their swords.

*

Septimus stood tall at the head of the assembled men. The ranks behind him were swelled by fifteen *praetoriani*, the consul releasing them in the desperate bid to take the Carthaginian flagship. They were the cream of the Roman army, each man a veteran of battle, and their strength re-invigorated the battered demi-maniple. Septimus waited as he judged the distance to the enemy deck, his *hastati* once more armed with deadly *pila* spears. At ramming speed the moment would soon be upon them.

At fifty yards Septimus could see the Punici form up into a knot of men on the main deck. They were well over one hundred in number. Beside them the rail of the foredeck was lined with archers.

'Raise shields!'

The first of the Carthaginian arrows soared across the closing gap, many with their tips aflame. At thirteen knots, the *Aquila* was a difficult target, but the close range allowed for near-flat trajectories and Septimus felt the arrows slam into his shield on the exposed foredeck. Behind him he heard shouted commands as fires were doused on the main deck and one man cried out as an arrow found its mark.

'*Hastati*, prepare to release on my command!'

The junior soldiers shifted their weight behind interlocking shields as they prepared to target the massed formation on the enemy main deck. Septimus breathed out slowly as he judged the distance with a trained eye. The volley would have to be perfect if the necessary chaos was to be instilled in the enemy ranks. He picked out individual men in the enemy formation, their shouted war cries lost in the noise of battle. Their faces were masks of fury and blood lust, of intense hostility. They would not die easily.

'Loose!' Septimus roared, as his body instinctively braced itself for the oncoming collision of the two ships.

The bronze ram of the *Aquila* struck the *Melqart* dead amidships, its blunt-nosed point striking the hull cleanly, the four-inch-deep cork-oak timbers splintering with the force of the collision. The *Aquila* seemed to reel from the blow, the impact transmitted down the long axis of the hull, as if the galley had struck solid rock. For a long second the men on both ships staggered under the impact, their balance and focus lost with the brute force of the blow.

Septimus didn't wait for his men to recover. Knowing there would be no retreat, he swung his *gladius* in an arc to sever the line holding the *corvus* aloft. The ramp crashed down onto the main deck of the Carthaginian galley, crushing a man beneath its weight, its foot-long spikes biting down on the deck timbers to bind the fate of both galleys.

'Advance!' Septimus roared, running at full tilt across the twenty-foot ramp, never looking behind him, sure by the cries he heard that his lead was being followed. The massive centurion raised his shield to chest height and angled his body to put the weight of his shoulder behind the charging wall of reinforced, canvas-covered timber. Septimus's momentum was duplicated to his left and right by the legionaries, who threw themselves across the six-foot-wide ramp. As one they slammed into the enemy formation, the brass bosses of their shields crunching bone and cartilage.

'Wedge formation!' Septimus ordered as the legionaries deployed from the head of the *corvus*.

Another Carthaginian fell under the centurion's blade as he heard his *optio*, Drusus, shout orders to dress the flanks of the wedge. Septimus continued to push deep into the enemy's centre, aiming to create a bridgehead that would allow his troops to form a solid line of battle. The gamble was significant. The wedge formation would shock the enemy and slow their response, but it was brittle, the thin edge exposed to the enemy on two quarters.

Septimus clearly heard Punic commands shouted in the pitch of battle. The Carthaginian commander was rallying his troops, aiming to reverse the momentum of the Roman charge. Septimus almost sensed the change in the enemy formation before it occurred, the Carthaginians at the rear pushing forward to check the retreat of their front line.

'Line of battle!' the centurion roared, an instant before the Carthaginian thrust reached the front.

The wall of interlocking shields formed up to create a semi-circle around the boarding point.

'Steady the line!'

The legionaries roared their acknowledgement of the command. Unable to advance against the mass of the enemy pushing against them, they would hold the line of battle where they stood. There would be no retreat, no forfeiture of the deck already held. From this moment their mettle would be tested. Whichever side broke first would be slaughtered.

'Push them back into the sea!' Gisco bellowed as the Romans' initial thrust was checked.

From his position at the rear of the formation he watched the first steps backward as the Romans surged into his men. The sight enraged him and, sensing the panic ripple through his men, he watched for the first sign of retreat. A young soldier turned his back on the fight, a moment of hesitation that cost him his life as Gisco ran his sword into the man's chest.

Gisco stepped over the body and pushed his way into the formation, his personal guard and Khalil following, forming a solid knot that drove directly at the apex of the Roman wedge. His shouted commands and presence amongst his men overcame the first heated moments of panic, and the Carthaginians turned into the fight with renewed vigour. Five men back from the front line, Gisco watched the Roman line re-form into a seemingly impenetrable wall of shields. His eyes scanned the Roman line for the man he sought and found him at the centre of the formation, his height setting him apart from the men on his flanks. Gisco turned to Khalil to single the man out but the Nubian had already identified his prey.

Gisco renewed his cry to advance and his men surged forward, the momentum allowing Khalil to push through to the forefront of the formation. Within seconds he would be poised to attack the very centre of the enemy line – his target, the Roman centurion.

Atticus ignored the strike of the arrow on his *hoplon* shield as he stood on the foredeck of the *Aquila*. From the moment Septimus had led his men across the *corvus*, Atticus had realized the magnitude of the task set for the legionaries. The enemy outnumbered them by at least two to one and, after the initial shock of boarding had been overcome, the Carthaginians would fight fiercely to defend their ship.

With victory in the balance, Atticus had assembled on the foredeck the best fighters from amongst his crew. The twenty men were veterans of countless battles and skirmishes with pirates, and they stood stoically as the battle unfolded before them. Eight of Atticus's crew were skilled with a bow and they worked to keep the Carthaginian archers at bay, their own arrows seeking targets on the decks of the *Melqart*. Atticus suppressed the urge to rush across the *corvus* as he saw yet another legionary fall under the enemy's onslaught. Atticus and his men knew nothing of legion tactics and would hamper the strict discipline of the line formation. If the enemy broke through, the battle would descend into a mêlée. Only then would Atticus unleash his men.

Septimus grunted as a fresh surge hit the shield wall and he shoved his shoulder forward to counter the lunge. His *gladius* sought the gap between the shields and he struck low, seeking the groin of an unseen enemy. His sword connected with flesh and he twisted the blade, hearing the cry of pain as yet another Carthaginian fell under the Roman attack. He withdrew his sword, its blade dulled with anonymous blood, before sending it out again to maim and kill.

Septimus's shoulders and upper arms ached as he reversed the thrust. The physical stress of the battle was beginning to take its toll on the legionaries. In a land battle the three-line, *triplex acies*, formation allowed for troops to be rotated from the front line to let men rest before rejoining the fight. In a demi-maniple on the deck of a Carthaginian ship, no such respite could be granted. The legionaries would have to continue fighting until the fight was done. Stamina, willpower and courage had become the foundations for the last line of defence.

A guttural war cry cut through the air and Septimus arrested his next sword stroke, his warrior instincts screaming at him to beware. The shield of the legionary to his left was struck with a force that pushed the man off his balance, exposing a small gap in the shield wall. The next legionary along the line thrust his sword into the breach but it was instantly struck down, the attack anticipated. Septimus bellowed for Drusus to cover the possible breach, unable to help the man to his left without turning and exposing the flank of the man to his right. The legionary's shield was struck again, this time with a ferocity that caused the soldier's legs to buckle, and Septimus was given a glance at the enemy warrior forcing the breach. His eyes widened in shocked awareness as he recognized the figure of Khalil, Scipio's Nubian slave. The man's face was twisted in grim determination as he bore down on the legionary, battering his sword like a hammer on the anvil of the shield. A final thrust tore through the legionary's defence and he fell, clutching at the mortal blow to his stomach.

The Carthaginians screamed in triumph as the breach was made. Time seemed to slow for Septimus as he watched the enemy ranks swell in anticipation of exploiting the gap. Survival and victory for the Romans now depended entirely on discipline. With the line breached and their backs exposed, there was the immediate threat that the legionaries would panic. If they fled they would be cut down. If Septimus re-established order they would survive and counterattack. Everything now depended on his command. As the order formed on his lips, Septimus instinctively threw up his sword to counter a thrust from Khalil. The Nubian had not rushed through as anticipated, but instead had turned into the centurion, focusing his attack on the embattled commander.

Septimus was forced to parry another blow as Carthaginians surged through the gap made by Khalil. The centurion took another step back under the onslaught, the Nubian's blade seeming to strike in two places at once as the speed of the blows intensified. A tiny portion of Septimus's mind registered the need to regain control of his men, but the thought was overwhelmed by his survival instinct as he narrowly defended a counter-thrust. He raged at his incapacitation, his inability to command his men when they needed him most. As he readjusted his balance and took a further step back, he planted his feet firmly on the deck. Steady the line, he thought grimly as another blow was parried. The battle for the Carthaginian flagship might be lost but Septimus would ensure that at least his fight for the legions would be won.

*

'Breach!' Atticus roared as he pointed to the emerging gap in the Roman formation with the tip of his sword.

'Men of the *Aquila*, to me!'

Atticus raced across the *corvus*, his men at his heels, shouting the name of their galley as they charged. The captain swerved into the line of the breach in time to see a powerful black warrior step through to engage Septimus. Atticus recognized him immediately but his mind swept the shock of recognition clear as it focused on the vital action needed to save the Roman line. Another legionary fell and the charge intensified, the breach widening.

A dozen Carthaginians were through the breach, their cries of triumph causing the Roman line to waver as the legionaries felt their backs exposed to encirclement. The men of the *Aquila* crashed into the charge at full tilt, their attack cutting the premature cries of success short. Atticus brought his *hoplon* shield high to block an overarm blow of a Carthaginian axe, driving his sword underneath into the exposed flank of his attacker. The strike knocked the Carthaginian off his feet and Atticus twisted the blade to release the weapon from the man's ribs. His men overwhelmed the breach, their frenzied attack causing the Carthaginians to hesitate at their expected moment of success.

'Men of the Fourth! The line is held!' Atticus roared, his eyes scanning the backs of the Roman legionaries. The Boars of Rome roared as the tide was turned again and they intensified their defence.

The Carthaginians trapped behind the now solid line fought with the desperation of doomed men. At their centre was Khalil, his focus entirely on Septimus, their fight exemplifying the intensity of the bitter struggle. The centurion's spirit rose as he registered the shouted acclamation of Atticus, the captain now engaged in the front line. The battle was once more finely balanced and victory was there for the taking.

Septimus stepped inside another strike from Khalil and reversed his sword to rake the Nubian's stomach. Khalil bunched his shield into the assault, narrowly deflecting the blade against the shield edge. The men were mere inches apart, their combined skills keeping the combat close, their blades a whirl of iron. Septimus focused his mind on the movements of his attacker, searching for a weakness, a way through. With the clarity of discovery, Septimus realized his advantage over the Nubian. Khalil was using his rounded shield for defence only, his sword the only offensive weapon in the attack. The legions had taught Septimus differently.

Khalil kept his attack high, forcing Septimus back on the defensive as he parried a sequenced series of blows. The Nubian suddenly inverted the attack and Septimus cried out in pain as Khalil's sword swept the back of his thigh. The wound itself was not mortal, but it would kill him nevertheless as his balance crumbled, his body automatically favouring his uninjured leg. Against an opponent of Khalil's skill, the end would come swiftly. Septimus had mere seconds to react.

The centurion attacked with ferocity, forcing Khalil to throw up his shield, keeping his sword low, poised, waiting for the opportunity to counterattack. Septimus registered the stance, the coiled energy of the Nubian, waiting for his own chance to end the fight. Septimus ground his teeth against the pain and shifted his weight onto his injured leg. He could feel the severed muscle buckle under the strain, and his cry of pain mingled with a vicious roar of attack. He lunged forward with his *scutum* shield, striking the Nubian's sword arm with the copper boss of the shield, the unexpected blow throwing Khalil completely off balance, causing him to stumble backwards. Septimus resisted the intense urge to ease the pressure on his injured leg and he continued the lunge, committing himself fully to the desperate attack. Khalil's arms raised fractionally to balance himself and Septimus seized his chance. He whipped his *gladius* high through the opening, the blade cutting cleanly through Khalil's arm, severing the sword hand from the wrist. Khalil screamed in pain, dropping his shield as he grasped the stump of his injured arm. He bowed over the wound and Septimus reversed his swing to bring the sword down in a killing blow. At the last instant the centurion stayed his blade and he struck Khalil on the top of his head with the iron hilt of the *gladius*. The Nubian collapsed, unconscious, before he hit the deck.

Khalil's fall was registered by the front line of the Carthaginian formation and their will cracked at the loss of such a powerful warrior, the only man who had forced a breach in the Roman line. Septimus straightened up slowly as the last of the Carthaginians trapped behind the line was dispatched by Atticus's crew.

'Advance the line!' Septimus ordered, finally released to command his men.

The legionaries stepped forward under the familiar command of a centurion, their swords exacting a terrible price from the Carthaginians on the front line. A ripple of panic ran through the Carthaginian formation, a ripple that soon became a wave as Carthaginians turned from the advancing wall of shield and iron, the vacuum created by their retreat hastening the advance of the line. Almost as one they finally broke, their resistance buckling, and they fled the main deck as one. The Romans cheered in triumph as the pressure against their line dissipated.

'Drusus!' Septimus called, the *optio* immediately by his side.

'Two parties, fore and aft, clear the decks and then sweep below. Wipe out all resistance.'

The *optio* nodded and left to command the legionaries. Only then did Septimus collapse from his wound.

Hamilcar was staggered by the sight before him. Everywhere he looked Carthaginian galleys were locked in hopeless fights against an enemy that had somehow turned the naval battle into a land war, immediately making a mockery of the generations-old superior seamanship of the Carthaginians. The Punic warriors, so skilled at boarding and shock attacks, were completely outclassed by the efficient butchery of the Roman legionaries, the wall of shields an impenetrable barrier that swept each deck in turn.

Hamilcar's quinquereme, the *Byblos*, sailed unopposed around the flank of the battle, her superior size deterring any Roman attack against her hull. The *Byblos* was surrounded by Carthaginian triremes milling in abject confusion, their initial escape from the dreaded Roman boarding ramp, and the witnessed destruction of their sister ships, compelling them to withhold from re-engaging the enemy. The sight made Hamilcar nauseous, the shame of his countrymen's timidity and fear coursing through his heart.

Even at a mile's distance he had seen the *Melqart* re-engage, her distinctive size distinguishing her from the surrounding vessels. The Carthaginian centre was completely collapsed around her, the quinquereme flagship lost in the maelstrom. It was a sight that sobered Hamilcar, forcing him to rationally examine the situation as a commander. Gisco had failed. The battle was lost. With bitter resignation, Hamilcar realized the decision that needed to be made, the unendurable order that needed to be given if the remainder of the fleet was to survive. With the taste of acrid shame in his throat, he issued the command to withdraw, cursing the admiral who had once again led the sons of Carthage to defeat.

Gisco bellowed with rage as his forces fled past him for the main deck, leaving the admiral standing alone with his personal guard of a dozen soldiers. On the brink of collapse, Gisco had watched in desperation as the Carthaginian war cries gave way to muttered sounds of panic and furtive glances over shoulders as men sought avenues of escape. Gisco had seen Khalil fall, the massive Nubian warrior clearly visible even in the maelstrom of battle. The fall was immediately followed by a shouted Roman command to advance as the centurion once more took charge of his men. The moment of victory had been snatched from Gisco by the re-formation of the Roman line and the Romans' success in holding the breach. One man had brought about the recovery of the Roman line; one man who Gisco had seen run across the boarding ramp at the very height of the battle.

The *Melqart* was lost but victory was still in the offing, a victory that now depended on Gisco avoiding capture. He quickly ordered two of his men to launch the skiff and bring it alongside, making ready the flight he now knew was inevitable. Only one task remained before his escape, one vow to fulfil, one man to send through the gates of Hades. The man who had precipitated his defeat, the captain of the *Aquila*.

Atticus cheered with his men as the Carthaginians fled before the Roman line, the enemy split down the middle as men ran towards the fore and aft of the ship, seeking refuge and escape below decks. As his eyes scanned the chaotic scene before him, Atticus noticed an unmoved knot of men formed at the far rail. There were maybe a dozen in total, their leader standing tall at their head. Atticus recognized him immediately, although it had been months since their first encounter. He was the commander who had chased the *Aquila* from the Strait of Messina, and Atticus realized in an instant that the commander of the Carthaginian flagship was the admiral of the Punici.

Atticus bellowed a challenge to the Carthaginian, the remaining men of the *Aquila* immediately forming behind their captain as they saw the reason for his outburst. Gisco had been scanning the deck himself and the shouted defiance focused his attention on the man he sought amidst the chaos.

'You!' Gisco roared.

For a heartbeat the two men locked eyes across the blood-soaked deck, their mutual belligerence forming an inescapable bond. Gisco's mind swam with visions of defeat at Agrigentum, of humiliation in the Strait of Messina and the doomed fleet surrounding him. Atticus saw only the massacre at Brolium, the defeat at Lipara and the vow he had made to a centurion many weeks before.

With a visceral cry both men charged across the deck, their crews following recklessly behind. The two forces met in the centre, the groups overlapping into a mêlée of tangled, individual contests. The fight was vicious, the men of the *Aquila* outnumbering the Carthaginians, and within seconds the balance of the struggle was set.

Atticus and Gisco fought in the middle of the fray, their fury turning the fight into an uncoordinated brawl, both men using their swords like clubs in the frenzy of attack. Within seconds the contest became one of brute physicality, anger and hate suppressing all skill. Gisco's strength, forged by thirty years of combat, pitted against the speed of a younger man.

Atticus was first to regain his wits, and he focused his mind to channel his aggression. Gisco's attack filled his vision, the endless blows numbing his sword arm, and Atticus sidestepped suddenly to gain a heartbeat's respite. His speed fooled Gisco, the admiral immediately trying to re-engage, but Atticus side-stepped once more to keep the Carthaginian off balance.

Gisco roared in frustration as the Roman captain continued to elude his sword, the younger man's superior speed now dictating the focus of combat. Gisco realized that within a dozen strikes the contest would be lost, its end inevitable. The adrenaline and blood lust in his system rapidly cooled as his body sensed the failing strength of his arm and he stepped back for the first time, his eyes seeing a look of triumph cross the Roman's face. With a final ferocious roar Gisco summoned up all his rage, all the hate within his soul for the enemy he could never overcome, and he grabbed the man to his left and hurled him at the Roman captain.

Atticus reacted instinctively to the sudden attack, the oncoming Carthaginian completely off balance from the unexpected push. Atticus drove his sword forward, putting his shoulder behind the thrust and, although the Carthaginian guardsman reacted instinctively, he could not avoid the outstretched blade, the *gladius* striking him full in the chest, the momentum of his charge and the force of the strike burying the blade deeply. Atticus was shoved off his feet as the full weight of the guardsman hit him, the Carthaginian dead before both men struck the deck. Atticus kicked wildly to free himself, twisting his blade to release it from the clinging flesh, the rush of blood warm over his hand. He pushed the Carthaginian to the side and clambered up, immediately regaining his balance and adopting a defensive stance in the midst of the dying fight around him. His eyes sought out the Carthaginian admiral, expecting to see him directly in front. It took a full second before Atticus realized his enemy had fled.

Gisco reached the side rail at full tilt, diving over the side in a single movement. He fell ten feet before striking the water, the weight of his armour and the height of his fall driving him deep beneath the surface. His powerful arms struck out and he regained the surface, the salt water bitter in his mouth. Strong hands grabbed his arms and lifted him cleanly from the water into the skiff, the two men immediately retaking the oars and sculling with all speed away from the flagship. Gisco coughed and pulled himself up to look back at the rail he had just jumped. The Roman captain was standing there, his face twisted in mottled rage. Gisco felt the equal emotion swell within him and his anger burst forth.

'The curse of Mot on you, Roman!' he screamed. 'This fight is not over . . .'

'Archers!' Atticus roared for the second time, the impotence of his rage clouding his mind. The Carthaginian commander was escaping, the arch-fiend who had slaughtered Atticus's countrymen at Brolium and brought the legions of Sicily to their knees. Atticus's gaze swept the sea before him for another Roman galley, for any ship that could cut off the Carthaginian's escape. He swung around in agitation, searching the deck again for archers. There were none. His eyes sought out the skiff again, watching in bitter frustration as the three men shouted to a Carthaginian galley beyond the entangled line of battle, her course change answering the call. Atticus threw his sword to the deck in anger, his mind barely registering the clarion calls of victory emanating from the Roman galleys on all sides.

Duilius walked slowly across the *corvus*, his eyes ranging over the scene of carnage before him. He had never witnessed a battle before and the adrenaline and euphoria of victory were lost at the sight of slaughter. He choked down the bitter taste of bile in his throat as he fought to control himself. The smell of battle was overwhelming, the air filled with the scent of blood and voided bowels, of burnt timber and flesh. Romans

– legionaries, sailors, marines and *praetoriani* – lay strewn amongst the Carthaginian dead, their shared fate marking them as comrades in the hard-fought victory.

The Roman centurion, Capito, was lying on his back on the deck, his wound being tended to by one of his men. Beside him lay a huge Nubian warrior, his face bloodless in shock as he nursed the bloodied stump that had once been his hand.

Captain Perennis stood by the mainmast, surrounded by the remains of his crew, men who had rushed headlong across the *corvus* to seal the breach in the Roman line and save the battle for the Carthaginian flagship. He was issuing orders to his second-in-command, orders that would secure the Carthaginian vessel and release any Roman slaves below decks.

Beyond the *Melqart*, the sea to the west was strewn with fleeing Carthaginian galleys. Over half of their fleet was escaping, many scattering in panic and confusion, while a core number followed in loose formation behind the quinquereme. Duilius had stayed the order to pursue, conscious that the element of surprise that the *corvus* had afforded them was lost, and in the open sea the Carthaginians still held the advantage. He regretted the lost opportunity to eradicate the enemy fleet, knowing that soon the *Classis Romanus* would have to face them again.

Duilius watched as the *optio* led a group of slaves up from the lower decks. His eyes passed over their number without interest, their pathetic condition failing to evoke pity in Duilius's weary soul. He was about to turn when the last man in the group arrested his attention. He was filthy, his only clothing a soiled tunic, but he stood tall, his eyes alive with intensity, and it was only when those eyes looked at Duilius, and the light of hatred cast itself upon him, that he finally recognized Scipio.

*

'Curse you!' Gisco bellowed as he stormed down the gang-plank onto the dock at Panormus, his sword raised in anger, his face demonic at the sight of shattered crews disembarking their dead and wounded onto the dock, the spirit of each man broken by the sudden reversal in fortune. 'Get back to your galleys, all of you: this fight is not over . . . !'

The Carthaginian crewmen on the dock scattered before Gisco's flailing sword, some running back to their galleys but many more fleeing towards the town. A vacuum formed around Gisco on the dock, an empty void that he filled with his frustration and anger. He recognized one of the galley captains and ran towards him, grabbing the petrified commander by the arm before bringing the tip of his sword up under his chin, forcing the captain onto his toes.

'Who gave you the order to abandon the battle?' Gisco spat, twisting his blade until a drop of blood appeared.

'Commander Barca . . .' the captain stammered, his eyes alive with fear.

'Barca!' Gisco roared, throwing the captain to the ground. He twisted his sword and began to beat the captain with the flat of the blade, snapping the man's forearm the instant it was thrown up in defence, his anger knowing no bounds. The captain cried out for mercy, his pleas ignored by the fanatical Gisco. Suddenly the fall of his sword was stayed by an outstretched blade, the unexpected strike causing Gisco to loose his grip on his weapon.

'Seize him!' Hamilcar commanded, keeping his sword charged against Gisco's throat.

Hamilcar's guards rushed forward and took hold of Gisco's arms, the admiral struggling against their superior strength.

'Release me! I will have you all flogged raw for this insult! And you,' Gisco rounded on Hamilcar, his face a mask of fury, 'I will have you crucified for cowardice.'

'No, Admiral,' Hamilcar replied, his voice cold and calm, 'it is I who will have you crucified for failure.'

'You cannot!' Gisco railed. 'I command here. These men answer to me!'

'They answer to Carthage!' Hamilcar roared back, his temper unleashed. 'And on the island of Sicily, I am Carthage!'

'You cannot!' Gisco repeated, his voice now tinged with fear.

'I am an envoy of the Council and a son of Carthage and you have failed both . . . Take him away!'

The guards hauled Gisco towards the barracks, the admiral bellowing a tirade of hate laced with accusations of treachery. Hamilcar ignored the shouts, ordering the men to continue their attendance of the wounded and dead.

The slain were laid ceremoniously in ranks, their arms folded across their chests, waiting patiently for their journey to the world of Mot. Hamilcar looked upon them with reverence, marking their faces in his memory. They had fought well for their city and Hamilcar murmured a prayer to Tanit, the queen goddess of Carthage, for their souls, his mind already picturing the funeral pyres that would cleanse the mortal remains of the fallen and release their spirits to the gods.

Today Hamilcar would grieve with honour for the dead. Tomorrow, he vowed, the living would pay the price for failure. And as the ashes of the pyres grew cold after the inferno, so too would Hamilcar harden his heart for the terrible retribution to come.

EPILOGUE

Gaius Duilius raised his hand in victory as he entered the Forum Magnum at the head of the triumphal parade. The whole area was thronged with the people of Rome, their number swelled by the promise of wine and food, a celebration of victory for the *Classis Romanus* at the Battle of Mylae four weeks before. Duilius wore the *corona graminea*, the grass crown, upon his head, an award given only to commanders whose actions saved a besieged army, and he was dressed in a ceremonial toga, its cloth solid purple, embroidered with gold, a gift from the gracious people of Rome.

The consul's gaze swept across the crowd in front of him before resting on the men gathered on the steps of the Curia. Every senator was present, ally and foe alike, all save for one man. Duilius smiled at the sight, a response to the summons he had issued that none could ignore for fear of crossing the most powerful man in Rome. As tradition dictated, a slave stood behind Duilius on his chariot, whispering in his ears the words, 'Memento mori; remember that thou art mortal,' a reminder from the gods that he was just a man. Duilius ignored the slave, the truth of the words lost in the heady wine of victory and the potent aphrodisiac of power.

Atticus rode in a chariot directly behind the consul, the

place of honour insisted upon by a grateful Duilius, even after the captain had requested leave to return to his galley. Many in the crowd recognized Atticus from the stories told by the orators that Duilius had hired to spread the tale of their victory all over Rome, and they called out his name in tribute. Atticus acknowledged the cries with a nod, unsure of how to respond as he kept his right hand firmly on the reins, his left gripping the shaft that held aloft the new banner of the *Classis Romanus*.

Atticus smiled inwardly at the sound of Roman voices heralding a Greek name, and his thoughts returned to the constant conflict of emotions that symbolized his loyalty to Rome. On this of all days he couldn't help but feel part of the surging crowd that surrounded him on all sides, their cheers infectious, their own unquestioning loyalty to Rome impossible to ignore. It was a city like no other, populated by a race of men who constantly strove to expand their world at the expense of others, and Atticus looked over his shoulder to see what that ambition had wrought. An army of slaves followed behind, carrying the bronze rams of the captured enemy galleys, rams that would adorn a new column being raised in the Forum to mark Rome's victory.

Atticus turned once more as the parade came to a halt at the foot of the steps of the Curia. He watched as Duilius dismounted from his chariot, his arm raised once more as the renewed cheers of the crowd mixed with the constant clarion calls of a thousand trumpets. The consul turned slowly to face Atticus, gesturing with his hand for the captain to join him on his triumphant walk up the steps of the Curia. Atticus stepped forward, never relinquishing his grip on the banner of the *Classis Romanus* as, side by side, the two men began their climb.

*

The sound of distant trumpets sent Marcus running up the steps leading to the parapet above the main gate. His heart soared at the sight before him, the long train of red- and purple-clad warriors approaching to the sound of drums and cheering from the men within the encampment. Two days before, on the ninth day, a troop of fifty Roman horsemen had reached Makella with news that the legions were following on a forced march from Brolium. The camp had cheered at the news before unceremoniously slaughtering the cavalry's fifty mounts, the horse meat sustaining them as they waited for the coming rescue.

The gates below Marcus were opened without command and the legionaries of the Ninth spilled out to line the road to the camp. Marcus recognized a tall centurion accompanying the first maniple on horseback, his gaze steady, his back straight in the saddle. He rushed down from the parapet and pushed his way out into the middle of the road, standing with arms akimbo, a broad smile across his face. Septimus spotted Marcus immediately. He issued a terse order over his shoulder for an *optio* to take over, before dismounting and covering the last few steps on foot, his determined stride marked by a pronounced limp. Septimus had requested temporary leave from the *Aquila*, a request readily granted by Duilius; Septimus had arranged to be in the vanguard of the force that would relieve Makella and Segeste, wanting to personally discharge his promise to his old commander.

Marcus strode up to Septimus, his hand proffered in comradeship.

'Welcome to Makella, marine,' he said with a smile.

'You look hungry,' Septimus replied, shaking the centurion's hand, marking the last time they had exchanged the gesture and the vow that was now fulfilled.

*

Scipio swallowed another mouthful of wine as the sound of the cheering crowd washed up from the Forum half a mile away. His town house was deserted, the servants dismissed, his guards commandeered for the triumphal parade of Gaius Duilius. Scipio's hate swelled inside him at the thought of the consul's name, a man who had taken everything that was rightfully his. He vividly remembered their last encounter on the deck of the Carthaginian flagship, the look of disdain and disgust on Duilius's face, his dismissive tone as he ordered Scipio to be taken on board the *Aquila*, his rank of senior consul ignored. He also remembered a similar look of victory and success on the face of the young Captain Perennis as he stood amongst his battle-hardened crew. It was a sight that was for ever burned into Scipio's soul.

The triumphal parade was coming to a head in the Forum Magnum, the crowd being whipped to a frenzy as Duilius marched victoriously up the steps of the Curia. Once there, the Senate would crown him with a golden wreath of olives, an everlasting symbol of his victory. Scipio retched at the sight in his mind's eye, at the thought of the accolades stolen from him through deceit and betrayal. There was even a proposal before the Senate to award Duilius with a cognomen, an honorary title in recognition of his victory. Scipio's political rivals had already bestowed on Scipio a cognomen of his own: *Asina* – 'donkey' – in recognition of his ignominious defeat at Lipara.

Scipio stood up suddenly as a figure entered the room. It was Fabiola, his wife. She approached slowly, her expression hard and cold. She took the goblet of wine from his hand and laid it gently on the table.

'You were betrayed,' she said simply.

Scipio nodded and sat back down, his hand reaching for the wine goblet again.

Fabiola stayed his grasp before taking his chin in her hand, raising his face so she could look him directly in the eye.

'You were betrayed within this very house, by one of your slaves, a man in the service of Duilius.'

Scipio absorbed the words slowly.

'You know his identity?' he asked.

'Yes, and he is oblivious.'

Scipio nodded, understanding immediately. If the traitor within his midst was unaware that his true identity was known, Scipio could manipulate the information Duilius received. He smiled at the thought, his expression mirrored in the face of his wife. Scipio closed his eyes as the cheers in the Forum reached a crescendo. For the first time the sound did not disturb him, and he filtered out the noise to allow his mind to focus on the faces of his enemies, the faces of senators and a naval captain, enemies that would pay dearly for their disloyalty and betrayal.

Gisco roared in agony as a second nail was driven through his right hand. The hangmen worked with silent efficiency, ignoring the grotesque, maniacal expression of their charge as they bound his wrists to the crosspiece. Hamilcar viewed the condemned admiral dispassionately, his disgust at the obscene ritual hidden behind a cold expression. Only yards away, Boodes screamed a silent scream as the garrotte around his neck was given one final turn. He collapsed to the ground, his swollen tongue purple from strangulation. Two guards walked forward and lifted the lifeless body of the former squad commander, throwing it onto the fire already fuelled by the bodies of the six other commanders of the fleet.

The hammer blows continued as Gisco's feet were nailed to the sides of the cross, the position designed to support the upper body and prolong the agony. Gisco's screams of pain continued unabated, the strength that had carried him through life depriving him of the oblivion of unconsciousness. The cross was hoisted up and made fast, the transfer of weight onto Gisco's tortured hands and feet robbing him of every vestige of dignity, and he begged for the release of death.

Hamilcar ignored the cries, turning his back on Gisco to look out over the harbour. Ninety-six galleys lay at anchor in Panormus, ninety-six that had escaped the disaster at Mylae, a hollow prize given the loss of so many. Hamilcar would report the summary execution of Gisco, the admiral's life a token consolation, along with a request to the Council for full command of the campaign to be given to him immediately. His first action would be to summon the fleet at Malaka on the southern coast of Iberia, a fleet of one hundred and twenty galleys that could be in Sicilian waters within a month.

Hamilcar turned once more to Gisco, the admiral's screams now abated to a low murmur of incoherent cries. For an instant his senses seemed to return and his eyes looked past Hamilcar to the shattered fleet he once commanded. He roared a visceral challenge, the incomprehensible words born from an unrecognizable emotion. Hamilcar nodded to himself, deciding Gisco's final fate. Tomorrow he would order Gisco's legs broken, ending the admiral's life by suffocation, the weight of his own body constricting his lungs, the end coming swiftly.

Hamilcar dismissed his guard and walked back along the beach towards the port. He cursed the island of Sicily, hating it anew, its arid shore and coarse mountains so different from the fertile hinterland of Carthage. The defeat at Mylae was a dark mark against the pride of his city, a mark he felt on his own heart, a mark that could only be removed with Roman blood. The enemy were now poised to strike at Thermae, the only other port the Carthaginians held on the northern coast. The Romans would become careless in the aftermath of their victory, their confidence blinding them into believing the Carthaginians were all but beaten. Hamilcar vowed to shatter that illusion.

Atticus looked down at the Carthaginian war banners that carpeted the steps of the Curia as he and Duilius made their way up to the assembled Senate, remembering when and where he had last seen them.

'You belong in Rome, Atticus,' Duilius said suddenly, his voice barely audible over the constant cheers of the crowd. Atticus looked over at the man by his side, the consul's expression proud and magnanimous.

'Join me on my staff,' he continued, 'and I promise you, the city will always be at your feet.'

Duilius held Atticus's gaze for a second before turning his face upward once more as they covered the last few steps to the top, the members of the Senate moving back from the edge to allow a place in the centre for their consul. Atticus walked on behind Duilius before turning, his breath catching in his throat as he drank in the sight before him, the assembled masses of Rome spread out from the foot of the steps of the Curia, the entire city at his feet.

Waves of sound crashed over Atticus as he watched Duilius being presented with a golden wreath of olives by the Senate, and he closed his eyes against the noise, his mind transposing the sound into that of the crashing waves of the sea against the cutwater of the *Aquila*. In that instant Atticus was sure his place would always be on the aft-deck of his galley, and in his mind's eye he could see the clear horizon over the bow of the *Aquila*, taste and smell the salt-laden air of an onshore breeze, hear the sound of the canvas sail catching the prevailing wind in a crack of cloth and rigging as the finely balanced hull of the *Aquila* sliced through the white horses of the wave tops.

Atticus opened his eyes once again as Duilius turned to accept the adulation of the crowd, but the sense that he belonged elsewhere stayed with him in his heart. Rome would never be his home but Atticus knew that for now his destiny was intertwined with hers, his fate and future commanded by a city his forefathers had called their enemy. He, like the *Aquila*, was no longer alone, no longer a solitary warrior of the sea. He was now a commander in the Roman fleet and the *Aquila* was a ship of Rome.

HISTORICAL NOTE

The First Punic War began in 264 BC when the inhabitants of the city of Messina, fearing occupation from Hiero II, the tyrant of Syracuse, sent envoys to both Rome and Carthage pleading for an alliance that would protect their city. Carthage was the first to react and after persuading Hiero to call off his advance, promptly occupied Messina themselves, installing a garrison and effectively taking control of the city.

Rome had been slow to react, believing the conflict between Syracuse and Messina to be an internal conflict. However the permanent presence of a Carthaginian force so close to Italy prompted the Republic to land a force of their own on Sicily, the first time the legions had ever deployed off the mainland. By the end of 264 BC, and after several defeats, Hiero concluded an agreement with Rome that allowed Syracuse to remain independent but confined her forces within her own borders on the south-east corner of Sicily. The conflict was now transformed into a contest between Carthage and Rome with each vying for complete control of Sicily.

In 262 BC the Romans besieged the city of Agrigentum. The siege was finally lifted after several months by the Carthaginian navy but in the ensuing land battle the Romans prevailed and the city fell into their hands. The city's commander, Hannibal Gisco did not suffer censure for the defeat although the loss of Agrigentum was considered a significant blow.

Polybius, the Greek historian, states that the Romans did indeed build an entire fleet within the space of two months. For narrative purposes the Roman fleet in *Ship of Rome* consisted entirely of triremes however it is generally accepted that the majority of the fleet were quinqueremes based on a captured Carthaginian galley. Gnaeus Cornelius Scipio, the Senior Consul in 260 BC, was given command of the fleet while Gaius Duilius, the Junior Consul, was given command of the army.

Roman history records that the Carthaginians tricked Scipio into sailing a small detachment of approximately twenty galleys to Lipara in the belief the city was poised to defect to the Roman cause. The Carthaginians, commanded by Gisco and Boodes, were lying in ambush and the inexperienced Roman crews promptly panicked and surrendered. Scipio was captured and was thereafter given the *cognomen Asina* to signify his foolhardy mistake.

Little is known of Gaius Duilius before his election to Consulship in 260 BC. As a *novus homo*, a new man, his family lineage was not of historical importance. After the capture of Scipio at Lipara, Duilius was elevated to command the new fleet and led them into battle at Mylae.

The Battle of Mylae took place in late 260 BC. The sides were evenly matched although the Carthaginians anticipated victory given their superior experience. The inventor of the *corvus* is not recorded however the device is similar to the one described. It was this that assured the Roman fleet's first victory, an invention that allowed them to deploy their superior soldiers at sea.

Gisco escaped after the Battle of Mylae although his flagship was lost in addition to half his fleet. The remaining Carthaginian galleys fled to Sardinia where Gisco was relieved of his command by his own men. He was subsequently crucified for his incompetence. A commander named Hamilcar replaced Gisco although it was not Hamilcar Barca as stated in *Ship of Rome*. I have introduced Barca at this earlier stage in the war for narrative purposes.

Scipio was shamed upon his return to Rome but his career survived and he subsequently returned to power. Duilius enjoyed a triumphal parade for his victory and a column was raised in the *Forum* in his honour, the remains of which are enshrined in the Capitoline Museum in Rome. Although he secured Rome's first naval victory he never again commanded the fleet.

The command structure on board a Roman galley was as described, with a naval captain and a marine centurion sharing authority. It involved a delicate balance, a partnership between career officers, men like Atticus and Septimus.

The Battle of Mylae was a significant victory for Rome but the Carthaginians were far from beaten. They would reform and challenge the *Classis Romanus* again and within a short time the two fleets would meet in the largest naval battle of the ancient world, the Battle of Cape Ecnomus.